GAS, FOOD, LODGING

Michael Payne

To the boys at Mojo's Dunk Tape.
Rileigh, you know what you did.
Samantha, don't ever change.
And Lynn. Always Lynn.

He couldn't see the use in spreading sadness
So he took his dark depression
And went home

"Wednesday" /
Drive By Truckers (Patterson Hood)

PROLOGUE

April 1999

T he way I heard it, long after it was over, my friend Police Constable Jim Edwards saw the body first. I wasn't there, of course, but in my mind now, I can hear the echoes of a dark night and see the patrol car moving slowly, the searchlight turning black into white. Jim is riding shotgun, and when the patrol car stops and the searchlight settles there is an unexplained shape on the beach but human, clearly human. Has to be a drunk the two policeman figure, because nobody sane and sober sleeps on the sand at Vancouver's Crab Park at three in the morning; at least, not in the rain.

Beer cans, condoms, syringes, torn mattresses and maybe a body litter a landscape that is joyless even in the sun, let alone now. Sand, dead grass and spray-painted concrete come into focus as the cruiser slows to a stop, headlights pointing at the harbour. Tankers and cruise ships are close enough to swim to, so tangibly real that they must be an illusion. The water is still, absorbing the rain but protected and calm beside the chaos of garbage that is the beach. There is no energy here, none at all, no indication that in a few hours this harbour will beat with life. There are no street lights here, at least none that work, and the only brightness comes from the police car as the bubble lights flash and Jim Edwards trains the searchlight on the sleeping man. Jim, first out of the car, walks through the light and unsheathes the heavy night stick he carries. He is thinking nothing more and nothing less than *one more drunk to roust.*

"Hey, buddy," he yells from fifteen feet away. Edwards' voice is deep and rich. The policeman himself is huge, six-foot eight inches of muscle slowly turning to fat, and he doesn't particularly enjoy this shift or this part of town, littered as it is with other peoples' trash. In two long strides, tremendous steps, he is on top of the man, who is well dressed: suit, tie, cap-toe oxford shoes. This is odd, and should perhaps have tipped Jim that something other than the usual is happening here, where filthy army jackets and blankets are the normal camouflage. Three blocks to the south, the streets teem with business men and strip clubs but the suits don't come to this place.

The policeman doesn't think about this, however, nor does he question the leather briefcase on the ground, about a foot from the unconscious man. This too should give Jim pause, and in my mind, I alert him—a gentle reminder that anything not chained to a guy like this would long be in the possession of strangers. But Jim Edwards misses these things because he is bored and wet and tired, tired of the same old crap night after night. Or maybe fate is against him and makes what happens next inevitable.

The policeman is not wearing a poncho, and the rain beats on both men. Jim takes off his hat and shakes the water onto the man, who does not move. With side-burns and shaggy hair, Jim is not the ideal Vancouver Police Constable, in appearance or, these days, attitude. "Dead to the world," the police giant grunts at his partner, who is just now getting out of the car. Jim drops his hat to the ground where it somehow illogically, improbably, stays through everything that happens next.

Jim pokes the man with his blackened nightstick, stained dark with use, hard. "Subject does not respond to pain stimulus," he says into his shoulder mic, letting the dispatcher know what is happening. He then hits the man in the flesh of the thigh, at first lightly but each subsequent blow hardening, and still there is no response. At this point, as the story is relayed to me, my mind is screaming at Jim, but he can't hear me and he continues with the job at hand. Perhaps his stomach grows cold as he bends over the man and swears; perhaps, like a dog, he sniffs the air because he can sense something is wrong. But I'll never know. I wasn't there. But whatever my friend is feeling is pushed aside as he concentrates on this man on this beach in this city that he loves less and less each day.

There is an Irish expression that says God watches out for drunks and fools. But although he has been both, right at this moment in time, Jim Edwards is neither. In fact, there is no God on this night and the policeman doesn't stop to consider the situation fully and instead does his job. As his partner gets back in the car to call for an ambulance, Jim kneels beside the man he thinks is simply passed out from drink or something stronger and reaches towards him. After feeling for a pulse —"Faint but present" he tells dispatch—Jim undoes the man's suit coat and opens it to look for a wallet, for identification he is not sure he will find, and he dies. The simple act of opening the man's coat triggers the bomb that blows pieces of both their beings against the cruiser, the beach, the cement seawall, the night. For a little while, there is a mist in the air that does not come from the rain, reflected in the cruiser's lights, red then blue, blood after bruise.

By the time the rain has ended and morning has come, the crabs and the birds and the tide and the police units have come and gone and taken with them the body but not the memory of my friend Jim David Edwards, sixteen year Vancouver police veteran and his unknown eternal companion.

Only the fact that he is back inside the police cruiser when the bomb blows saves Kyle Richards' life. Kyle has been Jim's partner for three years and friend for ten. Kyle is keying the radio when half a pound of explosive goes off, half a pound that is wired to a man and left on a public beach on a rainy night in the cruellest month. With his face towards the blast, Kyle is quite badly lacerated by shards of window glass and metal. He is blinded by his own blood and temporarily deafened by the fearful sound of the bomb and the after blast. He fights unconsciousness, wanting to remain awake, to somehow call for help and save his friend, but he loses, of course. As he fades, Kyle knows clearly that he is alive, but that this surely must be hell, for what else could it be?

When it starts, Kyle's thumb is on the transmit button of the two-way radio. Then it happens and the Communications Officer who answers the call hears everything. She hears the air shatter and the glass break and the bodies tear open and the ground heave and then she hears nothing, for there is nothing left to hear. She calls for assistance and the ambulances and fire trucks and bomb squad units and every police officer in the downtown area arrive but there is little they can do. By now, of course, it is too late for Jim and the only one to save is Kyle.

And for Kyle, salvation will come, but it will bring unimaginable costs.

*****

This is how it starts, with an eruption of violence and emotion on a nearly empty beach in a driving rain. I don't really know how it ends, or if it does end, because now life is forever because of this event. And some of this is good. Much of this is good. But now I know things that I never wanted to know and can't forget and, sometimes, at night, in those honest hours we all face when we are truly alone and maybe even frightened or who we are, I try to remember how things were before... and I can't do it.

I try to remember how it was before this started and how it could still be if only for the accident of now. But I can't remember and I can't forget. And when this happens, I remind myself again that much of this is good. But I know some of the things that I have learned were better left unknown; I have learned that darkness exists that is separate from the night. I have felt it, embraced it, and come back from it. But, here in the daylight, sometimes I long for the darkness. Ask me today if I believe in God and I will share the only truth I know: Yes, I believe in God, but he hasn't always believed in me.

CHAPTER 1

February 2000

My name is Ryan Simms. I turn 30 this year, and I'm not dealing with it very well. I started not dealing with it well when I was 26, but some things you can't rush into.

When people ask me what I do, I used to tell them I was a baseball player. "Any good?" they'd ask, and I'd smile and shrug with the false modesty of the truly confident. That all ended thirty-two months ago in the basement of Calgary's Frank Claire Stadium, home of the Triple A Calgary Cannons baseball team. I was playing for the visiting Phoenix Firebirds at the time, but it was there in Calgary that the parent San Francisco Giants chose to tell me that the franchise wanted to go in a different direction, one that didn't include me.

In reality, my baseball dream—the only dream I've ever had—ended nine months previously in Chicago's Wrigley Field, the oldest ballpark in Major League Baseball.

I've relived that catch every day since. Sometimes it is a dream of pure joy, the childlike thrill of the chase; other times it is a nightmare that wakes me up. In the mornings, I see the scars from multiple surgeries and feel the pain when I lift my arm over my shoulder—all for a few seconds of youth, the glory of the moment and then the finality of the wall. And every day, some days more than others, I wish that the chase had not happened—or, more honestly, I wish that time had frozen at the exact moment when the ball hit my glove but before I shattered like a porcelain doll against one-hundred year old brick with a thin coating of ivy. I could have lived with that, I think now, more easily than I am living with this. *For what is this, if not someone else's life?*

And I often wonder, usually while drinking, how life's highlight can be followed so readily by pain and sorrow.

Now, when people ask me what I do, I have no answer. "I drink" is accurate but only begs more questions that I don't want to answer. "Nothing" seems dismissive and is not entirely truthful. Telling them that I made friends with an old baseball fan, a Calgary Private Investigator named Seth Pinel, who brought me into his business to learn while I told him stories, takes too long.

"Mostly what I do," I say, "is find things." It's a skill I've developed while getting lost myself as I wait for the seconds to become hours to become days and for life to continue without me.

The name of my bar is Ivy Green.

CHAPTER 2

I've considered changing the name of the bar many times, or changing the bar to suit the name. Both seem like a lot of effort. Despite having a Calgary address, there are no rodeo decorations on the walls and we play no country music on the stereo. The bar itself is in the Beltline District, home to a nice mix of bearded guys and women who make them look dumb and everybody loves my dog. She's a one-hundred pound Malamute who has free reign of the place, and people come specifically to see her. They certainly don't come to visit me.

The bar itself is in a cross-over phase. It was a chain restaurant before, so the bones are good. I'm slowly trying to make it into something more my style—but I lost track of my style quite some time ago. Over time, on nights I can't sleep, I've taken out the vinyl booths and put in live-edge tables, lengthened the bar with hand cut timbers and used a lot of barn wood, so there are parts of the place I really like. And there are parts that look like a failed chain restaurant. But I keep the drink prices low, created most of the food recipes myself, and the people in the Beltline seem to appreciate the effort—or lack thereof. Even if it's just the prices, we are almost always full. There is nothing ivy-like or green about the place.

This is my life. Worse than some, better than others. What are you going to do?

We were starting to fill up on a February Tuesday when Karen Temple walked in out of the cold and snow. She was wearing a violet raincoat that looked like silk but wasn't offering much protection to the weather. It was an easy twenty below outside, and there was ice in her hair, melting into her jacket, in a puddle at her feet.

A lot of eyes were on Karen as she entered, but the empty stool beside me is where she headed. As she skirted the tables between us, ice melted off her jacket leaving a clear and obvious path from door to bar. Before she arrived next to me, I finished my drink and ordered another.

At first, I didn't recognize her. Just a déjà vu feeling that I ignored with beer. Striking, rather than classically pretty, Karen has curly dark hair and confidence in equal quantity. I struggled to place her, and drank more beer in case it could help.

"Nothing for me," she said without being asked. Looking directly at me, she added this: "Might be enough for you as well."

"You talk too much," I told her and looked at my fresh beer with every intention of drinking it, and maybe a few more besides. Since I owned the bar where we were sitting, this is mostly what I did. "And you need a winter coat."

"Cold," she said and I think she meant the weather. "You haven't changed, Dirt," she added. "One liner and a beer too many. Maybe a few extra pounds."

In Calgary, where I live, you can sometimes smell the frozen heart of winter; when I caught her eyes in the mirror behind the bar, I could see it, and I looked away. I drank from my beer for warmth.

Realization dawned, and I spun on my stool to face her. "Karen," I said to a woman I once knew well despite only meeting a handful of times. "Nobody's called me Dirt in a long time," I told her. "I'm sorry, I should have been there."

I hadn't seen Karen since the last time I'd been home. Karen was Jim Edwards' wife and I hadn't even gone home for the funeral. Despite this cowardice, Karen embraced me tightly and either melting snow or tears fell on my shoulders and, maybe, even her jacket.

Jim's partner, Kyle Richards, has been my best friend since we were six and I have talked to him twice in the last year.

"Help me, Dirt," Karen said. "Help us." As I spun my beer in circles on the bar, Karen took a notebook from her purse; in the notebook were a number of newspaper articles and things that looked like insurance claim forms and some handwritten notes. She spread all of this on the bar and I moved them around, looking at the headlines and taking it all in. Most of the articles I was familiar with, they were about Jim and I knew about Jim, of course, because even drunk I can read and even hungover like I'd been much of the past three years, I can watch TV. Hell, living in the bar as I do, I can watch fifteen at once.

"I'm sorry, Karen," I said. Unsure of why she would need my help and ashamed that I might not want to know, I managed to say, very softly, "help with what?" But she heard me.

"Something Jim and Kyle started. I don't know it all and now Jim is gone, of course, and Kyle has been suspended," she said, "without pay."

I am surprised to hear this, but not surprised I didn't know—for the last year I have left messages for Kyle where I know he isn't and I don't have voicemail for when he calls back. But what she tells me next is truly shocking: the Vancouver Police Department, despite burying Jim with full honours, is denying Karen and their daughter widow's benefits. All other legal rights have been refused as the 'member's resultant death was a direct result of prolonged criminal activity and specific and personal persecution of members of the *Silent Saint Motorcycle*

Club'. This meant nothing to me then; it means something now.

"I'm going to win the war," Karen told me, "but I need help with the battle. And," she added, "maybe learning which is which."

As I take this in, Karen motions for two more beer, a comforting and familiar gesture. Absurdly, I choose that moment to wonder how many drinks I've had since last seeing her. This is an impossible number to discern; in fact, even now, I am probably drunk. As we sit at my bar, unsure of what to say next, it is Tuesday afternoon and I am pretty sure that, minus a few breaks, I have had a beer in front of me since Thursday evening.

But that is not entirely accurate; in all honesty, I've been drinking now for the better part of three years straight—ever since the San Francisco Giants cut me loose. I was in the minor leagues on another rehab assignment, hoping against hope to make it back to the Major Leagues when they made that decision. We were in Calgary at the time and I never went back to Phoenix, a city I quite enjoyed; in fact, I haven't left Calgary since that day. I sent for my dog and my truck and now I own and live in a bar. Is fate funny or cruel—how do you decide?

But here, right now, my mind is reeling and it isn't totally from the drink.

*****

Karen tells me what has happened to Jim posthumously. How he has been branded as dirty and how the police brass have made it seem that only death has saved him from certain disgrace and dismissal, and jail. This is not the Jim I knew. And it is not the Jim that Karen and their daughter loved. Karen, as a Provincial Prosecutor, does not need the money that is being withheld; what she needs is for Jim's legacy to be as clean as her memories of him, unsullied by rumour and accusations of deeds not done.

"They're saying Jim was heavy-handed with some of the people he arrested, that he was negligent in his duties to pursue 'individual enrichments', whatever the hell that means, and that he negotiated arrests for money and drugs. And," she added, "that he ran a string of strippers/prostitutes throughout BC."

She drank some beer. "He was brought up on charges internally. But the union argued there was no evidence and his record prevented him from being fired. He was demoted though. The Chief got that, at least."

"Jim?" I asked, seriously stunned. "Jim Edwards? Hookers and strippers? Jim couldn't even talk to girls, let alone run a stable of prostitutes. They would have eaten him alive."

"Tell that to the ass who signed this letter," she said and handed me the notice of loss of benefits. "He didn't seem to believe me." The letter also mentioned witness tampering and destruction of evidence.

"Apparently," Karen added with enough heat to dry the melted snow on the floor, "Jim was busy. And now they're doing the same to Kyle. His suspension is the real deal and being fast-tracked."

"Suspended for what?" I asked, an obvious question but obvious is all my brain could process right then.

"I have a tape of it at home," she says. "The short version is that he called the Vancouver Chief of Police a murderer during a televised press conference. But, really, it's for believing in Jim." She drank some beer. "The long version starts four years ago."

"Why me, Karen?" I asked. "I sort of checked out a while ago."

"Answered your own question," she said. "You don't know

anything about what has happened, and nobody in Vancouver knows who you are. You've got a license and I assume some training; Kyle speaks well of you." She paused—self-doubt can do that to people. "At this point, that's all I've got."

For the first time in a long time, I pushed away a nearly full beer. "Tell me," I say. "Tell me everything."

*****

Telling the story takes an hour. I asked very few questions because, truthfully, I didn't know what to ask. I slowed down on the drinking while she spoke, but Karen sped up, so the consumption remained consistent. Around seven, we went across the street for dinner, more for a change of scenery than anything else, and since neither of us was particularly hungry, it was a quick meal.

Even though there was a lot still left to say, we barely talked. When we were through, we boxed our leftovers for Nesha and Karen grabbed a cab and headed to her hotel. I agreed to pick her up at seven the next morning; she was going to ride to Vancouver with me. That was obviously the intention all along as she hadn't booked a return ticket.

At 6:57 the next morning, I was standing in the hotel lobby, two travel cups of coffee in my hands. If I wasn't exactly bright eyed and bushy tailed, I wasn't a drunken slob, so I counted the morning as progress. Karen had a full-size suit-case, but there was plenty of room for everything in my Bronco—even with Nesha, all 100 pounds of her, taking up a disproportionate amount of space.

Although I wasn't sure how long I would be in Vancouver, my packing had been fairly easy. Truthfully, it took me longer to choose my sneakers for the trip than my clothes. I own doz-ens of sneakers, but my wardrobe consists almost entirely of San Francisco Giants hoodies and shorts and t-shirts from my minor league stops. A few of each in an old leather duffle, and I was ready to go.

There are two ways to drive from Calgary to Vancouver. One is due south from Calgary on what's known as the *Crow's Nest Highway*, a route that essentially parallels the Alberta / BC border until it hits the Canada / US border, and then turns due west. In the winter, the danger on this route isn't extreme as it manages to avoid most of the high elevation passes that the Cascade and Rocky Mountains present, but it takes fourteen hours.

The second route, up and through the Rocky and Selkirk Mountains and then south to Vancouver along the new Coquihalla Highway, is ten and a half hours under ideal circumstances; obviously more in the snow—and it was snowing heavily. In fact, five inches would fall on Calgary that day; considerably more in the mountains we had to drive through. I chose the Coquihalla route, even though I'd never driven it before. *Could be sunny up top. Ten dollar toll, how bad can it be?*

I wasn't thrilled about the driving conditions, but the Bronco did have push-button four wheel drive and snow tires and I promised myself to take it easy—especially through Rogers Pass, one of the world's most active avalanche zones. Even with that much time in front of us, there was only going to be one topic of conversation, and it wasn't going to be the worsening weather.

"Can we run through this all again?" I asked Karen as we left Calgary proper, following the Bow River west. "I knew Jim had a sister who died, of course, but the other stuff... I just don't know what to think or how to fit it all together." I looked at her, hoping sincerity and not residual hang-over was showing.

"Start with Kylee, okay?" I said. "I really need to get my head wrapped around what I heard and think I heard last night."

"You and me both," she said, and sighed. Not out of frustration about telling the story again, but simply because the story is incredible and frightening and sad. Looking for attention, Nesha stuck her head into the front-row and sighed like Karen. Karen scratched the dog between the ears and told us about decorated police constable Jim Edwards and his high-school valedictorian and all-Province volleyball player sister Kylee, dying within months of each other by violent means. With the scratching, Nesha was instantly in a happy place; Karen and I were not.

"Kylee and Jim were thirteen years apart," Karen started. "Despite that age difference, they were very close. Even though he had graduated and was in the academy and then on the Force, he went to her basketball and volleyball games when she was in high school. Their Dad died when Jim was eighteen, so Kylee was five. Their Mom didn't work, so they only had Mr. Edwards' pension and not much else, so Jim always made sure Kylee had what she needed—latest jeans or whatever.

"As a teen, Kylee was often at our house. When their Mom died, she moved in. Rileigh, our daughter was six, and they were inseparable. I would have sworn Kylee was happy. All-Canadian kid, you know? Blonde and pretty and smart and athletic. She had multiple scholarship offers for volleyball. A million friends; definitive plans."

"And it changed," I said.

"Overnight," Karen replied. "It was really that fast." Karen had stopped patting Nesha, who was now gently protesting by nudging Karen with her head. "The spring before graduation, the taste of freedom she was getting meant that, for Kylee, there were all these new experiences waiting and she had to do them all at once."

"And that's where the *Silent Saints* come in?" I asked. "The romanticized criminality of a motorcycle gang?"

"They call themselves clubs, not gangs," Karen said. "But, yeah, that's where she ended up. But it wasn't a straight line descent. There were stops and detours along the way." She paused for a few seconds to gather her thoughts. "But it definitely ends with Anthony 'Agony' Baker—he's the CEO of the West Coast branch of the *Silent Saints Motorcycle Club*. What a piece of shit."

I let that one lie, but the dog heard something in her tone and she put her head between the seats again and tried to get her head under Karen's arm. Karen obliged, and said "Maybe not Baker directly, and Jim probably forced the issue with the *Saints*. But there's no doubt they took Kylee from us."

"But it started with somebody else, right?" I asked. "The Hanson brothers?"

Karen smiled without meaning it and shook her head. "Hadden," she said. "Josh and Darryl Hadden." Done with the patting, Nesha had laid down in the back seat, but Karen stayed half-turned in hers, looking at me and not the falling snow.

"In Grade 10," Karen continued, "Kylee became friends with Emily Hadden. Emily seemed okay, but her brothers were a different story—quite a bit older and low-level bikers with the *Saints*. Officially, they were hang arounds."

"Right. You said that last night—hang arounds. That means they were but weren't club members?"

"More or less," Karen said. "Motorcycle clubs have their own cultures and traditions. A full patch member has four patches —the club insignia—for Baker's crew, that's a rip off the Munch *Scream* painting—and then three other panels."

She looked at me with a bit of a smirk. "Stay with me now, this part lost you last night."

"I'll do my best," I told her. "Please use smaller words than you did last night."

"Hang around is like second level—after a lengthy trial period, a decision is made that you are worthy to continue with the club. So you go from nothing to having some status—hang arounds get invited to some club events and can mingle with members at gathering places. The Clubhouse, rides, public events, etc. But a hanger on does NOT receive a patch.

"From there, after a year or two, a hanger on can be promoted to 'associate'. This is more status than hang around, obviously; and as an associate, you get your first patch—the club insignia. Prior to that, you can wear the colours only."

"Colours are like your uniform, right?" I asked. "So you know who to hit in a brawl?"

"Exactly," Karen said. "And from associate, if you follow the rules and hand your home work in on time, you graduate to prospect. This takes at least a year. As a prospect, you can participate in club activities, but you have no voting rights as you are still being evaluated by the club leaders."

"Seems like those two levels are reversed," I said. "Shouldn't an associate out rank a prospect?"

"I've always thought so," she replied. "But criminals don't think like we do, so who knows? A prospect," she continued, "can wear two patches—the insignia and a 'rocker' with the club's territory name."

Karen took a sip from her now cold coffee. "Is this a good time to mention that it's snowing even harder?" she asked.

"Wait until we get to Banff," I replied. "Mention it then, if you must. For now, tell me about Full Patch."

"Full Patch is the highest membership status—it's the full meal deal," Karen told me. "All four patches—which, interestingly, actually remain the property of the club and can be taken away at any time—and you've got the keys to the Kingdom:

"First, there's the insignia for whatever club you are with. For Baker's *Silent Saints*, it's a really weird 'Scream' rip off, like that painting could get any weirder, and I simply don't get the connection.

"Then there is a square patch that says 'MC' for Motorcycle Club and a small patch that denotes your territory—in case you forget, I guess.

"And finally, you get the last patch—the top rocker—and this makes you full patch. It's another small one and only states your club name."

"In case you forget that, too, I guess."

"Probably. These guys are typically not that bright, until you get to the top at least," she said. "To be full patch, you have to be sponsored by another full patch and win a unanimous vote of full-patch members to be officially recognized."

"That's a lot of patching," I said. "And, ultimately, we end up with four levels of douche-baggery. Doesn't seem that complicated."

"On the surface, it isn't," Karen replied. "But, again—motorcycle clubs have an intense ingrained culture and values that they absolutely will not deviate from. As 'straights', we think it's warped; they, however, think we have our heads you know where."

"Okay," I said, "and Karen, I'm sorry if any of this hurts, but I'm trying to make sure I have it all straight." She waved my concern away. "Kylee's in with a bad crowd, maybe on the edges of the *Saints*, but I don't see a connection to Baker yet, or even understand why Jim went after them so hard."

By this point, we were entering Banff National Park of Canada, and the mountain straight ahead was either Mt. Rundle or Mt. Cascade—either way, we were in the Rockies. When we saw the first exit sign for the city of Banff itself, Karen simply raised her eyebrows at me and pointed her head at the direction of the windshield and the blowing snow. "Hold that thought," she said. "We need to talk about the snow."

Banff National Park was Canada's first national park, and the world's third. At more than 6,600 square kilometres, it houses black and grizzly bears, wolves, cougars, elk, deer, bighorn sheep, bald eagles—basically, if you're afraid of it but it isn't poisonous, it lives in the Park. The city of Banff itself is everything a resort town should or shouldn't be, an amazing combination of mountains and hot springs and money. It's one of Canada's most popular and expensive vacation destinations.

As we hadn't eaten much the night before and had only had coffee this morning, we agreed to stop at The Grizzly House for something warm and to consider our options. I let Nesha out, and she immediately started to roll in the snow and dig a snow cave to lie in. I didn't have the heart to put her back in the truck, so I clipped her leash to the winch on the front of the Bronco.

Karen asked me about the winch, and the tow hooks. "Never realized you were so country," she said.

"Not country," I replied quickly. "Definitely not country, just an easy mark." She laughed. "Actually, the winch and hooks and lift are for my land up Roberts Creek. It's off a fire road, but there is access to the Ocean. I bought it with my bonus money from the Giants, and I bought the truck too." I made sure the leash was attached and gave Nesha some biscuits. "Kyle and I were going to clear the land ourselves, haul the logs to a local mill and build a cabin. That's why I had this stuff installed." I looked at the winch and felt foolish. "Another dream that I guess isn't going to happen," I said.

Changing the subject, I pointed at the dog, who was now lying in an eight-inch hole she had dug. "She doesn't actually need the leash," I said. "She's not going to go anywhere. But she's so big, people seem to feel better knowing she's attached to something."

"And you're just going to leave her there, in the snow?" Karen asked.

I just shrugged and said "She's a Malamute. Look at her. She loves it."

We turned and headed for the restaurant. By the time we made it inside, we were covered in snow, which was getting heavier and building up on the sides of the road where there was no traffic to melt it as it fell.

CHAPTER 3

Inside the restaurant, we exchanged some observations about the weather with the hostess and were seated by a window where I could keep an eye on the dog. Beyond the dog was the Trans-Canada Highway and an increasing convoy of sand-trucks and snow-plows and road graders. Karen ordered an egg-white omelette and I had coffee and sausage, with a side of bacon. When the waitress left, Karen toasted me with her water.

"You take a girl to the nicest places," she said, looking around at the 1960's décor—including beads in doorways and lots of tie-dye. "But it is getting bad out there. You okay to continue, or should we call it a day—okay, a quarter-day—and start fresh tomorrow. Or whenever the snow stops."

Banff should have been a ninety minute drive, but it had taken us an hour longer than that. "We'll only have snow for another six hours," I said. "Give or take. I mean, theoretically it can snow all the way to Chilliwack, but the next few hours are the worst." I looked at the highway trucks, still rolling.

"I was trying to save time," I said, "but maybe we should have taken the Crow's Nest. That adds three or four hours, but I know that the Coquihalla has some seriously high elevations that you avoid on the Nest."

"Never made the drive," Karen said. "Either way. But let's be careful and not heroes."

"It's only snow," I said, "it'll be fine." But I don't have a lot of experience driving in the snow, so I'm not sure how confident I really was with that comment.

The waitress dropped off our drinks. Karen added milk to her tea. "Okay," she said, "Jim and the *Saints*." She stirred her tea, and her hand was shaking enough that some spilled onto the table. I pretended not to notice. "Jim hated the Haddens. That's where it started."

"Makes sense," I said, "right? Jim knows who and what they are, and Kylee thinks they're just having fun."

"We have to back up for a second," Karen said. "The Hadden brothers were officially *Saints'* associates, but by all accounts they were on the fast track. Because they could grow pot like nobody else. I don't know if this is true or not, but they have been credited with making BC Bud even better, and before they were on the scene, BC pot was already winning awards in Europe."

She paused and smiled. "It *is* pretty good," she said.

"Karen, I'm shocked," I said with mock-indignation.

"Like you've never," she said.

But truthfully, I haven't. My last couple of years playing ball in the states, BC Bud was all the rage—top price, but apparently top buzz. To this day, my only vice is beer. Maybe a Caesar or two if the hangover is really bad and the day needs a jump start. But never dope or anything stronger. Marijuana was everywhere when I played and is maybe even considered normal now—in fact, there is talk of it becoming legalized, at least in Canada—but beer has always seemed to do what I needed it to do, so why change what's working? Plus, in a lot of places in the States, beer is cheaper than water and that's important on a minor-league salary.

Karen lost focus for a second, but gathered herself. "So that's where Emily was at two years ago. She basically dropped out of school after Christmas of her senior year, when volleyball was over, but she had enough credits to graduate. She was spending more time with the Haddens, and their friends, and the Hadden brothers were living large as celebrities in that culture."

"There's a celebrity ladder of gangbangers?" I asked her.

"In a way," she replied. "Remember I said that motorcycle clubs are hierarchal?"

"I do."

"So there's a social ladder within the club itself that the Haddens were fast-tracking because of the potency of their pot *and* their ability to grow it almost anywhere."

"And with that came money and fame, I guess."

"Yeah," Karen replied. "It absolutely did. And this is the world Kylee joined. Ryan, Emily always had money—when she and Kylee first started hanging out, Kylee was often dropping hints to Jim about 'needing' this or that, something Emily had. By Christmas of the next year, those hints had stopped and Kylee often had clothes and purses, shoes, whatever, that Jim or their Mom hadn't given her money for or bought themselves."

"What did Kylee say?" I asked.

"At first, she said Emily had leant whatever it was to her, then it was Emily had bought it for her, and then it was she was working part-time. But she would never say where.

"And then, one day, she had a car. A Honda, but not the beat up old Civic Jim and I bought her—a brand new CR-X SiR. It was nicer than my car, and I'm a Provincial Prosecutor.

"Jim lost it," Karen said. "It was insidious... Kylee slipped away day by day." Karen drank some more tea and visibly gathered her thoughts. "But that was her world." Karen might have been crying. "*Our* world," she said.

She continued. "Kylee started smoking pot in Grade 10. It was a little of a rebellion towards Jim and his uniform but, hell, Kylee knew the stories about Jim when he was in high-school and he was no kind of angel." We both smiled. "It seemed under control though—she never missed school or showed up at our place stoned-- and she swore there was nothing harder.

"Her grade 12 year, though, Jim really started to give her a hard time. He had worked on some motorcycle gang related stuff and knew enough to be scared for her, I guess, as she was spending more and more time with Emily which meant more and more time with the brothers and other low-level associates. Karen even told us of a few 'stories' she'd heard—some robberies, a few violent fights—and we were worried that she wasn't rejecting this as strange."

"Jim must have been losing his mind," I said. "I can't even imagine."

"And I was travelling a lot, back and forth to Victoria for work, so that didn't help. Later I found out that he tried to scare off the Hadden brothers, keep them from spending time with Kylee. I asked him to leave it alone, let Kylee work it out on her own. Truthfully, I didn't know if that was the right approach either, but Kylee saw him as interfering, even bullying.

"For Jim," she continued, "it became an obsession. 'Kylee,' he would plead, 'what normal twenty-two year old guy goes to watch high school volleyball games?' 'You go', she'd reply and Jim would turn red. 'You're my sister!' he'd say—but then she'd counter with 'and Emily is theirs'. He'd try to explain it's not the same, that he wasn't selling pot out of his car, but I think she was having fun trying out this new rebellious attitude."

Our food arrived, and the waitress gestured out the window

and said "Can't even see your dog no more, she looks like a Yeti now! You sure she's okay?"

"That dog would love to be a Yeti," I replied. "I can never get used to how much she loves the cold and snow. In fact, if the Himalayas came with opened bags of crunchies and peanut butter treats that weren't too hard to find, she'd leave me in an instant." The waitress walked away shaking her head and laughing.

"Look at that dog!" she said to the next table. "It's the damn-dest thing, but I guess she's in the right place. Won't stop snowing here until May." I shuddered at that thought; even though I live in Calgary, I hate winter. I grew up in Vancouver and played baseball all my life—neither of those things involves snow.

Despite her earlier misgivings, Karen tried to tuck into her omelette. It didn't quite work. And despite the bacon and sausage sitting in front of me, I stayed with coffee. Looking at Karen, I thought two things. First, I realized that Karen is far more than striking, she really is a beautiful woman; Jim definitely punched way over his weight-class. And secondly, I realized that I need to spend more time with grown-ups and less time with myself and bar customers. *There's a world out there, Dirt. Might be time to see it.*

And then I had a third thought, that compared to Karen and others I know, maybe I'm not ready to be an adult. Wearing button-fly Levis, an aforementioned Giants' hoodie and tri-colour Nike Air Max 90 trainers on my feet in a late winter blizzard, I was glad Karen was with me to do the heavy thinking.

Of which there was plenty left to do.

*****

"Jim and Kyle were beating up on the *Saints*, in every way possible. Ryan," she said, "they were pounding on the *Saints*. Rob a bank, and pass by a *Saint* standing on the sidewalk? They arrested the *Saint*."

"Seems like they had reason," I said. "If not cause."

Karen arched her eyebrows. "Legal scholar," she said. "Or did you get that from TV?"

"I don't watch TV, except sports. Must have picked it up from you last night when you thought I wasn't listening."

"Right," she said. "Every *Saint* they saw they were hauling in; Ryan, I swear to God Jim laughed one day that he busted a guy for a broken tail-light, and the guy was *walking*."

"So, for the *Saints*," I said, "that got old fast."

"It did. And Jim and Kyle heard about it from both sides— the *Saints* called a town-hall to discuss 'ongoing police harassment' and the cop brass told them to knock it off."

"Were there threats from the *Saints*?"

"Only implied. Just questions and pleas for 'understanding and compassion', some BS like that. The threats actually came from Jim's superiors." I looked up. "They even busted him down a rank when he didn't stop—conduct unbecoming and all that crap."

"Wow," I said. "You'd think the brass would applaud actual policing."

"Yeah, I know. But understand that Jim was seeing nothing but *Saints* at this point. Everywhere he looked. And this is *before* Kylee overdosed.

"*That's* how she died?" I asked. "It makes sense given everything, I guess, but Karen—I swear I had no idea."

Karen pursed her lips and shrugged. "I didn't mention it last night," she said. "I'm not looking for sympathy, only answers. And Jim obviously didn't make a public thing about it. If you had come home, Ryan," she added, "you would have known."

I dropped my head in shame and looked away. What else could you do, being called out on stuff you should have done?

Karen wasn't being unkind. Guilt is always self-applied. "I'm sorry Karen," I said. "What you guys were going through… and I was selling drinks to people I can't remember. Or drinking with people I can't remember."

She let that lie for a few seconds.

"I suspect now," she said, "that Jim's pressure on Kylee to leave before she became a *Saint* punching bag or fall guy made things worse for her. She was stuck between two worlds—and Ryan, the *Saints* and the other clubs glamorize the living hell out of their life style and lack of respect for squares—you know, people like you and me. And they hate, *hate*, cops or anyone in law enforcement. I think that Kylee being the sister of such a large and well-known police officer made her a bit of a celebrity in that world."

"Making that side of the equation even more exciting for her," I said.

"Right," Karen said. "And the *Saints* loved having her 'on their side'.

"'Where's your sister tonight? Jimmy', they'd say. 'Oh yeah, she's working for us tonight'. One night, a full patch *Saint* named Pistol said he'd seen Kylee on stage at Brandi's." Brandi's is a high-end strip club in the heart of downtown Vancouver. Karen paused. "We know definitively that Brandi's is owned by the *Saints*."

Vancouver is world famous for its strip clubs; in fact, Vancouver is one of the very few places in North America that allows full nudity on stage. It is no secret that the Vancouver's strip clubs are run by motorcycle clubs—drugs for the girls, muscle for the customers who step out of line, and plenty of cash for the owners.

"This Pistol guy," Karen continued, "was full patch *Saints* and described what he saw in graphic detail. Then he showed Jim pictures. Ryan," she said, "he had *pictures* of Kylee dancing."

I let that one lie—what could you say?

"Kyle said after those pictures came out, he thought he was going to have to pull his gun on Jim to get him out of there before anything happened."

"I'm so sorry, Karen. I can't even imagine what Jim was feeling."

She shrugged. "And we were at the point that Jim couldn't even talk to Kylee, it was like she wanted nothing to do with him." Karen's voice was low, the strain of these memories obvious in her tone.

"And any time I saw her," she continued, "even when it was warm, she had long sleeves or even a jacket. She'd been so sweet, Ryan, so sweet." Karen stacked the salt shaker on top of the pepper for something to do with her hands. "Kylee was still in there, Ryan, but Jim definitely wasn't scaring her straight and I feared we were losing her. Long sleeves was not a good sign."

"Hard drugs?" I asked.

"She wasn't cold in August," Karen said. "But you know what I thought, Ryan?"

"Karen," I said, "I have no idea."

"I thought—long sleeves, that's a good sign, right? Right? If she's doing hard drugs and her arms are marked up, she isn't

dancing. *That's* what I thought. That guy Pistol is lying."
Karen's anger—at Kylee, at Jim, at the *Saints* and all their
fucked up little kids playing tough guys, at herself (for what I
didn't know)—was real. I had no idea what to do or say. *Maybe
being a grown up isn't something I'm interested in. It's too damn
hard.*

"Ryan," she said in a whisper, "Kylee was dancing."

She looked at me, and this time she was definitely crying. "Can
we go?"

*****

I dropped some cash on the table, including a few of our
new Canadian one-dollar coins, and we headed for the truck.
Nesha, an entirely black dog, was as white as a Pyrenees. She
took nearly five minutes to towel-dry, at which point I was a
Yeti. I slipped off the wet hoodie and replaced it with another
(this one from the Shreveport Captains) and we let the truck
run for a few minutes to warm up and for the windows to clear.

After the snow and ice had melted and the truck was warm, we
headed for the recently plowed highway.

Karen took a deep breath and started to apologize for breaking
down at the restaurant. Not being a complete ass, I didn't let
her finish, and reached out to take her hand, but Nesha's head
was in the way. How dogs know when they are needed most is
a mystery.

"The *Silent Saints*," Karen said, "are what we law-enforcement
types refer to as 'One Percenters'. This goes back fifty years
and refers to a comment made by the American Motorcyclist
association that 99% of motorcyclists are law-abiding citi-
zens. *Silent Saints* belong to the other 1%--outlaw bikers. 'Respect few; fear none'. That's a *Saints'* mantra.

"As the best of the worst, clubs like the *Saints* completely reject what we think of as normal; they play for shock value from the rest of society and support themselves in ways you would expect: drug dealing, stolen goods, old fashioned extortion. Their prostitution and strip club businesses are pretty slick, borderline human trafficking as the girls work a programmed circuit with absolutely no say in their 'careers'.

"That particular file has its own cabinet in Victoria."

"And Kylee?" I asked. "Where were you guys at? I mean, Jim must have been losing his mind, even just thinking she was being seduced by white trash like the *Saints*."

"It's what they prey on," Karen said. "So many kids—suburban, urban, whatever—so many kids think they don't have a chance. And, Ryan, some of them may not have a chance—I get that. But Kylee had *every* chance.

"But the 'life'," she said with air quotes, "is so glamourized that you've got all these kids trying to prove their worth to people who, ultimately, are the worst people alive. So these kids sell drugs and kick the 'profit' upstairs, collect debts... they do whatever they can to get noticed by a member of a viable motorcycle club—with the stupid hope that they will ultimately get sponsored by this club."

She turned in her seat, but couldn't reach the dog who was lying down again.

"It's so stupid, of course, to potentially put your life on the line for people who don't give a crap about you, but the lure —I guess—of the life style is too much. And the motorcycle clubs, Ryan," she said, "they don't care. They're just happy to have so many naïve kids do their bidding." She wiped her face with one hand and then the other. "That's the world Kylee had entered."

Karen started to play with the vents in front of her, pointing them in different directions. "Jim, on shift or off, would go to *Saints'* hangouts looking for her. These were mostly downtown eastside places—The American, the Ivanhoe, the Turf Hotel. He never found her with the *Saints,* but within an hour or so of his being there, she'd either call or show up, so she was getting the word somehow." She closed her eyes and leaned back in the seat.

"And then she didn't go to graduation," Karen said. "In fact, she went missing."

"Missing?" I said. "What happened?"

"We didn't see her for three months," Karen answered. "We knew she was around at first, at least periodically. Food was getting eaten, laundry was being done, and there were gifts for Rileigh almost every week." Rileigh is eight year's old and growing up without a father now. "But we didn't see her, or hear from her directly.

"I was scared; Jim was destructive."

"Was that as bad as it sounds?" I asked.

"It was," she replied. "For a lot of reasons. We knew Kylee was alive, because after the visits when nobody was home, Rileigh started to get post cards instead of gifts." Karen pressed her forehead against the passenger window and drew a stick figure family in the condensation from her breath. At least I think it was a family; she wiped it away with some finality. "She was dancing the circuit: Seattle, Vancouver, Calgary, Prince George...

"And then we got the call. Kylee was dead. They found her in her car, parked in long-term parking at the airport. Heroin."

We were silent for quite a distance. The kilometres went past, one after another, like days in the week. Soon, we were at Lake Louise, and even though it's only 1,600 metres above sea level, you would think Lake Louise is the top of the world. It is a pure turquoise colour, the result of rock flour carried into the lake by melt-water from the Victoria glacier. When the lake freezes, and at only 70 metres deep, it freezes every year by Halloween, the water stays that incredible colour, and it's like skating over open air. It's terrifying or electrifying or something in between.

"After," Karen said, "after... it didn't seem possible to do, but Jim somehow took his quest to eliminate the *Saints* by any means possible to new heights. I begged him to take time off and I could not believe his superiors weren't demanding that he do so. I think now, they wanted him to snap, to do something that couldn't be taken back."

"Jesus," I said. "That's cold."

"You haven't met the Chief," Karen said. "And remember those papers in my purse? These aren't nice people—on either side."

She continued. "For a long time, Jim had been a part of the Inter-Divisional Motorcycle Gang Task Force. It obviously wasn't healthy for him, but he had certain attributes the brass valued."

"Size and strength and a willingness to ask questions second?" I asked.

"Predominantly," Karen replied. "But he suddenly became the focus of the brass. And he was part of Task Force events that were just weird: raids were hitting the wrong addresses, evidence was going missing, and witnesses in *police custody* were not making it to court to testify. And," she added with equal parts flint and hurt, "*nobody* was getting convicted. Of anything." She looked at me but then turned to pat the dog. "These were *Saint* specific events," she said. "*Saints* drugs not being where they were supposed to be, houses being empty, *Saint* evidence gone. And all the little *Saints* Jim and Kyle went out of their way to bust were going free." She smiled without joy. "It was not a happy time at the Edwards' house. And that meant hell to pay for the bad guys Jim thought needed a little correcting."

I let that ride for a few seconds. "Isn't that sort of stuff pretty normal in law enforcement—evidence going missing or witnesses flaking out? And," I added, "my American friends constantly remind me about how Canadian courts favour the criminal."

"Some of that is true," Karen replied. "There is a certain amount of wastage, for lack of a better term, for sure. But what stands out now is how Jim was on *every* single one of the failed raids, was the *last* person to sign off on the missing evidence, and was the *officer* with the transportation detail on every late witness." Karen adjusted herself in the passenger seat, and made herself so comfortable that I was jealous. I mean, I bought the truck to have room, and included the custom soft-top, but at 6'5", the seats were still a little tight. Not so for Karen.

"Jim spent a lot of years on the VPD with nothing but commendations," she said. "Despite his size and reputation, there were no negative notes in his file." She smiled and shook her head. "I've seen it. And to your point, in terms of the courts," she added, "that criticism is usually reserved for 'light' decisions—six years for murder, like that. Here, the Task Force is losing evidence, losing witnesses, asking for inappropriate charges, on more than half their busts. And Jim was the common denominator on all of these cases."

"So he's being set up by someone," I said. "But it's a little too obvious, isn't it? I mean how careless is one cop going to be?"

"The pubic never knew about Jim's connections with the failures. The Chief was careful that, when she talked about 'non-successful campaigns', she never spoke of commonalities or coincidences—she just played them up to bad luck or timing."

"But she talked it up internally, didn't she?" I asked.

"She did," Karen said. "She started to question Jim's loyalty and even fitness; and then came the demotion, busted down a rank for 'continued harassment of members of the public'." Karen laughed a cheerless laugh. "The members of the public, of course, were all *Saints*.

"Jim's diligence was held against him. He arrested thirty-four *Saints* in February and sixty-one in March, the two months prior to his death. All but two made it back to the street with no charges."

"That's less than two percent," I said. "What's normal?"

"To be charged? Maybe 80% of arrests are ultimately charged." Karen sighed, and then her shoulders visibly dropped. "The Task Force overall has a 70% charge ratio."

"How the fuck does that work?" I asked.

"It's pretty easy, actually," she said. "The rest of the Task Force targets other clubs." She pounded her fist on the dashboard so hard the music skipped. "I've checked the numbers—the Task Force as a whole targets every club *except* the *Saints*. VPD is protecting the *Saints* and hunting other clubs."

"But Jim and Kyle did the opposite," I said.

"Exactly. Therefore, Jim and Kyle have to go."

"Karen," I said, "I think that's a stretch. At least for now. But help me with the math. Jim has a less than two percent conviction rate for February and March, and he's killed in April?"

"And disgraced by summer," Karen said. "Welcome to my world."

*****

"That night," Karen said, "when Jim was killed, he and Kyle

were asked to work a double shift. That never happens—Ryan, it's not allowed to happen."

"I would hope not. Sixteen hours is too long to be on the street."

"And they hadn't worked Crab Park in years—they'd been posted to their zone for years."

"Okay," I said, "so they find themselves somewhere they're not supposed to be, and things go horribly wrong."

"That's one way of looking at it," Karen replied.

"What's another?" I asked.

"The *Saints* set up this kill zone, and Kyle and Jim walk into it."

"Come on. That is a crazy stretch."

"Not really. Double shift. New zone. *Saints* territory. Easy enough to control."

"Karen," I started, but she cut me off.

"It's a pretty deserted area," she said. "That was their sector that night, one of them was going to find the bomb."

"Reminds me," I said, "what led them there, to find what they found?"

"911 call," Karen replied. "Somebody phoned in a suspicious package—but Kyle and Jim never got to the package. They found the body, and then everything ended."

I had a random thought. "Do they know who the other guy was?" I asked.

"They do, and I don't know how." Karen looked out the window for a very long time. "There was nothing left of Jim to bury. It was the same for the other guy. Ryan, they were basically soup." She looked back at me and then quickly away. "I wish I hadn't eaten those eggs," she said.

She drank some water and continued. "They did find some ID that survived the blast. The other guy was an accountant or something, his name might have been Small, something like that. I don't think he was looked into very hard—he had no connection to anything while the two cops on scene were getting off on taking the piss out of the *Saints*." She moved the water bottle from cup holder to cup holder. "I think he worked for Engs & Associates, for God's sake, a massive accounting firm."

"E&A," I said, "that's a national company—global, even."

"Exactly—no connection. Jim and Kyle were the targets, not some random guy."

I couldn't let go. "Karen," I asked, "is there any way that Jim wasn't the target that night? I mean, who would have known he was going to be there?"

She seemed to consider what I had asked. "Ryan," she said, "the *Saints* are as cold-blooded as it gets. And they hated Jim and Kyle. Now Jim is dead, and Kyle was badly injured and is suspended." She turned in the seat to face me directly. "They have the means, the knowledge and the people to set it up. Someone changes their assignment, the bomb is planted, and the only sector car in the area finds it. Only the *Saints* win with how it played out."

"Okay," I said. "I get that." I hit the wipers, front and back, to clear the snow that had fallen since we left the restaurant. "It's too windy for it to stick," I said. "I don't know if that's good or bad, but it makes driving fun." I hit the wipers again. "Can we table this Engs & Associates guy to look at later?" I asked. She shrugged. "All I'm wondering, is what if Jim wasn't the target?"

"You're wrong," she said. "But consider it tabled. It should be easy enough to check."

"Thank you," I said. "I just want to know more about this guy."

*****

At this point, we were in BC -- nearly to Golden, the last real stop before the long uphill climb to Rogers Pass and then down the other side to Revelstoke. There was no homecoming parade to greet us; *probably the snow keeping everybody away*. And although the highway had been good since leaving Banff, we had also been tucked behind a convoy of snow-plows and sand trucks. With the snow and breakfast and the snow-plows, we were five hours into a three-hour trip. Without the convoy in front of us, I had to use the high beams a few times, it was that dark.

To me, the snow seemed quite heavy. But since I hate being cold I haven't really spent a lot of time in heavy-snow situations. Karen, being from Vancouver, was also no expert on the subject. That left the highway as our only recourse for information—and it was covered in snow to our left and right and we seemed to be the only passenger vehicle around.

"Might be time for some highway information," I said. "Can you check the radio for updates? The signs on the road said AM 840 is the highway report."

"Your radio console is like a spaceship," Karen said. "I didn't even know cars could have CD players."

Neither did I, until the Ford dealership upsold me. I didn't mention the six-disc CD changer was an $1,800 addition; when I bought the truck, the changer held six more CDs than I owned. "There's a manual for the console somewhere, or you could just hit the button marked AM/FM."

Karen figured it out, and *The Violent Femmes'* self-titled debut album was replaced with static at first, and then a road report. Compared to the report, I much preferred the first track on that album, which is actually just Gordon Ganno leaving a voicemail to another band member about how he couldn't make practice that night because his Dad had locked him *inside* the house. According to the radio, being locked inside was a pretty good idea.

"I don't know, Karen," I said. "That road report scares me a bit, and we really just started." I glanced at her—but only quickly. Even in four-wheel drive on a plowed road, the conditions were less than optimal. And I am not a great driver. "But, we do have an abominable snowman in the back who can dig shelters to keep us warm and forage for food if necessary." Nesha perked up at the word 'food', but then lay back down, staring wistfully outside at the falling snow. "You're call."

"I've never actually made this drive," she said. "What happens in Golden or beyond?"

"Nothing happens in Golden," I replied. "But then you're in Glacier National Park and Rogers Pass, which can get so messed up that traffic is stopped for hours at a time with nowhere to go—and if you run out of gas while stopped, you freeze."

"Sounds lovely," she said. "Does Golden have an airport? Maybe I could fly home."

"No way," I said. "We're in this together, remember? Besides," I added, "you don't want to miss watching the military shoot off howitzers in order to set controlled avalanches and prevent cars from getting swept away." Rogers Pass is in the Selkirk Mountains and at 4,360 feet above sea level, it averages more than 400 inches of snow per year. Looking at the side of the road, I was fairly confident this had been an above average year.

"It's still early," she said, "but you're driving." She looked at the side of the highway, where the plowed drifts were easily ten feet tall. "I'm okay to stop, though—there's no real hurry. Rileigh is with her grandparents, and there was no real plan for how long I was going to be away." This confirmed my 'stay until Ryan agrees' theory.

"In case I was a hard ass," I said.

"Yes," she said simply. "That."

"When we get to Golden, let's check that the tank is full."

*****

I did top up in Golden, and Karen bought some coffee and road snacks. We both consulted independently with the highway and weather experts inside and outside the gas station, and decided to temper our expectations for the day and shoot for Revelstoke—about the half way point of our trip. In current conditions, that would probably be another two, maybe two and a half hours. But after that, we were assured that the weather should mostly be behind us and the Coquihalla was expected to be sunny and clear the next day. "That'll work," I said and put a very unwilling Nesha back in the truck.

"She really does love the snow and cold," Karen said.

"As far as I can tell," I replied, "it's her only character flaw."

Forty minutes later, we were at an impasse. Just the other side of Blaeberry, a mining town of about two hundred people, a semi-trailer had flipped and was blocking the Columbia River Bridge in both directions.

"Gonna be a couple of hours, at least," a very cold-looking RCMP officer told us. He was wearing a heavy parka and a fur hat, but his lips were blue. "Gotta bring a rig in from Parson," he said. "Usually, it'd come from Revelstoke, but it looks like they're gonna be shuttin' the Pass down to set off some controlled avalanches." We were at 3,800 feet and the temperature was surprisingly cold given the snow.

He read my mind. "Usually it's one or the other," he said. "Cold or snow, not both."

Karen offered him her coffee. "Haven't opened it yet," she said. "Still warm."

"Much obliged," he said. "Wish I could send you on your way through rather than send you back." He drank some coffee. "But even if we could squeeze you through, you'd just get stuck at the Pass, who knows for how long. At least here there aren't any avalanches."

"Where's the driver?" I asked, nodding at the flipped rig.

"Talking to my partner in our car," he said. "Where it's warm." He laughed. "Neither of 'em is in a great mood right now, though. Safer out here, directing traffic that isn't coming."

"Good luck with the rest of the shift," I said. "Hope it gets better from here."

The plows and other heavy equipment we had been following earlier were stopped haphazardly across the highway, stuck like we were someplace they probably didn't want to be. "Crappy to be on the other side," I said, "with the plows over here."

"Got that right," he said and slapped the roof twice. "Thanks for the coffee. Be careful on your way back."

Even with the scattered plows and graders, I had plenty of room on the deserted highway to make an easy U-turn. "Where is everybody?" Karen asked.

"Staying safe and warm in Golden, I guess. We'll find out soon."

"Oh joy," she replied. "At least the company is fair to middling."

"For me or you?" I asked.

She smiled. "Hopefully Golden has a bar and a hotel." She paused. "At least a bar."

"I know they have a liquor store," I said. "I can't vouch for those other things."

Thirty minutes later, I took the first of three Golden, BC exists at maybe twenty kilometres an hour. I had to break through a small drift of snow left behind by the convoy of plows. Before I'd straightened the wheel, we were downtown. And it was snowing even harder.

CHAPTER 4

Golden itself is in the Canadian Rockies, and surrounded by six National Parks—Yoho, Glacier, Banff, Jasper, Kootenay and Mount Revelstoke. It was established in the late 1800s as a construction camp for the Canadian Pacific Railway workers building a rail route through the Selkirk and Rocky Mountains. Initially called McMillian's Camp in honour of the man who led the railway survey crew, the town became Golden in 1884 when a lumber camp in Alberta began referring to itself as Silver City.

Today, Silver City is an infrequently visited Ghost Town deep inside Banff National Park. Apparently there is a nice plaque, although I've never seen it. Compared to Silver City, Golden has done quite well for itself; perhaps due to its proximity to Rogers Pass and the strain mountain grades put on older vehicles, Golden has more car repair businesses per capita than any other Canadian city. There are nine licensed repair facilities for three-thousand residents; by contrast, there are only three schools.

Downtown Golden was packed. "Weird how we didn't notice how busy it is on our way through," Karen said. "Maybe because everyone is inside?"

I shrugged. "Technically, we by-passed it," I said. "But it might explain why the highway was so empty."

The sides of the road were packed with plowed snow, and as we drove down the main street, the hotel and motel parking lots were packed with cars. We pulled into the Swiss Inn, which looked a little less packed than others. In hindsight, maybe we should have wondered why they had spaces left and everyone else was full.

The parking lot was narrow and recently plowed, although it needed it again. Pulling in, I had to navigate carefully around two tricked out pick-up trucks that dwarfed my full-size and lifted Bronco. Each truck was parked lazily and taking up multiple spaces; each was pulling an open trailer filled with new snowmobiles and carefully protected motorcycles. I don't know much about truck paint and day light and optical illusions, but I swear as I drove between the two of them that one truck changed from red to blue and the other from blue to red.

"Boys and their toys," Karen said. I disagreed—I've never ridden a snowmobile or motorcycle. Karen, however, rolled her eyes and waved her hand expansively through the cab of the truck. I conceded the point by pulling the truck onto a three-foot pile of snow, collected and dumped by the hotel's plow.

"Found a spot," I said. Karen just shook her head. She had to struggle out of the cab and down to the ground. *Small victories.*

Inside, the lobby reminded me of Switzerland. I've never been there, but I was convinced. Woolen blankets and chunky sweaters, cuckoo clocks, skis, fire places, views in every direction of snow-capped mountains. If not Switzerland, than at least Kimberly BC, the self-proclaimed Bavarian City of the Rockies, two and a half hours to the south. I've been there a number of times. The Swiss Inn was clearly a mom and pop operation, and mom was at the counter and highly distracted. She was everything you would imagine the proprietress of a Swiss Inn would be, like a skinny Mrs. Claus.

Mrs. Claus was wearing jeans and a flannel shirt and hiking boots and her hair was pale blonde with a hint of grey and done in a tight braid. She looked like she belonged outside, certainly in our mountains if not the Swiss Alps, but it really did seem that she would rather be outside than in here with us. *Not very welcoming, despite the comforting ambience.* I wondered why the paradox and, in hindsight, it's one of those things I could have done without knowing.

There were three or four people in front of me, but Mrs. Claus kept looking into the restaurant and losing track of what was being said. I peeked into the restaurant too, but could only see half of the room and didn't see anything other than a couple of harried servers and some college age customers. Too few people to account for the noise. Karen had stayed outside to play with Nesha for a few minutes, and by the time they came into the lobby, I was at the counter.

Everyone in front of me had been turned away and I was expecting the same, especially given a very obvious 'No Pets Allowed' policy. I was hoping Nesha would win over the owner and maybe she did. We were in luck— even with the dog, two rooms were quickly found. One of the rooms, Mrs. Claus said, wasn't great, but she assured us the food in the restaurant would make up for it. The sign outside did promise "World's Greatest Schnitzel", so I handed her my credit card. She didn't run the card right away as she was busy fawning over the dog and I swear she asked Nesha if she liked to chase *Bose Menschen.*

I was about to ask what that was when a significant number of glasses fell in the dining room, and there was some obnoxious laughing. I heard a man with a loud and deep cigarette voice say "Hang on Chief, we'll pay for the glasses, but we need more beer!"

"Somebody's having fun," I said. Mrs. Claus handed my card back without taking an imprint and said, simply, "we can do this later." *I wonder where everybody is right now?* People were being turned away at the front desk, yet the lobby was empty and the restaurant was far louder than it was full. Given that the Swiss Inn was the only place we had passed with a restaurant, I wondered if it was empty because of the food or the tricked-out trucks parked outside. I hoped it wasn't the food.

Karen was preoccupied with thoughts of home and work and said she wasn't hungry. Sensing she needed a friend, the dog stayed with her. I'd only had coffee and some bacon to eat earlier, so as she headed to the nicer room to connect with her office and to let her folks know we were delayed, I headed for the restaurant disappointed that the promise of schnitzel wasn't enough to entice Karen to join me. Mrs. Clause seemed relieved that Karen and I had made the choices we did.

I turned for the restaurant. *You're losing it, Dirt. There was a time....* To prevent the self-pity, I instantly started to think about how good lightly breaded and deep fried pork with lemon tastes. *Besides, there was never actually a time where you would make a pass at a friend's widow.*

In the restaurant, the scene was familiar and strange. It had all the trappings and things you would expect in a small-town mountain restaurant, but there was a significant tension in the air. Two dishevelled and obviously tired teenage servers were huddled around the bar. There was an elderly couple seated at a window and four college kids, cutting class and heading east to Banff or west to Revelstoke for some fun in the snow, sitting two by two behind them. The kids looked like they were getting ready to leave but were having trouble with something. Maybe the bill, I thought. Math can be hard.

The only other customers were a group of a half-dozen hard looking guys of different sizes and shapes having an inexplicably good time. There were easily two dozen empties on the tables in front of them. I made an educated guess as to who owned the poorly parked trucks outside.

A white-haired gentleman I assumed to be Mr. Claus had a

broom and was doing his best to sweep up broken glass. The yahoos weren't making it easy, and kept kicking larger pieces around the floor or grabbing his broom.

One of the waitresses, a pretty blonde with a pencil behind her ear, pointed me at a table near a fire place. Or maybe she was pointing at the fireplace itself. There was a nice fire going, three crackling logs and what looked like four winter jackets. The college kids were all staring at the fireplace with shocked expressions, like even though they had been there, they couldn't believe what had just happened. "That was my sister's jacket," one of the girls said. "She's going to kill me." The boyfriends were of average size and doing their best to look tough, but the group of six weren't impressed. Truthfully, I wasn't either, but at least the kids weren't' afraid of me.

All six of the ass-hats were white although, oddly, two of them were clean cut. There were four of them huddled around one table, large and hairy and all wearing the biker uniform of greasy t-shirts, denim vests and Timberland boots. Two of them had face tattoos, but I couldn't make out what they were. I hoped never to get close enough to find out.

The other two were at a separate table; it was obvious the four-top the gorillas were crowded around had been an eight-top a little while ago. The two at their own island of Formica were small and wiry with perfect hair and manicured nails. They were wearing actual khaki pants, collared shirts and golf sweaters, although I had a difficult time believing golf had been on the daily calendar. One of them had a blazer draped over his chair and yet, despite the veneer of business success, *mean* was the word that came to mind when looking at them. Maybe even feral. One was dark with a prominent nose and wearing a red sweater, the other was almost ruddy in complexion with very fair hair and wearing a black sweater. Without speaking Swiss, I suddenly knew what *Bose Menschen* meant. These were seriously bad men.

It was obvious the two sweaters were in charge and they somehow seemed to not notice or care about anything while simultaneously noticing and caring about everything. Red Sweater looked at me and then away, clearly unconcerned by what he saw. That hurt my feelings—usually I have to say something stupid before being dismissed so quickly.

While the sweaters discussed stock options or off-shore banking, the four hairy guys noticed me for the first time. Each of these guys was bigger than the one beside him and, because of the way they seemed to sniff the air, they reminded me of poorly trained dogs on long leashes. They lost interest in me and went back to giving themselves a show and the waitresses a hard time. As one of the girls tried to clear the table of the remaining empties before more could be broken, there was some grabbing that was clearly unwelcomed. The pretty waitress who'd pointed me to the table came by with a menu and a grimace. Her name tag said Amy. She was wearing faded jeans and a UBC sweatshirt. There was nothing provocative about her in any way. The other waitress was Sarah, and she could have been Amy's dark-haired twin.

"Thanks Amy," I said. "You doing alright? Looks like an interesting crowd."

She shook her head no, but said "It's good. Thanks." She had her back to the Mensa meeting, and the four gorillas were staring. "Oh, I do like *this* view," one of them said and the others hooted. "I prefer the front view," another said. "High and round, like God meant 'em to be." Amy blushed, and over her shoulder the four wise men were so busy congratulating themselves for knowing that many words that food and drinks were spilling.

"How long has this been going on?" I asked her, using my head to point at the wildlife exhibit.

"They showed up last night," Amy said. "When we closed,

they didn't leave. We had to have the cops come, although they didn't do much good. When they finally left, I thought they were gone for good, but they showed up again about an hour ago." She looked at me directly for the first time. "All they do is drink and grope."

"Hey," the largest gorilla shouted and Amy visibly shuddered. His hair and beard were so red, he was probably closer to an orangutan. "Order your food and move on, Slick. We need that piece back here. Our drinks spilled."

He actually called me 'Slick'. I wasn't convinced it was a compliment.

"There's a napkin holder on the table," I said. "As a group, you can figure out how it works."

 Amy's eyes were wide. "Don't," she whispered. "Please don't. It's okay."

"Give her back," one of the face tattoos said. "You got your own girl, and she's sweet. We saw her when you rolled in."

"Yeah," the other face tattoo said. "Where's she at? Getting started without you?"

"That's it, "a third guy chimed in. "Everybody knows blondes are so stuck up that they take a while to warm up. Right, Amy?" The laughter was ugly and the back slapping was intense.

I stood up and suddenly Amy was gone. I couldn't really blame her, I wanted to be gone myself—but where was I going to go? They'd already spotted me, and at 6'5", 230 pounds, I don't disappear that easily. My size means that I've been challenged to a lot of fights by a lot of different guys for a lot of different reasons over the years. But, off the baseball diamond, I've had exactly one fist fight: with Kyle when we were twelve. Not fighting, however, is completely different than backing down;

that, I don't do. Fortunately, my mouth has gotten me out of as many situations as it's gotten me into over the years; I've probably had as many drinks with guys who wanted to tear me apart minutes before as I have with friends. But here in Golden, BC of all places, I was severely outnumbered and didn't understand the hostility. Of course, I don't spend a lot of time with the sleeveless denim vest and face tattoo crowd, so maybe this is just how they roll and I was in the wrong. *Maybe we're bonding.*

"Listen," I said to the group at large. "I just want some schnitzel, and maybe you could show Amy and Sarah some courtesy. They're kids."

The orangutan stood up. He towered over me. I'm pretty sure his movement was enough to tilt the earth's axis. On his jacket, there was a horse with a dagger through its head, exactly like the medical snake and sceptre except completely different and far scarier.

"Amy," he grunted. "Oh, Amy, come out come out wherever you are!" His three buddies fanned out and started towards the bar and the kitchen behind that. "Oh Amy," they all shouted, "we just want to play!"

"And our table cleaned up," another said. "Do your damn job, woman!"

One of the face tattoos—it actually looked like a Maori symbol—found Amy in the kitchen and dragged her to the bar. I did not like where his hands were. The other face tattoo went in the kitchen and found Sarah. He was even more handsy than his buddy.

"Guys, they're kids," I said again. "And terrified." The guy who grabbed Amy squeezed her breasts with both hands and actually said "Honk, honk". That killed his buddies—"honk honk" they all repeated, "honk honk". Amy, god love her, didn't flinch even as the other two bikers headed to the bar making squeezing motions with their hands. "Honk Honk!" The second face tattoo—his was just words nobody could read —was holding Sarah in front of him and had one hand inside the waistband of her jeans. "We're going to have some fun tonight!" he said. One of his buddies had reached the bar and cleared everything off the top—bottles and glasses breaking on the floor while the Maori lifted Amy onto the bar with one hand. I felt like we were recreating the opening scene from *The Accused*.

Mr. Claus ran for the bar, but one of the four tripped him and he went down hard. The two sweaters still hadn't moved. "Oops," the mountain said. "Clumsy you."

"Hey, time out," I said and made an actual T with my hands, like it was a football game and I was the coach. Four blank faces looked my way. The sweaters still hadn't moved. "I'm not getting my schnitzel, am I?"

Nobody laughed; weirdly, I remember being disappointed because I thought it was a pretty good line.

"Don't worry," the biggest one said. "We share."

"Chromosomes," I said. "I can see that. But come on, guys, what do you say? Let the kids go, I'll buy you a couple of drinks for the road, and everything's cool."

"Please don't hurt them," the wife said. "I beg you to leave them alone."

Maori had Amy pinned on the bar top. Two steps, and I pushed him off. Amy ran to the other side of the room and when Word Face let Sarah go so he could grab me from behind, she was able to escape as well. At least temporarily. Why they didn't leave altogether, I'll never know. While Word Face held me, the orangutan punched me in the head—left eye, right eye, and one in the gut for fun. My vision exploded, but my head stayed attached and I stayed on my feet—mostly because Word Face was holding me, but still. Small battles win the war.

Even though there was a pretty significant cut over my left eye and what was left of my vision was blurry, the stomach punch hurt worse. "That's not going to help my hernia," I told the two blurry orangutans who seemed to be causing the pain. *Not fair, there was only one when this started.*

Through the sparks in my eyes, I could see the husband was up, and I noticed that the college kids weren't moving in our direction. Maybe they'd already had their dance, I thought; after all, their jackets and not mine were in the fireplace. Amy stopped the husband from getting any closer.

"Dancing bears like you guys belong outside," I said. "In the mountains, maybe find a nice Sasquatch to mate with, you know, mix with your own kind?" Another stomach punch, this one softer, or maybe I was still feeling the first one. "What do you say, guys? Feels like we've had our fun tonight."

Additional blows never came. "Axle," Red Sweater said and snapped the orangutan's leash. "Let our new friend have his schnitzel. And *we* will buy *him* a drink." Despite, or maybe because of, his careful enunciation, there was no hint of an accent. "I'm Malone," he said. He did not offer to shake hands. In my mind, he looked nothing like a Malone; he was significantly more Mediterranean than Irish. "Please forgive my colleagues. Snow makes them tiresome."

"Nothing to forgive," I said, "but thank you." Word Face let me go. I threw an overhand right and hit him flush on the side of the jaw. I don't think he even noticed.

"Enough," Black Sweater said.

"I'll buy my own drink," I said, rubbing my hand. I decided to push my luck, because that's what I do. "Amy is pretty scared. A nice tip might help with that."

Malone dropped two $100 bills on his table. "Gentleman," he said, "we ride." The gorillas stood up and moved to the outside exit rather than into the hotel lobby. Each did his best to scare me to death as they walked away. Malone simply nodded at me and followed.

Black Sweater hadn't moved and had said just that one word. When the rest of his crew was outside, he stood and dropped another two hundreds on the table. "You weren't afraid," he said to me, his lips curling in a cold smile. He peeled off another bill. "Buy yourself some stitches." He put on the blazer. "Down the road," he added with absolutely no emotion. He was wrong though—Black Sweater did what the other five had not: he scared me to my core.

"Dancing bears," he said, heading out the door. "Sasquatch. I like that."

*****

I sat back down and the college kids toasted me. One even called me 'Dude'. "Sorry about your jackets," I said. There were a lot of handshakes and hugs and then the college kids got busy helping the owners clean the broken glass and bottles from the floor. Everybody does what they can, I guess.

Sarah handed me a cloth of ice and some towels for my face. "You're going to need stitches," she said. "Or that cut is going to scar." She looked at me kindly. "My gramma used to be a nurse, maybe she can help with that."

I asked Amy to repeat what she had told me earlier about my new friends and she explained in greater detail: they came in about eight the night before and didn't leave until well after closing and with some inexplicably mild prompting form the cops. The bikers—for what else could they be—hadn't been happy to learn that a Swiss restaurant didn't have chicken wings, but they made up for it in beer. They paid for very little and had been handsy enough that two regular waitresses hadn't shown up for work today. Amy picked up the $500 the group had left on the table. "This will cover most of last night and the stuff they broke." She hugged me carefully. "Thank you."

I'm not rich—I was going to be, but a brick wall got in the way—but I'm not struggling in any way. I said, "No, that's for you. The sweaters were clear about that. Whatever you're short from yesterday, you can put on my bill." Amy started to cry and Sarah drew her close, exhaustion getting the better of them both.

"Taken another punch," one of the students said to me, "and maybe they would have left enough for new jackets."

He paused to make sure I knew he was joking. I did. "Laughing hurts," I said. "Please, no more jokes."

"Or at least better ones," one of his buddies said. I laughed again.

The husband and wife owners appeared at my table. The wife, like Amy, was crying. "I am Hans," the husband said in a clipped accent I assumed was Swiss. "My wife is Gwen." They both reached out to shake hands at the same time. That was awkward, so Gwen just hugged me and wouldn't let go. "You have met our grand-daughters," Hans said.

"Sarah and Amy?" I asked, but who else could it have been? "They're very brave," I said. "Amazing kids. I'm Ryan."

"Speaking of brave," Gwen said, "let me see that face." In just a few minutes, she had applied some homemade butterfly bandages. "It will scar, she said, "but not too badly."

"The girls love scars," Hans said and we all burst out laughing.

"You have no idea what you have done," Gwen said. "Thank you."

"I have some idea," I told her. "I just hope it's over. Man," I said, "I just wanted a place to sleep and something to eat. Schnitzel made it seem like an even better idea."

"That group arrived yesterday, but only the two in the sweaters came inside. They booked four rooms, but we never saw the other four people." Hans looked at his wife.

"But," Gwen continued with far more of an accent, "we have seen their rooms today."

Hans sighed and slumped into one of the seats. "It will be months before we are able to rent two of them again."

He grabbed my arm. "The toilets," he said, "are missing. Who steals a toilet?"

"That didn't stop them from going to the bathroom," Gwen added.

At this point, Karen entered the dining room. Nesha had stayed in her room. Oblivious to everything that had happened and why the floor was covered in glass, there were jackets in the fire place, and teenagers were crying, she looked at me like she hoped this wasn't my fault but expected that it was.

"You know," she said, "I am a little hungry after all."

Gwen jumped to her feet and gave Karen a hug. Karen patted Gwen's back, but was understandably confused. Karen gave me a wry smile and Hans stood up and clapped his hands. "Tonight," he said, "*we* will cook for you. Amy, Sarah, call your friends, we will have a party! Ryan, get the dog—I hope she likes schnitzel!"

As Hans and Gwen went into the kitchen, a few more customers appeared. I assumed they were staying in the hotel and had passed on eating when they noticed the earlier lounge act. There was a light round of applause; it wasn't much applause, but it was clearly directed at me. Amy appeared again, with more ice and clean towels and another hug.

When we were alone, Karen touched my face and asked an obvious question. "What *the hell* did I miss, Ryan?"

"I'll tell you," I said, "but you won't believe a word."

*****

Obviously, there was beer that night. Despite the name, the Swiss Inn only had bottles of Labatt/Molson/Kokanee products. I had been hoping for something more European. As I was getting ready to settle on Kokanee Gold, a brand new entry to the Kokanee shelf which now stood at two, Hans arrived with some *Quollfrisch*, a very nice lager. "From my private collection," he said with a wink.

For an hour, Karen grilled me like the prosecutor she is. When I described the logo that I had seen on the Four Horseman's jackets, she grabbed her phone and made a call to a friend of Jim's in Vancouver. Advanced technology comes with a speaker function, so Karen put the phone on a table and we could both hear without having to share the headset. Rich Koleman, a guy I'd met a few times over the years, spoke to us from Vancouver. Captain of the VPD flag football team, Rich was a seven-year veteran of the motorcycle task force and a no-nonsense kind of guy. "Horse head and a dagger," he told us over a choppy line, "means *The Death's Head* out of Edmonton. They are a puppet group of the *Saints*. Strictly low level enforcement and intimidation."

"That explains the four mouth-breathers Ryan saw, but what about the two upper management guys?" Karen asked.

"Word on the street is that our little task force has been so effective here, that clubs are running out of management material," Rich said. "That includes the *Saints*, even though we never seem to touch them. Every dent that we make in their competition, the *Saints* are able to step up and fill the void. That means more soldiers and more soldiers means more generals."

"Hence the sweaters," Karen said. "Exponential leadership growth."

"You know," I said, "Karen said a similar thing yesterday, Rich. Why does the task force have such success against clubs that *aren't* the *Saints*?"

A decorated sergeant of the Vancouver Police Department paused. "I'll deny I said this," Rich said, "but you'd have to ask the Chief about that. Success is tied to effort, man, you know that Ryan—and our only consolidated efforts seem to be against other clubs. Those are the operations on our end that run clean".

"*Saints* are being looked after," I said.

"You said that, Ryan, not me. Now," Rich continued "from what you've said, the two sweaters are probably Roy Gaston and Jim Hodder. Gaston runs the *Death's Head;* Hodder is second in command for the *Saints* nationally. It definitely sounds like the *Saints* are on a recruiting drive."

"If that's the case," Karen said, "will there be more members on the way?"

"No idea," Rich said, "but I would expect so. Four soldiers sounds like a scout squad." There was silence and a strange static on the line. "I can't stress this enough, guys—these two are the real deal; in fact, Gaston is the only non-Anglo member of any *Saints* or *Saints* affiliated club in the country. That tells you what kind of juice he has."

"Both guys looked white," I said, "but one was maybe Mediterranean. He's the one who called himself Malone and he talked very carefully. He pronounced every syllable."

"That's Gaston, for sure," Rich said. "Malone is kind of his inside joke—one that only he understands. But Hodder is the guy you really have to worry about. Jesus Christ, Ryan," he said, "what have you done?"

"I just wanted some schnitzel," I said. "Nothing more, nothing less."

"Yeah," Rich said, "schnitzel be damned. Word is that Hodder consolidated biker power in Alberta by cutting off the ears and cutting out the eyes of his competition and sending those 'canapes' to the RCMP."

With nothing left to be said after that, we stammered some good-byes and hung up. "Ryan," Karen said softly, "I leave you for twenty minutes and you start a war with a biker gang."

"Club," I reminded her. "Biker *club*. And I swear it was closer to half an hour."

*****

The rest of the night is kind of blurry. The snow continued to fall, Nesha spent more time outside than in, and I know that I tried to beg off a couple of times only to find a new beer in my hand. Many of the college kids from surrounding hotels joined the party, as good news and good times spread fast. At one point, there were at least thirty people laughing and drinking —and eating. The food was excellent—and Gwen even found me some chicken wings. *Take that, you hairy fucks.*

Karen was having a great time, snowbound in Golden BC, hanging out with strangers. I thought about Jim and what Karen's life had been like since that night last April and toasted her strength silently with my beer. *She needs this. Probably the only fun she's had in months. It's worth a couple of shots to the head.*

I grabbed a six-pack and a significant amount of ice from Amy and headed to my room. Tired from the food and attention,

Nesha came with me—I had expected her to want to stay behind. New start, fresh beginnings, tomorrow is the first day... all those new-age sunshine thoughts were in my head. But, realistically, this forward motion thing was something very new to me. I may have been sitting at a bar with a beer in my hand, but it wasn't my bar and apparently I wasn't actually paying for the beer and—most importantly-- there did seem to be a goal in mind other than oblivion. The goal wasn't entirely clear right then, but I had just been beaten up by a three-hundred pound orangutan. And I knew that future days were going to be different from prior days and that was something I hadn't been able to say for a long, long time. I just hoped that immediate days didn't involve more conversations with high-level bikers in golf sweaters or their hairy friends.

Karen half-heartedly questioned why I was leaving, but I just pointed at my face. She kissed both of my eyes. "Thank you Ryan," she said and before I could respond she went back to the party. As I headed to my suddenly upgraded room, if I had to put a name on what I was feeling, I might have called it... hope. And what I've learned about hope is that it dies if you push it. So I left while it still seemed to be in bloom.

*****

In my room, fresh beer in hand, I found my calling card and dialed Kyle, but got his store-bought answering message. I also called my brother Jaxson and told his voicemail I was coming home. I remembered when I hung up that he was in England and likely didn't care.

I did think of calling Robyn, Kyle's sister and my first—and only—serious girlfriend, but it was after midnight and I have drunk dialed too many times. She lives in Kelowna, and I rationalized that since Kelowna *could* be on the way, we could find some time to stop. *Maybe we could have lunch. Or at least I could get a new calling card. Maybe even a cell phone.*

I did not remind myself that it's easier to get to Vancouver from where we were by avoiding Kelowna. And because I didn't puncture my own lie, that night I slept the sleep of the just, and not the damned—which is how I had spent the past 1100 pus nights. I did not dream of Wrigley.

CHAPTER 5

In the morning, I figured out how to use the motel-room coffee maker and intentionally didn't look in a mirror. I took Nesha outside and threw a half-dozen snowballs for her before Karen even stirred. There were still four beer on the dresser when I woke up, a sight I am unaccustomed to seeing. The dog didn't care or praise me, but at least she didn't call dibs on what was left. She just wanted to run and, maybe, move to Golden.

The back of the hotel was an empty field covered in at least two feet of unbroken snow. Because I'm right handed and it was my left shoulder that took on Wrigley Field, I was still able to get each snowball a good distance for her to chase, most sailed to the end of the field. Snowballs do not travel as far as baseballs, but I was pleased. For a major league out-fielder, sailing a snowball to the end of this field was probably average, but it was off the charts for a Canadian bar owner.

Heading back around to the front of the hotel, I could see the morning had already peaked and I hadn't even had a second cup of coffee. Red Sweater and Black Sweater were nowhere to be seen, but the four acolytes were front and centre. Denim vests had been replaced with down vests, I assume as a concession to the weather. The tricked out red truck was idling in the parking lot, exhaust slowly dissipating in the freezing air. The blue truck was nowhere to be seen and that told me the Sweaters weren't around to snap any leashes.

I heard the sliding doors to the motel open and hoped it wasn't

Karen, but it was. There were a few cat calls and multiple requests for Karen to take it off, but she didn't oblige. "Are you kidding?" she said. "Too cold." She looked at me. "Should I call the RCMP?"

"Just having a conversation with my friends," I said and asked her to go back inside. She stayed. "All good. I think they simply need directions."

"Kill joy," one of them said.

"RCMP? In Golden?" another said. "We'll be long gone before they show up. Plus," he added, "they didn't do much good the other night."

Orangutan made a comment about my black eyes, and being on the losing end of the evening.

"It's probably true," I told him, "but in a few weeks, I'll be better and you'll still be sleeping with your hairy friends. Who's really the loser?" I asked.

Obviously, Nesha wasn't on a leash and as Orangutan took a few steps forward, she moved directly in front of me and sat at my feet. I've had this dog for seven years; in fact, Robyn was there when I got her from an Arizona shelter. Nesha barks twice a year, if that, and I am convinced that she is incapable of anger. But the sounds coming out of her right then were not pleasant and I hoped Orangutan and his zoo could hear them. Later, I wondered if this crew reminded her of the group that had abandoned her in a shopping mall dumpster when she was eight weeks old. How the shelter knew she'd been left by bikers, I never knew, but that day she definitely seemed to be righting some wrongs.

Hackles up, she was nearly an inch taller than when calm. Fangs bared, looking from the other side, I would have been worried, if not terrified—and I'm a dog person. This group was clearly concerned, but didn't run away in fear. I gave them credit for being brave but then deducted points for being too dumb to know better.

"Jesus Christ," Word Face said. "He's got a fucking wolf. Nobody mentioned no wolf."

"She's a Malamute," I said. "Easy mistake to make. And," I added, "she's completely trained to attack on command." This was an outright lie, but all is fair in a motel parking lot. Nesha and I took a step towards them. "One, maybe two, maybe even three, of you might get away if you do anything stupid right now, but at least *one* of you won't." Nesha stayed beside me, but her growl was guttural and ancient. I was clearly on the dog's side, and I was unnerved. "So, who's it gonna be?"

"You know why we're here," one of the vests said. They all looked so similar I wasn't interested in differentiating who was speaking, only who was moving.

"I really don't," I replied. "I just wanted some fucking schnitzel, and then you proceeded to have a better time than I did.

"So, you know what guys? You can all fuck off or I can give you directions to where your sisters live so you can finish what you tried to start last night."

I'm not sure they got the joke. I'm not sure it was a joke. While we were talking, the face tattoos had moved, one to each side of my Bronco.

"We're leaving," Maori said, "but you, Fuck Head, are staying." They both took out folding knives and stuck them in the rear tires of my truck with significant strength.

I have never seen 100 pounds move so fast. Nesha was on Word Face before he could even stand up. She grabbed him by the ass and he went down face first in the snow with Nesha on top of him, ripping away at something. Word Face rolled over and the dog lost her purchase, rolling off him in a summersault. Word Face stood up and followed his teammates to the waiting truck, but there was no ass in his jeans. I was curious as to why Nesha didn't chase after them, but grateful she didn't. Instead, she trotted over to me, the back end of a dirty pair of jeans showing in her smile. At my feet, she dropped what was left of the pants and a greasy wallet.

"Good girl," Karen said from behind me. "Good dog." Nesha purred while Karen hugged her. Karen turned to me. "Sisters, Ryan, really?" I shrugged.

Hans and Gwen came out, and Gwen gave Nesha quite a bit of schnitzel. Hans handed me a case of *Farnsberger*. "More of my stash," he said.

There was $800 in the wallet. I gave it to Gwen and asked her to get the college kids new jackets.

The knives in my tires were in deep. Neither tire could be repaired and, like most people, I only had one spare. "Fuck me," I said softly. Hans overheard. "We will get you new tires," he said. "I know the guys at NAPA."

"That's not it," I said. "The knives don't even match. They could have at least left me a matching set."

*****

The cops came. Statements were made. Cautions were given. Tires were changed—paid for, despite my objections, by Hans. When it was time to leave, I had to wake Nesha up as she was fast asleep in Gwen's kitchen. End of the field in two feet of snow both ways, times six, followed by fending off an angry bunch of bikers is a good morning for one dog. And it was great schnitzel. Gwen gave me some as well, and added to the beer, I figured the morning was back to even.

*****

67

As we left the Swiss Inn and Golden BC, Karen said "you sure know how to show a girl a good time."

"I think you may have had more fun than I did."

She laughed. "Ryan," she said, "we spent the entire day talking about motorcycle gangs and drugs and Jim, and then you and your dog take on a *Saints* puppet club." She paused. "What the actual fuck?"

"Karen," I replied, "when we started this trip, I didn't think you even swore. Now, you're a sailor."

"I didn't, then," she told me. "But that was a lifetime ago."

Two days. Sometimes two days is a lifetime.

*****

The roads were compact, so I took the Bronco out of four-wheel drive. Truthfully, I was having trouble seeing thanks to the orangutan and would have asked Karen to drive; instead, I asked Karen about the night. She was certainly in no shape to drive. Apparently, she and Hans and Gwen and the staff and about a dozen skiers were now family. I was included—by extension as well as deed—and that made me smile as I still wasn't sure what I had done besides stand up for some brave teenagers.

Karen was in rough shape. Her sunglasses were on and she had pulled down the extra-large visor even though it was still snowing—although only a sprinkling compared to yesterday. I was oddly proud that I had beer left and no hangover and Karen was a mess. Score one for me, I thought, remembering her 'might be enough for you' comment. A good night's sleep can apparently make any of us a tiny-bit self-righteous.

An hour out, I asked Karen to back up to the point in the story where Kylee gets a new car.

"Kid gets an upgrade," I said. "What does that mean to Jim," I asked, "and independently of the family dynamic, to you?" I had my own ideas, obviously, but what did this new found display of independence and available cash mean to a sixteen-year police veteran and a Provincial Prosecutor?

"Drugs," Karen said. "Obviously. But what wasn't so obvious—despite the fact that the Hadden brothers were clearly growing whatever was being sold—is how the money came back to Kylee. Jim was convinced it was through the Haddens and—for lack of a better term—went on the war path. No Hadden or *Silent Saint* could avoid Jim."

"Right, we covered that," I said.

The Trans-Canada was in remarkable shape given the weather of yesterday. Rogers Pass came and went with only a high-way sign to make it memorable. There is an historical display and a plaque, like at Silver City, but I assumed without asking that Karen wasn't interested in stopping.

"Tell me about the drugs," I said. "I mean, I haven't lived in Vancouver full time since '88, and even then it was clear that there was a gang-war taking place." I took a quick look in the back of the truck, and Nesha was still sound asleep and purring. It's a weird thing about Malamutes, but they actually purr, like a cat. It could be snoring, but either way, I never hold that against her.

"There was," Karen said. "An obvious and bloody war that started in '85 as an effort to control the streets—most obviously for drugs, but extortion and hookers too—prior to Expo '86. In fact," she said, "between '85 and '90, my office believes that more than sixty people were murdered specifically because of involvement in the acquisition, distribution and sale of drugs."

She tapped her fist twice on the dashboard. "Those are the

legal words—basically, pushers and users getting killed like in a Montreal mafia war. But in Vancouver, it was the *Saints* who won the war and they have, basically, been in charge ever since." She held up one finger. "First," she said, "it was Anthony Baker Senior. He gained control of the streets for his crew." She held up a second finger. "And he held control until a year or so ago, and now it's his kid who runs things."

"This secession," I asked, "peaceful or forceful?"

"Mostly peaceful. Some of the old guard apparently don't like Junior's ways and his new-fangled ideas like bars and car washes instead of drugs and hookers, but you can't please everyone. And," she added, "make no mistake—Junior knows drugs."

 "But this turf war started," I said, "long before the Hadden brothers and their stuff even existed, right?"

"Right and wrong," Karen replied. "The *Saints* have always prided themselves on their stuff. And they have historically taken their best growers and treated them like Gods. Anything they want—lights, soil, hydro, sprinklers, just whatever.

"And, over time, the Hadden brothers got to a point where their stuff was so good that nothing else would do. In fact," she added, "the market even rebelled for a while when the good stuff was running low."

"How's that work?" I asked.

 "Control of the market became a blessing and a curse for the Bakers and the *Saints*. This was right about the time that Junior was looking for control, and Dad wasn't convinced he was ready. The Haddens, however, were producing amazing product but because they were so proficient, they were producing *too* much. The *Saints*," she said, "actually had too much product to keep prices high. They were struggling to maintain pricing."

"Supply and demand," I said. "Sure. But I would have thought with their success, they would have found new ways to distribute."

"Absolutely, they did. They went south. And then further south. Eventually, so far south they were in Mexico and trading BC Bud directly for 'horse'—or heroin. But the Haddens became so prolific at making this stuff under difficult circumstances that the *Saints* were having trouble getting rid of it all without flooding the market and crippling their own prices."

"Wait," I said. "They essentially blocked the market for themselves?"

"Which opened the door for other clubs and other growers and other strains, sold for a fraction of the cost."

"So now there's competition again," I said. "Which means more players and more violence."

"Exactly," Karen said. "And at the same time, the States is wanting more and more. And willing to consider other sources than the *Saints* if necessary, as production is dropping due to these 'internal pressures' at home." She punched my shoulder, once, twice, three times. "And all of this," she said, "is before Jim became a significant 'internal pressure' to the *Saints*."

"It's quite the compelling story," I said. "I wish it weren't real."

"Me too, Ryan, me too. Every damn day." She put both arms in front of her, palms up, and made a sweeping motion, right to left so that she was motioning to the south. "And Junior realizes that he and his old man are sitting on the answer—move more product south, stabilize the market at home, make more money." She flashed a quick smile. "Literally sitting on the answer."

"Please tell me they didn't smuggle it into the States in their asses," I said.

"Smuggle, yes," she said. "Asses, no. The Baker family owns the biggest RV dealership in Western Canada. They have more than forty locations. In fact", she added, "that dealership in Golden where they changed your tires is one of theirs."

"RVs is not what I was thinking. But I like it. So how's it work?" I asked her. "Secret compartments?"

"Some," Karen said. "Lead lined in order to beat the drug dogs at the border. And an endless supply of Snow Birds to drive across with dope and drive back with cash. According to the border reports I've seen, less than eight percent of RVs are stopped at the border for any reason. And the number one reason they're stopped?" she asked rhetorically. "To pay duty on purchases."

"Eight percent," I said. "That's crazy."

"Those are the Canadian numbers," Karen added. "So that's on the way back, but by that point, of course, the drugs are gone and all there is cash. We suspect that many of the mules deliberately exceed their allowable spending limits duty wise and self-admit at the Border so they don't get stopped randomly or raise any suspicion. Instead, they park with hundreds of thousands in twenties in a secret compartment or maybe a suitcase and head inside the border station to pay a few hundred dollars in duty on legal purchases. And because they were honest, nobody checks anything or even thinks twice about what might be in the rig, even if it only left the country two days ago."

"Who's gonna check Ma and Pa Kettle," I said, "when they admit to having spent more than they're allowed?"

She raised both arms in a there you go gesture. "And some stay longer, of course, especially the ones making the California and Texas runs. But, ironically, the longer the rig is in the

States, the less suspicious it is. That's what they're made for, after all: road trips."

"I'm in the wrong business," I said. "We both are."

"No. No we're not," she said, but with no fire. I took a quick peek at her, not sure if she was speaking for both of us, or just her. "We can live with ourselves and what we've done."

So she was just speaking for herself.

"The Americans don't share their border stop numbers," she added, "at least not with me since it's not technically part of my purview. But since the Douglas and Peach Arch crossings are so busy—only the Detroit-Windsor border is busier—we know they don't stop many more than we do. Especially not gramma and grampa driving a brand new RV."

"Wrong business," I said again.

"You don't believe that," she said.

"Something to consider when I'm older," I countered. "Assuming I can learn to drive something bigger than this truck."

*****

"Okay," I said. "We've got all this dope and we've got to get it to the States." I thought back seven or eight years ago, when life was real and full of promise. "I do remember when I was in the minors teammates saying how great BC Bud was—even if it wasn't called that yet—and how shitty everything else was in comparison. In fact, when the guys found out I was from BC, man, they thought marijuana to BC was like cactus to Arizona."

"When was that?" Karen asked.

"I spent so little time in the Majors," I said, "that I don't know if pot was a thing there or not. But in the minors, pot was everything: affordable, not tested for, and if you knew the right dealer, potent. To answer your question, maybe '90 or '91 is when I first noticed it. It was worse after I was injured—everybody, including some of the trainers, wanted me to smoke weed to help manage the pain."

"Should have jumped on board," she said, "at least as an investor. Word on the street now is that the Haddens control as many as sixty grow ops between Whistler and Hope." She turned around and tried to pet Nesha, but with the dog lying down, Karen couldn't reach. The dog didn't stir, so Karen turned back around and looked out the window at ten-foot snow banks. "The pressure to find new markets was incredible —*incredible*—and that meant doubling or even tripling sales in the States." She grabbed an atlas from the glove box. "Further south each trip."

"So," I said, "the *Saints* gave the Hadden brothers, former douche bags—"

"Hanger-ons," Karen said. "Douche bags is only implied, not proven."

"Right. Douche-bagger-ons", I said. "And these guys went from something to *everything* in zero seconds and Kylee was there for the ride."

"Yeah," Karen said. "Ultimately. You know from being in the States in the early 90s how valuable—or valued—BC pot was, and that was before the market got really hot. And BC Bud is at the top of every 'daily catch' price list. So the *Silent Saints* are falling all over themselves to give the Hadden brothers whatever they needed to keep that monopoly alive."

She undid her seatbelt and used the extra reach to grab her oversized purse. Nesha lifted her head for a pat. Karen obliged and then pulled out maybe a half-dozen files and sorted through them before turning back around.

"Understand," she said, "the biggest thing the Haddens needed was space to grow. So the *Saints* found abandoned houses in the city, farm houses in Abbotsford or Langley, and a crew of current and ex BC Hydro employees who could wire the facilities and / or fudge the billing. Hydroponic shops," she added, "were everywhere a few years ago, and still are on the Kingsway corridor and places like that. To help you grow your tomatoes, of course."

"Remember," she added, "that until Expo '86, Vancouver was up for grabs and the *Saints* won—fair and square. Competitors came and tried, drugs were everywhere; hell, people were growing pot and selling it on the Expo grounds. Everybody wanted a piece of that global... I don't know, Ryan, global degeneracy?"

"Meaning what?"

"Meaning," Karen said, "the world came to Vancouver with only three things in mind: drink, fuck, get high. And the *Saints* won the Expo years and have been making those three things happen ever since."

"Okay," I said, "but that was fourteen years ago. What's the connection to now?"

"Jim caught the end of Expo, but with his size and attitude, he has been part of the motorcycle gang unit off and on for a number of years. Other guys on that squad worked Expo and lived those years. When the top cops started a joint unit between the Vancouver and Abbotsford police departments and the regional RCMP units from Surrey and Langley, Jim was asked to join."

"He seems like a natural," I said. "Even motorcycle gangs would be afraid of Jim."

"And the task force was necessary," Karen said. "Right around Expo, there was a Mafia head named Sabatino Nicosso arrested at the Port of Vancouver with nearly thirteen kilos of cocaine."

"Mafia?" I asked. "And coke? Aren't the streets getting crowded if we've got Mafia and motorcycle clubs?"

"They are," Karen agreed. "But that was one of the prizes for winning Expo—access to hard drugs and new markets. The Mafia guys had the connections for the hard drugs out of the states and even Mexico, so they worked with the *Saints* in particular to scratch each other's backs—that was Baker Senior's doing. BC marijuana is streaming into the States where it is prized and cash and coke are heading back to Canada, where coke is harder to find."

She turned in her seat to face me. "Here's what Baker Senior discovered, or manipulated, better than anyone else: it's easy to grow pot in BC. The climate, soil, whatever is perfect and the BC appetite for pot has been voracious.

"Sure," I said. "Lot of old hippies settled in Vancouver—Kitsilano, Commercial Drive, Sunset Beach…."

"It really is a doper's paradise," Karen said. "And Baker found a way to take the product grown outside and grow it inside and the Haddens perfected it. And because of the relative lax border protection with the States, the perception has become that it's easy to make unimaginable money by getting the product to the south."

"Easy?"

"The life is glamourized, everybody is driving a $100,000 car, criminals are heroes, music videos, rap songs…. Jesus," she said in an old man's voice, "I sound like a cranky senior—'you there, get off my lawn!'"

We laughed and she took a mock bow. "So the joint task force is created with a goal of trying to infiltrate, slow down and maybe even break up the motorcycle gangs in the Lower Mainland. And even though the *Saints* were the top of the list, there were, and are, a lot of them: *Grave Wolves, True Roadsters, Steal Vagabonds*... it's a long list. And even though a lot of the other clubs are puppets for the *Saints,* there were probably twelve or fifteen competing clubs by the time Expo ended. At least half a dozen still fly their colours on Vancouver streets. And, Ryan," she added, "violence is nothing to these guys."

I leaned over and took an obvious look at my face in the rear view. "I get that," I said.

Not knowing anything about drugs or the drug culture, I asked if, even in a city the size of Vancouver, it was really possible to get rich selling pot. "With that many people carving into the pie, how big could a piece be? I mean, what's a joint cost? Two bucks, six bucks, twenty? I really have no idea."

"Depending on the strain," Karen answered, "maybe four or five. But distribution is the key, and this is where the Haddens had an advantage, and it's also where Agony Baker enters the scene in a meaningful way."

'Right," I said. "Access to the States. Sometimes my criminal brain is slow to track."

"From a distribution stand-point, you need to be able to get the marijuana into the States to make drug dealer, *Miami Vice*, kind of money. The Haddens are masters at maximizing yield, and they had the entire *Silent Saints* club sourcing locations —large houses, especially outside the city, empty warehouses —and at least once, up near Hope, the *Saints* had a two-acre underground cave. That one collapsed or it probably never would have been found.

"The *Saints* had the technical expertise to by-pass Hydro and get power to the locations and, by winning the Expo wars, the man-power to staff them. So they bought a bunch of prop-erties, and bikers and their girl-friends, often with small kids in tow, would live in the houses and the warehouses became auto-body shops or tattoo parlours and even a diner in one place.

"Locations in Abbotsford and Langley are perfect because of the proximity to the border. I mean, in parts of Abbotsford, the border is just a road—Avenue Zero. Canada on this side, America on that side." She shrugged. "There isn't even a fence."

"You can't just walk that much dope across the border, can you?" I asked. "How much fits in a backpack?"

"$200 an ounce is a common price, and a backpack holds maybe fifteen pounds. So, doing the math, that's two-hundred and forty ounces… so a backpack holds nearly $50 grand." Karen said. "So a lot *did* walk across, but a lot more—a LOT more—drove across. Mostly in the RVs we talked about."

"Alright," I said. "A lot of moving parts. The Haddens are growing so much pot that the *Saints* are buying every house or building they can to grow more and more. And, I guess, they need places to store and process what they do grow. And Baker is moving it across the border. And Jim is involved with the motorcycle task force—probably not the best thing for him at that point, actively investigating the culture and life-style Kylee seems attracted to."

"It wasn't," Karen agreed. "Not at all. I begged him to ask to be reassigned, but he couldn't do that without admitting what was happening, or we suspected was happening, with Kylee. Instead, he didn't tell anyone anything because he thought he could fix it. "

"But he couldn't," I said. "Did he really even know what he was trying to fix?"

"He didn't," Karen agreed. "Other than separating Kylee from that culture." She shook her head sadly. "And then Kyle was transferred to the task force from the motorcycle squad. I thought that would make things easier for Jim. But it didn't. Instead, things got worse.

CHAPTER 6

As we neared Sicamous, famously known as the eastern gateway to Apple Country, there was something odd in the sky. Karen and I noticed it at the same time, but it was just the sun—something we hadn't seen for a few days. I grabbed my Ray-Bans from the visor and Karen remembered she was already wearing hers. The Bronco's weather station said it was seven degrees and we were headed south west; it had been minus-20 when Karen showed up in Calgary. I realized how much I missed BC weather—so what if it rains from September to March in Vancouver? You don't have to shovel rain and you don't need to own a down jacket.

I needed to make a decision quickly: the smart play was to continue on Highway 1 to Kamloops and then south to Merritt on Highway 5 and finally the new Coquihalla until Hope. From Hope, it's back on the One and straight into Vancouver. I'd sort of missed the boat back in Calgary if I wanted to avoid the Coquihalla—Highway 3 would have dropped us in Hope as well, but it was due south out of Calgary and not west. Both of these routes avoid Kelowna.

But now I needed to choose—straight, or left on Highway 97 to Enderby, Armstrong, Vernon and Kelowna? Either way, we were heading for the Coq, a highway through the Cascade Mountains that is often referred to as the *Highway from Hell*. At over 4,000 feet, the Coq has seen more than 400 crashes a year since inception, many of them fatal.

Right at that point, we passed the first road sign with a distance to Kelowna. "Hey, how's Robyn?" Karen asked.

Highway *to* Hell, I thought and stayed straight for Sicamous. Everybody likes apples.

*****

Three days before high school graduation, my entire life changed in two phone calls. First, the San Francisco Giants called to let me know they had drafted me late in the first round of the Major League Player Draft; they were curious if I was interested in joining their organization. I said that I was. Oddly, I can't think of that call to this day without picturing the phone I answered. It was an off-white colour, I think they called it bone, and it hung on the kitchen wall of my mother's house in Kitsilano. On the other side of the wall were the stairs to three bedrooms and a games room.

It was a sunny day, and the kitchen was bright and cheery and might have even been clean and life was great. 18 years old and headed to the Major Leagues. The world was mine. And, as I hung up, I remember wondering how the Giants got the number. My Mom has a different last name, so I most definitely was not in the book.

And then, maybe twenty minutes later, the phone rang again. And Robyn Richards, older sister to my best friend Kyle, said six words that forever altered the trajectory of my life: "Hey Dirt, want to go out?"

*****

For the last three years, I have done my best to put Robyn out of my mind, ever since she made it clear that I was not going to be allowed to occupy any additional space in hers. "I haven't seen her since my first year in Calgary," I said. "We still talk every now and then," I added, which wasn't really true. Mostly, I would drunk dial Robyn two or three times a year, and she would very gently and kindly tell me to grow up. "I was going to call her yesterday," I added, which was almost entirely true. "She's great," I said with absolutely no knowledge of that statement's truth since I didn't, you know, call. But it *is* what I hoped, so I figured saying it wasn't really a lie.

Karen had some follow up questions, but I deflected. I hoped she didn't notice I was avoiding this Kelowna dilemma I felt she had created, although, in reality, I created it two years, three years, five years, a life time ago. Okay, Karen had nothing to do with it, and it was snowing again.

*****

It feels like I've known Robyn my entire life and that's mostly because I have. I remember meeting her, although I certainly didn't think anything of it at the time—in my defence, though, I was six. Kyle, his Dad and I were sitting on their back porch in Point Grey, near the University of British Columbia's main gates, tying fishing lures when Robyn stepped outside to ask us if we wanted anything to drink. Mr. Richards owned a tugboat business that towed log booms in and out of storage in the Fraser River flats. He worked long days, crazy hours, in the snow, cold and rain and taught us all about the importance of work and honour. Those are lessons that maybe I've forgotten over the last few years.

Mr. Richards always put his kids first, and I was fortunate enough to be considered one of those kids while growing up. That particular day, Mr. Richards told Robyn to bring us each a beer, but she only brought one. Kyle and I settled for some orange juice. For the next ten years, I truthfully didn't think about Robyn very often; from sixteen on, however, the days I have thought about her far outnumber the days that I haven't.

Robyn is two years older than Kyle and me and she was my first crush, first love, first girlfriend, and about three months after that call, my first. She's the one who gave me the nickname Dirt: one day, after a little league game when Kyle and I were maybe ten, Robyn asked why my Church's Chicken baseball uniform was always so dirty and Kyle's always so clean.

When she called me, eight years later, I was shocked—shocked about the Giants, of course, but shocked that Robyn might want to hang out with me, without Kyle or anyone else. The next nine years were hard, and easy, and great and challenging and beautiful. The three after that have been hell.

Back then, Robyn was a full-time student, ultimately earning two masters degrees from the University of British Columbia and then the University of Melbourne. I was playing ball all over the southern United States and, then, briefly over two years, in the Major Leagues. But from Scottsdale Arizona to Shreveport Louisiana, Sothern Oregon to Australia, we made it work. Robyn made it work, until she didn't. To be fair, she believed in us a lot more than I believed in me after Wrigley.

On my twenty-eighth birthday, Robyn visited me in Calgary. I was wallowing in self-pity after being released by the Giants and the visit didn't go very well. I was living full time in the bottle, and my attitude to everyone who didn't have money in hand to spend at Ivy Green was antagonistic. Robyn wanted me to come home.

"Enough, Dirt," she said. "It's time. We need to do whatever comes next. It's a nice bar and all, but you know this isn't it."

"What do you mean, next?" I asked her. "What's better than this?" I continued and probably drained a beer. "I've been in the Major Leagues. There are other teams. You just want me to... what, sell insurance?

"Screw that," I finished. "Screw that. Insurance sucks."

She looked at me for a long time after that and I wished time could stop, but that's not how it is with people you love. I wanted to watch her eyes, to see if she would understand the things I couldn't say, but, incapable of dealing with my own pain, I looked away. I tell myself now that if I had had the courage to look at her then, things would be different. That's an easy thing to believe, but then cowardice is always easier than strength.

Robyn stayed for the weekend and then moved on. She runs the School of Landscape Architecture at the University of British Columbia, Okanagan campus now. When the University made that announcement, they mentioned that she was the youngest female department head in the ninety-two year history of the University. I, on the other hand, own a bar in a different province and have alienated anyone who's ever cared about me. Call it a tie.

Before she left that weekend, Robyn said something to me that I am only now beginning to understand. Maybe she did have the answers, even then, I just didn't know the questions. Grabbing me by the shoulders, with her face an inch from mine, Robyn spoke so softly that I might have been lip-reading instead of listening. "You think you've been drawn with magic ink, Dirt. Touched by a promise of greatness that just isn't there anymore. Maybe it was once, but now, guess what? You're shit flushes just like mine. Get over yourself, Dirt—San Francisco has. You aren't a dog they forgot at the park. Calgary is not the pound." She kissed me gently and took a cab to the airport. "They are not coming back for you."

God, I was an ass.

*****

Karen and I fell silent. I was spaced out, thinking about Robyn but pretending I was thinking about Jim and Kyle and everything Karen and I had been talking about. In Salmon Arm, I pulled into a 7-11 and asked Karen if she would mind pumping the gas. "I'll pay for it inside," I said. "But I need to put minutes on my phone card and make a call. If I'm not back before you finish, could you take Nesha to the grass and let her do some business? You won't need her leash."

As Karen and the dog took care of business outside, I headed inside to take care of my own.

Embarrassingly, I was relieved when my call went to voice-mail. I did not leave a message.

Back at the truck, Karen asked if I wanted her to drive for a bit. "Feeling better?" I asked, but really didn't care. My head was pounding, my stomach was sore and as mentioned, I'm not a great driver. I jumped at the opportunity to be a passenger. Nesha seemed confused by this, but got over it after about five solid minutes of head-scratches. As she settled into the back seat again, I told Karen that Robyn hadn't answered. She looked at me kindly. "If the weather holds," I said, "we're four and a half hours from home."

The word home surprised me. I was pretty sure I lived in Calgary.

Karen spent a minute or so adjusting the seat—I'm 6'5" and she is not—and familiarizing herself with the controls and adjusting the mirrors. She asked, politely, if as driver she had control over the stereo. I told her she did, but if she wasn't crazy about what we had listened to at this point, it wasn't going to improve. There were probably one-hundred and thirty CDs in the truck. "What would you like?" I asked her and started shuffling through them. *"Pearl Jam, Nirvana, Alice in Chains, Nine Inch Nails—"*

"Anything that isn't angry?" she asked.

"The Stooges, Black Flag, Rollins Band, Soundgarden..." I kept shuffling CDs. *"Faith No More, Guns N' Roses, LA Guns, Mother Love Bone, Rage Against the Machine...."* She didn't seem impressed. "I think there might be some *U2* under the back seat."

Karen asked me to stop. "Whatever you want," she said.

"We'll just play it softly."

"*Sneaker Pimps*," I said, proud I had found something. "They're British, how angry can they really be? And *Smashing Pumpkins*. Billy Corgan is sad, not angry. And the *Talking Heads*. Look," I said, "*Stop Making Sense*—the soundtrack of our trip. We're golden."

"*Sneaker Pimps*," she said. Touching my bruised face she said "growing up can be hard." She was shaking her head and smiling. I was glad she finally approved of our musical selections—there was no *U2* under the back seat.

*****

Another ten kilometres are so, and we started talking about Kylee again.

"You said Kyle joined the task force. How did things get worse?" It struck me as I said it that this was a fairly insensitive question, given that Jim had been murdered and Kyle severely injured some time later, but Karen knew what I meant.

"Besides the obvious?" she said. "The cops uncovered a pretty slick little operation. But," she added, "you really need a cell phone to play."

"I have a pager," I told her. "Would that work?" I paused. "Or had a pager." I shrugged. "Not even sure where it is, actually."

"When did you last see it?" Karen asked with a bit of a smirk.

I paused and gave the question some serious thought. "1998, I think. It was summer." Karen shook her head and the smirk became a smile. "People know where to find me," I said. "There's a phone at the bar."

"You would *not* be good at Dial-a-Dope," she said.

"That's not fair," I said. "I don't even know what that is."

She glanced at me quickly. "A little something that our friend Agony Baker came up with," she said.

"I wondered when we would get to him," I told her. "And I think Agony is a cooler nickname than Dirt."

Karen disagreed. "I don't know that it's a better name," she said, "but Baker is most definitely better at dealing drugs and running a criminal enterprise than you. In fact," she added, "Baker revolutionized drug dealing in Vancouver for sure," she said, "and maybe North America as a whole." I made a face to show I was impressed.

"It works like this." Karen said. "In the olden days—you know, when we were teenagers—to buy weed, you had to know somebody, or know somebody who knows somebody. Or maybe you find a guy on a corner somewhere, and he has what you need. But Baker and the *Saints* changed all this. What he did was brilliant, actually: he made buying dope as easy as ordering a pizza."

Karen reached into the pocket of her jeans, not really that easy to do while she was driving at full speed, and pulled out a business card. "I picked this up at Ivy Green," she said. "It was on one of the tables." I took it from her and looked at it front and back. It was solid black, with a phone number printed in white and a single word: Hibiscus.

"I've seen this before," I said. "I usually just pick them up and throw them away. I kind of always assumed call girl, though."

"Hibiscus is the strain of pot you're buying," Karen told me. "All the strains have different names and different alleged properties and effects. The phone number is your dealer. You call that number, talk to a nameless person, and a runner shows up with a package. It's slick and it's sweet and drug sales went from *here* to *there* overnight. Cops simply couldn't keep up."

"I'm impressed," I said. "And only Baker and his *Saints* had the capacity to supply this new demand, right?"

"Right," she said. "Others have tried. Competition between the motorcycle gangs is ruthless, but the *Saints* are the only real players in the weed game in the Lower Mainland right now. And that's by force." She shook her head slowly. "They are some Chinese and Vietnamese gangs on the edges, but basically it's a *Saints* show.

"Those sixty people murdered over marijuana sales in the Lower Mainland?" Karen asked. "Those killings were solely the result of motorcycle gangs, *Saints* in particular, claiming their territories. Small time dealers were absorbed or made extinct."

"Okay, walk me through it," I said. "No, wait, it's probably not that hard. I'll walk myself through it."

Karen nodded, and took one hand off the wheel and moved it, palm up, across the cab of the truck. "Let's hear it," she said.

"I'm Baker and I've got this amazing product piling up in warehouses and who knows where else. So I get some business cards printed—500 for $15 somewhere."

Karen held her hand up to stop me. "One point of clarification —club members *never* get their hands dirty. Everything has layers. The more patches, the more layers beneath you," she said. "In fact, it is very uncommon for a full-patch member to be arrested."

"Right, okay," I said. "Some lackey or wannabe is given the name of the strain and told to get cards. And then some runner—maybe for a free bag—heads out on the town, hitting bars and clubs and restaurants, and leaves the cards behind. And as it turns out, this particular night, I'm in the mood for drugs, so I grab a card and place an order. And then someone brings it to me and, what, I give him a tip?"

"Tipping is optional," Karen said. "No cheques or credit cards, but that's how it works. And," she added, "runners do it for much more than a free bag."

"I get simple," I told her. "But why is it so effective? Can't the cops just call the numbers and bust whoever shows up?"

"They can," Karen replied. "And they do. Jim and Kyle went crazy with arrests, but understand that these operations are everywhere." She reached into her pocket again and handed me two more cards. "The cops can't keep up," she said. "Here, these were at the restaurant we went to Thursday night."

I took them from her. One was white with raised lettering and one was red with black lettering. Hippie Dream and Sunset Mood. How do you decide? "I never liked that place," I said.

"They change the numbers all the time," Karen said. "The phones are basically disposable now: new cards, new phone numbers, new products almost every week."

She paused and looked directly at me, road be damned. "And then," she said, "one night, Kyle phoned in an order, and Kylee showed up to drop it off."

"Fuck," I said. "Fuck me large."

"Kind of Jim's reaction," Karen said, eyes back on the road. "Except, you know, his was completely different and bat-shit insane in every way.

"And you know what Jim said to me Ryan? He said 'at least she isn't dancing any more'. I didn't have the heart to tell him she was doing both."

*****

Karen reached up and adjusted the rear view mirror. For the first time, she noted the digital compass displayed there. That made me worry as she'd been driving for an hour and had apparently never looked at the rear view.

 "Remember that Jim and then Kyle were part of an official motorcycle gang task force with the cops," Karen said. "As lawyers for the province, we were investigating as well. In fact, because drugs are such a huge part of reservation life and that's my department, I was asked to join a panel that looked specifically at Dial-a-Dope. Our conclusion is not a surprise and is supported by the eye test: marijuana comes from the *Saints*.

"But, despite countless arrests, we weren't able to crack *anything*." She used her thumb to point to the back seat where her briefcase was getting covered in dog hair. "The study is in there," she said. "It's a little bit dry, and over 400 pages, but here's the breakdown:

"Dial-a-Dope started with marijuana but quickly spread to include harder drugs, like cocaine and heroin. Understand," she added, "the hard drugs come from the States and are always tied to BC Bud going the other way." At 120 kilometres an hour, she chanced a glance in my direction. "BC Bud has become the new barter system: X amount of bud for Y amount of a hard drug of your choice."

"Nice," I said. "Capitalism at work. John Addams would be proud."

She smiled. "It's almost like you went to school… almost. Ryan, answering the phones is absolutely an entry level job, usually for kids who have had it tough, or think they have, or just think they're tough. Mostly male, obviously, but not exclusively. These kids see glamour and power in the clothes and the cars and the women and the money they see—and can make—is *huge*, certainly more than they've ever seen in their pockets. Or their parents'."

"How much we talking?" I asked.

"My friend Dallas works as a prosecutor on the task force," Karen replied, "and she interviewed a kid from Prince George who'd been arrested with $13,000 on him. She asked the kid about it, and *he* asked *her* why would he ever give up the life? 'Do the math,' he said. 'How many fucking minimum wage hours is in my pocket right now?'"

I did the math. "Jesus," I said and I think that about summed it up—what else could be said?

Karen asked for some water and I found one in the back and took the cap off and handed it to her. We'd made the right turn out of Salmon Arm and were approaching Mabel Lake.

Karen took a few sips and continued. "The teens—and almost *all* runners are teens, although a few are as young as twelve, actually; there was a kid in Aldergrove who was *ten*—carry these phones, fill the order and make the delivery. If," she added, "the runners are old enough to drive, then they use their own vehicles because they won't get impounded."

"So there's really no risk to the *Saints*, or whomever is running the operation," I said. "And I doubt that a kid, if caught, is going to give up anyone above him."

"That's right," Karen said. "A runner gets picked up, and is back on the street in hours because they are too young to prosecute. And, here's something ironic, but getting arrested somehow makes it more real and meaningful—the arrested runner actually becomes... I don't know, revered maybe. Like he's not playing anymore.

"And," she continued, "because the low-level associates and hanger-ons are not as fortunate when it comes to the law in terms of arrest and release—they will go down for possession, if only briefly—they spend a significant amount of *their* time recruiting kids who are disenfranchised and looking for some excitement. In short, these bastards glamourize the life."

"Kids like Kylee," I said, unnecessarily.

"Yup," Karen said. "Like Kylee. And Emily, although she knew what she was getting into because of her brothers. It's kind of a pyramid scheme, really, except the results are legit: the more kids recruited to run drugs, the more everyone makes. And," she added, "the runners end up recruiting more runners and the network expands."

"And I've got to think," I said, "that the amount of drugs in a runner's possession is simply not enough for the cops to get excited about."

Karen agreed. "Basically, it gets confiscated and the kid gets kicked free."

Karen took her eyes off the road again. "This," she said, "is where we think Kylee got swept up—she knows from being around Jim that minor drug arrests are basically nothing, and she sees how much money is available. Plus, she kind of gets to throw a couple of middle-fingers at the establishment. And," she added sadly, "the risk just isn't that great—not for her, she's protected on one side by her age and on the other by the fact she's Emily Hadden's best friend. And Emily's brothers are the *Saint's* cash cow."

"There has to be more to it than that," I said. "At least for Kylee."

"I'm not sure," Karen replied. "Answer a call, go to a re-load house, deliver the drugs, and make $1,500 a night on a good night."

"Jesus," I said again. "$1,500?"

"Yup. Friday, Saturday for sure. On a Monday or Tuesday, maybe $300."

I let the numbers settle. "So," I asked, "a re-load house is what it sounds like?"

"It is," Karen said. "That's your brick and mortar location where the drugs are kept. A safe-house, usually rented in the name of somebody's grandmother or uncle, without their knowledge, or even a dead relative. The worker bees here supply the drugs to the runners. But," she added, "like the phones and runners, these locations change almost every day. And a runner, no matter how old or young, *never* gives up the re-load house."

"Christ," I said, just to change things up. "The reward really does seem to outweigh the risk." I thought about it for a couple of seconds. "But these re-load houses have to get supplied from somewhere, right? Can the cops catch that?"

"In theory," Karen answered. "But not in reality. There's actually a secondary location where the larger supply of drugs is kept and there is a separate and distinct supply line for each of those houses. If," she continued, "and it's a *big* if, but *if* that house itself can be hit, good things might happen. But that has happened twice that I'm aware of. And you would have read about those raids in the paper." She looked at me again. "There was a raid last year in North Van where the task force hit the *Grave Wolves* and came away with $2M in drugs and cash and twelve arrests were made."

At this point, Karen shrugged her shoulders. "Ryan, the *Wolves* have one fifth of the Lower Mainland drug trade. Maybe. But there was something crazy interesting about that bust —the number of patched *Wolves* that were involved. Usually, patched guys are untouchable. But here, almost the entire mid-level management team for the Canadian *Wolves* was picked up in one swoop."

"Interesting," I said. "Why would so many mucky-mucks be in one place?"

"Nobody knows," she replied. "But the suspicion is they were planning some kind of action against the *Saints*. Action," she added, "that didn't happen."

"Convenient," I said. "So, if I'm following along correctly, the *Saints* are now better off because of a raid of some other bad guys that netted two million dollars in cash and product?"

"And guns," Karen added.

"And somehow," I said, "mysteriously, the *Saints* were in a perfect position to step up and fill the void this raid created."

"Yes," Karen agreed. "Anthony 'Agony' Baker and the *Silent Saints*. And Jim went crazy." She touched my arm. "That raid did not make Jim happy." She put her hand in her lap, and then picked it up again and put it back on the wheel. "Jim was only happy hunting the *Saints*, and they have never been touched. Not in any way."

"It's almost like they're protected," I said.

"Yes it is," Karen agreed. "It is very much like that, Ryan." She banged the steering wheel with both hands. "That is *exactly* what Jim thought."

CHAPTER 7

A few more kilometres ticked by and we were on the other side of Kamloops, starting on the #5 and pointed at the Coquihalla Summit.

"I was making a bad joke," I said. "At least, I think I was. How did Jim react?"

"Not well," Karen replied. "Although he did try to strip himself out of the equation, and look at Task Force numbers as a whole. And he found that there were some major inconsistencies with how the Task Force was watching and reporting the *Saints* versus other clubs. At one point, he calculated that 70% of arrests were non-*Saint* affiliated, which makes no sense because probably 80% of the drug scene is controlled by the *Saints*. And almost all the strip clubs and massage parlours and car washes and other primary cash businesses in Vancouver proper are controlled and or owned by the *Saints*. Hell, officially Baker is a restaurateur, with a long list of establishments—including a Brew Pub downtown that you'd probably really like."

"Brew Pubs are going to catch on. Big Brewery won't like it, but people like good beer. I've thought about it for Calgary, but ran out of momentum to do anything. But," I added, "you don't have to be a bad guy to own a bar."

"We'll leave that comment for later," Karen said. "The jury is still out on that," she added with a smile that was dazzling, especially given the hangover.

I laughed and made a show of checking my face in the visor mirror. I sort of wished I hadn't as my eyes were a little yellow, and a whole lot of red and purple.

"Jim's guesstimates weren't far off the reality. And he was also part of two operations that ended up with nothing to show," Karen said. "Raids of *Saints* hang outs that were empty when they got there. 'Fool us once,' he said. 'Fool us twice and I'm going to stick a 2x4 up somebody's ass'."

"He did always have a way with words."

"Yeah, and at first that 2x4 was headed straight for the *Saints*. He started spending a lot of time—a lot of time—at strip clubs and other places of ill repute."

*****

As a kid—okay, as a boy—strip clubs seem far more exciting than they actually are. But maybe that's only true if, as a kid, you actually grow up when it comes to nudity and sex and women as equals—I say that because I have a long way to go to grow up, but I left strip clubs behind long ago. Probably even before I was legally old enough to drink in them.

Karen knew a lot about strip clubs in Vancouver.

"Here's the thing," Karen said. "I didn't want to learn about strip clubs, believe me. But if this is where Kylee was at and I couldn't stop it, I had to do something." She hit the steering wheel in frustration. "Where do you want your lesson to start?" she asked me, at 140 kilometres an hour.

"If we could keep this on a need to know basis, I would really appreciate it. I know a lot of people think it's cool, or sexy, whatever—it's never really been my thing."

"You try to hide it," Karen said, "but you're a good guy Ryan. Really."

"This isn't a morality thing, trust me. Or judgement. I know there are many reasons to strip, or work in the trades—and, like sports, money is one of them. Sex for sale just isn't my thing.

"And, as for the 'good guy' comment, you'll deny you said that later," I said and we both smiled. "And there is plenty of evidence to the contrary."

"Ass or not," Karen said. "I need you to concentrate."

"Back at you, Karen. You've got the wheel."

She eased off the gas, slightly. "Strip clubs are legal in Canada," she started, "but each individual province and city decides how to regulate them through what are known as 'nuisance laws'. These laws are different province to province and even city to city. They determine the amount of nudity allowed (above the belt only or full, pasties or no), hours of operation, if liquor can be served and the amount of space required between the drunks and the girls and a bunch of other stuff that really makes no sense. In the States," she said, "most strip clubs are top off only and very few, if any, can sell booze." She looked at me, and I confessed—even on a minor league salary, that the boys sometimes went out and paid crazy high 'membership' dues to drink flat pop and look at bored girls dancing with no top.

"In Yakima," I said, "there was a place called *Hundreds of Beautiful Girls and Three Ugly Ones*."

Karen gave me a quick smile. "In Vancouver, though," she said, "it's a whole different world, nuisance laws be damned. The ratio is exponentially greater."

"That's a lot of beautiful girls," I said.

"And in Vancouver," Karen said, ignoring me, "anything to do with sex is owned lock stock and barrel by the *Saints*. In fact," she added, "our friend Agony has made controlling the sex trade in Vancouver as big a mission as his father made the drug trade. I've heard that he somehow thinks it's cleaner."

"Victimless crime paradigm, maybe?" I said. "Or a guilty conscience."

"Either or," Karen said. "Sure. But either way, most of the places you probably remember are long gone. There are really four key strip clubs left, and they are all *Saint* owned."

"Mission accomplished, it sounds like", I said, probably unnecessarily. "Baker now owns the two biggest vices in the world—sex and drugs? I should get him to run my finances." Karen looked at me. "Except," I said, "for all the illegal and creepy stuff." She nodded. "And police are hands off?" I asked. "So to speak," I added, conscious of the implications.

"For the most part," she replied. "And like the drug trade, the *Saints* have taken the sex trade by force. They are bigger and badder and smarter than everyone else, and there are a hell of a lot more of them. And what they can't do by smarts," she added, "they do by terror."

She slapped the steering wheel again, but this time we were at least at the speed limit. "They are like the god-damn mafia," she said. "They never do anything wrong *themselves*; instead, they set up a hierarchy all leading down from that damn full patch, and they invest their money in legitimate business. Money that is made off the backs of young women and smoked away by stupid teenagers or old men trying to stay relevant. All for the promise of membership in some stupid club that likes to ride motorcycles and punch baseball players in the face.

"And," she added after a few seconds of silence, "they killed Jim."

I left that one alone.

*****

"Something about Vancouver strip clubs," Karen continued after a few empty kilometres, "is that from a viewing perspective, the city has a niche—like Montreal—as being entertainment focused rather than simply tits and ass."

"You've changed, Karen," I said. "Three days with me and you could give any red-ass ballplayer a run for his money language wise."

"I blame you, "she said with some heat, "all you men. And I've kept this anger in for too damned long." She made an effort to put the anger back, at least temporarily. "Montreal," she said, "has one headliner a night who has costumes and music and lights, and then the rest of the night is filled with what they call fillers—girls whose only job is to get you into a VIP lounge.

"In Vancouver, clubs like *Brandi's* really try to put the 'exotic' in exotic dancer. Girls at the high end places put a great deal of effort into their shows and costumes." She smiled sadly. "Maybe not so much on amateur night at *The Sundowner*," she said, naming a low end bar on the border of Delta and Surrey. "But it works. Jim couldn't see it because he was blind with rage, but there is a real element of stage and magic."

She was quiet again, clearly thinking about something specific. "One night," she continued at a much lower volume, "Jim was in Prince George for some damn rugby tournament and I was 'doing research'." She made air quotes with both hands. "I left Rileigh with my folks and I took myself on a date to *Brandi's*—women never pay a cover charge, by the way—and was maybe hoping to find Kylee and bring her home. Didn't happen.

"But, Ryan, I swear to God, I did see a fire-breathing devil, the ghost from Ghostbusters, and an astronaut who did an entire routine suspended from the ceiling."

This is the world Kylee had entered.

"So Jim and Kyle continued their mission to destroy the *Saints* by themselves," Karen said. "And I continued to hope she would need us as much as we needed her and come home."

"But it didn't work," I said.

"It didn't," Karen agreed. "Kylee wasn't interested in being saved. She called me one night and said she appreciated our concern, but she was just having a good time and had registered for university in the fall." She sighed and shook her head sadly. "'No tattoos', she said, like that's what was important."

"Karen," I said, unsure of what I was going to say next.

She held up her right hand in a shushing motion. "No tattoos didn't appease Jim. Life with Emily and the *Saints* had become more than simply a good time for Kylee. And Jim and Kyle continued to arrest every *Saint* they could find. And the other motorcycle clubs were fine with this; in fact, Jim and Kyle ended up with quite the network of informants as low-level guys at other clubs realized these two larger than life cops were really not interested in small time infractions that they or theirs might be committing. Non-*Saints* affiliated bikers were falling all over themselves with information for the gang squad. People I've talked to said the downtown eastside was empty of *Saints*, hardly a patch to be seen. For a while."

"Sounds like progress, maybe?" I said. "Assuming the arrests actually stuck."

"They didn't," Karen replied. "Nothing good actually happened because of this street cleansing. And then it didn't matter anymore," she said, "because Kylee died. It was ruled an accidental overdose, but Jim never thought that for a second. They didn't put the drugs in her, but Jim knew the *Saints* killed Kylee."

Karen played with some buttons on the stereo mindlessly, and clicked the high-beams on and off with her foot. "I told you where she was found. I didn't tell you they got to her while she was still alive. Another anonymous 911 call, but she didn't make it to the ambulance."

We were silent for maybe two kilometres. "And then," Karen said, "Jim and Kyle *really* went to work. And the Blue Wall made Kylee a cause of their own."

*****

 "For the Vancouver police," Karen said while we drove through the Great Bear Snow Shed, "affiliation no longer mattered. There were so many associates—for all the clubs—in jail or detention that biker reinforcements had to be brought in from other cities. But, from our perspective as prosecutors, it was like catch and release—the police were catching them, but we couldn't hold them."

"So everyone who is arrested is back on the street?"

"Not immediately, but yes," she replied. "But that inconvenience of being detained for forty-eight to ninety-six hours was sufficient to create *some* chaos on the streets. That's why the reinforcements were needed—to maintain day to day operations. And new arrivals were coming faster than the police could arrest—non-*Saints* affiliated bikers were like 'Game On'. Every club thought this was there big moment."

"Because it was mostly *Saints* getting busted," I said.

"Right." Karen sipped some water. "It got to the point that the Task Force members were told to cut it out. It was chaos. Jim and Kyle were hauled on the carpet and told to cease and desist. And the craziest damn thing is that it was the Chief of Police who delivered this message, not a sergeant or captain, or, you know, the leader of their squad."

"Well, you said the Chief headed up the Task Force, right?" I said. "So if Jim and Kyle were making waves, maybe the brass figured the message was significant enough that it was justified coming from her?"

"Maybe," Karen said. But she didn't believe it.

"Was Jim seeing ghosts"? I asked. "Kylee's mixed up in something she doesn't understand, he blames the *Saints* and this Agony guy for cultivating the Haddens, he feels like he's losing something with Kylee... and, then, of course, she's gone. And Jim knows just who to blame. That must have sent him spiraling."

She was silent. "Yes. No. Maybe. All of the above, Ryan. How are we to know?"

Not for the first time, I wished for something profound to say. Instead, I asked this: "How does Kylee's death link to Jim's and then to Kyle yelling conspiracy theory at the Vancouver Chief of Police?"

"I don't know," Karen said quickly. "Yet. But two months ago, the *Vancouver Province* ran a front-page story about '*Dirty Cop Exposed and Killed*'; next day I got that letter I showed you about all benefits being denied.

"Make no mistake," Karen said. "None. I intend to find out."

After a few more kilometres, Karen said "There was something about the *Province* article that didn't ring true. Not about Jim, of course, that was all lies, but about the information and how it was presented. There were things quoted as fact that a reporter wouldn't or couldn't know."

"Like what?"

"First," Karen said, "the story stated that Jim was friendly to clubs like the *Wolves* and *True Roadsters*. Nothing could be further from the truth—own a denim or leather jacket, Jim hated you. That," she said, "was clearly part of the smear on Jim. But what was the point? *'Two dead at Crab Park'* should have been the story, not *'Dirty Cop Killed'*. Four hours after the explosion the *Province* went to press and, Ryan, how had there been time to leak shit to the press about Jim?"

"I don't know," I said. "Or why?" Karen shrugged. "What else?"

"The detonator," she said. "Only a cop would know that they found parts of the detonator at the scene—which they did—but only long after the *Province* hit the streets. But the story said that this clearly linked the bomb to similar bombings out east that had been committed by the *Wolves*.

"Ryan, they hadn't even finished putting Jim back together or getting Kyle to the hospital when the *Province* hit the street. But they somehow wrote about the detonator, *before* it had even been discovered."

"So the story about Jim is clearly pointing at the *Wolves* or some other one-percenters? You think the *Saints* wrote the story?"

"Well," Karen replied, "top lieutenants of three other clubs were named." She took a deep breath and changed lanes, just for something to do. "In *The Province* article, every club *but* the *Saints* was mentioned as being complicit in something. Businesses were named—*The Elephant Car Wash, Victory Motors* on West Forth, *The Rembrandt Hotel*... Ryan, these places weren't in the Top 100 of businesses being investigated by the cops or us. Mostly because they aren't affiliated with the *Saints*. Hell, *The Rembrandt* moves *one-tenth* the dope that *Brandi's* does. Maybe less."

"Okay, weird", I said. "So what does that mean?"

"What I think," Karen replied, "is that with the Task Force going after the *Saints* so hard, they were impacted more than any other club. So others, like the *Wolves*, saw an opportunity to gain ground that wasn't generally available."

"Makes sense," I said.

"So the other clubs went hard at *Saint* owned avenues and, by all accounts, they made some significant progress. But," she added, "then their shit hit the fan, and the Task Force had their number. *Wolves* busted in North Van, *Vagabonds* busted in Aldergrove, *Roadsters* busted in Merritt. Ryan," she asked, "how did that happen?"

"The *Saints* were fighting back," I said. "And they never had to before." I paused. "And they seem to have had help. But how do you know all this?"

"The busts were easy to see—hell, the Chief made sure of that with her weekly press conferences. But I decided to pull rank and I asked for all the Task Force files. The files take up an entire closet in my office. And what jumps out is what *isn't* there: the *Saints* and Agony Baker own Vancouver, Ryan. So why aren't they in the files if Jim and Kyle aren't involved?"

"I'm not a trained legal expert," I said, "but that seems like a really good question for a trained legal expert to ask."

"Noted," Karen said. "And something else—the story 'exposing' Jim was in the *Province*, but there's a reporter at the *Vancouver Sun* who writes specifically about crime and motorcycle clubs and drugs in the Lower Mainland. Her name is Terri Clement, and she was as curious about that *Province* article as I was." Karen looked at me for what seemed like quite a long time, given that she was driving. "Are you in, Ryan?" she asked.

I wasn't entirely sure what she was asking, but I didn't hesitate in my reply. "I'm in Karen. I'm sorry it wasn't sooner."

"Good," she replied. "We meet with Terri on Tuesday."

*****

By this point, we were in Port Moody, a Vancouver suburb about thirty kilometres from Vancouver. Burrard Inlet was to our right. Burrard Inlet is a coastal fjord that essentially separates Vancouver from the North Shore Mountains and moneyed communities like West Vancouver and Lion's Bay. On any day of the year, it is also home to dozens of tankers and cruise ships. Four hours had evaporated since our last stop and the snow was a distant memory. It was overcast but a pleasant twelve degrees. With all the time I spent figuring how to avoid Kelowna, I realized that I had absolutely no idea what to do with myself now. I dropped Karen at her parent's place in Greektown, a part of Kitsilano not far from where I had grown up. I declined her offer to come in and rest; instead, we hugged and she kissed me softly on the lips. "Thank you, Ryan," she said. I deflected, and we agreed to meet at the *Vancouver Sun* building on Granville Street at 10:30 AM on Tuesday. I may have even agreed to buy a cell phone.

I now had a weekend to kill, and I knew where I was going to find somebody to kill it with.

*****

When I walked into the Bel Air Sports Bar and Grill, a long name for a crappy little bar, it was pushing four o'clock on a Friday afternoon. The same time of day that Karen had found me in Calgary. Located on Broadway between Cambie and Oak—three of Vancouver's busiest streets—the Bel Air was in a great spot, basically in the shade of City Hall and Vancouver General Hospital. It is a classic dive bar, and although it looked like it hadn't been cleaned since the last time I had been there, it was packed. People love dive bars.

Kyle was sitting exactly where I expected him to be, right at the turn of the bar. But the person I saw in Kyle's spot was not the Kyle I've known all my life. Instead, it was someone wearing a poorly fitting Kyle Richards suit. It wasn't just the physical changes in his appearance that shocked me, although they were startling; it was his eyes. It could have been the reflection from the dusty bar mirror, but Kyle's eyes are the colour of polished steel; the eyes I looked into were the colour of an ordinary nickel, long past its prime. They could have been the poorly painted eyes of a child's cheap doll.

With absolutely no judgement, I asked the bartender—a good guy by the name of Thunder Bob—how long Kyle had been there. We shook hands and did the bro hug.

"What day is it?" he asked. That told me everything I needed to know.

I could see an ugly scar above Kyle's right eye. And the weight loss was noticeable, an easy twenty pounds off an athletic frame. Mostly what I noticed, though, is that his body lacked ignition; it was like his internal engine had seized. In twenty years, I've never seen Kyle entirely still. Even sitting, his body is constantly in motion, like he knows there is something that needs to get done and he is going to be first in line to do it. This energy and motion made him an all-Canadian safety for two years at Concordia. But he was entirely still today, a stranger I had known all my life. Same six-foot height, same bow legs and giant belt buckle, but a completely different Kyle.

"You look like shit," I told him, the first words we'd spoken in person in almost a year. "Maybe not that good."

"That's better than I feel," he said, catching my eyes in the mirror. He spun his bar stool around. "Nice face," he added. "So I'm still prettier than you. Some things never change." We hugged unashamedly in the crowded bar.

"Damnit, Dirt. I've missed you," he said. I hugged him tighter.

"Gonna deck me now or later?" I asked him. "I swear, Kyle, I swear I had no idea. About any of this."

"Later's good," he said, letting me go. "Maybe when you heal. I don't think your face could take another punch." He laughed, one bark, but it was a start. "Let's just drink right now."

And we drank.

At some point, Thunder Bob went and got Nesha from the truck and stashed her behind the bar. He fed her a couple of burgers, and I'm sure she managed to steal or beg a few more bites through the night. Kyle and I didn't do a lot of talking, but we did keep checking to see if the other was real. Somewhere late in the evening, or maybe early in the morning, and long after he had switched from beer to scotch, Kyle said this:

"It's like I've taken a long vacation, Dirt. Somewhere I don't want to be and it's dangerous but I don't know why and I don't want to be there. I'm afraid, and I've never been afraid before."

"Do they have baseball in this vacation paradise?" I asked him.

"They do," he said. "But the players are good, so you won't be able to play."

"Probably for the best," I said. "But if they have baseball, how bad can it be?" He shrugged. "Let's embrace it. We'll grab a cooler, some of the guys, and we'll plant some lawn chairs down the third base line and have ourselves one hell of a time. Maybe after, we'll go fishing."

"That sounds good," Kyle said. "I think I'd like that."

I know we hugged again, but I don't remember much after that.

*****

If there had been some unfamiliar moments over the last few days—like actually moving and talking to people and maybe even thinking—Friday found me in more familiar mental and emotional surroundings. Badly hungover and unsure of where

I was, it took me a few minutes to recognize the Richards' basement. I was wrapped in a Vancouver Canucks blanket and had a couple of matching pillows and I was staring up at my dog, who was sleeping soundly on the couch. *Some things never change.* And although I'm pretty sure Nesha knew how we came to be where we were, she wasn't telling.

Despite the aesthetic, there are some things to appreciate about the Bel Air, and one of them is that they take very good care of their regulars. I made a mental note to thank Thunder Bob and maybe slip him a couple of fifties when he wasn't looking. Judging by my head, there is no way I had anything to do with getting us to Kyle's place.

I don't wear a watch, so I had to fumble with the TV remote to figure out what time it was. Apparently, it was one in the afternoon. Learning that I have lost a half-day usually brings me great satisfaction, maybe even joy. I am often thrilled when time is gone and I had absolutely nothing to do with it— you see, that's the thing about drinking, it makes time easier. Sunday into Monday, Monday into Tuesday, everything just bleeds together and soon you have ordered enough drinks and the week has passed.

This day, however, despite the hangover, I was ready for something to happen. But then something did happen, and maybe I wasn't so ready.

Fully dressed from the night before, I folded the blanket, kicked Nesha off the couch and headed for the stairs and hopefully some coffee. On the move, I flashed to a muddled memory from the night before. Sometime after midnight but before closing, I remember grabbing Kyle's cell phone and misdialing a number two or three times.

"She's not there, Dirt", Kyle said.

"How do you know?" I asked, stabbing the buttons even

harder, wondering how he even knew who I was trying to call.

"Because I know where she is," he said softly, but I had stopped listening because the phone was finally ringing and I was in no shape to do multiple things at once. In hindsight, I probably should have followed up on what Kyle was saying, especially as the phone call went to voicemail again.

Now, I was at the top of the Richards' stairs and it was too late to reconcile what Kyle had said the night before. I could see into the kitchen and noted that the coffee maker was full. From the dining room, I heard a memory.

"Ryan 'Dirt' Simms," Robyn Richards said. Her voice was happy, which was unfamiliar to me. For the past three years, I had only heard sad. And despite being as Canadian as the Goods and Services Tax, her voice has a southern lilt to it that has driven me crazy forever. "Number 13 in your program, and somewhere else in your heart." That kind of stung. "One hundred and twenty-seven hits in three-hundred and eighty-two at bats over parts of two seasons with the San Francisco Giants," she continued. "A .332 life-time average, with twenty-four homeruns, twenty-two stolen bases and seventy-three runs batted in."

I still hadn't spoken or, unsure of what I was hearing, even turned around. My hangover and confusion were telling me that maybe we were still at the Bel-Air; maybe we hadn't left?

"Seven outfield assists," she added while walking into the kitchen. I turned to face her, and then she put her left hand on my chest—God help me, I checked for rings—and kissed me softly on the cheek.

"Two outfield errors," I said.

"Both on overthrows where you got cocky," Robyn said. "Welcome home, Dirt." Since she gave me the nick name, Robyn has never once called me Ryan. "It is great to see you." She wrinkled her nose. "Smelling you, though," she said, "not so great."

Nesha was losing her mind and this gave me some time to find mine. Robyn was there at the beginning with Nesha, and I know the dog has never really forgiven me for not making it work with Robyn. Seeing Nesha run circles, jumping on Robyn and doing her weird purring thing, I realized that this was indeed real. Welcome to Friday.

"That's what he meant last night," I said. Robyn looked at me, puzzled. "Kyle," I said, "something he said last night...." I shook my head hoping for clarity, but none came. Unsure of what else to say or do, I sat. "I've been trying to call," I stammered.

She hushed me. "Get some coffee, Dirt. If you're hungry, I can probably whip something up."

"We are five or six hours from food," I told her with absolute conviction. I reached across the kitchen counter and poured some coffee. "Kyle up?"

"Up and gone," she said. "He is in significantly worse shape than you," she said with a smile, "and judging by appearances, that is saying something." She laughed and I wished I could be like the dog, running and jumping and barking with joy. "He has a meeting with his union rep and then an appointment with a psychiatrist to 'assess his suitability for return to work'." She put her arm around my shoulder and squeezed gently. "A night out with you is probably not a great way to demonstrate his suitability for anything," she said. She touched both of my eyes and said "ouch", then she went to pour her own coffee.

Red haired and athletic, Robyn is 6'1" and covered in freckles that used to embarrass her and make me insane. With a body that I have made no effort to forget over the years, she still looked like the three-time NAIA all-star small-forward she had been at Simon Fraser University. She was wearing Simon Fraser sweats and—this actually made my heart skip one hundred beats—a Sothern Oregon Timberjacks t-shirt. I had played for the Timberjacks my second year in pro ball. Seeing her, breathing her, after three wasted years, I felt sixteen again —awkward, smelly, tongue-tied, nervous and horny.

"Robyn," I said, and then promptly forget every word I had ever learned. I drank more coffee.

"We've got some things to talk about," she said, not unkindly. "But I am *not* here because you are here. These are unrelated occurrences, and I need you to understand that, okay?"

"Sure," I managed. "But if you're not here for Kyle, then why?" I asked. "I was just in Kelowna," I added unnecessarily.

"I know," she said. "I talked to Karen last night. But for Kyle, he's a big boy. I will help and support him anyway I can, but he's certainly not telling me everything."

I nodded. "I had no idea," I said, "that he had even been suspended."

"Have to answer your phone, Dirt," she said.

I grimaced. "What Karen's told me...? Robyn, I'm not sure I can even digest it." I looked at her and repeated my earlier question. "If not for Kyle, why are you here?"

"The University has asked me to take over the entire department, and not just head up the Kelowna satellite," she said. "That means moving back here."

"That's incredible," I said. "Congratulations Robyn. I assume you said yes?"

"Thinking about it still," she replied. "There really isn't anything holding me in Kelowna. I saw you check earlier and, no, there isn't anybody in my life, but I do love it there. It's a really comfortable fit, you know? And Vancouver has changed for me since Mom and Dad died." She looked at me for what was probably five or ten seconds but felt like five or ten lifetimes. "And you stopped coming home," she added.

"Home," I repeated. "This is a lot," I said. "All of it."

"We'll talk," Robyn said. "But let's not get ahead of ourselves yet."

I swallowed too hot coffee. "I've never stopped loving you, Robyn, you know that. A rambling phone call at three-thirty in the morning every couple of months probably isn't the best way of showing that, but you know it's true."

She smiled. "I know," she said.

"But you broke up with me, remember? 'You go hit baseballs again, Dirt', you said. 'I have a real life to get started'."

"I didn't say that."

"Word for word. You were wearing faded jeans and a white polo shirt, and Fila sandals. It was a Monday." I sipped from an empty coffee mug. "Robyn, you took a cab to the airport."

*****

The Richards' house is on a hill with an amazing view of Jericho Beach and English Bay and then West Vancouver and the mountains beyond the water. Mr. Richards had knocked out walls before open concept had even become a thing. From the kitchen counter, you look straight through the dining room and then into the living room and out the bay window and you see sand and water and mountains and imagine people living the life you have always wanted. The house I grew up in was twenty blocks away, in a neighbourhood desired by many for its proximity to the beach and, apparently, the good life. But growing up in the Vancouver neighbourhood of Kitsilano was always lacking for me. Point Grey was better, and the Richards really did have greener grass. I realize now that was mostly because I was never home to mow ours.

My house was eleven blocks closer to the beach and nine blocks to the east. It had no view but was kitty corner to a pair of baseball diamonds. Those diamonds are where I learned to play baseball and, later, where I got to first and second base when I was learning about Robyn.

I did wonder briefly why I was at Kyle's, and not my Mom's place, or maybe Jaxson's, whose basement apartment is only a few houses from hers. But then I remembered that Jaxson was in England, finishing his law degree with a Fellowship at Oxford. Wired very differently than me, Jaxson was drafted by the Texas Rangers in the seventeenth round after high school. Our kitchen phone had been replaced by the time the Rangers called him, but he never even discussed his future with them. Instead, he took a baseball scholarship at the University of British Columbia, stayed home and started working on a future.

Our sister Liz and her girlfriend are living the Hollywood dream, working in the movies and living in Venice Beach. Liz is a set builder and Jeina is a head-lining magician at a number of well-known comedy clubs. Jaxson and Liz are happy, maybe success and confidence in yourself makes that possible, but I'm really not sure. But I do know that they have always believed that if there is nothing they need, then they have everything. Me? Whatever I have, it has always felt like there is something else I need. Except when I had Robyn.

The fact that the all the kids are gone from the family home, though, doesn't mean it's empty. Our Mom still lives there with a cat and a dog in a five bedroom house. I made a mental promise that I would go and visit.

*****

I didn't keep that promise, not that weekend. Friday was already half over, and I just let the rest of the day go. On Saturday, though, Robyn and I went to Granville Island and bought organic meat and wild flowers and then rode the Seabus to Lonsdale Quay in North Vancouver for African food and German desert. Sunday, we took the dog to Steveston to run in the tidal flats and bought Salmon and prawns from the fishermen at the Richmond docks. We barbecued the seafood and I made a broth from the leftovers.

Those were good days, exactly the kind of days Ice Cube had in mind.

CHAPTER 8

Monday rolled around, and I wanted to catch up with Kyle. He had been kind enough to stay busy on the weekend so that Robyn and I could be alone for the most part, but I did need to know where his head was at—after all, while I was drinking my way through all of this 1,000 kilometres away, Kyle was living it.

There are no shortage of parks in the Richards' neighbourhood. Around noon, we took advantage of the spring like weather and walked to the nearest one to throw a football around. It was warm enough that Kyle wore shorts; adverse to cold as I am, I wore sweats and a hoodie.

We were walking side by side, and were silent the first few houses we passed, each thinking about how something so familiar—us being together for a catch—could be so strange. "What do you want to know, Dirt?" Kyle asked. "I love that you're here, but I'm not sure why Karen went to get you." He tossed the ball high in the air and left it for me to catch. "Jim's dead," he said. "The *Saints* killed him and Kylee. The Chief of the Vancouver Police Department is as dirty—and not in a good way—as she is hot, and I'm suspended for bringing it up." I tossed the ball back, high, and he moved to catch it behind his back.

Nesha was five or six houses ahead, sitting at the corner like she's trained to do. "I'm looking forward to the video," I said. "Karen said it was a 'theatrical performance for the ages'."

"Could've been," he replied. "I don't remember much about that afternoon."

We'd caught up to the dog, and I told her she could cross the street. On the other side was the park, and she was gone in a flash. "Impressive," Kyle said.

I nodded. "Listen," I told him, "whatever else, I'm here for you. I need to make sure you are okay."

He waved that off. "Not necessary," he said. "We are big boys and have been for a long time. Some beds are just meant to be slept in."

"Okay," I said, "that's true. But if you don't need help personally—and I won't push—let's help Karen with this. She needs something—closure or some other new wave bullshit, I really don't know. But she's hurting and thinks I—we, hopefully—can help."

He threw the ball about thirty-five yards and Nesha chased it, temporarily forgetting about the squirrels she was hunting. "We can," he said.

"So where do we start? I can't piece everything she's telling me together and get the same picture she's created in her head. What am I missing?"

"I don't know, Dirt," he said and jogged after the dog. "Depends on how much you hate the *Saints*, I guess." He threw me the ball from about twenty yards, a tight spiral but it lacked his usual zip.

Despite the beautiful day, we were the only ones in the park. I returned the toss.

"That all you got?" he asked.

"Just matching you," I said. "I know how delicate you are."

"Person bomb beats brick wall," he said and threw the ball

back with some heat, but still not his best effort. The dog was running back and forth between us, tail wagging like she thought she might intercept a pass.

I took a couple of half-speed steps to my right and threw on the run. "I guess I'm struggling with the *Saints*," I told him. "I get it—they're everywhere and they've fucked with your lives." He caught the pass, and then did the same half-roll out. I held my right arm high and away from my body, and he hit it with a perfect spiral, a little more on it than the previous throws. "But Kyle, I ask this with all love my brother, but why the fuck do the *Saints*—Canada's largest motorcycle club —care so much about Jim and you?"

I led him two or three steps with my return throw. He didn't move to catch it; instead, the dog jumped on it like a fumble. "Dirt," Kyle said, "that's a great question." Nesha had rolled the ball back to him, and he picked it up. This throw had some real heat to it. "I guess maybe I've been thinking *around* that, but not actually *about* that."

I threw the ball on a bit of a loop and over his head so he had to retreat to catch it. We were now about thirty yards apart. "Some of it is retaliation," he said. "Jim and I messed up some of their operations—and operatives—pretty good. And Jim was *calm* after I joined him, compared to when he was on his own." His return throw was dead centre and stung my hands a little. "But the motorcycle clubs don't kill cops," he said. "It brings them too much grief."

We were throwing loose and easy now. I gestured with the ball, and he broke to his right. Perfect throw. "And Kylee," I said, "wasn't targeted, you know? That was bad luck and circumstance—the *Saints* didn't pick her out specifically to recruit."

"Yes," he said. I waited for more, but that was it. His return throw was again chest high and hard. If I hadn't caught it, it would have knocked me down. "Let's just throw," he said. "Helps me think."

We stayed at the park for close to an hour. At the end, it was a battle of wills to see who would stop first. My shoulder was killing me, and I could tell Kyle's was as well because his throws were starting to drift. That being said, if it weren't for the dog, we might still be there, one pass after another until all we could do was throw underhand with the wrong arm. It was Nesha who said enough.

"Good dog," I told her when Kyle was distracted. "Good dog."

*****

Since it was afternoon, we took a bit of a detour on the way back to the Richards' place and headed to *Dentry's* on West 10th. Neither of us had our wallets, but since *Dentry's* was Mr. Richards' local—and Kyle's go to spot for over a decade—our money wasn't needed. We both made a mental note to head back later to settle up and tip the server—who was also the owner and recognized me from years in the past. Nesha was welcomed; in fact, if I remember correctly, she enjoyed a few servings of left-over fish and chips.

"Remember when this would have been early for us to be drinking?" Kyle asked.

"I think so," I replied. "But truthfully, since I hit that wall, I've stopped worrying about time. Besides, by two or so every day, my body is already telling me it's five o'clock somewhere." We toasted ourselves.

"Here's to five o'clock," he said. We were drinking Guinness. "Better get the next ones started, Maggie," Kyle said to the owner. "We know how particular you are in your pour." Maggie laughed, but did start pouring the next pints—a proper pint of Guinness does take a bit of time.

"So what did our thinking lead to?" I asked. "Anything good?"

"Here's where I'm stuck," Kyle said. "It's a great point about why the *Saints* care—or cared about Jim and me, and I hadn't thought about it before. But, Jesus Christ, Dirt—if they didn't' kill Jim, who did?"

I shrugged. "Not to be delicate, but shit happens, right? Wrong place, wrong time?"

"But it was a set up. Jim and I weren't supposed to be there that night. That wasn't our sector, and we were working a double. That never happens, and it was orders from above that put us there."

"Kyle," I said, "I think you're making my point for me. You've been thinking that it was the *Saints* who set it all up and manipulated everything so you two would be there; just blind luck you weren't both killed, I guess." I was finished my beer and Maggie was coming with another. "But why would they do all that? I'm not saying they *couldn't*, or *wouldn't*, I'm asking why."

"Sorry to interrupt, gents," Maggie said and sat down the refills. "Bangers and mash or lamb stew?" I went with the stew, Kyle with the bangers. "I'm bringing you extra," she said to Kyle. "You need some weight back on you."

"Thanks Maggie," he said. Then, to me, he said, "let's take it easy on the Guinness right now. When we're done here, we're going downtown to ask the *Saints* your questions. We can drink their beer."

And we did. Quite a few, in fact.

*****

Once back at the Richards', we moved in a hurry. We wanted to be gone before Robyn returned from the university and we had to explain ourselves. Kyle dressed cowboy because that's what he does, and I coordinated a black velour Air Jordan sweatshirt with grey Air Griffey's with a black velour swoosh. We took Kyle's truck because he knew where we were going and in fifteen minutes we were underneath the Granville Street Bridge and looking for a parking spot on Granville Island.

"We'll start at *Monk's*," he said, naming a high-end seafood place. "If there's nothing shaking there, we'll head over to the *Granville Island Hotel* and see if any of the ladies are working. They'll know where the Monday action is if we can't find it ourselves." By ladies, of course, Kyle meant escorts. "From there, we'll start swimming downstream, but each stop we make, the class of people we meet will decrease."

"I'm interested to see how many stops it will take for us to blend in," I said. "And what are we doing? Looking for *Saints*, you said. But why exactly?"

"You've got questions," he said. "They've got answers. Will they share them? Probably not. We will need to be persuasive." He parked the truck and killed the ignition. "Look, Dirt, I want to know now more than ever if the *Saints* are behind what happened to Jim. I know they're behind what happened to Kylee, but Kylee has to own some of that too. But if the *Saints* didn't kill Jim and try to kill me, then I am going to find out—we are going to find out—who did."

"So our plan is to bluster around like bears at a campsite?" I asked.

"Welcome to police work," he said. "Hey, Ryan? Whatever happens tonight, no matter how nice people are being, be memorable, okay? Flash some cash, try to be charming. We want the word out that we are out and about."

"I thought you'd never ask," I said. "I have some brand new material."

He looked at me. "Maybe leave the charm to me. You can flash the cash."

Monk's is an old-fashioned kind of place. High ceilings and dark wood, and servers in black dress shirts and long white aprons. Since it looked like we were going to eat there, I was glad I had spent those months in the major leagues. I quickly calculated the food cost and wished my bar could maintain these margins.

The Hostess asked if we would care to sit at the bar while they prepared a table for us. We said we would. The bar had an excellent view of the Granville island harbour, with long boats and canoes and a few run-arounds. If Kyle had been his sister, it would have been an excellent start to the evening.

"Don't get me wrong," I said and drank from my $6 Stella Artois. "I love seafood—and living in Calgary, don't get to eat it that often. But why are we here?"

"Baker owns a big chunk of this place," Kyle told me. "And the chowder is really good. I know that you are going to be talking about it forever, trying to duplicate the recipe," he said disparagingly.

"At least I don't dress like a cowpoke," I said.

He smiled, but didn't mean it. "I figure if we start here, at the top, by the time we get to the bottom, world will be out and we'll find somebody to talk to." He drank from his Negra Modelo. "The problem is, though, that when you poke the bear, sometimes the bear pokes back." He took another pull from his beer. "So we should take it easy—easyish—on these because it could be a long night."

"Understood," I said and ordered two more beer.

When the bartender—a young, good looking kid probably working his way through University—brought the new drinks, Kyle asked him if Anthony was around. "My apologies, Sir, but there are a few Anthonys who work here. Could you be more specific?"

I handed him a ten. "Baker. Your boss."

The kid took the money, but said he didn't know an Anthony Baker. "I haven't been here that long, though. Perhaps I can ask around?"

"Please," Kyle said. "We'd appreciate that. And while you're doing so, could you ask if there's anywhere around here where we might meet a couple of like-minded women?" Kyle slipped him a matching ten. The kid was unimpressed.

"Like minded?" I said after the kid moved to the other end of the bar.

"Told you," Kyle responded. "Charm. Or, at least be memorable."

Our table was ready. Not sure if they thought Kyle and I were a couple, but they gave us a lovely window seat, all mountains and water and boat lights. The chowder was, in fact, excellent, as was the seafood fettuccini.

Baker never showed, and by the time we were finished our meal, our young bartender was gone.

"Let's see if we can get a date," Kyle said.

We couldn't. The *Granville Island Hotel* was the hot-spot Kyle had made it out to be, just not for us. The bar was full and there were million dollar water views and expensive canapes and a lot of chandeliers and marble, but there were no ladies of the night. Hardly any ladies at the bar at all, in fact. And the only person happy to see us was an ageing, overweight security guy in a blue blazer and cheap polyester pants. He met us in a narrow hallway, spacious rooms to either side.

"Help you gentleman?" he said.

"For now, we're browsing," Kyle said. "But I'm not seeing what we are after."

Blue Blazer made a subtle show of pointing us one direction while keeping us from another.

"Maybe," I said while making it obvious I was looking over his shoulder, "we can sit over there instead?" I put a twenty in his blazer pocket. Over there was a big room, couches and fire places, and a half dozen pretty people of both genders setting up tables and bar stations. "How's it going?" I said into the room, but no one responded.

"My apologies," the Blazer said in perfectly enunciated syllables, "that room is reserved for a private party. I am sure you will be quite comfortable at the bar. Enjoy the harbour view and small boats." He seemed to emphasize *small.*

"Too early for the good snatch, huh Chief?" Kyle said. I looked shocked and put another twenty in the guy's blazer pocket.

"My friend," I said, feigning shock and surprise. "I apologize."

"I get that," Kyle said to the Blazer. "We'll be over here when the party warms up." Kyle patted the guy dismissively on the shoulder and we headed to the bar. "Save us a place. I'm partial to blondes."

The Blazer was gone, closing a formidable set of sliding doors behind him. We were alone in the entrance foyer.

"Drink?" I asked.

"Seems like a good idea," Kyle said. "What do you think happens in there?"

Our bartender this time was another good looking kid, no older than twenty. She was no more helpful than the kid at *Monk's*, but she was significantly more talkative.

"How do we get invited to the big party?" Kyle asked.

"I don't know," she said. Her name was Amber. "I've only been in Vancouver three days, and this is only my second shift here. People just seem to know which side of the bar to go to." Kyle and I turned to face the room.

"Three days!" Amber repeated. "And I already have this job, and the manager here helped me get a great apartment in False Creek. I can walk to work and all the celebrities stay here! Yesterday, I was working on the other side, and made Mel Gibson a million drinks!" She noticed her exuberance and apologized. "Nothing like this ever happens in Blind River. It's too good to be true, you know?"

I tipped her heavily. From what I knew and from Kyle's posture, I knew her bills were coming due sooner than she was expecting. "Welcome to Vancouver, Amber," I said. I wrote my name and number on the back of one of Kyle's generic VPD business cards. "This is not a line," I told her. "Just please keep this and call us when—if—things change."

Amber gave me a puzzled expression, but put the card in her pocket. "Okay," she said. "Thanks, I guess. Hey—do you want me to see if I can get you into that other room?"

"Please," Kyle said and Amber left through a door at the back of the bar.

Kyle and I turned to face the room again. It was a beautiful room, very modern and streamlined. And it was close to full, important looking people in groups of three or four. Everyone was better dressed than the two of us, but clothes don't make the man. Unless they do. Either way, there were no woman looking for companionship—at least, not from the likes of us. "Weird," I said to Kyle. "Most people find us delightful."

Kyle ignored this. Not because it isn't true, but because at that exact moment, two new blazers showed up and asked us to leave. These ones were bigger and considerably younger than the first blazer.

"Pretty early," Kyle said. "We really just got here."

"We think you will be happier elsewhere," one of them said. "The *Granville Island Playhouse* is doing improve tonight. You guys might do well there—it's a more... pedestrian crowd. Look around, finish your beer, and off you go."

People were noticing our conversation and turning to stare. Four big guys and some tension to go with your after work martini. Good times. Amber had not returned.

My understanding of our goal was that we wanted to be noticed. Felt like mission accomplished, so I drained my beer. Kyle finished his and made a show of placing a fifty on the bar. "This," he said, "is for Amber. Please give her our thanks."

We both stood and Kyle looked at his watch. "Still early," he said. "Let's roll." The blazers were not unhappy to see us leave. "Tell Baker we dropped by," Kyle told them. "We'll catch him down the road."

They smiled while motioning us to leave. At the door, one of them gave Kyle a bit of a shove in the back which certainly seemed intentional. We stood our ground, and nothing more happened.

"Hey, do you guys have a wing night?" I asked once we were outside. They backed away, and the sliding doors closed. No answer to the wing night question. Knowing they were watching, I flashed a double bird. Kyle laughed.

"Classy," he said. "Nice."

We headed back to the truck. "I should have gotten my twenties back from that guy," I said. "And given them to Amber. She's going to need them unless her life stays perfect."

"Fuck it," Kyle said. "This isn't working."

"How so?" I asked. "First Blazer was definitely keeping us from something and Blazers Two and Three weren't surprised when you mentioned Baker."

"Not what I mean. We haven't been taking it easy beer wise. I'm not driving. There's a cab stand back at the hotel."

"Kyle," I said, "how many great mysteries have been solved by heroes in cabs?"

"One," he answered. "This one."

*****

Our cab driver was somewhere between our two bartenders on the talkative scale. "Know Anthony Baker?" I asked.

"Yes," he said.

"Know where he lives?"

"No."

"Okay," Kyle said. "Take us to the *Side Door* instead."

Truthfully, I was surprised the *Side Door* still existed. It was old and seedy when Kyle and I started drinking there, a thousand years ago. At the corner of Broadway and Arbutus, the *Side Door* was bar service only. No food, no servers. Just electric beats and synthesizers and wet T-shirt contests every second Friday. At thirty, Kyle and I looked twenty years older than the other patrons.

"Stay here," Kyle said to the cabbie. "Turn off your lights, turn down your radio. Maybe grab a nap. We'll be forty minutes at the most—probably closer to ten. Be here when we get back, okay?" He gave the guy a twenty to stay.

We didn't make it inside. There was a line up to get in, and when it was our turn, the bouncer made a show of checking his clipboard and looked at us both. "You're in," he said to me. To Kyle, he said, "You're not. No country here, and no cowboy boots." To be fair to Kyle, every other person was wearing boots—most of them were women, but still.

"Doesn't seem fair," I said. "What if a line dance breaks out? What am I going to do?"

"In or out?" the bouncer said. "I ain't got all night."

"I think you do," I replied. "I mean, this is your job, right? Where else you going to go?"

"In or out?" he asked again.

The crowd behind us was starting to grow restless. There was some gentle pushing and some less subtle whining. We were all that was standing between them and $2 Budweisers. "Letting underage girls in without checking their ID," I said, "making sure the pretty ones get over-served. What time do you close? I mean, this is what you do for another eight hours. You have all night."

"But you don't," he said. And the first move was quick. His hands were at his side and he tensed to give me a shot in the kidney, but Kyle was quicker. Before the blow could land, Kyle had the bouncer's hand in his.

"Tell Baker we want to talk," he said. The bouncer relaxed, perhaps foolishly. Kyle gave him a shot in the kidney that was so fast, I don't think anyone in line saw it. Kyle's smirk was anything but friendly. "We're going to *Bimini's*."

"Cool," I said. "I've always liked *Bimini's*."

And that was true. *Bimini's* was probably my second favourite bar in Vancouver. My favourite was the *Fogg 'N Suds* kitty corner to the baseball diamond where I learned to play. They let us drink there long before we were legal, and they even gave us a passport to stamp beer from around the world. It was a

127

block and a half from my house. Kitsilano was a good place to grow up—a little baseball, a little beach, a few beer and an easy walk home.

Bimini's hadn't changed. Two stories, wood and neon and open to the street, cheap beer and surprisingly decent bar food. We were able to grab a standing two-top on the second floor, and it was obvious they were expecting us. Before we had even settled, there was a server with beer and wings in front of us. "Welcome, Mr. Simms," she said. "Mr. Richards. This is an Espresso Stout made for us by *The Trestle Bridge* and we've got hot and salt and pepper wings." Kyle doesn't do spice. "Enjoy." And she was gone, we didn't even catch her name.

The wings were good, the beer was great. Nobody knew Anthony Baker and there were no obvious *Saints* associates around. I think I was at nine drinks, and that was taking it easy. Number ten came and went, and nothing happened. The Canucks lost at home against Montreal, and after that the bar cleared out. We drank number eleven, and then it was closing time. Our cabbie drove us home, and the ride had been pre-paid.

"Damn," Kyle said. "Just damn. That might have actually worked."

CHAPTER 9

And suddenly it was Tuesday. Although I was used to the hangover, I wasn't used to the thinking and I had a lot of it to do. About the previous night, obviously, and Kyle and Jim and everything Karen had told me, of course, and how I couldn't make sense of it, and now there was Robyn. I hadn't thought about her at all the day before, and now I was a bit panicked. The weekend had been fun and romantic without actually being romantic. Were we friends now, or on the way back to something else? Friends was probably more than I deserved; something more than that was unimaginable.

I grabbed a quick shower and a cup of coffee and made it out of the house without seeing anyone. At 9 AM, I was standing with Karen in the lobby of the *Vancouver Press* building, home of both Vancouver newspapers—the V*ancouver Province* in the morning and the *Vancouver Sun* in the afternoon. We rode the elevator to the seventh floor and the reporter, Terri Clement, met us in the reception area.

She was an incredibly beautiful woman. 5'8", straight black hair to her shoulders and green eyes. Boots added another inch to her height, and her curves were not hidden at all by jeans and a man's Oxford cloth dress shirt. It had never occurred to me that a crime reporter could look like this, and that made me feel some brief shame. Obviously, I was staring at her.

"I get that a lot," she said even though I hadn't said anything.

"I'm sorry," I said, flustered. "You really are beautiful." Karen looked at me like I had lost my mind. Truthfully, I may have, at least temporarily. Struggling for words, I managed, "does that help with the guys you deal with?"

"Thank you," she said, not at all irritated or surprised by my forward comment. "And it does help," she told us. "Until you get to the very top, most of these motorcycle guys do not have a brain between them, and none of them take me seriously—which means they talk to me more than they should." She laughed. "I most definitely use anything I can to my advantage. And," she added, "I'm pretty sure they don't read the stories I write. That includes the cops," she shrugged. "Maybe half the cops."

She showed us into a well-appointed conference room. There was bottled water and coffee already on the table, and a nice assortment of pastries. "Help yourselves," Terri said. "Everything is on the house as long as you understand that what we talk about is going to be in the paper. How we attribute it, we can work out later. And guys," she added, "if the *Saints* are tied to Jim's death like Karen thinks, this is going to be one hell of a story." She laughed quickly. "Hell, it already is." With that, she sat down and motioned us to do the same. Terri looked at me gently. "Does that face hurt as much as I think it does?"

"Only when sober," I said. "So it hurts until five o'clock." I looked at Karen. "We are a long way from connecting Jim's death to the *Saints*."

"Not as far as you might think," she replied. I pursed my lips and shook my head softly.

On cue, Terri passed each of us a file folder that was half an inch thick. "This is everything I've written on the *Saints* and the interdivisional motorcycle-crime Task Force. All the facts and numbers come from very reliable sources," she said with a glance at Karen. "Very reliable."

"You and Jim?" I asked Karen.

"Who knows?" she replied, with a wink.

"Bottom line," Terri said, "is that my *sources*"—both women smiled—"can prove that, since the inception of the Task Force, *Saint* arrests result in a seven-per cent charge rate."

"Charge rate," Karen jumped in. "*Not* conviction rate."

"And," Terri continued, "sources and court documents reveal that, in this same time-frame, non-*Saint* biker arrests have resulted in an eighty-three per cent charge rate and significantly higher conviction rate than for the *Saints*."

"Weird," I allowed, "but what does it prove? Maybe the *Saints* are better at crime. "And," I added, "if the *Saints* are getting away with everything, less reason to go after Jim and Kyle."

"The charge rate is the key," Karen said with determination. "The word is coming from above that *Saints* are protected." She looked at us both in turn. "I just don't know how high. Not yet."

"In the last three months," Terri continued without checking any notes, "fifteen high-level non-*Saints* have been arrested and one-hundred and twenty-seven charges have been laid. In the same time frame," she continued, "zero high-level *Saints* have been arrested and zero charges have been laid. Almost the only *Saints* that have seen the inside of a police station, let alone a court room, in the last year are the ones that Kyle and Jim took there."

I shrugged. "And no *Saint* arrests since Jim and Kyle...." I let that trail off. "My point still stands," I said.

"Ryan," Karen said, "what did the folks in Golden tell you about the cops?"

I thought on that for a second. "Amy said the cops had come

the night before we had our fun, but really didn't accomplish anything. Didn't even try to persuade our friends to move along."

"Right. And then when they came about your truck?"

"They actually seemed to be more concerned about Nesha's rabies tag and if her other shots were up to date than they were about my truck or who did it," I said. "Hell, we know who did it." I shrugged. "Maybe I was too pissed off to notice at the time."

"And," Terri interjected, "that was in Golden, not exactly the metropolitan capital of anywhere."

"But the first night was totally random," I said, unconvinced. "We could have stopped anywhere and they could have been anywhere. It was just some random thugs, pissed about the snow and looking for a fight. My face just happened to be there for the punching."

"What did Rich tell us?" Karen asked. To Terri, she said "Rich Koleman, task force veteran."

"I know Rich," Terri said. "He's one of the cops who can read."

"Rich said the trained monkeys and their handlers were probably on their way to Vancouver, but so were we. I don't think that proves anything."

"On their way at the request of the *Saints* to add muscle..." Karen was getting frustrated. "Recruited to help expand their drug and cash monopoly," she added with some heat, "while their limited competition is being rounded up by the Task Force."

"Still a long way from Jim," I said.

"Let's close the gap," Terri said. "Last six, seven months, it's been a point-counter point between the *Sun* and *Province.* We say the Task Force is corrupt, they say it's working. We say the *Saints* are running amok, they say motorcycle crime is at an all-time low."

"And," Karen added with emphasis, "*they* say Jim was dirty."

"Okay," I said, resigned to a long meeting. I poured more coffee. "Let's start with Jim."

Terri nodded. "There is a lot to cover. But first, do you understand how unusual it is for a police force to try and discredit a deceased member? Even dirty cops get buried with honours and then everything gets swept under the rug. No laundry gets aired."

"I do get that," I said. "No sense in the police tarnishing their own—just creates questions and distrust in the public."

Another folder was shared. "This one," Terri told us, "is a selection of Vancouver *Province* articles." I opened my folder and shuffled through the pages. "You'll see that they focus on Jim as a counter-balance to the Chief. Basically, the morning paper contends that despite this dirty cop, the Chief is having tremendous success."

"And it was Jim alone," Karen said. "No conspiracy, no rogue cops—one man trying to bring down the entire department. It's been like a series of old-fashioned cliff hangers," she added. "Stay tuned to see what happens today."

"The stories in this folder," Terri said, "document a series of failures: raids that turn up empty, busts that are disallowed, evidence that goes missing, witnesses that don't make it to trials."

"Karen told me about some of this on the drive. What's the connection to Jim?"

Terri tapped two fingers on the file. "I'll give the *Province* this," she said, "everything they say is true: Jim was assigned to every one of those broken raids, failed busts, or tied to all of the missing evidence and misplaced witnesses."

"Compelling," I told them. "But obviously it can be explained, right?" I looked at them both. "Why was Jim being scape-goated?"

"Near as we can figure," Terri said, "to get him out of the way so the *Saints* could continue to prosper without interruption."

"And that's why they killed him," Karen said. "So they could continue their reign of terror."

"Karen," I said, "I am on your side. 100 per cent. But this is thin. Motorcycle clubs don't kill cops. Jim's death still seems random."

Terri put her hand on top of Karen's. "Ryan," she said, "do cops kill cops?"

*****

We were silent for a bit. I think they might have been letting my brain catch up to what was being said. It was ten thirty and the coffee was well finished. Terri said she would get us a refresh. Instead, I offered to run down to the café in the main lobby and grab some fresh coffee and snacks. I purchased a surprisingly nice assortment and managed to not drip filling on my only clean sweater—a V-Neck from the Gap that the sales girl said really highlighted my eyes. I mentioned this to someone the last time I wore it and they reminded me my eyes are brown, so everything matches. Buying trucks and sweaters is not an area in which I excel. Fortunately, I don't do it very often.

When we had sat down earlier in the morning, Karen and Terri had both placed briefcases on the seats beside them. I didn't have a briefcase—everything I need fits in the pocket of my hoodie. This particular hoodie was one of my favourites: a grey and orange hold over from the 1989 World Series. I had only been drafted the year before, so I was nowhere near that team, but when I did get called up in '92, there were boxes full of them in the club house and the equipment guys said I could help myself. I took two boxes and gave most of the sweat-shirts away as Christmas presents.

Terri took a video cassette out of her briefcase, and then found a remote on a shelf beside the door. She pointed the remote at the white board behind Karen and a combination TV-VCR unit appeared as the white board disappeared.

Terri took a few strides, which I tried but failed not to watch, and put the video in place. "Your Vancouver Chief of Police," she said, and pressed play.

We watched the video, and it became boring in its repetition. It was a compilation of the last eleven Task Force conferences. When the video was over, Terri had handouts.

Street level crime in Vancouver is predominantly the domain of motorcycle clubs, but the *Saints*—the single largest club in Canada by a wide margin—are innocent on the streets of Vancouver, at least according to the VPD. On average, each of the Chief's press conferences mentioned 'Motorcycle Club' thirteen times, but the *Saints* were never named. In fact, the only time the *Saints* were mentioned was by reporters asking questions at the end of each session and every time, the Chief answered in generalities:

"We're seeking all violent perpetrators."

"We continue to take guns and other weapons of the streets."

"The *Grave Wolves* and *Steel Vagabonds* are known offenders and two of the most violent criminal groups in Canada."

"The Lower Mainland has long been part of a drug trafficking corridor, to the Southern US and even beyond. This will end."

"There has been a significant decrease in violent criminal activity, directly attributable to the success of our motorcycle crime task force and successful busts of the *Wolves* and *Vagabonds*."

At some point, my eyes glazed over. My attention span has always been attuned to the next pitch—if the next pitch was the same as the last pitch and the same as the next pitch and same as the last pitch... man, I would have hit a thousand in the big leagues.

Ultimately, where we landed is here: *Saints* (by not being mentioned) are good. Clubs like the *Grave Wolves* and *Steel Vagabonds* are bad. Here are some bars and businesses to avoid based on your own morality and desire to be safe. There is no quid pro quo of marijuana for hard drugs across the border. Our border with the US is the most securely patrolled and defended in the world. Conviction ratios are through the roof and guns and hard drugs—including opiates and heroin—are at an all-time low on Vancouver streets.

The video ended with the Chief's assurance that criminal activity, in any form, will not be tolerated in Vancouver and the *Saints* are being pursued and prosecuted to the fullest extent of the law, as are all criminal enterprises. She actually held up a *Vancouver Province* front page with the headline "*Tough Talking Chief Backs Words with Action.*"

At that, I laughed, but perhaps I was viewing facts with jaundiced eyes, yellow as they were by multiple Orangutan punches.

"No violent or drug related criminal activity," the Chief of the Vancouver Police Department concluded, "will be tolerated. Take your shameful behaviour to another location, one that finds you charming or amusing. Vancouver is not that place." The Chief did not offer a suggestion of where that other place might be.

Our viewing pleasure ended with Kyle's press conference. Ostensibly, it had been called for the Chief to brag about a $7.2 million dollar drug and arms raid in Aldergrove that all but crippled the *Grave Wolves* in BC, but it will always be known as Kyle's press conference.

In it, clearly inebriated, he walks through the middle aisle of press seats and stops about ten feet short of the stage, where the Chief is standing with other police officials and Task Force members. Kyle doesn't look good and is wearing a plaid work shirt, untucked, ripped jeans and a huge belt buckle that oddly catches the stage lights like a watch reflects the sun.

The room is silent. "Officers," the Chief says, "remove this man."

Kyle's opener is a classic. "Fuck you, bitch," he says. "They should be removing *you*—you're a fucking liar and a killer."

Things got pretty chaotic after that.

*****

We took another break, to stretch our legs and Karen and Terri checked for messages. I sat staring at the screen, Kyle frozen in mid-yell, a cop on each arm clearly confused by knowing what they had to do, but recognizing Kyle as one of them, and a friend.

"This is my fault," Karen said. "Kyle came by one night after Rileigh was asleep and I showed him Jim's journals and all the research Terri and I have done.

"The two of them had done so much on the street, and after Kylee, their only focus was the *Saints*. I can't remember how many times they'd been called on the carpet—even having to speak to the Chief directly." She made her voice deep, a passable imitation of the Chief. 'Do your jobs, officers. These ranks and positions are not rights but privileges bestowed by me'."

"She's a publicity whore," I said, "but Chief is a political position, so it's to be expected." I looked at them both in turn. "I'm still missing a connection to Jim. Isn't it possible that Jim's sense of justice was skewed and didn't align with the VPD's?" I asked. "Why didn't she just remove them from the Task Force? It's not like they were going to stop hunting *Saints*."

"We think it's pretty simple," Terri replied. "You said it before, Ryan—the Chief and the Task Force needed a scapegoat. Someone to blame when evidence was missing and raids were turning up empty. Someone to take the heat when the Chief's pet project was questioned—'what do you mean we aren't pursing the *Saints* with the same diligence we are other criminal clubs? They're have been a number of unfortunate circumstances around the prosecution of members of this particular club, but the Task Force is committed to pursuing all offenders to the full capacity of the law. Responsibility has been taken for those mistakes and corrective measures put in place'.

"It's unfortunate but undeniable that Jim is the common denominator between all the failures."

"Assigned in each circumstance," Karen said, "*by* the Vancouver Chief of Police."

"Pretty compelling evidence," I said, "to present to the media to say that something is rotten inside the Task Force, and not at the top. And that, of course, allows the *Saints* a pass."

"After the last failure," Karen said, "a raid on a transfer house in East Van that turned up empty, Jim was removed from the Task Force and, like I said, bumped down that pay grade. Didn't help his mood," she added, "or his passion for hunting *Saints*.'

"And after Jim was removed,' Terri said, "nothing but wins for

138

the Chief's project."

"I know about some of the wins," I said. They made the news in Calgary—the bust in North Vancouver, the shipment confiscated at Peace Arch Park, the grow op in Abbotsford."

"It's a perfect storm in so many ways," Karen said. "The end of the mistakes and empty raids is tied to Jim, the secondary players like the *Wolves* are being harassed and removed, and the *Saints* are picking up sales and ground in the few areas they weren't already dominant."

"And prices go back up," I said.

*****

We decided to break for lunch. I knew Kyle was heading downtown in the afternoon for an appointment at Police HQ, a building they call the Cop Shop, so I invited him to join us. He drove over the Burrard Street Bridge instead of the Cambie Bridge to the island that is downtown Vancouver and met us at the *Vancouver Press Club*. Meeting Terri, Kyle's eyes immediately regained some spark and his energy improved. She is that beautiful. Kyle was wearing one of his ridiculous oversized belt buckles from some rodeo that Terri instantly recognized.

"Don't tell me you're a cow girl?" I said.

"I won't," she replied, "but I've been barrel racing all my life."

"Aww, jeez," I said. "Not another one." Kyle's love for rodeo and all things cowboy has been a constant battle between us over the years. It's one of the reasons I try to drive when we're together—my truck is a no-country zone.

The *Vancouver Press Club* is a fairly fancy place on the outside, so I wondered if I would be under-dressed. Turns out, though, that since the restaurant caters to newspaper and media types, my hoodie was perfect attire. Even my black eyes didn't draw any attention.

I ordered a Cobb salad and felt like a grown up. Everyone else had a burger with fries. If one of them challenged me to a race after lunch, I was confident I would win. Alcohol was discussed, but we decided we were working so we all abstained. If they had been drinking, I definitely would have won any races, especially since Kyle and Terri were wearing cowboy boots.

After lunch, and too many conversations about horses, Kyle hung a right and headed east to Main Street and his mandated counselling session and Karen, Terri and I headed back to the seventh floor boardroom.

"Did something just happen?" I whispered to Karen.

"Boys," she replied while shaking her head. "You are all so clueless."

I took that to mean something had happened.

*****

Back in the boardroom, I asked the first question. "Is it possible the chief isn't as squeaky clean as she presents herself?"

"That's something we are looking into," Terri replied. "Our focus to this point has been motorcycle crime in general and the Saints in particular. She came from back east after a series of impressive corruption busts."

"That's interesting," I said.

"She is losing some of the media," Terri said. "She's always played favourites and those on the outside are getting tired of drinking the pre-made Kool-Aid. The tone and dexterity of the questions she gets asked at her monthly press conferences has changed dramatically."

"Guys," Karen said. "The Saints. Please."

"Right," Terri said. "Ryan, are you up to speed on how these biker clubs work?"

"That's pretty much all Karen and I have been talking about since Calgary."

"This will be fast, then," Terri replied. "But Karen said you guys predominantly talked about the hierarchy, and drugs specifically. I want to discuss these clubs on a more holistic level.

"But," she said, "before we get to the fun stuff like drugs and hookers and beatings—sorry Ryan—we need to do a quick overview of how clubs like the *Saints* and *Grave Wolves* operate."

"I'll put my hand up if I get lost," I said.

Terri smiled. "All motorcycle clubs operate the same way. And," she said with emphasis, "they are *clubs*, not gangs. You want a quick punch in the face with brass knuckles or something worse, call an associate or patched member part of a gang."

"I will try and remember that," I said. "I've already had the punch in the face."

"And you came out the other side," Terri said. "Not gonna lie, that's not always the case. I am suitably impressed." I assumed she was kidding, but part of me was hoping that she wasn't.

Terri passed us another folder, this one was thin and held nothing but glossy pamphlets and press releases warning the public of the danger of motorcycle clubs. The top pamphlet was printed by something called the *Canadian Integrated Response to Organized Crime Unit.*

On the cover, there were a lot of pictures of drugs, money and motorcycle folks—minus club colours, which I thought odd— having a grand old time. I picked mine up and opened it. Inside, there were a few more pictures, including guns and for some reason, numchucks. I wasn't immediately convinced to *not* join a motorcycle club. There were also a whole lot of words in a small font that I gathered were intended to convince me to stay on the straight and narrow. I was on the fence —those guys in Golden sure seemed to be having a good time.

"The *Saints* have been around for quite a while," Terri said. "They opened their first chapter in East Vancouver in late 1983. You know from being born here that the Downtown East Side is some of—hell, maybe the—richest drug selling territory in the country. By '98, they had chapters in Burnaby, Richmond, Surrey and what was then Haney, now Maple Ridge."

She passed over another brochure, this one from the *Biker Enforcement Unit* (BEU) of the RCMP.

Karen jumped in. "Law enforcement in Canada defines an outlaw motorcycle gang or one-percenter club as any group of motorcycle riders and supporters who have made a voluntary commitment to band together, abide by organizational rules, and commit crime. The *Saints* and *Grave Wolves* are the most common clubs in BC, the *Vagabonds* too."

 "The clubs," Terri said, "counter that—contrary to media portrayal—they are 'simply like-minded individuals who share a common goal of enjoying life to the fullest'. That's from a *Saints*' recruiting brochure."

Karen continued. "Membership to these clubs is not complex. To become a *Saint's* prospect, for example, you need a valid driver's license, a motorcycle over 750cc (you do not need to actually know how to ride it) and 'the right combination of personal qualities'. Apparently, they shy away from child molesters and anyone with an interest in becoming a police officer or prison guard."

"Good to have standards," I said.

"It is," she replied. "And there's clearly something compelling about the life of crime. According to the BEU, growth in identified gang members has been substantial and alarming. Five fold in ten years."

"In the last ten years or so," Terri said, "the price of drugs has remained relatively stable, so clubs need territory to make money—new markets. Accordingly, conflict between clubs has increased exponentially. We've got growers, dealers, smugglers, gangsters, shooters, fighting violently on a daily basis."

I looked at the brochure again, and learned that the *Saints* now have fifteen chapters in BC, eight in Ontario, five in Quebec, three in Alberta, two in Saskatchewan and one in Manitoba.

"Here, I quote myself," Terri said: 'Canada has more self-proclaimed motorcycle enthusiasts per capita than any other country, including the U.S., where motorcycle clubs are thought to be much more common'."

"They're called OMGs, for Outlaw Motorcycle Gangs, in the States. Here, we usually just call them MCs, for Motorcycle Clubs. They first appeared in the southern US after WWII as jobless soldiers tried to stay connected to something, stay part of a brotherhood. The Hell's Angels came to be in 1948 in San Bernardino, California and now they have more than 200 chapters worldwide. And," she said, "they're in places you wouldn't expect: Sweden, Iceland, New Zealand."

She tapped the brochure. "By the mid-eighties, the Hells Angels were mandating that any new chapter must have permanent members 'with expertise in profitable criminal activities'. This is the model that Baker Senior followed with the *Saints*.

I read aloud from the first brochure: "'Across the country, MCs,

143

particularly the Silent Saints, are involved in money laundering, intimidation, assaults, attempted murder, murder, fraud, theft, counterfeiting, loan-sharking, extortion, prostitution, escort agencies, strip clubs, the possession and trafficking of illegal weapons, stolen goods, contraband, and illicit alcohol and cigarettes.

"'A chapter operates in a given city or region and maintains independence over internal discipline and criminal activities of the chapter in its region. Wearing colours that bear the insignia of the gang is the culmination of the biker's training period. A fortified clubhouse equipped with a sophisticated security system serves as a chapter's meeting place. Patches and tattoos show members' status within the organization.

Such gangs threaten communities' safety through violent conflict with rival gangs. Living near an outlaw motorcycle gang can affect your safety and decrease your property value'."

"They didn't call them clubs," I said. "That's going to hurt someone's feelings. And my suspicion is that a lot more people look at the pictures than actually read this brochure."

"Like I said," Terri told us, "most of these bikers can't read. And I think they use the pictures like some perverse bingo card: Got it, don't got it, got it, need it."

Karen and I laughed. "But here's what it's trying to convey," Terri said. "Outlaw bikers have a total rejection of social constraints. And they play to the audience in a number of ways; ultimately, they choose money over everything, but shocking 'the squares' is a close second."

"They basically beat my head square," I said.

"*Respect few; fear none.* That's the Saints mantra," Terri said. "You will see *RFFN* tattooed on patch members, low and mid-level guys for sure. The higher ups tend to be clean cut and well put together, at least on the surface." She pointed to a blown up picture of a biker with more tattoo than face. "Another tattoo you will see is *SFFS*, for *Saints forever, forever Saints*." Terri tapped her index on the top folder at her place at the table. "You will see in the research that tattoos mean a lot to these guys. Every tat has a meaning of some kind—most speak to fidelity to the group, but some mean killer or speak to some other role in the club."

"I think that's what the guy had tattooed on his face, *SFFS*" I said to Karen. To Terri, I added "the guy who held me had some words, or I guess letters, across his cheeks." I might have emphasized 'the guy who held me' a bit. "Now, with some context, I think that's what it was."

"Face tattoos," Terri said, "in particular, are a way for those who need a helping hand up the ladder to show allegiance." She passed her hand up and down in front of her face. "Hard to drop out or change clubs when you have *Saints*' idioms written on your head."

I spread the other papers in front of me and held up the thickest one. It was a collection of Task Force press releases.

"Chief Callan's personal propaganda machine,' Terri said.

"This looks like some light reading," Karen said. "Maybe I'll pour a bath and have a glass of wine tonight while reading this."

"Won't be relaxing," Terri replied. "And you will most definitely spill your wine." She smiled. "Instead, let me give you an overview—I have all this crap memorized I've been writing about it for so long."

She sounded like she was reading from a government text: "Cops across the country know that motorcycle clubs are criminal groups. Period. That's from the press releases," she said. "Think RICO in the States. But law enforcement has not been able to get a single conviction on this basis."

"Why not?" I asked.

"Who the fuck knows, Ryan?" Terri said. "It's a trend that shows no sign of slowing. Despite years of work by police agencies, motorcycle gangs simply never get broken. And whenever good seems to be winning, the clubs simply go on a recruiting drive and we start all over again."

"Legally, Terri said looking directly at Karen, "it's a case of 'amoral familism' versus 'amoral individualism'."

"Okay," I said, "I'm tapping out early. Explanation, please."

"'Amoral familism', Terri said, "is action undertaken solely and specifically for the betterment of the economic interests of the family unit. That unit does not have to be a family in the *strictest* terms of the word. Think mafia—family (mafia) above all else and nobody acts against the family."

"Okay," I said. "Got it. Did you go to Stanford with Karen?" I asked.

"Carleton," Terri said. "But they had big words there too."

Karen took over. "'Amoral individualism', on the other hand, stresses the importance of the individual. In this context, it means that a member must show allegiance to the membership, but is free to commit criminal acts without thinking solely of the betterment of the family."

Terri agreed. "This is the heart of the MC legal argument," she said. "Everybody has free choice—that is why *club* is such an important word to them—and since everyone is independent and just graciously kicks money and drugs and women up the ladder out of their inherent kindness, there is no systemic culture of corruption."

"Makes sense from where I sit," I said. "It's kind of brilliant, actually. From the lowest hanger on to associate to full patch member, the club has no moral or legal responsibility for you."

"Yup," Terri said. "One of Agony Baker's most quoted expressions is that 'when we do right, nobody remembers; when we do wrong, nobody forgets.' Hence, the altruism. Baker is the primary benefactor of the Children's Hospital; shit, the gym at one of the local colleges is the Baker Bowl, named for his family."

"That's right," Karen said. "I drive by it so often the name has lost meaning."

Terri took a deep breath and let it out slowly. "So," she said, "clubs like the *Saints* and the *Wolves* and the *Vagabonds* fill their memberships with rapists and pushers and murderers and whatever else, but it's all okay legally, because it's simply like-minded people sharing their interests—like a fucking horticultural club. And this, Ryan, has been repeated—successfully—all over the world, like one of those stupid chain letters you get every Christmas."

"Clubs think collectively but act individually. They identify themselves through patches and tattoos and write and obey constitutions and bylaws, they own and operate legitimate businesses that make a shit-load of money, but they are not— legally—criminal enterprises. She flashed one of the world's most beautiful smiles. "Shit load," Terri told us, "is not an official term. It's more of an approximation."

Karen took over. "Additionally, each club trademarks their club name and logo, and then makes money from selling clothes and flags printed with said trademarked names and logos. They even sponsor charity events to help cultivate and grow a positive public image. Ryan," she asked, "who is the primary sponsor of the annual Vancouver Santa Clause parade?"

"Not a clue," I said.

"Baker RV," Terri said without hesitation. She sang a little of what I assumed was a radio jingle: "'Home is wherever you are parked'."

"Exactly," Karen replied, "although your singing needs work." Terri feigned hurt. Karen continued. "But according to club doctrine, each individual club member acts in his – and it is 99% male-- best interest at all times. It's the 'one bad cop' argument, reasoning that criminal activities are isolated occurrences."

"It's a compelling argument," I said. "This guy is bad, or did something bad, but that doesn't mean we are all bad. Like a cop gets pulled over for driving drunk—that doesn't mean all cops are drunk or do illegal things."

"Right," Terri answered. "And that distinction that even if MCs do, in fact, have nothing but criminals for members, the club has no legal responsibility for individual actions has become of vital importance to bikers." She continued. "And with this structure they've created, that every member is free to act independently, has killed conviction ratios because the law keeps trying to argue that the acts are part of a conspiracy. Baker perfected this. That's one of the reasons that the *Saint* conviction ratio is zero."

"And," Karen said, "the other clubs have adopted the same strategy. So even if the Crown does get a conviction, the sentences are light because the facts of what happened often can't be argued, but conspiracy *can*."

With that, there was one last piece of paper. "This," Terri said as she passed copies to Karen and me, "is a list of mistakes made by the Task Force." It was a long list. "Jim was the senior officer in charge for each incident."

I skimmed the list. "Failed raid. Illegal bust. Guns and other weapons missing from evidence locker. Illegal detainment.

Another failed raid resulting in civilian injuries. More missing evidence. Witnesses not appearing."

"That one," Karen said, "nearly cost Jim his job. "He was working with the Sherriff's office to bring a witness from the Burnaby Remand Centre to Vancouver for the day. Ryan," she said, "Jim's orders were that the trial was in Surrey. That's where they went. Fortunately, the dispatcher was honest and backed Jim's claim."

I put the paper down. "Looking at this," I said, "the Task Force is not working, no matter what the Chief says."

"Keep in mind," Terri said. "For every failure, there is a public win. And each of these losses is specific to a *Saint's* operation. Each of the wins the Chief talked about?" she asked rhetorically. "Connected to another club."

With that, we mutually agreed to call it a day. Before we left, though, Terri said one final thing.

"It feels like a two-pronged attack. Bikers on one side—led by the *Saints*—and then something rotten at the VPD. I don't want to make light of it, Ryan" she added. "Given your face." She stood up. "But people who end up in the middle have a way of getting hurt." She took a quick look at Karen. "Or worse. It's hammers and blow torches, that's what these guys use now. Hammers and blow torches." She smiled, but not her lightning smile. "Welcome home."

Terri walked us to the elevator, and gave us both quick hugs goodbye. In the elevator, Karen said "is that a new phone in your pocket, Ryan, or are you still thinking about Terri?"

I *was* thinking about Terri, but I didn't tell her that. And it was a cell phone. I had bought it Sunday and the only person who had the number was Robyn. But I didn't tell Karen that either. A guy has to be allowed some secrets.

*****

That evening, Karen brought Rileigh over to the Richards' house, and I made Greek for dinner. Grilled pesto lamb chops and chicken souvlaki, homemade pita and a quick salad heavy on the Kalamata olives. Karen grew up in Greektown, and I grew up on the edges—some habits are hard to break. While I was mixing the marinade for the lamb, the doorbell rang and it was Terri. She had a bottle of Ouzo, so some preplanning had clearly been involved.

That distraction was welcome, and while I did most of the cooking, Kyle concentrated on the Mythos lager we had found at a specialty liquor store and Terri. I held my own on the beer, of course, but with Kyle busy elsewhere, his cooking duties fell to Robyn, and we spent quite a bit of time together. Rileigh and Nesha became best friends on sight and even though it was February, we were in Vancouver and it was twelve degrees, so there was a lot of time spent outside.

Twelve degrees in February is a little warm for Vancouver, of course, but it's not that far off the norm. On this particular day, however, I think it was a bit of a goodbye wave to Calgary. I was beginning to accept that life was now different and Ivy Green was part of the past. Home is where they have to take you, right?

We talked a little about the meeting with Terri, but mostly we didn't talk about anything to do with anything that night. Instead, we just had fun as friends. About 9 PM, Rileigh passed out and Karen took her to one of the guest rooms. Nesha went with her. Around midnight, Karen said she was exhausted and Robyn showed her to the other guest room. That left the Richards and Terri and me, and I haven't laughed that hard or felt that comfortable since… I don't know when. But it was probably at their house.

Around three, Robyn headed upstairs and I took my usual

position in the basement, but with Nesha upstairs, I was able to sleep on the couch.

Progress. Feels like progress.

*****

Wednesday morning interrupted my Tuesday night with not enough time in between.

But a hangover earned with friends and laughter is a lot different than one earned through apathy and shame. I felt I was ready for whatever the new day had to offer.

CHAPTER 10

J ust before seven AM, Wednesday morning got off to a noisy start. Rileigh was looking for breakfast, and Nesha was helping her by knocking things off the kitchen table and counters with her tail. Karen and I arrived in the kitchen at the same time and each took care of our respective noise maker. Despite my disparaging comments about his hosting skills, Kyle had remembered to set the coffeemaker, so the first crisis of the day was averted.

"Come on, Dog," I said to Nesha. "Find your leash." She was reluctant to leave Rileigh and all that free food, but ultimately she decided on the walk and found her leash hanging in the mud room. We went out the back door, through the back gate and walked the two blocks to Camosun Park. From there, we crossed a creek and were in the primeval forest, cliffs and bogs of Pacific Spirit Regional Park. I didn't plan on running all sixty kilometres of trails, but figured three or four would be enough to get the blood flowing and the mind working. The park is dog friendly, with most of the trails being leash optional. I asked her, and Nesha opted for no leash.

Unusual for a Malamute, Nesha loves the water. She doesn't swim so much as she high-steps, immersed up to her shoulders. But once she's in, she's hard to get out. About three kilometres in, we found a dog-accessible creek and sand bar, and she began to splash. I picked up some rocks and threw them for her to chase, each one a little deeper than the prior.

"Big dog," a stranger said. "Weird way of swimming." He was

6'2" and dark haired. His beard was fashionable stubble—the kind I wish I could grow—and he was wearing Nike sweat pants and an Air Jordan zip up jacket. On his feet, he was wearing grey and black Nike Air Griffey IVs, a shoe I know isn't available in Canada. I was wearing a pair the night before.

"Nice kicks," I said, legitimately impressed.

"Yours too," he said. "Nice to meet another sneaker head." I was wearing a vintage pair of Nike Air Trainer SCs, the 'Bo Knows' shoe. The stranger reached down and unclipped his dog, a beautiful black Komondor.

"She's a beauty," I said. With thick, dreadlocked hair, Komondors are often referred to as 'Mop Dogs'.

"This is Sasha," he said and then his dog and mine did that butt-sniffing things dogs do and decided there were best friends and began running in circles at full speed.

"That'll tire them out," I offered.

"I hope so," he replied. "But even if it does, a half hour nap and she's back at full speed." He held out his hand. "Anthony Baker," he said.

"Ryan Simms," I replied and shook. "We were looking for you last night."

By this time, the dogs had expanded their circles and were about fifty yards downstream; simultaneously, Anthony whistled and I clapped and the dogs came sprinting back.

"I know. But I wasn't in the mood. Hard day at the office, you know?" His smile was self-deprecating, and he shrugged. "You've had worse," he said with a genuine smile. My turn to shrug. "You probably get this a lot," he said, "but I remember that catch. Man, you were something else." He smiled and shook his head. "Gotta ask," he said. "Did it hurt as much as it looked like it did?"

"It did," I said. "Still does at time. Booze helps."

I guess he thought I was joking, because he laughed. "I get that," he said. "It's why I own a brewery."

"Agony Baker," I said, wondering what would constitute a hard day at the office for him. "I was having this conversation with a friend of mine the other day: I think I like your nickname better than mine. She disagreed."

"Dirt is definitely a great name for a ballplayer. "'Agony'—I don't know, it's a tough one to explain." He shook his head. "Image, man, it will wear you down. That's not who I am, but it's what people think."

"Based on the name," I said, "I would have pictured you with a Bull Mastiff or at least a Doberman."

"There you go," he said. "Image."

We walked about fifteen yards to a bench, which the dogs checked out for us before we sat down. At least they were both female, so neither of them pissed on it.

"I always rooted for you to make it back—local kid makes good, and then good again, you know? In fact," he added," I've got a framed picture of the catch on the wall at the pub. And we make a beer in your honour: Left Field Fences."

"Ouch," I said. "Maybe I'll take you up on the beer and can sign the picture for you," I said. "Would make it worth even less, though."

He laughed again. "With you and Larry Walker in The Show at the same time, almost made the National League interesting." Larry Walker is an eventual Hall of Fame outfielder who started with the Montreal Expos and is now with the Colorado Rockies. With all due respect to Terry Puhl, from Melville Saskatchewan, who spent sixteen years in the Big Leagues and was my inspiration growing up, Walker will go down as the best Canadian baseball player ever. Fergie Jenkins will have to settle for best Canadian pitcher.

"It was a fun few years," I said. "I'm not going to lie."

"I think you paved the way for quite a few Canadians—Kirk McCaskill, Cory Koskie, Rob Ducie, Matty Stairs... it's getting to be a long list. And this Morneau kid the Twins have- watch out. And there's a kid in Sechelt, Ryan Dempster, who throws bullets."

"They're paving their own ways," I said. "But Canada is on the map now from a talent evaluation standpoint, I agree. But not because of me—because of everybody. We've earned it. And," I added, "I've still got friends in the game and they tell me Morneau is the real deal. Hit .400 in the Gulf League. And I know the Dempsters, I've got a place up Roberts Creek."

"Miss it?" he asked. "The Show?"

"I do. Took a while for it to sink in that it was gone."

And now?" he asked. "You own a bar in Calgary... what brings you home?"

"I think you know that, Agony," I said. "I doubt this was a random meeting, but how you found me here is impressive."

"Happy coincidence," he replied. "I live nearby and Sasha and I are here all the time. I figured you would stay with your friends and sooner or later, I'd run into you and today happened to be the day. Much quicker," he added, "than I was expecting."

"I don't know about quick," I said. "This is my third day back and you found me. You must have something on your mind."

He pointed at my face. "I see you've met Dewayne."

"I call him Orangutan," I said. "But how do you know we've met?"

"Orangutan suits him better. He's not much good for anything other than breaking stuff that isn't his. As for how I found out," he said, "Ryan, not every policeman is faithful to his or her code—or they have a code of their own. This allows our operation a great deal of latitude where we need it most."

"The cops told you," I said. "You've got people in Golden BC? What the hell for?"

"The RCMP can be hard to pin down, since they move so frequently. Although everybody does ultimately have a price. But you met Roy at the restaurant—he can be most persuasive. After your encounter, he wanted to know more about you; he liked your style. Or, as he put it, 'the cut of your jib'. Said you saved him from having to stop, or perhaps even clean up, some unpleasant business."

"Did he tell you what the unpleasant business was? It was gang rape."

"No," Baker said. "He didn't tell me that. I'm glad that you did. That will be addressed."

"Okay," I said, "cut to the chase."

"Yes," he said. "The chase." He put both arms between his legs, for all the world like a defeated version of *The Thinker*. "I didn't know your friends sister—"

"Her name was Kylee," I said with some heat.

"I knew that, Ryan. I'm sorry, I should have been more respectful." He paused and looked at the dogs, lying in the creek, tongues hanging out. "I didn't know Kylee, or what had happened, until well after it was over. We don't mess with cops, or their families. Candidly," he added, "it's not good for business."

I shrugged. "What are you telling me?"

"With my dad retired, I prefer to focus on delayed gratification —everything is a long game. What happened to Kylee was nonsensical and was clearly in response to Jim Edwards' war on the *Saints*. It was short-term thinking. We don't mess with cops," he said again.

"But you did," I said. "And now my friend, and his sister, are dead. Jim had a daughter. She's eight."

"Ryan, you can believe me or not, but we had nothing to do with Jim's death. Nothing."

"I admit," I told him, "that I've been struggling to figure out why you would, especially such a public execution. But bombs are a biker-tradition."

"So are motorcycles," he replied. "How do I get my dog on a motorcycle?"

"Would be something to see," I said.

"Sometimes, you know, what we see is simply what we are expecting to see. Perception and reality are not always in alignment." He stood up and whistled for Sasha. Both dogs came running. "Killing Jim makes no sense from our perspective, because suddenly the entire Blue Wave or Wall or whatever is gunning for us. Deals and agreements are no longer valid, protection is removed. It's become exponentially harder to conduct business." He clipped the leash back on Sasha, and the juxtaposition of a high level gangster clipping a leash on his well-behaved dog in a no-leash park made me laugh. "Has anybody," he asked, "checked out the other guy that died with Constable Edwards?"

That certainly caught my attention. Try as she might, Karen had never convinced me that Jim's death was, at best, random or, at worst, intended by the motorcycle club he was trying to destroy. Perception and reality, I thought.

Anthony Baker offered me his hand again. I stood up to shake.

"Ryan," he said, "I admit that I am using you as a go-between right now. I feel it's inappropriate to approach Ms. Tanner directly, so I am asking a favour of you that I have no right to ask, given our short relationship." I said nothing, although I think he had expected me to.

"Please tell Ms. Tanner what you will of this conversation, but reparations have been made and those responsible for Kylee's immersion into the less savoury side of our business have been removed. Permanently." He handed me an elegant business card, this one for a lawyer and not drugs. "A trust for Rileigh Edwards has been established with a donation of $50,000. My lawyer will have the details."

"I'll let Karen know," I said. "What happens from there, I have no idea or control."

"Understood," he said with a nod. "I think that under different circumstances, we could have been friends. I won't be presumptive and assume that could happen now."

As he said that, I was thinking the same thing. Damnit, he was right. We could have been friends.

*****

Back at the house, the craziness was over. Everybody was fed, Rileigh was ready for school, and everyone was on their second coffee. By the time my second coffee was poured, Robyn —always a late riser—had joined us. As we watched Nesha clean the floor of left-over cereal, Robyn said "what about the money?"

"I don't think cereal really costs that much," I said. "But I'm sure Karen's good for it."

Robyn ignored me. "You know what I've been thinking?" She didn't wait for an answer. "We've been talking a lot about motorcycle clubs and we know they have a lot of cash: what do they do with all those twenties?"

"What do you mean?" Karen and I asked simultaneously.

"Think about it," Robyn said. "You've got all these legit cash businesses—strip clubs, dirty bars, car washes, even massage parlours—taking in how ever many thousands per day, which is all well and good. Obviously that money is clean and going into legit bank accounts."

"But that money is dwarfed," Karen said with the beginning of a smile, "by the money being made illegitimately." She actually gave Robyn a high-five. "They teach that in the first hour of every law enforcement seminar—follow the money."

"My work here is done," Robyn said as her toast popped, but she had no intention of leaving.

"I'm not a criminal mastermind," I said, "but—"

"You're not *any* kind of mastermind," Robyn said and bumped fists with Karen. "You used to be able to hit a curve ball," Robyn said, "but now...."

At least Nesha cares for me, I thought, but when I saw her eating cereal off the floor I realized I had lost her forever to Karen's eight-year old.

I pretended I couldn't see or hear them. They didn't care. I persisted. "You're calling legit money illegal, aren't you? It's Canadian twenties, fifties and hundreds. Nothing wrong with those," I said.

"There is in volume," Karen said. "Remember when we were talking about Gramma and Grampa Snow Bird coming back across the border with hundreds of thousands of dollars from selling the BC Bud?"

"I do," I said, and Karen quickly explained to Terri. Rileigh and Nesha went outside. Early February morning and nobody needed a jacket.

"So the question becomes," Robyn said, "what do you do with these suitcases of money?"

"That's right," Karen said. "I mean, you could obviously bury one in the yard and grab some cash when you need it, but the *Saints* and the other clubs are making *millions* of dollars. Where is it?"

By this point, Kyle had joined us. He looked much worse from last night than I felt. That made me happy. Personal growth is measured in very small increments, and maybe even other peoples' pain.

"We know there's a laundry," he said. "Or a series of them. " He grabbed a mug and held it out, but nobody moved to fill it for him.

He poured his own. "It hasn't been a high priority for us because we've been busy trying to keep the drugs off the street and, you know, disrupt the criminals before they make money." He took a bite of toast off Robyn's plate, something I happen to know she hates. "But, interestingly, there were some Feds a couple of months ago asking about a guy named Johnny Zags." He reached for more toast, but Robyn intercepted. "I don't remember the guy's real name. The Fed asking was small but intense. Her name is Stephanie something, I think." He drank some coffee. "I've got her card somewhere. She seemed righteous, though, and didn't care for college basketball—a position I support. Apparently this Zags guy loves Gonzaga basketball."

"Go Bulldogs," Robyn said. "Although I still prefer Gary Payton over John Stockton," she added. Gary Payton, 'The Glove', is Robyn's all-time favourite player. Mine is Michael Jordan and always will be, a debate we have had over the years. John

Stockton is a multiple-time all-star guard for the Utah Jazz and perhaps Gonzaga's most famous alumni.

"Let's not get distracted," Kyle said, "by basketball." Kyle's jump shot couldn't hit water if he was shooting into a full swimming pool. "I wonder if anybody has actually ever looked at the money with any real interest?"

"Terri might know," Karen said.

"Let's head to the office," Terri said coming down the stairs. "I'll check our files."

By our nonchalance, I think we gave our surprise away. Kyle looked sheepish, but not for long. Overall, I think we recovered nicely, and I remembered other mornings at the Richards with a kitchen full of people. *The more things change... but this time we are grownups. Some of us.* Robyn solved a logistical issue by agreeing to drop Rileigh at school on her way to the university and the rest of us headed to the Press building. In exactly sixty minutes, we were eating yesterday's donuts.

*****

"Johnny Zags is a name our crime guys have heard," Terri told us. "But there's nothing really attached to it." She passed some Xerox copies across the table. "You do hear the expression 'Chinese Laundry' when it comes to the *Saints*, and 'shirts' seems to be a pretty common synonym for a thousand: 'I'm picking up a hundred shirts tomorrow' meaning one hundred thousand." She motioned to the handouts. "That's what I could dig up on the Chinese Laundry." She shrugged. "It's not much, but what there is seems connected to our Mr. Zags." But Terri was smiling.

"What?" Karen said. "What are you about to tell us?"

"Speculation from on high," Terri said, "is that Zags' real name is Faas Xhang." She handed us some more folders. "The connection isn't substantiated and comes from sources out east—law enforcement sources. Mr. Xhang is infamous in Vancouver for being the unrepentant owner of a number of happy ending massage parlours and supplier of party girls to the Hong Kong elite while they enjoy the Vancouver scenery." Terri's smile got bigger; her smile was lighting the room. "Everyone loves a happy ending," she said. Kyle looked away.

"But there's nothing locally linking Zags to Xhang?" I asked.

"Nothing," Terri said. "But interestingly, Mr. Xhang has been on the BC Lottery Corporation radar for at least three years as the potential source of 'significant amounts of unregistered money'." Her smile reached maximum radiance; I was both blind and dumb. "It gets better," she said. "We know this because two years ago, Xhang was banned by Lower Mainland casinos as undesirable." She let this sink in. "If we want to follow the money, Mr. Xhang seems a great place to start."

Kyle had recovered enough to ask a question. "This guy is banned from BC casinos, but he is *not* a person of interest to the Vancouver Police? That seems strange, doesn't it? You know, given that his prior line of work was indiscreet, shall we say. There should be some interest in him."

We all nodded agreement. "It can't be that easy," Kyle said.

"Easy?" I asked. "I'm not ready to cross whatever bridge it is your building from here to there. What's the connection between this guy and anything?"

"Jim was killed by the *Saints*," he replied. "He—we—were causing some pretty significant disruptions to their businesses that meant a loss of money—crazy amounts of money. If the *Saints* aren't making deposits, the laundry isn't working at capacity. Hence, additional pressure on the *Saints* to take action. This guy might be that laundry."

"Hence?" Terri asked. Kyle shrugged.

"I get it, I guess," I said. "Seems thin. After all, you guys were causing an inconvenience more than a disruption—nothing was sticking."

"It's a hell of a lot fatter than anything else we have," Kyle said. "Just before all that shit at Crab Park went down, the Feds I mentioned were asking about this Zags." He looked at Terri. "I think you just found him." To the room at large, he said "This is where we are at: *Saints* have money and need it cleaned, we disrupt their programs and Jim is killed, and now we have a lead on Zags, which is a place to start."

He stood up, and picked up every file and paper that was in the room. "And I've got an idea", he said. "One I should have thought of before. The Vancouver Chief of Police is the factual and titular head of the motorcycle club task force. But she has a civilian counterpart, who happens to be the head of the BC Lottery Commission."

"Titular?" Terri said.

I was slow to catch on. Karen wasn't. "Collectively," she said, "they would be in charge of any money laundering investigations." Karen and Kyle bumped fists, and then he looked directly at Terri again. I couldn't blame him. "I don't know his name, or hers" he said, "but I know where to find him. Or her."

"It's a he," Terri said smiling, "and his name is Gareth Davis. And he and the Chief lead the *Independent Commission of Inquiry into Money Laundering in British Columbia*. Don't ask me how they came up with that name, I think they get paid by the word."

"Okay," Karen said. "Let's go talk to him."

"No offence, Karen," Terri said, "but you guys are a collective mess and probably shouldn't talk to anyone. Individually or combined, you don't have any standing."

"Well, I am a cop," Kyle said. "And Karen is a provincial prosecutor."

"Kyle," Terri countered, gently, "you are suspended, for very public reasons. My favourite was 'get down here and fight me!'" Kyle looked at the floor and I would swear he was blushing. "And Karen, you're a provincial prosecutor, but you work land claims and treaties, not gang or financial crime. Ryan," she added, "I don't even know how to explain you, but I don't think you guys can just show up at this guy's office and say, 'hey, we have some questions about money laundering and maybe even motorcycle clubs'."

"We will use our grace and charm," I said. "At least Karen will."

"Or," Terri countered, "you can use me. I'm a reporter. I get paid to ask these questions." She looked very quickly at Kyle and then me, and then back to Kyle. "Karen and I might get somewhere with grace and charm. You two need to sit this one out."

*****

Gareth Davis was easy to find. As head of the British Columbia Lottery Corporation, which has complete oversight over all casinos, lotteries and even bingo halls in the province, his office is prominently listed in the phone book. Terri used the phone on the conference room table and Davis answered his own phone. I liked him immediately.

Terri introduced herself and Davis cut her off.

"How soon can you get here?" he said, with a light Scottish brogue. "I have a meeting I can't get out of at two; that gives you four hours."

Terri made the meeting details and hung up. "See," she said with a smile that could light a train tunnel. "Trained professional."

Richmond is about thirty minutes south of where we were, essentially Granville and Broadway just this side of any number of bridges from downtown Vancouver. We decided to take two cars, and as we were heading against traffic, we made good time to the Lottery Corporation offices. In reverse, at that time of day, the trip would have taken an easy hour. As had become our norm, I was with Karen and that left Kyle with Terri.

"Think they'll find anything to talk about?" Karen said.

"I think they'll struggle along, but ultimately be okay," I replied. "Kyle's been working on his banter."

"Unless he used it all last night."

"Maybe. And maybe she slept in the games room."

The lottery building itself was wide and low, five stories of glass and concrete just over the Fraser River and about five minutes short of Vancouver International airport. Davis met us in the lobby. He was six-feet tall and wearing beautiful wool slacks with a double pleat and a tweed sport coat, everything in shades of brown. *Exactly how I'm going to dress when I grow up.* Davis looked sharp and fit and I was glad he was on our side in whatever it was we were doing.

Inside, the building was wide-open and bright and there was a large water feature complete with Koi in the middle. Introductions were made, and it was clear that Davis was having trouble understanding why we were all there.

"Nice to meet you, Gareth," Karen said. "Terri, give me a shout when you're done. I'm going to take these two for something to eat and run some errands."

Kyle and I were slow to catch on, but after a look from Karen, we did. "I could eat," Kyle said and we left Terri and Gareth Davis looking at the Koi.

Outside, I mentioned that Terri was under no obligation to share anything with us. "In fact," I said, "we may have just locked ourselves out of whatever this is."

"Don't worry," Karen said. "I have resources and information that Terri wants to access, and this meeting was our idea. She'll share."

"Besides," Kyle said with a smirk, "I think she likes me."

Karen just shook her head. "Boys never change," she said.

*****

It was two o'clock exactly when Karen's cell phone rang. "It's Terri," Karen said and I had no idea how she knew that. "Call display," she said while answering. I wondered if my phone had that feature. It had still only rung twice and I hadn't answered it either time; although maybe if I had known who was calling, I would have. Probably not.

Deciding on a late lunch on Richmond's No. 3 Road was an easy decision. Deciding where to eat, however, was much more complicated as the food in Richmond—if chosen properly—can be just as good as the food in Vancouver's China Town. We settled on *Hon's Noodle House* and were not disappointed.

Over a spicy hot pot, Sichaun pork, shrimp in garlic sauce, dumplings, some vegetable dishes and Peking roasted duck, Terri told us what she learned from Gareth Davis. "He is fully willing to be quoted," she said. "And he is sitting on a bomb shell." Here she quickly looked at Kyle and the scar over his eye. Kyle shrugged. Terri grimaced and nodded an apology his way. "If what Davis says is true, Jim and the *Silent Saints* are just the beginning. And maybe the ending." Terri served herself some hotpot. "I'm not sure Jim was the target that night."

I sipped some Tsing Tsao and looked at Karen. She tilted her head in my direction. I met her nod with one of my own and started to look in vain for a fork.   I was the only one at the table without food.

"It's about the money," Terri said.   "Robyn was right.   And," she added, "nobody who should care seems to actually give a fuck."

*****

"I'm going to need some help filling in some of these holes," I said.   "Jim and the *Saints* are obviously connected, but mostly by their actions"—I included Kyle in this statement and he just shrugged—"and murder and money laundering may seem like an easy connection, but I'm not seeing it.   At least," I added, "not here and not yet."

"Hang on, Dirt," Kyle said and looked at Terri intently.   "I think I know some of this," he said.   "We know that money laundering is most definitely on the radar of some heavy hitting federal units, and we know that the *Saints* must be involved because of the sheer volume of their cash operations."   He grabbed some pork and ate it just to spite me.   "But the Feds were not gang specific, and took more than they gave."   He used his chop sticks to eat rice.   I have never hated him more.   "What are we missing?"

"I don't know," I said, "but, Kyle, you accused the Chief of Police of being a murderer.   That's a leap."

"Dirt," he said.   "We're not talking about drunken leaps, not right now.   But she is," he said definitively.   "The current Vancouver Chief of Police is a murderer, and I think Terri is going to get us there."

"Ryan is right," Terri said.   "Let's not get ahead of ourselves." She paused.   "Guys, this is all fucked up.   There are too many moving parts."

"Tell me about it," Karen said.   "We have files too—criminal activity after criminal activity. But we simply cannot connect them." Her chopsticks were lightning fast and she grabbed the duck I was eyeing. I was close to using my fingers, manners and protocol be damned.

Karen continued. "I'm not on the financial crimes detail, but we talk about it often in departmental meetings and regarding specific cases of course. But I have never gotten the sense that it was a high priority provincially. There seems to be a reluctance somewhere along the chain." She paused and looked at each of us in turn.

"So why isn't it pursued more vigorously?" I asked. Karen simply shrugged.

"Gareth," Terri said, "asked me one question when we sat down: where is unlimited cash never questioned?"

"Never questioned?" one of us said.

"*Never*," she replied. We were in need of a clue. "There's such a place down the road a bit, over Kyle's left shoulder."

Light bulbs went off: "Casinos," we all said. Richmond's *River Rock Casino* was just down the road, maybe a three minute walk.

"*Casinos,*" Terri agreed.

I still didn't have a fork.

"And here's something that we knew, but didn't know we knew," Terri said. "Gareth couldn't believe that no one put it together. Now, though, I think maybe it was kept silent. Or," she added, "maybe the misdirection was amazing."

We all looked at her expectantly.

"Kyle," she said, "what was the name of the man you and Jim found at the beach that night?"

Kyle studied his plate for a brief second. Then he looked directly at Terri. His eyes, I noticed, were definitely bright again, not at all like when I found him at the Bel Air. "He was identified—and I don't know how, because there was nothing left... nothing—as Denis Sault. He lived in Southlands. If I remember, he was an accountant." He paused. "No wife or kids, thank God."

Southlands is as pricey as it gets in Vancouver. Bordering the Fraser River, it's almost exclusively estates—eight bedroom homes and guest cottages and room for families of horses. If you've seen pictures of Vancouver, you've seen pictures of some of the water-side homes on Marine Drive—most probably the Casa Mia, 20,000 square feet of waterfront once owned by Peter Pocklington, the man who traded Wayne Gretzky.

"That is a pricey postal code for a single guy," I said. "Even if I'd had five years in the majors, I don't think I could afford Southlands."

Kyle was going to make a joke, but Robyn stopped him. He looked at us both, wondering. I was trying to suppress that unusual emotion again: hope. *Maybe,* I thought, *maybe.*

"Family money?" Karen said. "Who knows? Why is it important?"

"According to Gareth, who knew him personally, Denis Sault was not just an accountant. He was a senior partner at Engs & Associates. And accounting firms are like law firms—billable hours make you rich and famous." She sipped some beer. "Sault was directly in charge of the BC Lottery Corporation accounts, and this includes all BC Casinos."

"That's a lot of billable hours," I said.

*****

"Here's how Gareth laid it out," Terri continued. "Casinos in Canada, at least in BC, are obviously significantly different than they are in the states—Nevada, Atlantic City, etc. *Most* obviously, there is no free booze in BC. And no cheap slots; in fact, there is a much lower proportion of slot type machines than in most US casinos."

"I think I can see where this is going," Kyle said. "If there are fewer slots, and no cheap slots, the emphasis on table games probably means an emphasis on high-stakes games." He stole the dumpling I had stabbed with a single chop stick. "That means high stakes."

"Exactly what Gareth said," Terri told us. "BC casinos have bags and bags of cash coming in on a daily basis. Literally, bags: hockey bags, duffel bags, IKEA bags, shopping bags. Amounts, Gareth said, that defy logic." She spun the table insert and located the garlic shrimp. "And whether the cash is the chicken or the egg, the casino culture in BC now is that this is the norm—and no one is prepared to ask where the money comes from."

"But where is the crime?" I asked.

"Here's where it gets criminal," Terri said. "Potentially." She ate the last garlic shrimp. "After the cash has been traded for chips, some gambling takes place, and then the money is cashed out."

"And it's clean now," Karen said, the thrill of the hunt becoming obvious in her face. "And from a verifiable source."

"That's right," Terri said. "Gareth has videos and stills of people trading these bags full of cash at the casino tellers for chips. Some people, 'whales' they're called, have cashed in $15 to 20M in a single month. And," she added, "the majority of the cash is in twenties.

"Ironically," she continued, "in order to combat money laundering, the Lottery Corporation has actually made it *easier* to clean it. Because any cash out over $10,000 is mandated to go into a Personal Gambling Account, or PGA, which is exactly what it sounds like—a bank account specific to casino spending."

"Wait, wait, wait," Karen said. "Don't tell me this PGA gets cashed out by cheque?"

"I won't tell you," Terri replied, "but it does. Or bank draft. In fact," she continued, "Gareth escalated a case of a particular whale who cashed $200K of twenties for six straight days. He didn't even bother gambling. For six straight days, he just cashed a suitcase of cash into chips and went straight to a different teller and put the chips into his PGA.

"Then," she added with some weight, "on the sixth day, he cashed out and left with a bank draft for over one million dollars."

She grabbed the full beer that was in front of Kyle.

"Gareth escalated this," she continued. "But word came from on high—Chief Callan and Gareth's immediate supervisor for the Province—that it was 'categorically not Gareth's job to investigate'."

"And so," Kyle said, "he's essentially hamstrung."

"Can't do his job," I said, the hunger making me the master of the obvious.

"He claims there were other times as well that he was told, specifically, to not do his job," Terri said. "In fact, at one point, like we were talking about earlier, Faas Xhang had been banned from BC casinos as 'a person of questionable character'. But despite Davis' concerns and evidence, Xhang's ban was quickly lifted and the police never moved to investigate him for anything."

"Take a step back," Kyle said, and I'm sure his mouth was full. "Think about this," he asked rhetorically, "who has more access to twenties than a motorcycle gang?"

"Bingo," Terri said. "The first thing you need to launder money is money—and massage parlours, drug transactions, strip clubs, protection rackets, bars, greasy spoons… well, they give clubs like the *Saints* almost unlimited access to cash."

"And," Karen interrupted, "this guy is talking about *suitcases* of cash."

Terri had ate more duck. "*Every single day*," she added. "And the volume is important. Because maybe you can buy a crappy used car with cash, or a home entertainment system, but you can't buy a new car with cash. Or a house."

The waitress came by and cleared some plates. She was no Amy. Terri and Karen had a quick conference and ordered some more food. Terri took pity on me and asked for a fork. I was looking forward to eating.

"Understand," Terri said, "that Gareth is the head of anti-money laundering for the BC Lottery Corporation, the Crown Corporation that oversees all legalized gambling in the province. And he has meticulous records." She ate the last gyoza and definitely looked at me while she did it. "Gareth mentioned we should talk to Mark Caldwell at the *River Rock*."

"I know Mark," Kyle said. "Quite well. Good guy. Mounted squad—was hurt when a couple of tweakers on dirt bikes surrounded him and his horse in Stanley Park and he was thrown. The skells then ran over Mark a couple of times each, but his horse kicked one of them and that guy is in a wheelchair. I knew Mark took disability but I didn't know, or maybe forgot, that he was at the casino."

Randomly, Terri asked me how much the house I grew up in was worth.

"No idea," I said. "Haven't been home in a lot of years." I picked up my beer since I had nothing to eat. "My Mom, on her own, bought that house in 1974. I think she paid $14,000." I felt that making sure it was understood she had bought it on her own was equivalent to a visit.

"Where is the house?" Terri asked.

"Fifth and Blenheim."

"Okay. Today, conservatively, that house is worth $750,000. And it's not because you once lived there."

"Well, partly," I said. Nobody laughed. At least Terri smiled. "Real estate developers believe that even the smallest house in Vancouver will be worth more than a million dollars in the next few years."

"So why are people coming here with suitcases of cash?" Karen asked. "Not all of them are interested in buying Ryan's old house."

"If we're talking about money," Terri said, "Chinese Nationals are prominent. And they add a second layer of complexity to the so–called 'Chinese Laundry'."

The conversation was moving too fast for some of us, mostly Kyle as he was using chop sticks to eat all my food. "Here's the issue," Terri said. "Chinese Nationals are not legally allowed to move more than $50,000 per year out of the country—yet we know, for example, that Richmond is forty percent Chinese." She moved a bunch of empty plates around to demonstrate sleight of hand, but I took it as a personal affront. "And the percentage of homeownership is consistent with other BC cities, but the percentage of mortgages is not. In fact, there are fewer personal residence mortgages in Richmond than in any other BC city."

"So," Karen asked, "where is the money coming from to buy

these properties?"

Terri paused for effect. "Gareth explained all that and the Chinese Laundry...." Here, she paused. "Politically correct or not, that's what Gareth and his team call the cash coming in—the Chinese Laundry. That's where the term comes from and now it's part of the police vernacular. And the laundry is funded by two sources: proceeds of illegal crime here and deposit payments made over-seas. Guys," she said, "the amount of money Gareth is talking about is unfathomable."

"There was a raid on a *Wolves* club house last month," Karen said, "and they had nearly eight-hundred thousand in cash on hand."

"So we have that," Terri said. "And Gareth explained about imported players. The overseas players at the high stakes tables." She stopped herself. "Sorry. I was getting carried away. We were about to discuss how this dirty money is collected and sent for cleaning." She looked at Kyle and me specifically. "So let's slow down on the Tsing Tsao until we talk about that."

We shrugged. "No promises," I said. "Some food would help," I added.

"No promises," Kyle echoed and ate the last dumpling.

"You're an idiot," Terri said to him, not unkindly. "Actually, you're both idiots."

"Matching pair," Karen said. "Can we get back on track?"

Ironically, Terri took a long draw on her beer. "So," she said, "if Chinese law prevents an individual from taking or transferring more than $50K per year from the country, Gareth wonders how he has records of dozens of Chinese nationals showing up with $300K *or more* in shopping bags and suitcases at BC casinos.

"Okay" Karen said, "very interesting. That seems like a pretty obvious question to ask: if these folks are showing up at the casinos with money they couldn't legally take out of the county, where did it come from?"

"And," Kyle added, "why are they here? Why not Macau or some other money-centric local?"

"To Karen's question," Terri said, "nobody seems to care. To Kyle's question, easy access to cash is the primary reason, and Vancouver real estate is very popular. You cash out from the casino with clean funds, make a legitimate bank deposit, and now you can buy anything you want. Or anyone."

The waitress came with my fork, but not the additional food the girls had ordered. I remained hungry.

"But," Terri continued, "we've got the *Saints* in particular with cash heavy businesses and now we have overseas 'whales' with suitcases of money—and they are all landing at places like the *River Rock Casino* over Kyle's shoulder, the *Parq Vancouver* and the *Starlight* in New Westminster."

"So what does the Task Force—on which Gareth and the VPD chief are key members—think about any of this?" Karen asked.

"Gareth thinks the Task Force is being played," Terri said. "Or, more likely, that it is playing everybody else. 'Sound and Fury', he said, but nothing happens. He has definitive proof of Casino activities that are in violation of stated policies, but nobody cares. 'They move the penalty kick whenever it suits them' is how he put it. 'And it's hard enough for the goalie to make the save when he knows where the shot is coming from'."

With my fork, I ate the last piece of Sichuan pork and there was nothing left but the hot pot broth. The extra food never came. Terri tilted her head the way all beautiful women do when they have one last thing to say.

"Davis," she said, "is convinced that Sault was going to go

public with something to do with the BC Gaming Commission books. And he doesn't think Sault was delivering a gold star for honesty and transparency."

*****

With three of us full, we left the restaurant and turned toward the water and made the short walk to the *River Rock Casino*. The casino itself is billed as a luxury riverside resort and it is attractive if overstated, all natural rock and timber and glass on the outside and sweeping marble stair cases inside. The casino is primarily in the middle of the building and there are hotel towers on either side. At the entrance, there is a huge silver dragon, ten feet tall and fifteen feet long, made out of steel that I couldn't stop looking at. It shimmered in the sun, colours reflecting off intricately carved scales. I have most definitely stayed at worse places.

On arrival, Kyle and I asked to speak with Mark Caldwell. It wasn't a long wait. Mark and Kyle were clearly tight, and they spent some time catching up. The girls faded into the casino, and Kyle explained who I was and why we were there.

"There's something," Caldwell agreed. "Money shows up, money leaves, and nobody cares where it comes from or where it goes." He laughed. "They pay me too well to actually care," he said with a look that made it obvious he cared. "Seriously," he said, "more than I've ever made and no overtime."

"Johnny Zags?" Kyle asked. "Fass Xhang?"

"Don't know this Zags guy," Caldwell said. "But Xhang is known for not being able to attend our daily festivities. He's banned, and every entrance and new security guy have his picture."

Kyle shook his head and shrugged. "Don't give up, young man," Caldwell said. "Our ever seeing eye doesn't' just cover inside the casino."

"What do you mean?" Kyle and I said in unison.

"We know for a fact," Caldwell said, "that when we banned your guy from being *inside* the casino, he just had flunkeys deliver to *outside* the casino."

"Deliver?" I asked. "Deliver what?"

"Xhang is your bag man," Caldwell said. "The bags of cash you are talking about? Xhang delivers them."

And you know this because…?" Kyle asked.

"Because I fucking followed him," Caldwell said. "That's how. I can tell you exactly where he went." And he did.

*****

We found the girls, and collectively spent an hour or so breaking even at the black jack tables. Caldwell gave us some tokens to spend at the bar, and I managed to grab most of those—I was still pissed off about lunch and needed to get my calories one way or another. At least they had snacks.

After the black jack, and maybe a few hands of poker—and one misguided attempt at pai goa—Karen drove me home and Kyle went with Terri. They all made me promise to answer my new cell phone in the morning so we could arrange whatever needed to be arranged.

Karen dropped me at the Richards, and it was only five o'clock and I was starving. We arrived at the same time as Robyn, so Karen passed off ownership of me and went home to Rileigh. I grabbed the dog from the house, and Robyn drove us down the hill from Point Grey to the fruit and vegetable markets on Broadway. We bought some strip loins at Kefekes' Meats and a celeriac at the stall next door and some broccoli for Nesha —she loves the stalks. I made a celeriac mash with bacon and green beans to go with the steaks, and we had Robyn's house to ourselves. Despite the success of the meal, and a liberal application of alcohol, Robyn kissed me quickly on the lips when the night was over, and we went to bed in separate rooms. Hope stayed strong, but was beginning to fade ever so slightly.

I'm not going to lie: when Kyle didn't come home that night, I was jealous. Not of the night he had had with Terri, but of the night that I hadn't had with Robyn. With Robyn on the top floor and me in the basement, Nesha was confused and slept in the kitchen, equidistant between us.

CHAPTER 11

Thursday passed, and mostly I was alone with the dog. We had heard from Kyle, but he was in no hurry to come home and hang out with us when he could be spending time with Terri. Robyn spent the morning at the university. Karen was back on Vancouver Island, catching up on some work at her office at the Provincial Legislative building in Victoria. She promised to gather some information specific to the death of Jim and Denis Sault as well as anything she could find on Kyle's suspension and the work he and Jim did to disrupt the *Saints*. She said the file on Agony Baker would fill the trunk of her Honda del Sol. I admired her bravery and calm when talking about Jim.

Nesha and I spent a couple of hours running in Pacific Spirit Park, which was good for us both. My metabolism and infrequent guilt runs have helped me stay relatively fit. Despite the years of excess drinking and bar food, I still have a flat stomach and no man-boobs. Wind, on the other hand, was getting hard to find as Nesha and I ran through the mud. When we were done, I was able to find a groomer who would take a 100 pound dog as a walk-in and the end result was spectacular, although I don't think Nesha liked the pink bow the groomer put in her hair.

Around noon, Robyn came home and threw an old canvas gym bag at me, this one from the Tacoma Raineers, another minor league stop. I have no idea where she found it or why she had it. "We're going to have to hurry," she said. I opened the bag, and inside, I found an old pair of Jordan XIIs—the first Nikes to feature Zoom Air—and some new ankle socks and a pair of basketball shorts.

"You shouldn't have," I said. "I hope these shorts are baggy—I gave up short shorts a long time ago."

"They are," she said. "No one wants to see you in short shorts. Now, hurry up, we're going to get a run in if you can kick it into gear."

"I already ran today," I said. "Just got back."

She just looked at me and turned to leave. "By the way," she asked over her shoulder, "when was the last time you played?"

"Basketball?" I asked, dumbly. "Two years, maybe." I paused. "Is the Kerrisdale Community Centre still running that high-level afternoon game?"

"Yup," she said. "We're going to see how high level you are."

Robyn and I have had endless debates over the years about who is the better athlete, but there is no debate about who is the better basketball player—she is. I was a Provincial all-star in high school, but Robyn dominated the sport at the highest Canadian level for a lot of years, even playing three dozen games for the national team. "Pretty sure I'm going to puke," I said.

"Yup," she said with a grin that was pure evil. At the gym, while stretching, she pointed out the other players. Of the fifteen or so guys warming up, I lost track of how many were former college players. There was another woman warming up, Dana Britton, who played with Robyn at Simon Fraser and on the national team. "This is definitely going to hurt," I said.

Robyn elbowed me in the ribs. "Suck it up, Dirt," she said. "It's go time."

Robyn knew the players well enough to manipulate the teams,

and somehow I wound up guarding her for most of the first three games. Rusty, I simply concentrated on hitting the glass and passing to Dana, a strategy that was good enough for us to win one of the games. The other two games, Robyn ate my lunch, out-quicking me on the perimeter to get to the hoop and then pulling up if I over-played. On offence, I posted whenever I could and had some success, but mostly in getting my own rebound and scoring that way.

Heading into a fourth game, I desperately needed a blow. To my surprise, Robyn subbed herself off as well. I sat on the bleachers, feet still on the court, spread out as big as I could get hoping that would create more oxygen. Robyn stepped well into my personal space. "Not bad," she said. "Not great, understand, but better than I expected." She put her hands on my shoulders. "You were quite physical, Dirt. I liked that." And she was gone.

I couldn't breathe for fifteen seconds. And I was very glad that I was wearing baggy shorts.

*****

Robyn had dinner with the faculty staff that night and Kyle never showed. After running with the dog, and then being run *like* a dog on the court, I was in bed by 9. I was fast asleep when Robyn came home, but I swear she kissed me before heading upstairs. If that was a dream, it was welcomed. *On the other hand, hope can be a dangerous thing.*

Dream or not, I woke up Friday morning thinking about an old minor league coach, Dude Atchinson. Dude's real name was Millard, and he hit 438 homeruns in the big leagues. For a guy like me, he was as legit as it gets. Dude had been in the Big Leagues and dominated—nobody called him Millard.

In my dream, I was back in Double A, and had a particularly rough game. Maybe it was the Raineers bag that took me back,

I'm not sure. But I had been really bad that game—maybe 0 for 4, maybe worse. I'd definitely struck out a couple of times and I remember making a throwing error and getting picked off first after a force out. It had been get-away day, which means we had to be on the bus thirty minutes after final out.

Bad luck is contagious, so nobody wanted to sit with me, and I was by myself maybe half way down the bus. We had a crazy long drive in front of us, maybe San Antonio to Nogales and I wanted to be alone. My hair was still wet when Dude came and kicked my legs until I moved them out of the aisle. For the first few minutes, he was silent. But then he said, "On your left, son. What do you see?"

"Road sign, Dude, not much else."

"Try again, son."

"Highway sign," I said. "There's an exit coming up. Not ours, but somebody's."

"What did the sign say?" he asked.

"I just told you—exit up ahead."

"No," he said with some heat. "What did it say? There weren't no words. You want to play baseball and you can't read signs?"

"Okay, Dude," I said. "It was pictograms. Gas, Food, Lodging. We see thousands of those signs while we travel. Why does this one matter?"

"We never know which one matters," he said. "But trust me, one of 'em does." He waved at the bus in general. "It may not be tonight. Hell, it's not tonight—tonight was nothing. And you, son, got days ahead of you. Better days, maybe great days." We caught eyes in the window. "But, son, I'm a tired old ballplayer and I've been around this world. Shit, I saw Sadahoro Oh hit one in Ozaka that ain't come down yet.

"I don't know how many I hit," he said, "but you're going to hit more IF—and, son, it's a great big if that is up to you, but you can hit even more. That left handed swing of yours, if you could bottle it you'd be rich—forget about what the Giants want to pay you. But do you want it?"

I told him I did.

"Alright," he said, "I believe you. But nobody's ever beat the system. There ain't no easy way, only shitty breaks. And ain't nobody knows where they're going to be, only know where they think they're headed." Dude Atchinson, hitter of more than 400 major league home runs, grabbed my shoulders until I was looking directly at him.

"Tonight," he said, "I need you to remember this: this bus has gas to get us where we're going, there is plenty of food in the back if you're hungry, and you'll have a roof over your head whether we get there tonight or not."

He slapped me on the shoulder with force. "You can drive fast or slow," he said, "but there ain't no way to shorten the miles you gotta go.

"Gas. Food. Lodging." He stood up, on his way to the front of the bus with the other coaches. "Son, let the rest of that shit go. Otherwise you end up in a bottle. That ain't no way to live."

*****

I shook off the dream and headed upstairs for coffee. Terri was most definitely the topic of conversation at the breakfast table. The coffee was Venezuelan. The *Vancouver Sun*, the afternoon paper, had released a special morning edition with multiple pages devoted to Terri's by-line. The headline read:

Lower Mainland Casinos Knowingly Accept Millions in Suspicious Cash.

Robyn and I tried to read the paper at the same time.

The Vancouver Sun has learned that a high level British Columbia Lottery Corporation Manager believes that, at any time of day, BC casinos have millions of dollars at play that simply cannot be sourced. Despite the province publically claiming to have some of the world's toughest money laundering policies, Gareth Davis, the head of BC Lottery Corporation's anti-money laundering division, says that suspicious cash problems are serious and being ignored.

Unsourced money, Davis says, is flowing like an open faucet, including hundreds of thousands weekly from VIP gamblers that have been previously banned from BC casinos.

The scheme in play is so successful that it is now famous throughout the world and called, simply, "The Vancouver Model". This is how it works:

- *Money needing to be 'cleaned' is deposited in an underground bank, location currently unknown to law enforcement*
- *This cash is then 'loaned' to gamblers and money exchangers*
- *The 'borrowed' money is gambled at BC Casinos and then cashed out*
- *Loans are repaid to the underground bank, with the house getting a substantial cut*
- *Provincial lawyers believe that this now 'clean' money is then used to front illegitimate businesses and even the purchase of vast quantities of illegal drugs, including fentanyl and heroin*
- *These drugs are then sold on the street through a series of well-established distri-*

bution channels and the cycle starts again

The current Canadian anti-money laundering rules are to act much as the recently revised mortgage and banking cash transaction rules: any transaction over $10,000 cash is to be reported to the X. However, Davis says, this is simply not the case when it comes to BC's cash friendly casinos.

"Any buy in over $10K," Davis told me yesterday in his bright corner office in Richmond, "is to be listed and reported by BC's Gaming Policy and Enforcement Branch.

"But pick a day at random," he said, looking out the window at the Fraser River and North Shore Mountains beyond. He reached into a stack of files nearly six inches thick on the credenza behind his meticulous desk. "Here's one," he said. "First Friday in December." He placed the report on his desk. "We saw buy-ins at our Georgia Street location of $60,000, another for $45,000, and one for $85,000. That's $190,000 in three transactions in one day—and all the bills were twenties and fifties."

"And these were reported?" I asked.

"They were," Mr. Davis replied in his soft Scottish brogue. "As have countless other transactions been reported."

Amazingly, during Mr. Davis tenure as essentially the head of casino financial transactions in BC, there has been no action taken as the result of any of these suspicious activity reports. In fact, Davis has been told, "without equivocation that it is functionally impossible to launder money through BC casinos because of all the controls that the BC Lottery Commission and police fraud units have implemented. Mr. Davis picked up the papers he had been looking at and let them fall. "This reporting," he said

185

heatedly "is the primary control. And it is being ignored at every possible step by every possible person."

BC's top casino cop continued: "The reality is that this happens every day. We have made a decision," he said, "to be completely and wilfully blind to where all the money is coming from. We are literally and figuratively drowning in twenty dollar bills."

Mr. Davis has been in charge of BC's Casino Money Laundering unit for nearly two years. Prior to taking over this position, Davis was the Head of Security for Richmond's River Rock Casino. In that role, he became quite familiar with many of the gamblers he now feels helpless to investigate. Through his experience in both roles, he is singularly suited to speak from a positon of knowledge, and—he says now—shame.

"Do you think anybody is really interested in finding the source of all this money?" I asked him.

"I do not," he replied. "I have filed the reports and... nothing. I have never received any feedback on those reports or even been told if anything was being done. Ultimately," he said, "no one wants us to know where this money comes from."

The Vancouver Model is shockingly simple. It starts with cash, bags and bags of cash. Gareth Davis says he has seen them all: hockey bags, IKEA bags, duffel bags, suitcases, even cardboard boxes of cash brought to BC casinos every day. And the people arriving with this cash openly admit that they don't know the source of the money they are endlessly trading for chips. Essentially, they are mules: they arrive in Vancouver, go to a pre-determined location, pick up the cash, and gamble. When they are done gambling— and none of them appear to be poor gamblers—they cash out. Because of the sums involved, Davis explained, cash-

ing out involves making a deposit into a Personal Gambling Account; ironically, the casinos are more worried about the cash that leaves than the cash that arrives. Sums over $10,000 require the use of a PGA.

When cashed out, these PGAs are paid by cheque or money order, written from one of Canada's oldest and most respected banks. And, just like that, hundreds of thousands of dollars are laundered. Every day.

Mr. Davis has no knowledge of what happens next, but he —as do sources at the Vancouver Police Department—believe that this casino-washed money is then deposited into legitimate bank accounts; however, since the source of the funds is obvious and legitimate, no red flags are raised despite the amounts. After deposit, the suspicion is that the money is then shuffled from bank account to bank account and, somewhere along the way, used to pay back the original cash loans—here, or more likely abroad—as a legitimate business transaction. These legitimate bank accounts are controlled by the original 'source' of the gambled dollars. But where does this money come from and, perhaps more interestingly, where is it kept? According to Mr. Davis, the location of this money is 'Ground Zero'.

In Vancouver, the speculation is that Ground Zero is funded through the criminal activity of motorcycle clubs. And motorcycle crime in Vancouver almost always begins and ends with Anthony 'Agony' Baker and his Silent Saints Motorcycle Club.

At this point, the story continued on an inside page, and Robyn went to pour us coffee. I separated the front page from the rest and gave Robyn the inside page to read. Neither of us had spoken since we started reading.

The second page of Terri's story was even better than the first.

Last year, the Joint Investigation Gaming Investigation Team (JIGIT) was created to determine the scope and probability of large-scale money laundering occurring in British Columbia. The team is a blend of law enforcement and governmental departments and is led by Vancouver Chief of Police Tara Callan. Mr. Davis is the civilian head. Earlier this month, the Task Force delivered a report to the Prosecutor of Financial Crimes in Ottawa. Mr. Davis was not willing to sign his name to the final report.

Cutting to the chase, the JIGIT told our Federal Government that a thorough review of anti-money laundering measures in BC casinos has determined that our province has the strongest anti-money laundering rules in place across the country, if not North America. Rules are sufficient, apparently, to make it nearly impossible for criminal activity to operate in a 'significant manner'. Mr. Davis scoffs at this notion and has provided The Vancouver Sun *with a copy of this report.*

At first read, the conclusions seem unsubstantiated.

Chief Callan, of course, is more commonly recognized for her prominent role as the head of the inter-divisional Motorcycle Gang Task Force that includes the Vancouver Police Department, multiple attachments of the RCMP, as well as the singular police forces of North Vancouver, West Vancouver, Aldergrove, Langley and Matsqui. This task force was created to control and minimize the criminal reach of motorcycle clubs such as the Silent Saints *in the Lower Mainland. Chief Callan has publically praised the success of this team, citing the recent arrests of multiple high-ranking* Grave Wolves *club members and the confiscation of nearly one million in cash and $4.8 million in drugs and weapons from a North Vancouver residence.*

Gareth Davis, in a position to know the true reality based on his involvement with BC Casinos and the money-laundering task force, says that heading both committees presents too much of an overlap for the Vancouver Chief of Police, if not an out-right conflict of interest. He provides document after document that seem to demonstrate the two task forces do not work in concert despite having one overarching voice—that of the Vancouver Chief of Police.

Is there a connection between money-laundering and the lawlessness of BC motorcycle clubs? Most definitely. The Vancouver Sun *has published a number of articles detailing the intricacies of cash-heavy enterprises such as those owned and operated by the* Saints. *So is there a link between motorcycle clubs and the* Vancouver Model, *undertaken daily at BC casinos? Only the most naïve among us can assume they exist separately.*

Here, there was another page break. I was ahead of Robyn, so I fed the dog and gave her some water. Robyn hadn't seemed to notice Nesha's new bow. Robyn caught up and we moved to the third page.

It is well known that there is a significant motorcycle club war taking place on the streets of the Lower Mainland. In a battle for control of the streets and numerous illegal but profitable businesses, the only constant is cash—and lots of it. The $900,000 confiscated recently, and lauded publically by the Chief, was headed somewhere. *The Head of the BC Lottery Commission thinks he knows where: the elusive Ground Zero and then to BC Casinos to be washed, dried and maybe even folded.*

Mr. Davis points to the public record and questions why the JIGIT is the second *task force created to investigate money laundering in BC when the results of the previous disbanded task force were ignored. Five years ago, the prior task force suggested the RCMP move to shut down BC casi-*

nos for the simple reason there was too much money that could not be sourced.

Of course, from a provincial perspective, any money is good money. The current estimate is that the BC Gaming Commission generates $3 billion in annual revenue for the province of BC.

What is not so easily understandable is why the original task force was sheltered last year and replaced with the current task force led by Chief Callan. Governmental gossip is that the prior task force has been discredited federally. Submissions under the freedom of information act have not produced a copy of the task force's conclusions.

What that leaves us with is speculation, yes, but also some undisputable facts. Two years ago, Mr. Davis—in his former position as head of security for the River Rock casino—gave a presentation to the Association of Certified Fraud Examiners called 'Spinning the Slot-Machine Wheel: How BC Gambling Complies with Existing Rules.' *In this presentation, Mr. Davis noted that in any given month, an average of 1,977 suspicious transactions are reported by BC casinos. Of these nearly 2,000 transactions, exactly* zero *are acted upon.*

Two years ago, Mr. Davis was stunned that nobody seemed to care. Today, however, he notes that people are beginning to ask questions and action has been taken. You would think that Mr. Davis would be pleased. He is not. The action has been words only.

"At some point," Mr. Davis says, "they realized this was too big to contain and was all going to be public, so they had to do something". The 'they' he refers to is, of course, the current Joint Investigation Gaming Investigation Team (JIGIT), led by Chief of Vancouver Police, Tara Callan. As the second most senior member of this committee, Mr.

Davis has met with the Vancouver Chief of Police and every ranking senior RCMP and municipal force officer every week for the past 42 weeks. No investigations have been opened, no arrests have been made.

I asked Gareth Davis why he was choosing to go public now. He answered that he felt he had exhausted all internal avenues and that something was changing, but not for the better. He was not able to say what or how, just that the amount of money coming into BC Casinos on a daily basis has hit historic proportions and is no longer feasible or believable. "And nobody cares!" he said.

His logic is compelling and everything he mentions is provable in the public record.

At the conclusion of our meeting, Mr. Davis gave me one final document. A summary of affairs from Acting Deputy RCMP Commissioner Ray Doyle. In this report, delivered last month in support of the current JIGIT task force's effectiveness, Mr. Doyle states that 'whales have been identified.' By this, he means that casinos and law enforcement are aware of people who repeatedly bring hockey bags of cash to Vancouver casinos. He mentions a gentleman who cashed $200,000 for six straight days at the River Rock Casino *in Richmond.*

These 'whales', once spotted and named, are now prohibited from entering BC Casinos where security is vigilant. According to the JIGIT, problem solved. According to Gareth Davis, the cash is now given to a 'sub-whale' in the casino parking lots and then brought into the casino, so nothing has changed except the addition of one more hand-off.

Doyle, however, Acting Deputy RCMP Commissioner, actually proves this point while attempting to argue the other. Mr. Doyle states that the BC Lottery Commission, has spoken directly with problem VIPS on numerous occasions and reached positive resolution. The reality, according to Gareth Davis who would know, is that—in every situation —casino managers have always spoken directly with these VIPs with no provincial representation. When told of this, Mr. Doyle stated that "we really have no idea if these meetings have taken place, but see no reason as to why they would not have occurred."

To this final point, Mr. Davis has added a note in red pen. His handwriting is neat and tidy and proper, very much like the man himself. "There was an integrated gaming unit, funded by the Province at $1 M per year with another half million from the City of Vancouver", he writes. "It was shut down by the Chief of Vancouver Police soon after it was established, with the main reason being a lack of cooperation between entities. Immediately after that, the RCMP Proceeds of Crime Units throughout the province were eliminated. After that, there was nobody watching the play house. Nobody." Nobody is underlined six times.

Mr. Davis has the last word: "All of these agencies, such as mine, are collecting evidence of large transactions, and yet the enforcement branch gets shut down, at a municipal and provincial level."

In conclusion, and just for fun, if you get a little extra on your pay cheque this week and decide to visit a BC casino, hang on to your cash for a few extra minutes and take a look around. If you look closely enough, you will see secret elevators to secret VIP rooms that you probably can't afford and you will hear rumours of $100,000 tables just out of sight, and you may just see a hockey bag of cash being turned into casino chips. And none of this is illegal.

Of note, Vancouver Chief of Police Tara Callan has not responded to an interview request. We are left with her

*public words on money laundering and motorcycle crimin-
ality: everything is fine.*

"She wrote all of this in two days?" Robyn said when we
finished reading. "How much could she have written if she
weren't being distracted by Kyle?"

The rest of the day passed in mundane style. Robyn had ap-
pointments at the University, and I kept myself busy by doing
some laundry and catching up on what was happening with
the bar. Around three, Robyn came home and said she and
Terri had decided we were going to the Vancouver Grizzlies
game. We invited Karen and Rileigh, but Karen begged off,
electing to spend time alone with her daughter instead of another late night.

Through the paper, Terri was able to get us good seats—
although, truthfully, with the Grizz already rumoured to be
relocating to Memphis, good seats were easy to find, and always had been in Vancouver. In fact, since inception, the Grizzlies have given away so many free tickets and counted those
tickets as paid attendance that the NBA actually changed at-
tendance-reporting rules for the league.

Terri was quite knowledgeable about basketball, which put
Kyle on the outside—which Robyn and I both enjoyed. We
teased him incessantly about Terri's infatuation with Michael
Dickerson, a lightning fast Vancouver shooting guard with a
pure stroke. Because Kyle was sulking, we made him buy the
beer.

While we drank and watched the Trail Blazers toy with the
Grizzlies, we talked about what we knew; embarrassingly, it
wasn't very much. We had run through it all by half-time and
sent Kyle for more beer.

Denis Sault, a partner at Engs & Associates, died at the beach
with Jim. Sault was the accountant in charge of doing the

books for the British Columbia Corporation and casinos. Sault may or may not have been planning a public announcement to do with the BC Lottery commission.

Jim, and later Kyle, were in a one and then two person war against the *Saints* while the rest of the task force—seemingly under orders from Vancouver's Chief of Police—focused on secondary motorcycle clubs with great and public success.

After Jim's death, Kyle examined every record and talked to everyone he could and came to the conclusion that the *Saints* were being protected from above. Kyle, over time, mixed his meds with booze and decided the right thing to do was call the Chief a murderer on live TV for how the *Saints* were being protected.

The convoluted thinking behind this assertion is that the *Saints* were responsible for Jim's death. We have VPD and provincial numbers that support the conclusion they are protected, but nothing demonstrating they were involved with Jim's death.

Terri's thought is that the Chief has been so public crowing about her success in cleaning up drug and street crime (the purview of motorcycle clubs) that no one has noticed the predominance of clubs other than the *Saints* getting busted in very media-friendly ways.

Third quarter break. Last call for beer. Kyle goes; this time, he brings popcorn too.

BC Casinos are inundated with money that needs to be cleaned and nobody knows where it comes from.

There is an underground bank, and our one lead has maybe connected it to a mystery man called Johnny Zags. Or maybe not.

It makes sense that the bank is funded by low level street

crime and cash transactions such as those controlled by the *Saints*. Why the *Saints* are potentially being protected, we have no idea.

A link between the *Saints* and the Chinese Laundry certainly makes sense.

Bombings, like the one that killed Sault and Jim, are pervasive enough with motorcycle clubs to be considered a trade-mark.

"If you squint hard enough," I said, "you can see a trail between the *Saints*, the Task Force and the underground bank. But it is not coming into focus."

"It will," Terri said. "It will."

When the game was over, we said our goodbyes outside of GM Place. Terri had thought ahead and, as 'confidential sources', she had arranged for the paper to provide a Town Car for Robyn and me. Kyle went home with Terri and I realized I was stuck in a kind of no-man's land—staying at the Richards' was all fine and good, but time was probably running out. I was thinking this through in the back seat when Robyn took my hand. That did not make thinking easier.

We made it through the night, comfortable with each other but not pressing. I was struggling, her proximity something I had never thought I would experience again. Robyn seemed less conflicted, but she didn't invite me upstairs. Nesha slept in the kitchen again.

Saturday morning, a week after returning home, all hell broke loose and our lives were pointed in a different direction yet again. This time, at least, old friends and new friends were in it together.

CHAPTER 12

Saturday, Robyn was the first one up. I found her sitting on the sun porch with Nesha. Robyn poured me a cup of coffee. "It's Guatemalan," she said.

"Do they have caffeine in Guatemala?" I asked.

"They do, in fact, and it looks like you need it."

I took the cup and added some cream. "Listen, Robyn," I started.

"Shut up, Dirt," she said. "You aren't going anywhere."

"How—" I started again.

"Just stay where you are for now, Dirt. We both have some big decisions to make, and we are each a part of the other's decision." Nesha's tail was thumping. "But right now, I want you close." She drank some coffee. "When I saw you in Calgary, I didn't think we could get to here. Not this fast. Do you remember what I said?"

"I remember it all," I replied. "You said I had to start liking myself again before you could commit to our relationship." I added cream to my coffee. "I'm a work in progress, Robyn. But I swear I'm trying. I was listening in Calgary, it just took me a while to hear you. "

"I can tell," she said. "And I said that I had enough love for both of us, but you had to remember who you were, outside of baseball. That hasn't changed." She smiled, and I swear my heart stopped. "Now drink your coffee."

I drank some coffee.

"Good answer," she said.

Before I could say anything else and screw up whatever had just happened, my cell phone rang. It took me a few rings to realize it was mine. It was Kyle, and he stopped our morning cold with a story of gunshots we didn't hear or even know had been fired.

A few minutes after 8 AM, Gareth Davis was killed on the porch of his Marpole home. More than one hundred bullets had been fired and twenty-seven had been found embedded in the porch and stairs and wood of Davis' three story house. One bounced off an iron railing and went through a neighbour's window. Seven of the bullets passed through Davis; six found their way into his four year old son. Both Davis died within seconds of each other. One can only hope the terror they felt was brief.

Kyle had phoned me from Terri's land line. He had his own cell phone pressed to his other ear and was giving us updates as he received them from the scene, which was understandably chaotic. Despite his suspension, Kyle was still quite popular with the Blue Wall and was being fed information in real time. We learned that there were at least a dozen witnesses and multiple shooters involved and that two as yet unidentified males had also been killed, and one unidentified male injured. Kyle told us that these three victims were Asian and all had obvious gang tattoos. The survivor was not cooperating with police.

That all three were Asian and gang affiliated was immediately odd to all of us, as Marpole is not an area known for crime or somewhere you would go for an early morning stroll if not a resident. Early speculation, therefore, was that these men were the intended victims and the Davis were unfortunate and unintended casualties. No shots had been fired in retaliation and none of the victims were armed with anything beyond knives.

Marpole is a family neighbourhood with deep lots free of hedges and all fences are low. Violence is non-existent. People were stunned; panic was immediate. Police presence was substantial. Marpole is the most southern Vancouver neighbourhood, bordered by Richmond across the Oak Street Bridge, so there was a significant RCMP presence as well.

Neighbours on their way to work or looking out their windows to get a sense of the day, saw a blue Jeep Grand Cherokee drive around the block very slowly, two, maybe three, times. Davis' house was on a corner lot, and on the Jeep's third—or maybe second—trip around, the three strangers turned the corner just as Davis and his son emerged and gun fire erupted from the front and rear passenger side windows of the Jeep. It was over in fifteen seconds. With four dead and one injured, that was one casualty every three seconds. The only survivor rolled under a car to escape; that's where the police found him.

Kyle relayed what kind of guns had been used, but that meant nothing to anyone except Kyle. My knowledge of firearms ends at water pistols, and I hadn't fired one of those in fifteen years or more.

There wasn't much else to be learned. Multiple witnesses saw the Jeep, and a few saw the shooters—but the shooters were "definitively" white and large. Obviously, the plates didn't lead anywhere and the Jeep itself was found at Richmond Centre Mall hours later.

Kyle told us that he and Terri had heard about the shooting on an illegal police scanner she keeps on her kitchen counter, next to the toaster. Terri headed for the scene immediately, and Kyle hadn't spoken to her yet. He hung up and headed back to Point Grey from Terri's townhouse in East Vancouver. By lunch, there wasn't much left to be seen on site, so Terri made her way to the Richards' house and arrived the same time as Karen. Terri made Kyle promise to tell her everything.

The major update was that the three other victims had been identified and were 'known to police', as they say. They were low level Vietnamese enforcers that were in the neighbourhood to collect money from a debtor on Davis' block. The shooters, police were set to announce, were *Steel Vagabonds* sent to enforce the idea of territorial management—Vietnamese gangs tend to be concentrated in the Kensington area of Burnaby. Vancouver Police Chief Tara Callan had called a 1 PM press conference to assure the city there was no imminent danger of gang war and that the Davis were truly innocents.

None of us were buying the gang-turf story the cops were selling. And as Kyle spoke, the mood was understandably subdued, except for Terri who was bouncing with so much energy that she was getting Nesha worked up and we had to put one of them in the yard.

"I am going to grieve for Gareth," she said, "but it's not going to be today. He was such a nice man, and I will spend some time thinking about if what I wrote made this happen." We all moved to speak, and she held her hand up forcefully.

"You can believe this is about gang retaliation, if you want. And you may even be right. But I don't believe one goddamned word the Chief speaks." She looked at each of us in turn. "I *will* grieve for Gareth," she repeated, "but not right now," she said. "Soon, but not now."

The room was quiet. "Here's what *wasn't* in the paper," Terri said. "It's *going* to be, but tomorrow, not today." She looked directly at Karen. "It's coming together," she said. Karen nodded once. Terri spoke for twenty minutes and for once in our lives, Kyle and I simply listened. Karen took notes, but asked no questions. Here is what Terri told us.

Five months ago, as head of anti-money laundering enforcement for the entire BC Lottery Corporation, Davis implemented a number of initiatives and directives that would prohibit individuals from using large amounts of cash until the source of funds was confirmed. Immediately after implementing these new policies, but before they were actually live, he was called to a meeting with BC Lottery Corp execs and the police leadership of the JIIGIT, led by VPD Chief Tara Callan.

He was ordered to remove these intrusive policies as they would have an immediate and detrimental impact on the BC Casino industry.

Davis refused. In fact, rather than capitulate, he doubled down and mandated that individual gamblers and whales and delivery men be 'named and shamed'. He urged police at all levels and in all jurisdictions to actively and aggressively investigate the endless lake of twenties and fifties flooding BC Casinos.

He even gave the Task Force a place to start: Chesapeake Financial.

"You know what?" Kyle said. "I swear that Chesapeake Financial is in Jim's notes. It's only mentioned once and there is no context or follow up, so I just assumed it was a dead lead or not relevant after he looked into it."

"I don't even remember it being mentioned," Karen said.

"I do," Kyle said.

*****

Karen was on the phone to her office in Victoria immediately. Even on a Saturday, there were people around—provincial crime never rests, I guess. Karen was able to learn things about Chesapeake Financial that we probably weren't' supposed to know. Licensed as an investment house and money lender, Chesapeake Financial was unusual in that the corporate hierarchy was quite convoluted and primarily consisted of numbered businesses. And there was no record of licensed financial advisors or mutual fund dealers attached to the company. Hard to give investment advice or negotiate a legal loan without actual employees with proper licensing in place.

Karen learned that there was also speculation of a connection between Chesapeake Financial and the Lower Mainland drug scene; in fact, the Vancouver vice-squad was convinced that Chesapeake was a multi-kilogram buyer of cocaine in the Vancouver area alone.

"That's strange," Karen commented, "because most cocaine enters Vancouver as a trade for BC Bud and cash. It's impossible to believe that that much volume isn't connected somehow to the *Saints*."

"Unless," Terri said, "someone who matters doesn't want there to be a link."

"Yeah," I said, "but this $7 million bust from Kyle's press conference—"

"Fuck you," he said.

"Kind of flies in the face of the Task Force not working," I continued. "And, maybe even more so, it kind of kills the idea of an underground bank."

"No," all three of them said simultaneously. Karen tool the lead. "Instead, she said, "it supports the idea of the Task Force being pro-*Saints* and that it's the *Saints* who control the bank."

"The public," Terri said, "doesn't care who gets busted or where—they just want happy stories about guns and cash and drugs off the street. I guarantee you that for every story like this there are four more busts that didn't happen. Call this one a loss leader, so to speak."

"That's a stretch," I said.

"No," Kyle said, "it fits." He jumped up, some of Terri's manic energy had obviously reenergized his inner perpetual motion machine. "Dirt, let's go. I'll drive."

"Where we going?" I asked.

"To finally do something," he said. "Karen, can you call us with the address for this Chesapeake place?"

She said she would. "Robyn, can you watch the dog?" I asked. Kyle had pushed me out the door before she could answer. "No country," I said to him as we headed for his diesel Dodge Ram 2500. "For the love of God, no country."

"Where are you guys headed?" Robyn asked.

"To blunder around like bears in a campsite," Kyle said. He gave me a quick smile.

"Well, at least you have a plan," she replied.

Forty five minutes later, Kyle and I walked through the lobby doors of a five-story Richmond office building and checked the directory to find our destination. We took the elevator to five. "I like my investment advisors to be on the top floor," Kyle said. I nodded agreement.

The elevator doors opened directly onto a marble foyer. There were two heavy and intricately carved wooden doors directly in front of us, flanked by statues of a dragon and a lion. At least, I think that's what they were. I didn't get a very good look as the doors opened as soon as we left the elevator. We entered the Chesapeake Financial office and the place was huge. Probably eight hundred square feet with a tremendous view of multiple parking lots and, on the north facing side, snow-capped mountains. The furniture was bright and shiny and plentiful. It was set out in sections that Kyle refers to as veal fattening pens. Despite it being a weekend, there were at least a dozen bright and shiny people hard at work, and they were all dressed very casually, which I found surprising. Chesapeake Financial has a nice, high-brow sound to it. I was expecting ascots, not sneakers.

Three of those employees, pretty but not beautiful in their similarity, were sitting at a fourteen-foot long reception desk and speaking on phones. All three were Asian and petite; far left hung up the phone and asked if she could be of assistance. I read Kyle's body language which told me to make nice and take charge.

I played it cool. "Hi," I said. Hard to go wrong with 'hi'. "I'm here for my appointment."

The other two gatekeepers had hung up, and my charm was met with three blank stares. "I talked to Judy the other day," I lied and said a silent thanks for name plates. "I'm early, but I have a three o'clock to talk about my portfolio. Mr. Rodriguez is expecting me."

"Not here," Far Left said. "Perhaps downstairs. There is a Sun Life office that I am sure would be able to help you."

I was dismissed. "I have substantial funds," I said. "I used to be a pro-athlete. I am sure my appointment is here."

All three shook their heads. Middle and Far Right stood up and moved to the back of the office. I saw Kyle's eyes follow them to the back where two walls had been built to create a very nice corner office.

"My friend Johnny Zags recommended you," I told Far Left. "He said he was getting about fifteen percent on his invest-ments. I don't even think I'm getting three per cent."

She looked clear through me, like she was searching for something I didn't possess. I knew it wasn't charm. I turned to Kyle. "That's what he said, right? Chesapeake Financial in Richmond?"

"Yeah, this is the right place. Johnny even mentioned the view."

But that was the end of our conversation. The two women who had gone into the back office returned, but this time they were two giant-sized Asian guys. Think James Bond Villain sized gentleman, and then add another four inches and sixty pounds. "Help you guys?" one of them said, again with absolutely no accent. Not Chinese, not French, not East Coast, not American. And I don't think he was serious about helping us.

"You Mr. Chesapeake?" I asked. "Or Mr. Rodriguez? I've got some money I want to grow and invest. Should we go in the back and chat?"

"No," he replied, rather definitively. "We should not, because I think you guys are just about to leave. I know that Mya has already referred you to Sun Life downstairs. It's for the best. You will not meet our standards as a minimum investor."

"But," I said, and the other guy cut me off.

"Besides," he said, "we don't know no Zags."

"Must be the wrong Chesapeake," Kyle said.

"It's a common name," I told him. "Sorry guys." They were still moving towards us and they had no pamphlets about investing strategies and potential yield. In fact, they really didn't seem to want our business, so we did the smart thing and left. The door clicked shut and there was a very distinct buzzer that locked the doors in case we wanted to try again.

"Interesting," Kyle said. I had to agree.

*****

On the way back to the Richards', Kyle turned the radio to CKNW 980, the all-news radio station. We were in time to catch the top-of-the-hour news report. The Marpole shooting was obviously the lead story; the radio station was calling it "Rain of Fire". I saw what they were trying to do, but I don't think it quite worked. After the details were explained and the dead and injured were named, the newscaster played a long clip from the Chief's afternoon press conference.

She spent quite a long time talking about gang violence in general and the destruction it brings to innocent people like Mr. Davis and his son and about her vow to clean the streets of Vancouver was working despite infrequent and unfortunate events such as this. It was a lot of political bull shit that sounded good if you weren't really listening and meant absolutely nothing if you were.

"Part of her is probably happy," I said. "She gets her face on TV and there is nothing she likes more."

"You notice how quick she was to blame the dead gang-bangers for being in the wrong place at the wrong time?" Kyle asked

"I did," I told him. "I also noticed how she named the *Vagabonds* as shooters despite any actual... what's the word you guys use...? oh, yeah—evidence."

"Speaking of evidence," he said, "how the *Vagabonds* were named is a mystery. Guys I talked to at the scene said none of the witnesses saw any colours. That makes no sense—these guys never go anywhere without flying their colours. Incognito is not something they understand."

"She did throw in some lovely platitudes about the Davis," I said.

"She did," Kyle answered. "And that only seemed to push them to the background. Everything else was about gang violence and guns and rampant crime and destruction and a bunch of other stuff I didn't listen to."

"So," I said, "as a trained investigator, was it also your opinion that the public is being skilfully manipulated to *not* wonder about Gareth's presence at the scene? Just an unfortunate coincidence that he happened to live there and be on his own porch at that exact time?"

"I did have that sense, yes."

"Interesting," I said. "I wonder what the girls thought—they would have seen the press conference live."

"We'll know shortly," he said.

"Hold that thought. Pull in here, I want to get a few things."

Kyle pulled his truck into the parking lot of the T&T Supermarket. The T&T is the biggest grocery store I have ever seen, and it specializes in Asian foods and spices. I hadn't gotten any of the Chinese food the other day, and had a craving for ginger beef. As I walked the aisles, picking up everything I needed to make the dish and then some, I sent Kyle across the street to get some Lucky Buddha beer. I don't know if it's authentic Chinese beer or not, but it comes in green glass Buddha bottles and makes me feel warm and safe.

At the house, while I minced garlic and chopped peppers, carrots and onions, Terri and Robyn—without prompting— agreed with our observations of the Chief's press conference. "Maybe," I said, "we are just predisposed to see what we want to see." But nobody really believed that.

Kyle then filled the girls in on what we had found—or not found—in Richmond. They were as confused as we were.

"Make enough for Karen and Rileigh," Robyn said about dinner, without offering to help. "They'll be here in half an hour or so."

"When did you learn to cook?" Terri asked.

"Crap," Kyle said. "Don't get him started."

"I'm serious," Terri said. "Not to be judgmental or sexist, but I wouldn't have expected a pro athlete and 'guy's guy' like you to cook as well as you do."

"Thanks, I think," I said. "Cooking is kind of an escape. I learned, basically out of necessity, when I was in my early teens. My Mom is a very good cook, but her food tastes run to the extreme and her efforts in the kitchen were sporadic at best. As much as I like things like mulligatawny stew and Ox Tail now, they weren't really big hits with three kids between three and thirteen, you know?"

I whisked some water into corn-starch until smooth, and then whisked in two eggs. When that was done, I added strips of flank steak and made sure they were well coated.

Robyn handed me a green Buddha and I tipped it at her in thanks. "My grandmother, God bless her, tried her best, but she was a terrible cook. Unwrap some ribs, add a bottle of barbeque sauce and bake until black was her go to recipe. And," I added, "we were lucky—despite being raised by a single mom, there was never any shortage of food. So I learned to cook— basic stuff, really, at first—roast chicken, meatballs—and as I got older, I tried more things."

"That reminds me," Robyn said. "Seen your mom yet?"

"There will be no questions at this time," I said and added one-quarter of the beef to hot canola oil.

"He's a great cook, but a really terrible baker," Robyn said. "And maybe not such a great son."

"I'll leave the son comment alone," Terri said. "But why can't you bake?"

"I think it's because cooking is feel and baking is science. Us manly ballplayer types don't do well with sciencey stuff."

Terri threw a bottle cap at me. I ducked it, and when all the beef was cooked, I drained most of the oil and then added the vegetables and cooked for about three minutes. Usually when I cook, I time things in beer—three minutes of cooking vegetables is roughly one beer. But oddly I still had the one Robyn had handed me ten minutes ago. *Falling behind, Dirt, and it's a good thing.*

Karen knocked at the door, and Nesha almost knocked Rileigh over she was so excited to see her.

I whisked sugar, rice vinegar, soy sauce, sesame oil and some chili flakes (not very many in deference to Rileigh) and added the beef back to the vegetables.

"Perfect timing," Karen said. "That smells great."

Robyn had set the dining room table, and made sure that I had a fork. In fact, she gave me two.

*****

When dinner was over, Karen and Rileigh cleared the table, and Robyn and Terri did the pots and pans. I am a very messy cook, so there was some good natured grumbling about the mess. Kyle used the built-in vacuum to vacuum up about half a dog's worth of Nesha's hair and then we ate ice cream. Rileigh and the dog went downstairs to watch a princess movie, and the five of us sat at the dining room table, unsure of what to do next.

"Is this a good time to mention Nesha made a new friend the other day?" I asked.

"That's nice," Robyn said, "but she's a very social girl."

"The dog's name was Sasha. Her owner is Agony Baker."

Collectively, they made enough noise that Rileigh came upstairs to see what was going on. Convinced we were all okay, she headed back downstairs. "You're telling us this *now*," Kyle said.

"Well, you and I went looking for him and he found me. He wasn't what I was expecting."

"Ryan," Karen said, "the man is a monster."

"Trust me," I told her. "I'm not looking for a new friend; I know what he's about. But he seems conflicted to me."

"You're fucking conflicted," Kyle said.

"Listen, we can talk about this however long you want and in however many ways. But the *Saints* didn't kill Jim—he has a long and compelling list of reasons why not. And this is no comfort, but he knew nothing about Kylee." I paused. "Pistol is no longer with the organization." Thankfully, no one asked about that. "And, Karen, he's established a trust for Rileigh." Karen said nothing.

The mood in the room was odd—intense, yes, but there was anger too. "Listen, I don't know why everyone is looking so angry. We set out to meet with him and ask questions—goal accomplished. He—they—didn't do it."

The room thawed about three degrees.

Robyn was the first to speak. "I can see what your new friend is saying," she said. "In fact, it's something Dirt said when he got here: Jim and the *Saints* is too obvious."

"Maybe," Kyle said. "I need to think about that some more. In a way, though, it's a perfect distraction—like a well-executed end around in football. Done right, everybody follows the guy *without* the ball. That's the *Saints*. So who has the ball?"

"I'll find out what I can on this Sault guy," Karen said. "I meant to do that before but got distracted." She looked directly at me. "I don't know what to say to you right now, Ryan. I asked you to help and you are, and I'm grateful. But there's something about your meeting with Baker that bugs the crap out of me, and I don't know why."

"I get that," I told her. "I do." She patted my hand. "Baker suggested we do just that—look at Sault."

"Okay," Terri said. "Between us, Karen and I will find out what he was about."

"It may be nothing," I said. "Their two deaths could be completely unrelated."

"You don't believe that," Karen said. "Even if you did, somebody planted a bomb on the head accountant for the BC Lottery Commission accounts, and nobody has thought to investigate that."

"Could it be random that Jim and I were the ones to find him in the park?"

"Don't know," we all said. "What are you thinking?" Terri asked.

"Like I said before, usually, Jim and I worked the West End, Stanley Park, up into Kits and even the University. That particular shift on that particular night was—we thought—a punishment shift. There was no reason for sectors to be changed."

"So it was totally random then," I said. "Nobody knew where you were going to be, so it's not like they planted Sault where only you two would find him."

"Fuck," Kyle said. "Fuck me large. Dirt, I think's that's *exactly* what happened. But if it wasn't Baker, then who the hell was it?"

*****

The next morning, Kyle and I were in his truck by 8 and down the street from Chesapeake Financial by 9, coffee and donuts in hand. We watched. We watched some more, and then we watched even more. And nothing happened. I don't watch any TV, except sports, and sometimes the news if it's on at the bar. I haven't been to a movie in probably five years, so I don't know how romantically Hollywood portrays stake-outs. However romantically they are portrayed, though, you can cut that in half. And then again, one hundred more times.

Kyle was excited because he felt he was doing something. I was bored out of my mind because we were staring at a building. It was a nice building, I guess, very similar in fact to the BC Lottery building. Same general location near the airport, same five stories and tinted glass. From our visit yesterday, I couldn't even waste time trying to imagine the inside of the building—like the outside, the inside was the same as the Lottery building. Same Koi pond and waterfall—hell, maybe even the same Koi. Maybe the company that looks after the plants moves the Koi from building to building so the tenants always have something new to look at. I would have liked to look at some Koi. Or birds. Or even a person other than Kyle, and we'd only been staring at the Chesapeake Financial building for twenty minutes.

"Lay it out for me," I said. "Leave out the part where you jump to conclusions about things we know nothing about."

"Dirt," he said. "According to Terri, Davis linked Chesapeake Financial to Ground Zero for the underground bank. I was on the Task Force for two years, and never heard of it. Jim never mentioned it to me, but it was in his notes."

"One time," I said. "And like you said, maybe that was random or unrelated. Maybe this place isn't linked to the MCs."

"I don't believe it," he replied. "Too many coincidences. This place is dirty; the guys at Vice confirmed that. And what Terri found out, or can't find out, regarding ownership and what they do is suspicious."

"Sure, I agree. But how are you linking *this* to *that*? Kyle," I said, "what's the connection to the *Saints*?"

"That's what we're waiting to find out. Now be quiet—you're scaring away the bad guys."

*****

By four in the afternoon, we had seen four people enter Chesapeake Financial. Not one of them had a suitcase or even a bag of any kind. Seven people had left, including two we had watched go in. No one who left had a bag either, although one had a purse. Kyle wasn't impressed, but I kept track on my own and didn't even need to write anything down.

"We'll give it 'til six," Kyle said. "It'll be dark then; hopefully money laundering is a day-time business."

It wasn't, at least not that day. But it was Sunday. At six exactly, Kyle put the truck in drive and we headed across the Oak Street Bridge into Vancouver, stayed straight on Oak Street and hung a right at Broadway. Five blocks later, we were at the Bel Air.

Thunder Bob made fun of my face, we ate wings and drank beer, and watched the Grizzlies lose on one TV and the Canucks lose on another. The evening was significantly more fun than the afternoon had been. Around 10, Robyn and Terri arrived together and we went our separate ways. "I'll pick you up at 7:30," Kyle said. "Bring something to read."

Something between Robyn and me had shifted, for the good

this time. She put her arm around my waist as we walked to her car. *Hope,* I thought. *Don't fuck this up again.* She told me that she was on the verge of accepting the University's offer, they were simply squabbling over fine print now. That meant moving, maybe selling their parents' place, finding somewhere to live in a crazy market... you know, life. "Robyn, I don't know very much about life as an adult," I told her. She stopped walking, but I was in a bit of a daze and took two more steps. When I turned around to face her, she surprised me and kissed me full on the mouth. For quite a long time. "We can learn together," she said with her hand on my chest. "How hard can being a grown-up actually be?"

Seven AM Monday, I woke up on the couch again. This time, Robyn was with me, and the dog was purring. Day number one of being a grown-up was off to a great start.

*****

Kyle was early but I was ready and we headed for Richmond, with a quick stop at a Tim Horton's for coffee and sugar.

"What do we do when we have to piss this out?" I asked.

"There'll be a washroom inside," Kyle said. "Use it. It's called reconnaissance."

We were in position a few minutes before eight, parked on the same street as yesterday, but facing in a different direction and maybe a half-dozen cars further away. Amazingly, by 8:05, there was an actual suitcase sighting. At 8:08, there was a hockey bag. At 8:12, the suitcase—much lighter—came back outside and two heavy liquor boxes went in. All deliveries, if that's what they were, were made by white trash—big guys, small guys and in between, but all with the same greasy hair and scraggly beards and dirty clothes.

"Either bikers or homeless guys," I said.

"Explains why they let you in the other day," he said. "You match the job description."

"I have much nicer shoes," I said. "And with all this traffic, if it keeps up, I'm going to have to take notes today."

Kyle flashed a wicked smile. "You owe me an apology," he said, "and I don't accept."

In all, by noon, fourteen bags and boxes of various sizes had entered the building, and only three had left. We couldn't tell for sure if those three bags had been ones we saw enter, the suitcases being used were basic black or silver hard shell wheelies. But we did the math and assumed that today was deposit day at Chesapeake Financial. "If those were all full," Kyle asked, "how much money did we just watch go by?" I had no answer.

With that, as a trained professional, Kyle started the truck and we drove around the block and parked on a cross-street. We ate some donuts and did some more watching. "Neither of us has done any reconnaissance," I said.

"Need to drink more water," Kyle replied.

We decided to give it two more hours, but maybe thirty minutes later—just as I was thinking about going reconnoitering—the same hockey bag we watched go in came out of the building. It was clearly heavy, as the woman sitting in the middle position of the desk yesterday was having trouble rolling it.

Middle struggled the bag across the street to a newly arrived Cadillac Escalade, a vehicle model I had never seen before. "Brand new," Kyle said. "But it has a certain appeal with a specific type of person."

"Who wants an SUV you can't take in the mud?" I asked.

"Mostly drug dealers," he replied.

The driver of the Escalade was a small man, Asian, wearing a red Adidas track suit, complete with white stripes down the legs and arms, and white sneakers. I hoped they were Adidas too, you know, to complete the look. Despite its obvious weight, the driver picked up the hockey bag and tossed it through the open back window as if it were nothing.

"If that's twenties," Kyle said, "that bag holds about $2 million dollars and weighs probably 100 pounds. He picked it up one-handed."

"If we have to fight him," I said, "you go first."

"Thanks Dirt. Nothing's changed—I'm always fighting your battles."

"Not sure that's true," I said.

"Grade 11 versus Notre Dame. Robyn's twentieth birthday at that place under the Burrard Street Bridge. The next morning at Denny's—"

"Look," I said, "the truck is moving."

The Escalade signalled—which I thought was strange given that there was nobody driving on the street—and pulled away from the curb. Kyle started his engine and pulled away as well, but he didn't signal. The driver clearly wasn't expecting to be followed, but I was impressed with how easily Kyle kept him in sight without being obvious himself—not easy to do given that the Escalade and Kyle's truck were the two biggest things on the road.

After maybe a fifteen minute drive through Richmond and another fifteen on Highway 99 and through the Deas Island Tunnel, we were in Delta. The Escalade took the exit for Tsawwassen, a gentle and well-to-do suburb that has a BC Ferry Terminal for trips to Vancouver Island and the numerous Gulf Islands.

"If he's getting on a ferry," I asked, "are we going with him?"

"Game time decision," Kyle replied. "Let's hope it doesn't get to that."

It didn't. Along with the ferry terminal, Tsawwassen is also home to one of the largest native-owned casinos in BC, *The Sundancer Gaming Palace*. The driver pulled in to their immense horse shoe driveway, eschewed valet parking, and headed for the visitor lot. Eventually, he pulled up beside a white Honda Civic, and the bag dance started in reverse. The new owner of the bag was another woman, also Asian, but instead of a track suit like her friend, she was dressed for a night on the town. If she had a million bucks in that hockey bag, like Kyle and I suspected, it was going to be one hell of a night.

"Should we join her?" I asked.

"Absolutely," Kyle said. "Beer's expensive here, but the tables are loose." He smiled. "So I've heard."

Kyle told the valet attendant we were on the job, and gave him a twenty to leave his truck in the horseshoe. We went inside and waited in the over-bright lobby for the hockey bag to appear. It took about three minutes, and then it, and its new owner, walked right through security and headed for the VIP section.

"We've lost her," I said. "We aren't getting in there."

"We don't need to," Kyle answered. "Follow me."

We headed back outside and Kyle opened his phone. "Calling Caldwell," he told me. Mark Caldwell answered, and he and Kyle spoke for about two minutes. I heard Kyle ask who Mark's counterpart was at the *Sundancer*, then Kyle smiled and said "I know Derek. Can you give him a call and let him know I'm outside?" There was a slight pause and Kyle said "Thanks, buddy. Appreciate it." He hung up and looked at me.

"Two minutes," he said. "In two minutes, we head to security and ask for Derek Peterson. By that time, Mark will have called him, and Derek will be our new best friend."

And that's exactly what happened. In two minutes, we were talking to security, and in five we were talking to Derek.

"You know this guy?" I asked during our short wait.

"On the periphery," he said. "Another retired cop. Haven't seen him in years, but he and Caldwell are still tight. Derek was my number one option on the flag football team for a while, but then he was hurt pretty badly in the 1994 Stanley Cup Riots. Took a disability, and now he runs security here. Pretty good gig, like Mark's, if you don't have to get hurt to get it."

Derek was quicker to find us than promised, and he and Kyle caught up in a hurry. "We need some help," Kyle told him. Derek started to protest, but Kyle cut him off. "Nothing official, Derek. I know I'm suspended. Just need some eyes on a lady who came in about ten minutes ago." Peterson wasn't budging. "Remember who threw you all those passes," Kyle said. "Made you a star. Come on man, nothing serious and nobody but us three ever knows."

Long story short, Derek took us back to the surveillance room, but we were too late. Our well-dressed friend had come and gone. "Shit outta luck," Kyle said. "Always the way at a casino."

"Not necessarily," Peterson said. "Tell me what's going on, and I'll find out whatever it is you want to know."

Kyle shrugged and filled him in. Peterson, apparently, was not a fan of the uninhibited amount of cash he sees on a daily basis, or Chief Callan. "Callan sold me out when I got hurt," he said. "Wanted my pension reduced despite my having my twenty because I wasn't 'sanctioned' to be working that night. Whatever the fuck that means," he said. "Every cop worked that night. Every single one of us." He shook his head. "What do you need?"

"There was a woman in a black pant suit and a yellow scarf. She had a hockey bag and headed to the VIP section. We want to know if it was hockey equipment she was dropping off for her kid or—"

"Or if it was a cash exchange," Peterson said. "Head to the bar, have a couple on me, and I'll let you know shortly."

Shortly was two beer for me and one for Kyle since he was driving. "Emma Corrales," Peterson told us. "BC driver's license says she lives in White Rock. That bag had more than $800,000 in it, and $550,000 of it was twenties, the rest fifties. No provision asked or answered."

"Gentleman," I said, "the game is afoot."

*****

Kyle and I were back at the Richards' by five. We had a quick conference and made the executive decision that even crooked bankers take time off, so instead of getting ready to stake out Chesapeake Financial again in the morning, we took the girls to Whistler for the night.

Whistler is two-hours north of Vancouver and is one of the largest ski resorts in North America. Maybe 10,000 people live there year around, triple that in the winter. It's breathtakingly beautiful and has a crazy-cool vibe to it, even if you don't ski. Which I don't. The roads were clear and we made great time arriving for a late dinner, even after dropping Nesha at a buddy of Kyle's who breeds and trains Avalanche Rescue Dogs. I'm pretty sure she spent the night outside, which she deserved after being cooped up for so long.

We had better luck on rooms at the *Fairmont Whistler* than

Karen and I had had in Golden. Kyle was even able to get us a preferred rate as law enforcement. When I looked at Robyn to see how many rooms for us, she held up one finger.

It was a very good night.

The next morning, Robyn and Terri were up early to maximize their spring skiing. Kyle and I took a hard pass on that and slept until almost noon. I don't do cold and Kyle doesn't like hurtling down snowy and icy mountains at dangerous speeds. Terri tried to get him to do the bunny hills, but he held firm.

We were back in Vancouver by ten o'clock Tuesday night, and even though it had been less than twenty-four hours, it somehow had felt like a full vacation. Even the dog agreed.

CHAPTER 13

Wednesday morning, eight AM, Kyle and I were back at Chesapeake Financial. This time, because we are savvy surveillers, we took my Bronco. For the first couple of hours, nothing happened. And then something most unexpected and unpleasant happened.

"Heads up," Kyle said. "On your left, Dirt."

I looked in the side view. "Are you fucking kidding me right now?" I said.

"You know these guys?" Kyle asked. "I've got one on my side too."

"My face is intimately aware of the guy on my side," I said. "You're guy, though, is a stranger."

"Interesting," he said, just as the rounded rear window on his side shattered.

I started to get out of the truck, but Kyle grabbed my arm to stop me. "Just a crow bar," he said. "Not a gun. Stay put."

By now, they were even with our doors. Orangutan saw me and did an actual double take. "I know this fucking guy," he said to his friend.

The guy on Kyle's side was a carbon copy of Orangutan, but dark haired. Black Beard tapped the crow bar very gently, almost politely, on Kyle's window, tap tap, tap tap.

Kyle slid the window down, showing absolutely no stress or

concern. My heart was racing, I think his heart rate had dropped. "Coffee, three cream," he said. He looked at me. "Anything for you?"

"Honey crueler," I said. "Please."

"Shut the fuck up," Black Beard said. "Get out of the truck."

"I don't think he heard our order," Kyle said.

"Could be out of cruelers," I said. "They often are."

"It's a popular donut," Kyle said.

"You ain't listening," Black Beard said and leaned into the open window, maybe to scare us with a closer look at his face. "Get out of the truck."

"No," Kyle said. And with the speed of a bantam-weight, his right hand shot out and grabbed Black Beard by the beard. Kyle yanked on the whiskers and slammed Black Beard's head off the closed door frame.

Taking my cue from Kyle, I put all my weight into opening my own door and caught Orangutan in the stomach, knocking him down.

"Now what?" I said to Kyle while existing the truck. If Kyle answered, I didn't hear it. I was concentrating on not letting Orangutan stand up. Not being skilled in street brawls, I kicked him. I felt some shame, but hell, he had a crow bar. I was aiming for his substantial stomach, but might have caught him lower. I decided not to care about this social faux pas and just be glad he stayed down.

And suddenly, there was calm—mostly because Kyle had found a gun. In my truck. *Wake up brain, he must have had it with him.* The gun was short barrelled and stubby looking, not like any water pistol I'd ever used. While I knew, definitively, that Kyle knew how to use it, the two grease-bags chose to simply assume he could. Wise choice.

Kyle motioned them both to the back of my Bronco, and I swung the hatch open. "Sit," Kyle commanded. They did. "Speak," he said.

"Fuck you," Black Beard said.

Kyle looked at me. "Totally my fault," he said. "I should have been more specific."

If Kyle was concerned about holding a gun on two people in broad day-light in one of BC's most populous cities, he certainly didn't show it. Instead, he turned the gun around in his hand and hammered Black Beard on the nose. There was blood everywhere.

"Carpet is so expensive to clean," I said. "Why not hit him when he was still on the street instead of in my truck?"

Kyle shrugged a mea culpa. "You know I'm a cop, right?" he asked our new friends. It was clear by their expressions that they did not, in fact, know that Kyle was a cop.

"Jesus Christ," Orangutan said while watching his partner bleed and try not to cry. "This guy's got a fucking wolf and this guy is a cop. What the actual fuck?"

"She's a Malamute," I said. "Is that why you broke my truck? 'Cause of that guy's jeans?"

"You guys been hanging out here," Black Beard said. He nodded towards Orangutan. "He saw there were two of you, and I offered to help." He smiled and it's not true what they say—not everybody is more attractive when they smile. "I like to help people, so here I am."

"You're a giver," Kyle said. "But why do you care if we sit here day after day? People have to be somewhere—and, besides, my friend and I are currently between jobs."

"Thought you were a cop," they both said.

"They are listening," Kyle said to me. "That's good."

"You're here every fucking day," Black Beard said. "Go somewhere else. Give us a break."

"Does this have anything to do with suitcases full of cash?" I asked. "It's tough to buy that the Orangutan here just saw us and decided to have some fun. Although I do buy that he needed you to hold my arms this time."

Orangutan smirked.

"Why aren't you guys working actual productive jobs?" I asked. "You could have called us, we could have done some resume workshops together."

"Wait," Kyle said with mock surprise, "maybe they are working. Like right here? You're watching us watch this building? This is what you do all day? Shit, Dirt," he said, "we can do what they do."

"We are, when you think about it," I said. "But we aren't getting paid." I looked at Black Beard's broken face. "Does Johnny Zags really pay you for this?"

The two beards looked at each other, and with that we knew.

"We don't know what the fuck you're talking about," Black Beard said.

"And we apologize for the misunderstanding about your truck," Orangutan added.

"That blood is never going to come out of that shirt," I said to his partner. "I'm afraid it's ruined."

"My fault," Kyle said and waved them off the tail gate. "Go away."

They left. "Nice truck," Orangutan said while they both made a concerted effort *not* to look at Chesapeake Financial. Black Beard picked up the fallen crow bar and ran a two-foot grove in a side panel. "You should get a shine coat."

I was proud of myself for not reacting. As we watched them leave, I turned to Kyle. "You know you're suspended, right?"

"Thank God," he replied. "I never could have done any of that if I was working."

*****

We drove to an industrial park in Richmond's River District where Kyle knew a guy who would fix the broken window for cash but, because the window is tinted and curved at the top, he needed to order one in. "Don't ask too many questions of where the window comes from, okay?" Kyle said. I agreed, and then we crossed the street for lunch.

"Things aren't moving fast enough," Kyle said.

"Wow. I was *not* expecting that," I replied.

"We need to get in there, see what's going on."

"You think they just leave bricks of cash lying around? 'You get one, you get two, one for you, three for you'."

"That is what I think," he said. "More or less. And we somehow need to find out."

We traded shrugs and two RCMP officers walked through the door. Kyle told me, quietly and instantly, that he didn't know either of them. "Trouble," he said softly.

"Buy you guys a sandwich?" I said. Neither of them smiled.

The two guys were definitely RCMP. Cops have a swagger, for sure, but RCMP somehow ratchet it up another notch. These guys were another matched set, like the bikers, one a negative of the other. The guy on the left was white, the guy on the right was black. That was the only way to distinguish them —they had matching haircuts, matching sunglasses in the grey afternoon, matching body armour and matching weapon belts. They were exactly the same size—not tall, not small— like if you'd bought two steroid crazed Ken dolls for your kids.

"This day," I said to Kyle. He shrugged, I sighed. "Man."

"No sandwiches," one of them said, like a directive. We ignored him. I think his name plate read McCurdy.

"Fuck that," Kyle said. "I'm eating mine. These guys import Mortadella from Italy."

"Which one of you clowns owns the Bronco across the street?" the other one asked. His name seemed to be McNare. Kyle and I put down our sandwiches and pointed at each other, back and forth—'you, no you'.

"Listen," Left Cop said, "one of you guys is coming with us. And we really don't care which one of you it is."

Kyle and I did the pointing thing again. Best advice I ever got about my swing was find something that works and stick with it. Seemed to apply here as well. The RCMP comedy team did not agree. "I guess I'm almost done," I said, "so why do you care about the Bronco?"

"It's not the truck, Jack Ass," Right Cop said, "it's the owner."

"Man," I replied, "if only in the year 2000 there was an easy way to figure that out. But, alas."

"Up," Right Cop said. "You and us are going for a ride."

"Down," I said. "I changed my mind and am going to finish my lunch. And watch your syntax." I took a bite. "If you want to be polite and tell us what's going on, we could and would probably help. I already offered you a sandwich."

"The Mortadella is *really* good," Kyle said.

"Listen," Right Cop said. I guess he had taken over the leadership role. "We get orders, we follow 'em. There's someone at HQ who wants to talk to you."

Kyle and I looked at each other and shrugged simultaneously. "In for a penny, in for a pound," I said.

"Where you taking him?" Kyle asked. To me, he added "I'll call Terri for a ride and then meet you there."

Turns out, it wasn't that easy. Wherever they had told Kyle I was going to be wouldn't have been correct. I had a busy afternoon ahead of me, and all I did was wait. Left and Right Cop each grabbed one of my arms as we left the sandwich shop. "So," I asked, "ever kick a guy in the nuts during a fight? Is that cool, or kind of frowned upon?" They didn't answer and put me in the back of an RCMP SUV. The ride to the RCMP station in Richmond took maybe four minutes. I didn't even have enough time to get uncomfortable. "Could've just phoned," I said, "I would have walked over."

Two police divisions moved me around like a domino from station to station and that managed to kill the rest of the day, which seemed to be their only goal. Maybe I should have been grateful as the day was already worth forgetting, but I wasn't.

At the third station, this one in Burnaby, I waited for another hour before two Vancouver Police officers showed up—a Neuveld and a Thornstenson. These guys were not a matching pair —one was short and looked like a balding rat, the other was tall and fat, with a black mark on his pale face like he had been stabbed with a pencil and the led broke off. "Had to get you a bigger name tag, huh?" I said. Again, no one laughed. But I was tired and bored and my brother's a lawyer... almost a lawyer... knows some lawyers, so I figured why not try and amuse myself? Plus, Karen is most definitely a lawyer. *Take that Thornstenson.*

Eventually, I was at the new Vancouver Police Head Quarters, just shy of downtown Vancouver. The old central police station was located in a less than desirable part of town—Main and Hastings—right in the centre of the Downtown East Side. Known mostly for its natural beauty and proximity to places like Sqaumish and Whistler and referred to as 'God's Country', Vancouver is home to the most luxurious postal code in Canada—the British Properties in West Vancouver—and Canada's poorest postal code, the Downtown East Side. The new Cop Shop is three blocks to the west of the old one. All communications personnel—mostly 911 operators—still work out of the old building. They walk through some tough territory to get to work each day.

Turns out, the person I was meeting, in heavy secrecy and after multiple transfers, was the Vancouver Chief of Police, Tara Callan. I didn't understand all the shuffling from station to station—it's not like I was blind-folded or would ultimately forget meeting with the Chief. Neuveld and Thornstenson had no opinion on this, and dropped me in her outer office and left without as much as a goodbye. "We'll have lunch," I said. "You guys probably love herring. I know a place." They didn't respond.

I was expecting a long wait. Instead, the Chief's personal assistant Barbara, a nice looking older lady, ushered me quickly through an impressive set of double doors and into the Chief's private office. Unlike everyone else I had met that day, Barbara didn't judge. "The Chief will be right out," she told me. "I'd offer to get you something, but she told me not to." This was said with a wink. "What would you like?" *That's me, Ryan Simms. 65 year old ladies get me.*

The office was larger than I'd expected, and I had expected large. There wasn't much view to speak of, but you obviously can't have everything, no matter how hard you try. The wood was dark and the furniture light. There were five or six bamboo arrangements of different sizes in glass vases filled with river rocks and the wall without bookcases was adorned with a silk triptych of Chinese characters in the upper left and bottom right surrounding a cherry tree in bloom. I'm not one for art, but it was stunning and I couldn't stop looking at it. There was something familiar about it, which was strange, because whatever I don't know about art, I know even less about Chinese art.

And I'm not sure what I was expecting a Chief of Police's office to look like, but this wasn't it. Instead, it had the feel of a private club, and when Chief Callan walked in, I wasn't sure I could afford the initiation fee.

Vancouver Police Chief Tara Callan stands five foot nothing and has a slim and athletic build. She is in her late thirties, with dark hair and very white skin. She was wearing a black pant suit with an open-necked white dress shirt with one too many buttons undone. I wasn't complaining. While not Hollywood beautiful, there is a primal quality about her. She photographs and televises very well.

"Beautiful triptych," I said. "I think I recognize the writing. What does it say?"

Not a believer in small talk, the Chief cut right to the chase. "It's about the tree and changing seasons," she said, standing behind a desk larger than many elementary school gymnasiums. She made no move to come around and shake my hand or extend any greeting. No offer of coffee or a Danish or banality about the weather. I immediately wanted Barbara back. "Simms," the Chief said, "what the hell do you think you're doing?"

"In life? With this shirt? In general? Help me out, Chief," I said while helping myself to a comfortable looking armchair done in a very fine, pale blue, silk brocade. It wasn't comfortable, at least for somebody my size. I was wearing faded Nautica button-fly jeans, an all-white long-sleeve Henley and an orange and white cotton palm leaf print shirt from The Gap, so I knew it wasn't my clothes—although I was afraid that my shirt might clash with the chair. I hoped there was no Black Beard blood on me. "What do you mean, exactly?" The chair was stiff, so I leaned forward—I had heard somewhere that doing so makes it seem like you are cooperating. Something I wasn't really planning on doing.

She ignored me. "You wake up drunk in Calgary one day and decide to move to Vancouver to solve crimes that don't exist?"

"That's a solid opening, Chief," I said.

She ignored me again. "Guess what, you are neither wanted nor needed. When there are actual crimes, we have trained and authorized police personnel to investigate them." She remained standing, probably a trick to demonstrate authority, but because I am nearly a foot and a half taller, it didn't really work. "What kind of authority does a Calgary liquor license give you?"

I gave her a two-shoulder shrug. "Not as much as I might have hoped," I said.

The Chief moved to the windows but rather than enjoying the limited view, she turned to face me. The sun was behind her, so looking at her then would have been exactly like looking at the sun; insubordinately, I looked at her ego wall instead. Nothing out of the ordinary—local politicians, a few federal, a couple of hockey players since traded and one Vancouver Canuck icon. Many people I didn't know.

Interspersed on the bookshelves were a number of smaller framed pictures of the Chief throughout the years and a half-dozen commendation plaques from Richmond businesses. Richmond, where we had met Gareth Davis and staked out

Chesapeake Financial, is a city of 160,000 or so, due south of Vancouver, and is forty per-cent Chinese. I found it odd that this Vancouver suburb would be so grateful to the Vancouver Chief of Police, who has absolutely no jurisdiction there since Richmond—as are all but two Lower Mainland suburbs—is policed by the RCMP. On another bookcase, there was something that looked like a bee-keepers hood, white with silver mesh.

"I'd be real careful if I were you," the Chief said, turning away and assuming I would stay to listen. "You're awfully close to an obstruction charge. We have cut you considerable slack because of the high emotions involved currently and because of your attachment to many of those who are seeing ghosts where none exist. But no longer." She walked to her desk and picked up a file, although I couldn't see what it contained. "Do you understand? We are not only talking about careers here, but lives as well.

"By the way," she added, "how is Mr. Richards? Still attending his mandatory counselling sessions I hope."

This last, she said in an almost playful voice. Men pay money to listen to voices like hers on the phone, probably set to speaker, but it was clearly a threat. To make sure I understood, she followed up with this: "Make no mistake, Mr. Simms. Lives *are* at stake—maybe even yours. You have no idea of the investigations you are jeopardizing." She paused, I think for effect. She took some full size pictures from the file and placed them on the desk for me to look at, one after the other. I obliged. There were pictures of me, pictures of my truck, and pictures of me with Anthony Baker.

"That's a great shot of my dog," I said, pointing at one. "Her friend's name is Sasha."

The Chief laughed. "Agony Baker is not someone an amateur should engage, whatever said amateur imagines has happened."

"Chief, I've met the man once. We talked about dogs and baseball."

The Chief of the Vancouver Police Department stepped back to her desk and gave a slight, but dismissive, wave. She smiled without warmth. "I understand your investigative training was liquid more than substantive." "In fact," she said with a nasty smile that somehow turned me on, "my sources tell me that you were a lousy baseball player and a lousy drunk. Maybe you are a lousy investigator of conspiracy theories as well."

That hurt; no matter the metric you choose, I am a great drunk. Easily a .400 hitter.

"You know," the Chief repeated, "I'd be careful moving forward. I hear Calgary is nice at this time of year. Maybe you should return." And with that, the meeting was over. "Please close the door on your way out."

Doing the math, I realized I had said less than seventy words since entering her office. "No", I told her, putting one more on the ledger and I left both doors open—another example of a small mind being easily amused.

*****

It was Robyn who picked me up. Unsure of how much she knew, I played it cool. "Yeah, so I met with the Chief," I said.

"Shut up, Dirt. Don't talk. In fact, you are on time-out. When we get back to the house and you are asked a question, you can talk. Until then, we listen to country radio."

I was very mad at Kyle.

When we got back to the house, everyone was there. Even Rileigh, who was upstairs asleep with Nesha. Kyle shot me a look that said it wasn't his fault. I had never suspected that it was, but I was still mad.

"Here's what we know now," Karen said. "While you guys have been fucking around with getting arrested, Terri and I were doing work."

"Only one of us got arrested," Kyle said, "and I don't think Ryan was fucking around. He seemed to do it pretty well."

"Says the guy with an illegal gun in his ass," said his sister.

I knew better than to say anything.

Karen, the Provincial Prosecutor, took charge.

"You two idiots," she said without real heat, "get yourself some beer and something to eat. We ordered pizza and there's Dos Equis in the fridge."

"Prison won't be like this," I said to Kyle as we headed for the kitchen.

"Take the fifth," he said. "No matter what they ask." I didn't know if he meant in prison, or now.

Rather than making us eat pizza standing up, the inquisition followed us to the kitchen so Kyle and I could eat at the breakfast bar.

"Same guy?" Karen asked me.

"At the truck?" She nodded.

"He didn't know it was me before they smashed the window," I said. "But, yeah, it was the same simian as Golden."

"Ryan kicked him in the balls," Kyle said.

"My hero," Robyn said, but I don't think she meant it.

"Easy to judge," I said, "you weren't there. But I do feel some shame—I asked the RCMP guys who picked me up about fight etiquette, but they wouldn't answer."

Karen, as the only parent in the room, hushed us. "Last year," she said, "there was a national investigation into money laundering. Kyle met the lead investigator—Stephanie Page. I talked to her today—I gave her some bullshit about missing reservation cash and I don't even know what else. She knew I wasn't being straight, but she still was happy to talk. That," she added, "is strange in and of itself."

Like an actor with great dramatic timing, she paused. "Stephanie stopped short of saying the Chief is being investigated at a federal level, but she certainly allowed me to think it." Another pause. "Guys, this is far bigger than any of the Chief's show ponies have let on." Like at a trial, Karen shook papers in the air and raised her voice. "How the Integrated Task Force hid this national investigation from us is a triumph of obfuscation."

"I recognize most of those words," Kyle said, "but what do they actually mean?"

"Means," Robyn said, "that you guys on the street have been getting played, and somebody pretty high up has been keeping secrets."

"Exactly," Karen said. "I knew none of this, and that doesn't make me feel good. I haven't talked to anyone in Victoria because I am not sure whom we can trust, but I have spent the day on the phone—mostly with Stephanie, and she even asked us to put a fax in the kitchen so we could share documents. Again, the fewer eyes the better."

Karen gave Terri a fist bump. "Stephanie loves your work, by the way."

Karen continued. "Federal estimates are that $500 million dollars *a year* are being washed through Lower Mainland casinos. And the investigation is three years old, and I found out about it today. Today!"

"Turns out," Terri said, that while we've been going along,

all 'hey, how you doing?', the Feds have been operating something called *EBluff*, which is only the biggest money laundering investigation in Canadian history."

Karen took a long pull on her beer. "Somebody," she said, "somewhere, could have mentioned this!"

Another pull on the beer. "It's embarrassing how easy this information is to access," Karen continued, "after the fact and now that we are looking for it, but *nobody* is talking to anybody else." She grabbed another Dos Equis from the fridge even though she wasn't finished with the one in her left hand. "I'm in charge of *millions* of treaty dollars," she said. "Don't you think it might be relevant, and that I should know, if there is a fucking highly scrutinized drug or money laundering operation taking place on one of the reservations I'm negotiating with?"

What do you say to that?

"I called a colleague back east," Terri said. "We went to school together and now he works for the *Ottawa Citizen*. Apparently, this money laundering investigation is well known in the capital. There was even a major operation in Quebec that essentially eliminated the *Doral Riders* by drying up their cash flow."

"A fricking illegal bank," Karen said, "supplying gamblers bags of cash, and I find out today because Ryan went to jail."

"Wasn't really jail," I said. "They never fed me. Or checked my wahoo."

Kyle checked the fridge and flashed me an okay sign. Plenty of beer left. He grabbed one and asked two questions. "Where are we at and what do we know?"

"What we know and can prove are very different," Karen said in her prosecutorial voice. "But I am convinced that what we are learning now is the truth." She finished her first beer. "Jim wasn't killed because of his hatred for the *Saints*." She looked directly at me. "Baker told you the truth about that." She opened her second beer. "That was a smokescreen, but for whom?"

We were all silent. Karen continued. "Somebody here—with the cops, with the province, with the fricking Lottery Commission is sandbagging a federal money laundering investigation and people, like my husband, are dying because of it."

"The Chief sure wanted me to go back to Calgary," I said. "And there was something weird about the meeting, you know? Like why bother—who am I to her?"

There were a few wise cracks at my expense. "But she sure loves Richmond, and Chinese decorations." I explained about the art work, and the commendations from Chinese citizen groups on display in the Chief's office.

"That is strange," Karen agreed. "And you know, she has access to everything," she added. "In fact, we've got all these moving parts—motorcycle clubs, crime, vice, prostitution, money laundering and whatever the fuck else, and it's all related to what I do, but I know nothing about any of it. But the Chief has access to everything all of these silos report. She chairs every committee, runs every unit, is on TV twice a day with her top button undone… what do we know about her?"

Karen's face was red, and I worried about her health. Apparently, Nesha was too and she butted Karen in the thigh. Karen visibly relaxed and sank into a chair with Nesha's head in her lap.

"We know Jim's death wasn't an accident," Terri said and headed to the fridge for a new beer. "Even If I don't win the Pulitzer," she said with her head in the fridge and her ass in the kitchen, "we are proving that."

With friends like these, the world is an interesting place.

*****

Calmer now, Karen maintained control of the room, if not the fridge. "This is all new to me, but three years ago, the RCMP opened an investigation into what they officially called the *'Investigation of National Laundering of Proceeds of Crime and Loan Sharking'*. Who the fuck even knows what that means?" she said. "*EBluff* is a result of that investigation, and I sure as fuck, never knew about it."

"That's a lot of fucks," Robyn said.

"It is," Karen agreed. "And I don't give a shit."

"Karen," I asked, "how is it possible you can learn about all of this so quickly? We've got federal investigations being ignored provincially, but this isn't news?"

"Guys," she said, "the information has been there, but it's been carefully manipulated so that everything we are talking about has been isolated. The provincial task force has determined money laundering is impossible in BC; therefore, no need to pay attention to what the Feds are saying. Or doing. And it took you two clowns a couple of days to close the loop."

"I think Robyn started us on this path," I said.

"Probably proves we aren't clowns," Kyle added.

"Ryan," Karen said, "was the Chief trying to scare you away from Baker because he's a bad dude and she is worried about your health, or could she have been trying to *keep* you away from Baker so you don't learn what he knows?"

I had no answer for that.

We were all quiet for a few minutes, but it wasn't an awkward silence. More like we were all trying to rethink everything we hadn't known through the prism of what we thought we knew now. It was Robyn who spoke first.

"We've made this too complicated," she said. "With all the moving parts, we focused in the wrong places. This has always been about money." She ate the last piece of pizza. "We need to know about the Chief and the accountant and the banker."

"And the candlestick maker," I said.

With that, we called it a night. Kyle and Terri took his truck and headed for her place, leaving her car behind as we agreed to make a plan over breakfast. With Rileigh already asleep, Karen headed for the smaller guest room so as not to wake her daughter or my dog, fast asleep in the larger one.

Robyn and I went downstairs and were asleep before our clothes were even off, at least she was.

CHAPTER 14

Thursday morning, and the candlestick maker proved elusive, but the other searches were fruitful. Kyle and I, deep off the record, drove out to Harrison Hot Springs to meet with his former sergeant, Andrew Robillard. Harrison is a resort community of 1,500 people about an hour and a half east of Vancouver. It is famous for an annual sand sculpture competition that draws contestants from all over the world. "Robillard moved out here," Kyle said, "the day after he got his 30—full pension and benefits."

"Subtle victim of the Chief?" I asked.

"I really don't think so," Kyle answered. "More a victim of the 30 years."

Robillard met us on the porch of his lakeside cottage. He looked exactly like the owner of a beautiful country cottage should look; he was tall with silver hair and a bushy moustache and was wearing faded corduroys and a yellow cardigan. His cottage was beautiful—knee high picket fence, Canadian and BC and Harrison flags flying in the breeze, shutters and clapboard siding. The backyard was about twenty yards of grass and then sand and then water. I wanted to take pictures of the place and make an exact copy of it on my lot in Roberts Creek.

In the way of guys everywhere, there was no small talk. Just handshakes and wise cracks. "You look significantly better than the last time I saw you," Robillard said. "Welcome back."

"We need help, Sarge," Kyle said. "It's why we're here."

Robillard arched his eyebrows. "I figured it wasn't to sign up to build sand castles," he said. "Not sure what you need, but I'm happy to try." He led us to an enclosed sun porch and told us to sit on an obviously homemade sectional.

"Great furniture," I said. "You make it?"

"I did," Robillard said. "Took me a weekend and I saved a ton of cash."

"Hand bent Teak?" I asked.

Robillard nodded. "I know a guy for the wood," he said, "and I built a steam box for the bending." I decided I would take pictures of the furniture too.

To Kyle, Robillard said "This one knows what he's talking about. Remember when you tried to help hang the siding?"

"Got hung, didn't it?" Kyle responded.

Robillard looked at me. "After I put him in charge of the cooler and the barbeque."

"Been there," I said.

"Yeah, you guys are riots," Kyle said. "Andrew, there's a lot of stuff going on and I'm not sure how much of it makes sense. But," he added, "I'm not crazy and I don't have a concussion this time, but we think—and can almost prove—that there's a connection between the Chief and the *Saints* and money laundering through Vancouver's casinos."

"And we think," I added, "Jim's death is somehow a part of this."

Robillard pursed his lips thoughtfully and held that pose for ten or fifteen seconds. He looked at Kyle, and nodded. "Okay," he said. "But that means the other guy—Sault?—was the target and their deaths weren't random."

"That's are working thesis," Kyle said. "Bombs aren't random. Sarge, you know that. But I obviously wasn't part of the investigation and can't access any records now."

"I never bought the *Saints* theory for that night," Robillard said. "What do you know?"

Kyle shrugged. "We know Sault was a top guy at Engs & Associates, the accounting company, and handled the Casino accounts. And apparently lived well beyond his means."

"We checked on that," Robillard told us. "But he was clean—made well into seven figures each year and started with family money. Apparently his grand-parents were big deals in France, but on the mother's side. Cursory looks into his finances maybe wouldn't show that."

"Damnit Kyle," I said, "Terri brought up his finances, and we blew right by it—just assumed he was dirty." I shook my head. "That put us chasing after the *Saints*."

"That might have been a mistake," Kyle said with absolutely no humour.

"But it was probably a logical conclusion," Robillard said kindly, "given Jim's hatred of the *Saints*, that they would do something dramatic to send a message and eliminate their greatest annoyance at the same time."

"Sault wasn't the smoke screen," I said. "Jim was. Jim was simply positive collateral damage."

We all let that one sit for a while and watched some gulls chase waves, in and out of the water.

"You remember you and Jim weren't supposed to be working that watch, right?" Robillard asked. "That shift change came from above, the day before. We were told there had been a meeting arranged with one of your confidential informants from the *Grave Wolves*. Obviously," he added, "that meeting never happened."

"And you didn't think it was strange?" I asked.

Kyle was shaking his head. "Ryan," Robillard said, "shift changes happen all the time. Guys are sick or in court or needed somewhere else. Changes don't usually come from above and aren't usually that specific, but no—not unusual."

"But Kyle," I said, "and Andrew, did I hear this right—you were told to change the shift because Kyle had a meeting with an informant."

"What I said," Robillard replied. "We weren't told Kyle had *set* the meeting, just that he had a meeting."

"Either way," Kyle said, "that seems like something I would have known about."

Robillard shook his head. "I'm sorry Kyle. I never even thought to ask."

"Why would you?" Kyle said. "Forget it."

"And Sault is single, no family, right?" I asked. "So there's no pressure from anyone to pursue what happened on his behalf. Just another tragic inexplicable event on the Downtown East Side."

"Nobody checked into Sault beyond crossing the Ts," Robillard said. "Good place to start before you take this conspiracy theory any further." He gave us both a smile, looking a little like the actor Sam Elliot. "But I'm on board with the conspiracy theory." He stood up and walked to the wall of floor to ceiling windows. "Here's why: all the little things that Callan tried to use to brand Jim as dirty were all explainable, but nobody looked. The weight of all the mistakes collectively became the proof."

He turned towards us. "Jim was the last one to sign the evidence card; but he wasn't the last person in the evidence locker. Jim took a witness to the wrong court house; but those were his orders. Jim led two failed raids; but it wasn't his sources that confirmed time and location. There is missing cash, but if Jim took it, where is it?"

He looked at each of us in turn. "It was just too damn convenient: Jim and all these black marks and his hatred for the Saints became an easy explanation for why they would want him dead." He rubbed his face with both hands. "Gentleman," he said, "I think about this every night: if Jim hated the *Saints* so damn much—and we know that he did—then why did all his 'mistakes', which were acts of commission and not omission, *help* the *Saints*?"

It was barely eleven in the morning. Robillard stepped into his kitchen and came back out with three cold Steam Whistle Pilsners from Ontario. "My daughter sends it to me," he said. We did a silent cheers. "Tell me about the money laundering," he said.

Kyle laid it out for him, including our stake outs of Chesapeake Financial and our trip to Tsawwassen following Emma Corrales, and everything in between. Robillard knew about Davis, of course. "The link between Sault and Davis is quite suggestive," he said.

"It is," I replied. "But I struggle to fit Jim into that particular picture. He wasn't chasing the money; he was busting heads."

"I think that's where you need to focus," Robillard said. "By busting heads, was Jim disrupting the money operation? Is there someone who would profit, so to speak, on both ends if Jim is gone?"

With that, our beers were empty. "Gentleman," Robillard said, "I would offer you another, but I have to head to a council meeting. Some nonsense about a commemorative plaque at the Visitors' Centre." He looked directly at me. "Ryan," he said, "I don't know you other than your taste in cottages and furniture, but take care of this guy. I don't want him hunting ghosts or doing anything stupid that he won't be able to recover from—personally or professionally."

I shook Robillard's hand. "Thank you, Andrew," I said. "We've been looking out for each other for a long time."

On the way home, Kyle was silent and I let him brood. Earlier, the girls had let me know that this was Italian night, so we stopped for groceries. I needed semolina flour and spinach and figured Kyle could use some Moretti beer. Actually, forget Sam Elliot, Robillard looked a lot like the guy on the Moretti label.

*****

By three in the afternoon, everyone was back in the living room. Rileigh was with her grandparents. "It's a bad habit," Karen said. "They all love it, obviously, but I need my kid and my life back."

It had been a very productive day. Robyn had been to the University to sign her formal acceptance and to meet her new team, and we briefly celebrated that with the booze on hand. "Champagne later," we said. "When this is all over."

Then Terri and Karen shared what they had found out about their respective assignments. With the entire research department and archives of one of Canada's largest newspapers at her disposal, Terri chose to concentrate on the Chief, and Karen put the law clerks and assistants of the Provincial Legislature to work digging into our elusive friend, Johnny Zags.

We gave Terri the floor.

"Chief Callan," she started, "is not native to Vancouver—but nobody really is."

Kyle, Robyn and Karen held up their hands. "We are," Kyle said.

Terri held up her hand. "Me too," she said. "But that is surprisingly uncommon. Forget being born in Vancouver—more than 45% of Lower Mainland residents are born outside of the country. Not the province, the country. Why I bring it up," she added, "is that for someone who is not from Vancouver, the Chief sure made connections fast. From the former Premier to the current, and the Mayor to a number of Vancouver's mover and shakers—they are all on her speed dial."

"She's a political animal," Kyle said. "But we already knew that."

"Plus," Robyn added, "she's easy on the eyes. There is a lot going on in that small package."

"It all helps," Terri said. "Ryan, I told you that on the day we met."

"Wildcat in the sack," Kyle said. "That is the technical term we police officers use."

Terri didn't look up from her notes. "Would make one of you," she said.

"Ouch," I said. Robyn arched her eyebrows in a 'who are you to talk?' sort of way. She sighed and shook her head. The girls laughed—pretty sure it was at our expense.

"The Chief was born in Southern Ontario," Terri continued, "Windsor. Her mom, sadly, was shot in a robbery while pregnant, and died in childbirth."

We all grimaced. "That could explain the law and order persona she presents," Karen said. "Something like that is obviously a life-changer, no matter how young you are when it happens." I'm sure she was thinking about Rileigh.

"Absolutely," Terri said. "She was in and out of the hospital for the first couple of years, but ultimately okay. After getting the green light regarding her health, Callan's Dad—Robert Chaston Callan—moved to Hong Kong for business when she was two, and remarried when she was five. Callan's step-mom comes from money—her family builds electronic components for a lot of the big players—Sony, Nintendo, and so on. The marriage was a bit scandalous at the time, as Mr. Callan's new bride was freshly divorced and had an infant son and was marrying an outsider. At thirteen, the Chief moved back, or was *moved* back—the records are unclear—to Ontario alone and was enrolled at Banksome Hall in Toronto. The step-brother stayed in Hong Kong."

"The school sounds snooty," Kyle said.

"You guys went to Vancouver College," Robyn said. "Remember, suit and tie and blazer?"

"Blazer or not, the Chief wins," Terri said. "Tuition at Banksome was $35,000 a year at the time. I'd call that snooty."

"Mr. Callan's Hong Kong business did well," Karen said appreciatively.

"I haven't found a lot on him yet, other than he didn't join his wife's family business. There are some notations regarding property development, but mostly he is listed as a 'Canadian philanthropist and business man'."

Terri was looking at me. "What, Dirt? Looks like you've got a hold of something."

I shook my head. "Not sure. Probably not. Keep going—if there is something, maybe it will come to me."

Terri continued. "After graduation from Banksome, she went to the University of Virginia on a fencing scholarship. Majored in criminal justice with a psychology minor. Graduated in three years."

"Go Cavaliers," I said.

"I didn't know fencing was really a thing," Kyle said. "I mean you see it on TV during the Olympics but that's it. Who knew they had scholarships for it?"

"I guess it is real," I said. "When I was in her office, I saw crossed-swords and what I thought was a bee-keeper's hood, but it was obviously a fencing shawl. And," I added, "her history in Hong Kong explains the Asian décor in her office."

"The Chief was good," Terri said. "Two time NCAA champion. She was also on the school biathlon team, which means she can shoot as well."

"It's interesting about Virginia," I said. "We think of Chesapeake as somehow romantic, at least I do, like maybe it's somewhere in Massachusetts where people like the Kennedy's play. There *is* a bay with money and boats and social events on the Atlantic, but Chesapeake itself is a good-sized city in Virginia. I played there in the low minors—great barbecue, although it's vinegar based, so not for everybody. It's also not where the university is, but it's a weird coincidence."

"Duly noted," Terri said, and actually wrote it down. "After graduation, the Chief moved to Hamilton, and based on grades and majors—and, ashamedly—being a woman, was hired by the Durham Regional Police Department over grade."

"Meaning," Kyle asked, "that she started a rung up the ladder and didn't have to climb that first one?"

"Yes," Terri confirmed. "That's exactly what it means."

"So," Kyle said, "she was already hated when she started… let me guess, she went into Internal Investigations and started spying on other cops?"

"She did," Terri said. "And, she was pretty good at it too." Here, Terri read from her notes. "Callan headed something called *'Project Phantom'* and, over six years, she busted a number of schemes where the estimate was cops had hauled in over a million dollars in bribes. One guy was getting $20K a month," she said appreciatively. "Of course, he's now in jail and will be for the next twelve to fourteen years. But still."

Back to her notes. "From her busts, the Crown filed twenty-four counts of obstruction of justice, breach of trust and cocaine trafficking against a dozen police officers. She is quoted in the Southern Ontario papers many times as saying 'Your badge stands for honour and respect; it is not an ATM machine'."

Terri handed us each a photocopy of a fax. "This is a transcript of her first official press conference from Hamilton. I haven't seen the performance, but apparently she was as polished then as she is now. "

One section of the handout was highlighted in yellow marker:

> *'Many, indeed most, of our police officers are good and true and honest, aware of the oath they have taken in everything they do. But not all. Some police officers—and one is too many—believe that illicit payoffs, illegal deals, and subverting police practices for personal gain is appropriate.'*

"She does have a gift," I said. "And, I know we talked about it, and it feels wrong to say, but she is really something to look at. There's something about her that says 'carnal'."

Terri nodded agreement. "Ultimately," she said, "the majority of the cases she brought forward were ones where – and here I air quote—'protection and advisements had been provided to the bad guys in exchange for cash and other considerations to the good guys'."

"That sounds *very* familiar," Kyle said.

"Far too close to home," Karen added, "given how many times Jim and his team went out excited about some information and came home with nothing except grief from above and public humiliation in the press."

Terri agreed. "There are a number of stories on a guy named Steve Lang, a Hamilton drug dealer. He was the guy who was *paying* the $20K a month and he says this allowed him to run free and do what he wanted, and nobody was going to tell him differently."

"This guy goes on to say—and I'm still quoting—'I would know when search warrants were happening, I would know who was ratting on me. I was allowed to sell drugs. Shit', "(this part is redacted, but four letters, starting with an s)", I get pulled over, I hang my phone out the window and the cops make it go away'."

"Until it didn't," I said. "What happened? Why was he caught?"

"Apparently, it was becoming too obvious—the vice cops and gang cops in Durham / Hamilton actually were airing dirty laundry and complaining about each other, so they spoiled their own party. My colleagues investigated and found systematic abuse."

Terri handed gave us another handout. "This," she told us, "is a copy of a story that my friend Daniel Haslem wrote six years ago for the *Durham Register*, specific to the police scandal in Durham and Callan's role as whistle-blower." The story started with a head-shot of Callan.

"I'm not going to lie," I said. "If I hadn't met her, or heard you guys talking about her, I would believe anything she told me."

"Boys are dumb," Karen said.

Five months ago, Staff Sergeant Tara Callan, Chief Investi-

gator for the Integrated Community Policing Committee *submitted paperwork to the* Ontario Civilian Police Commission (OCPC) *that clearly implicated Durham Regional Police Chief Patrick McCawl and others in a scandal of unbelievable proportions.*

On Friday, in an unprecedented move, the OCPC removed Chief McCawl from his position and placed him on administrative leave. Further investigations have been ordered into the behaviour of McCawl's top deputies and additional charges and suspensions are likely.

Based on information and witness statements from Callan's report, the OCPC began a full-scale investigation of multiple Senior Durham police officers regarding abuse of power and corruption allegations. Witness statements included in Callan's report were from active and retired officers as well as members of the public.

The Register has obtained a copy of Callan's report. It is a most interesting read as it details a crisis of confidence regarding the fitness of our police leaders to place community standards and interests above their own greed. The report states that there is a deep sense of mistrust in the judgement, integrity and capacity of police leadership.

Damningly, the report states that this "sense of mistrust is widespread in both sworn officers and civilian members of the service as well as the general public whom we are sworn to serve."

The report further alleges that McCawl, in his capacity as Chief, completely ignored (at best) or allowed and encouraged (at worst) serious criminal misconduct by his officers and acted to improperly influence and prevent investigations into alleged violations of Canada's Controlled Drugs and Substances Act.

As well, the report provides evidence that the former Chief frequently used threats of reprisal and / or formal complaints and suspensions to intimidate and coerce his own officers.

The committee's evidence was sufficient enough for the OCPC to declare a state of emergency in the Durham Regional District and immediately remove McCawl's powers as Chief Constable.

Staff Sergeant Callan has been named acting Chief.

"So there," I said when finished reading. "Take that Hamilton Chief!"

"And now Ms. Law and Order," Kyle said dismissively, "is promoted and covered in glory and ready for her next act."

"There's a really subtle difference between what happened in Hamilton and what has happened here," Karen said. "Does anyone else see it?"

"I think so," I said. "There, all the blame clearly fell on the cops for allowing the crime to get out of control and for being such active participants."

"Right," Karen said. "There, they tried to keep a lid on it and pretend everything was fine. But here, it's the opposite. The cops have been covered in glory for making the streets safe and for eliminating violent crime, but we know that hasn't happened."

"She figured out what was missing," Kyle said. "Call out corruption and chaos, and you won't be suspected of it yourself."

Terri held her hand up for a quick pause, and grabbed six beer from the fridge, even though there were only five us in the room. "All I could carry," she said. "And here is where I think we see the biggest similarities between what was happening in Hamilton and what is happening here: Hamilton drug dealers constantly went to court and pointed out the discrepancy between the cash they had on hand at the time of bust, and what was actually entered into evidence. One guy admitted that he had just counted $30,000 in cash before the cops broke in, but only $7,000 was shown as evidence in trial."

Terri handed Kyle a beer. "If," she said, "you follow the notes and do the math, as Karen and I did while you guys were out shopping, it's about a two-third split: one third gets entered, two thirds go missing."

"Jesus redacted Christ," Kyle said. "That is millions—*millions* —of dollars if true."

"Is any of this sounding familiar?" Terri asked.

We all smirked, shrugged, smiled or nodded agreement. But then we broke for dinner. My pasta dough was finished resting. I made *Spaghetti Aglio e Olio* with Wilted Spinach and Mushrooms. I add bacon to mine for substance, and bacon fat, of course, for taste. I make this dish a couple of times a month, it's that easy and that good. Ten minutes, start to finish, as long as your water is boiling when you start. At my current pace, that's not even one Moretti. *Progress and hope, hand in hand. Please let hope be dominant. I'm happy to stagnate growth wise right here.*

*****

Dinner was finished, kitchen cleaned, and the empties cleared away to make room for new ones.

"So let me guess," Kyle said. "Callan is the flavour of the day out East, we turfed our last chief for being caught with the Mayor's wife, and needed someone stable and virtuous. And Callan's star is shining the brightest of all applicants."

"She ticks a lot of boxes," Terri said. "Smart, female, gorgeous, tough on crime, politically savvy, decorated—she has two commendations for heroic action—and, by all accounts, righteous. Vancouver hunted her. She didn't apply. The only box she doesn't tick is race."

"And," Karen added, "Callan arrives in Vancouver, and history seems to repeat itself."

"Okay, wait," I said. "Let me catch up. We're saying that she cleaned up the Hamilton police force by taking dirty cops off the street and then came here and put dirty cops *on* the street? Or at least fronted for the *Saints*?"

"What my colleagues at the *Hamilton Spectator* say is that drug dealers were running amok in the Hamilton Durham region, with full cooperation and consent from the cops. But it was out of hand, so something needed to be done. Whether Callan was in the right place at the right time and was virtuous and law-bent when she started, we'll never know. But she went after cops with a vengeance."

"She was watching and learning," Kyle said. "How to play one side against the other and where the blind spots were. If I can jump to a conclusion," he added, "the cops in Hamilton got greedy and had to be cut off at the knees because they ultimately were hurting the drug dealers by stealing from them instead of working with them. That's what she learned—how to be a better partner so everyone wins."

"What happened when she got here and took over?" Terri asked Kyle.

"It was a purge," Kyle said. "Within the first two years, almost everybody who had already hit their twenty or beyond left. And it wasn't about change management, which is to be expected. It was about being told we were doing it wrong." His voice was pained. "Here we are in Vancouver, Canada's third biggest city with a crime rate that ranks thirty-first in the country, with almost zero gun crime, but apparently there are better ways.

"And these better ways come from Hamilton," he added, "number one in gun crime in the country." He took a deep breath and finished his Moretti. "There was zero experience on the street and, more importantly, up top. Sergeants like Robillard who had kept things normal through the riots and managed rosters and played the game were gone. Nobody trusted the 'new' management because, honestly, what the fuck did they know about anything? You had guys with five or six years on the job running desks and making assignments."

"But," Terri said, "the old guard tried to fight back, or at least hold firm."

"They did," Karen agreed. "In fact, there was legal action taken against the Chief. Jim was called to give multiple statements--"

"Me too," Kyle said.

"Right. I have that here," Terri said and passed us each a handout of important legal looking stuff. "Ultimately, the Union lawyers felt there was enough to go to the Civilian Oversight Committee here in Vancouver alleging that the Chief and her leadership team—including the Mayor— had acted and were continuing to act in an 'overbearing, intimidating, harassing and/or tyrannical manner towards both sworn and civilian members of the police service'."

"Oh, she was," Kyle said. "They were. Still are.

"But results," Terri said, "at least in how they are being presented to the public, are amazing." She dropped a lot of paper on the kitchen table. "We're not going through all of these, but these are the Chief's wins, as told through the press."

"And none of them," I said, picking up on the theme, "are *Saints'* losses, right? Man," I added, picking through the stories, "you guys have been busy while I was away."

"West Coast is the best coast," Kyle said.

"And that," Terri said, "is what we know about the current Vancouver Chief of Police. Ta da," she added with a flourish and did a full pirouette, complete with the classic hands over head and one leg bent ballet finish. "My book report is now complete." We clapped.

"Karen, the floor is yours."

"Right," Karen said. "Okay." She shuffled some pages and moved some paper from the bottom of the pile to the top. She looked at those pages, and then stuffed everything in her briefcase.

"Name two people who have never been seen together," she asked us. "Wrong," she said before anybody had responded. "The correct answer is Johnny Zags and Faas Xhang."

"Karen," Kyle said, "we've suspected that for a while."

"Did we also suspect that Fass Xhang is Chief Callan's half-brother?" she asked.

If four people do a double take at the same time, how many takes is that?

*****

Karen was buzzing. "You have no idea how many favours I've called in," she told us "or how cooperative different agencies —including passport and transportation—have been. It's not always this way—and my agency does a lot of passport control. Just believe me this never happens—thank you Stephanie Page!" Once again, Karen reached into the fridge for six more beer. "Johnny Zags," Karen said after delivering the beer, "meet Faas Xhang. She put two pictures on the counter. "Oh, sorry," she said in mock jest, "you've already met, since you're the same damn person."

I'm not good at recognizing people; in fact, if a teammate grew a moustache, sometimes I would wonder who the new guy was. But these two guys were the same.

We all opened our new beer, needed or not. It was something to do while we were smiling.

"Okay," I said, "I'll be the one to ask: what's the connection to the Chief?"

"Ryan," Karen replied, "I thought you would never ask. "Some of this," she continued, "was connect the dots. Funny thing is, all the dots have been there in plain view, just nobody has thought to draw a line from one to the other."

She held up one of the pictures. "Fass Xhang, brown on black,

five foot eight inches tall. Born February 8th, 1963 in the Sha Tin District of the Hong Kong Special Administrative Region of the People's Republic of Hong Kong. Master in four different martial arts. Officially, a British citizen." She put a badly printed reproduction of an old-fashioned birth certificate on the counter. "This character here," she said, "means father." The box was blank. Four shrugs. "This was, apparently, considered controversial." She placed another poor reproduction on the counter. "Especially as this document, a marriage certificate, shows a marriage date seven months prior to Xhang's birth."

"Shot gun wedding," Robyn said. "Happens all the time. Beck sings about it."

"'*Someone keeps saying I'm insane to complain / About a shotgun wedding and a stain on my shirt'.* No one seemed to enjoy my singing.

"Are you done?" Karen asked, maybe a little unkindly. I nodded. "Check out the groom's name," she said.

"Robert Chaston Callan," Terri read.

Four more double takes.

"Holy Christmas tree," I said, too excited to swear. "The Chief's half-brother is our underground bank!"

*****

Karen had more pictures and kept placing them on the counter, one on top of the other, almost too fast to keep up with.

"Here's Xhang at a ribbon cutting for a new building in China Town. You'll note who is on the far left." It was the Chief.

"Here's Xhang being recognized as the major donor for the Richmond Chinese Cultural Conservation wing at the library. With a better picture, you can see the plaque that lists other donors. *Coal Beginnings* is one of those donors—that's the Chief's horse farm in Abbotsford."

"Xhang's mug shot. The Chief isn't in this one."

"And my favourite," Karen said with a smile, "and this is from Stephanie's personal collection, is Xhang's new car—I believe it's called an Escalade." She tapped the picture twice near the end of the frame. "Ryan, any chance that's your Bronco here?"

"Jesus Christ," Kyle said. "The Feds were there and didn't do anything to help?"

"Probably a good thing," I said. "Remember the little matter of hitting a guy in the head with your gun?"

"Still," Kyle said.

We passed the pictures around; Karen did have more. We did this quietly, and Robyn was the first to break the silence. "CF," she said. "Chesapeake Financial or Callan / Faas?"

*****

"Holy shit," I said. "Terri, when you were asking earlier if I'd gotten a hold of something?" She nodded. "The Chief has this beautiful silk triptych front and centre in her office." Kyle was making 'go on' gestures with his hand. "In the top left, there were some Chinese characters that I thought I recognized, and in the bottom right, there were similar letters."

Everyone was looking at me, even the dog had entered the room. "You don't speak Chinese," Terri said. "You barely speak English."

"The chief handed me some bullshit about the characters referring to the changing of the seasons. But, guys," I said, "I swear to Christmas, when I was with the Giants—San Francisco obviously has a huge Asian population and they've been the most aggressive in signing Asian players. The Japanese market is the obvious one for proximity, but that's pretty well scouted. So the Giants had some players from Taiwan, and I would see them in spring training." Kyle ramped up the 'go on' gestures. "There was a pitcher, Chien Li, with a tattoo on his chest that was kind of cool—I asked him what it meant, and he said 'my brother'. *That's* the triptych I saw in the chief's office. I bet the other symbols were 'my sister'."

"My Brother / My Sister," Terri said. "Is it going to be solved by something hanging on the wall?"

"None of this has been easy," Karen said. "So we are due some luck." She handed me some paper and a pen. "My office has translators essentially on call. Dirt, write out what you saw, and I'll fax it right now."

In ten minutes, if my shaky recollection and even shakier drawing were to be believed, we had confirmation that what I had seen in the Chief's office was, maybe, 'My Brother / My Sister'."

Sometimes there are road signs, Dude, but you have to be awake to see them.

*****

"Guys," Terri said. "Can you take the dog for a walk? I need half an hour. I've got some calls to make and some favours to collect."

Karen, Robyn, Kyle and I walked the dog eight blocks to a Safeway. I had Nesha on a leash, which she wasn't thrilled about, but I prefer that to strangers being scared by a giant black dog at night. Karen and Kyle went to buy brownies and ice cream, and Robyn and I went to the liquor store to buy some champagne to toast her new job properly. I just threw the end of the leash over a bicycle rack so it looked like Nesha was attached. Strangers or not, I wasn't going to start treating her like an animal.

By the time we made it back to the house, it was pushing ten o'clock and the adrenaline hit off our earlier discoveries was fading. Terri made one last rally.

"It's time to call every single bluff and double blind," she said. "And I know how to do it." It took her twenty minutes to outline her plan—one she had already set in motion—and we all agreed that it was equal parts devious, dangerous and brilliant. And maybe foolish.

Terri's editors, with the involvement of legal counsel and the owners of her paper, had agreed to a significant marketing campaign to advertise a *Sun* exclusive story for this coming weekend. Over the next four days, TV, radio and of course newspaper ads would run selling the hell out of motorcycle criminality, some as yet unsubstantiated rumours about the VPD and specifically the Chief, and proof of money laundering through BC Casinos. "The ads will promise a story so big that 'it will change Vancouver forever'," Terri said.

She basically had the story written, we just needed to see it through, and Terri needed the strength and willpower to make all the puzzle pieces fit.

"We'll get our answers," Terri said. "Somebody's going to snap and point us in the right direction." We were all so eager for the plan to move forward we should have paid more attention to the potential cost.

*****

The next morning, the real world intruded again in a way that was neither kind nor cruel, just mundane.

John MacNally, my general manager at Ivy Green, phoned to let me know that the main water pipe had burst overnight and we had about a foot of water in the bar. There was a lot to take care of, too much to do from a distance. I booked a noon flight to Calgary, returning Friday. Robyn booked a flight to Kelowna to wrap things up there, and I knew better than to ask Kyle to look after the dog. Fortunately, Rileigh was thrilled to do it and I knew Nesha was in the best possible hands.

While I was dealing with insurance and claims adjudicators and by-law enforcement officers and plumbers and disaster clean-up crews in Calgary, Terri's editors were true to their word and ran newspaper, radio and TV ads for her Friday exclusive. They were calling it *'Rinse, Wash, and Repeat: How Dirty Money is Cleaned in British Columbia'*. I liked that better than what the radio stations had referred to the Davis' murder.

The ads were to run for one week, with the story slated for the following Saturday. On the sixth day, however, everything changed again and this time the intrusion was anything but mundane.

 At 7:28 exactly Thursday morning, Kyle and Terri were woken by a polite but firm knocking at the door of Terri's mid-city four-plex. Kyle remembers the time because he was awake waiting for the 7:30 alarm.

Terri answered the door and let her neighbour Mya inside. "I hate to ask," Mya said, "but my car is dead and I need to get downtown for a job interview. Can I borrow yours? It will only be a couple of hours, and I'll even throw in a wash."

"Kyle," Terri asked, "can I ride with you today?"

"I've got an appointment at one, but other than that, I'm all yours. Being suspended," he said to Mya, "has its benefits."

Terri handed her the keys. "Take it," she said. "Don't worry about hurrying back. If you've got stuff to do, take care of it."

"Thank you," Mya said. "I appreciate it." The girls hugged and Mya gave Kyle a high-five.

"If I'm not here when you get back," Terri said, "just drop the keys through the mail slot."

Sixty seconds later, Kyle was experiencing PTSD in real time as the windows in Terri's condo shattered due to the violence of the car bomb wired to the ignition of her Mini-Cooper. Terri remembers there being an absence of sound when she was expecting an excess of noise. Kyle found her in the silence, but who was comforting whom is unknown and perhaps irrelevant. Noise returned with the arrival of police, fire and ambulance, as did panic and chaos. Mya was gone, of course, and while Terri grieved for her friend, she was ashamed of her relief that it wasn't her. Kyle wouldn't let Terri go, even when the police wanted to question them separately. Fortunately, the cops on the scene knew Kyle and were kind enough not to press.

There were two injuries—a jogger on the other side of the street and down a few houses and a neighbour on his front porch. Amazingly, Mya was the only fatality, although the jogger lost a leg and the neighbour required hospitalization.

Kyle insisted to everyone that he was fine and Terri insisted she needed to be anywhere but there. With no reason to keep them at the scene, they were free to go—but how? Unimportantly in the scope of the horror, Kyle's truck had been destroyed. One of the patrol guys agreed to drive them to the Richards'. "Stay tight," they were told. "Let us know if you need to be somewhere, we'll see if we can help."

Knowing none of this, at noon, I picked my Bronco up from short-term parking and drove to the Richards' place. With no cars in front, I assumed nobody was home and was very surprised to see Kyle and Terri sitting on the couch, silently, holding hands and not moving.

I immediately panicked. "Robyn?" I said. "Nesha?" No response. "What's going on?"

Kyle simply shook his head, and pointed to the muted TV. I couldn't see it from where I was standing. When I moved so that I could see it, I wished I hadn't. "That's my house," Terri said. No other words were spoken for quite some time.

I called Robyn to tell her what had happened before she saw it on the news. She wasn't due back in Vancouver for a couple of days, but left for the airport while I was talking to her. Karen had already phoned Kyle, and when he didn't answer, she checked with her police contacts to learn that Terri and Kyle were okay. She said she would come over after work with Rileigh and Nesha. I don't know why, but I asked her to stay away and promised to stay connected by phone. "We have no idea what's going on," I said. "Obviously, Terri was the target. Might be best for us to stay away from here for a bit." She agreed. "I might take this group to a hotel," I said. "In fact, I will."

"Call me when you're settled," Karen said.

Terri phoned her editor, who was relieved to hear from her. I relayed this message as Terri insisted I do the talking. I think I did well given the circumstances, and the paper agreed to secure a two-bedroom suite at the *Fairmont Pan Pacific* on the Vancouver waterfront. If the *Pan Pacific* isn't the most expensive hotel in downtown Vancouver, it's close.

An hour after checking in, Karen arrived with Rileigh and the dog. The Fairmont provides baby-sitting, so Karen was able to send Rileigh to the pool. She and the dog had no idea what was going on, and we were all able to hold it together until Rileigh was swimming. But then there were hugs and some tears and considerable anger.

An hour after Karen's arrival, Agony Baker called.

CHAPTER 15

I still hadn't activated call display on my phone, so I didn't know it was Baker. I couldn't imagine who would be calling since the only people who had the number were here with me, but I answered anyway. Still shaken, instead of some clever opening, I managed "Hello."

"It's Baker," he said. "We didn't do this."

I believed him, but still asked to meet. "I'm at the bar," he said. "You can be here in ten minutes."

I didn't question how he knew where I was. Some things are better left unknown. Kyle wanted to join me, but I asked him to stand down. "Stay with the girls," I said. "Please. Empty the mini fridge and rent some movies."

The inside of *The Trestle Bridge* opens into a very large rectangular bar. I wasn't crazy about the train motif, but nestled as it was into the Vancouver Train Station, I was willing to accept. Baker and I caught eyes when I walked in, and by the time I made it to the far end of the rectangle, there was an Oatmeal Stout poured and resting.

"Left Field Fences," Baker said. "Enjoy."

I did, very much. I might have enjoyed more than one. "Low IBUs," I said. "Malty instead of hoppy. My kind of beer."

"Thought about you when we were making it," Baker said, pointing his own beer at the picture of me hitting the green Wrigley wall. "Maybe not you personally, but something about the game. The colours, the dimensions, the parks themselves. I don't know." He picked up his beer. "Said you'd sign it," he said.

"When it happened," I told him, pointing at the picture, "and this is something I've never told anyone else, but I was smelling grass and beer." He looked at me. "And that's fucked up, because I have no sense of smell. I have *no idea* what those things smell like, or anything else." I drank some Oatmeal Stout. "So somehow I knew I was going to catch it, but I also knew there was going to be pain. How much, and in how many ways, I didn't know."

"If you did know," he asked, "would you do it again?"

"In a heart beat," I said. "A heart beat." We clinked glasses and drank. "That exact moment in time, having the ball but before I hit the fence, was the happiest I've ever been. I would go back there in a second."

"Think about it?" he asked.

"Only every day. And not about the surgeries or the rehab, or the drinking. But about the joy. Doesn't diminish those other things, but it's given me something to hang on to while everything else went to shit."

"I've never had a moment like that," he said. "Not sure I've ever felt joy. Duty, honour, obligation—that's been my life. Even knowing what you went through, I still envy everything about it—does that even make sense?"

Before we could head deeper into the gestalt, there were chicken wings in front of us. There was no point in pretending I wasn't hungry; after all, we were two guys sharing.

"I don't know why," I said, "but it does. You didn't choose this life, right? You inherited it. Was there a chance to say no?" He shook his head silently. "I did get to choose," I said. "I mean, it was taken away violently and well before I was ready, but all the choices I've made from the time I realized I could hit—really hit—have been mine. That's not a freedom you've ever had.

"But, AB, everybody owns themselves, you know? I've got some friends helping me with that right now. It's something I forgot over the last few years."

"I don't have friends," he said. He whispered the word 'friends' like it was a foreign language. "Associates, sycophants, idiot fan boys—they're called soldiers for fuck's sake. I'm responsible for a lot of people, Dirt, most of whom I don't like in the least."

"Your guys are cold blooded killers and drug dealers and probably rapists and people smugglers and whatever else," I said. "But you—and I do mean *you,* not your crew—are not stupid. The worker bees, on the other hand, are honestly beneath you." I ate a drummette. "Good mix of flavours and heat," I said. "Got some butter in the hot sauce. Very nice."

"You know, Dirt," Baker said, "*this* is what I want to do." He spread his arms around the bar. "Fuck the trains, we do that for the tourists." He put both arms on the bar in front of him, with his beer exactly in the middle. "As fucked up as it is, the *Saints* were my Dad's deal. I just kind of fell into it. And what the fuck do I do now that I want out?"

"I've never been a part of a crime family," I said. "Not trying to be flippant, AB. I really don't know. Options seem limited."

"Try bringing this up with someone like Jim Hodder," he said. "He doesn't trust me anyway, because I want to do things differently than they've always been done. Those aren't fun conversations."

"I've met him," I said. Baker nodded. "Wasn't much talking on either side."

"I think we're similar," he said, "you and me. Opposite but maybe the same. All I've ever wanted to do, I haven't been able to, and all you've wanted to do was taken away." He signalled for two more beer. "And here we are," he said. "Want some ribs? We smoke 'em out back with hickory we import from Kentucky."

*****

The ribs were really good. Eight hours at 225 degrees, and you could see the smoke rings. Baker finished them with traditional southern flavours which are ketchup based while I prefer the vinegar blends, but these were first rate.

"Listen," I said after a rack or two of ribs and some more chicken wings, these ones smoked and done in a Memphis rub. "First, I need the Memphis rub recipe, but second, I need to know what the fuck is happening. I've got hold of so many ends I can't figure out which one to pull."

"We didn't kill your friend Jim," Agony said. "Or try to kill your friend Terri." He looked directly at me, and I swear I saw pain in his eyes. "If you aren't looking at the facts, it might look like we did. And the cops are happy to let people think we did. Fuck it," he said, "in a perverse way, the public thinking we do shit like this helps our recruiting drives."

"The *Vagabonds* are being blamed for the Davis," I said. He just shrugged.

"Like I said, wasn't us. I didn't know them. Or the guy who died with Jim. Only I give the orders for something like that, and it wasn't me. Wasn't us. Hasn't been us since Pistol."

I preferred when he wasn't admitting to murder. "And nobody acting behind your back?" I asked.

Baker just looked at me.

"Not Gaston, maybe, or Hodder? I heard what he did in

Alberta. They both scare the shit out of me."

Baker looked at me some more. "They still answer to me. Failing that, they don't go against my Dad."

"Okay," I said, "what I can't figure then, is who prospers by setting you up?"

"Maybe the same person who has pictures of you and me and our dogs," he said. "Were you curious as to why the VPD is following me if we—allegedly— are working together?"

I admitted that I had thought about this. "Purely a scare tactic," he said, "aimed at getting you to stand down."

"Stand down from what?" I asked. "This is where my head starts to hurt."

Baker took my beer glass and his, and grabbed an empty one from behind the bar. He moved them around in the traditional Monte Carlo style. "Who's hidden by the smoke, Dirt? We use the bank, but so does everybody else in our line of work. But for us, if it gets shut down, we go somewhere else." He reached over the bar and filled our glasses. "Twenty minutes of inconvenience. So who doesn't want you looking at the money?"

"Follow the money," I said. "I've heard that."

"What the fuck do I care about a couple of hundred shirts?" He looked me dead in the eye. "Dirt, there's two and a half million dollars in cash in the office safe." He started moving the glasses again. "There's more in other places. We're a smoke screen. Yeah, we put money in the washing machine, but we also aren't stupid, organizationally. We don't spend beyond our means and we hoard the rest. Those are my orders." He picked up one of three glasses, a full one so I knew it was his as mine was only half full. "If we get shut down," he said, and raised the glass as a question, "what still exists?"

I grabbed my glass and finished it. "The bank," I said. "With or without you, it still exists. Just the deposits get smaller."

We clinked glasses again and had fresh ones in front of us before our empties were on the table.

"Fuck me," I said. "There's no getting around it, is there? We're going after the Chief." Baker toasted me with his full beer.

"And a shit-load of dirty cops," he added. "Welcome to Hell," Baker said. "Welcome to Hell." He smiled sadly. "It helps that you speak the language."

I let that one sit for a while. Looking around the bar, except for the trains, I really liked what I saw. Friendly and enthusiastic staff, beer kettles and fermentation tanks through the back display windows, a great food menu and lots of brick and wood. *If I lived within an easy cab ride, I would call this my local.* Ivy Green was close, but not quite, at this level. *Maybe after the repairs.*

"So your deposits stop," I said, and Baker stopped me.

"Listen, Dirt, we may be the best, but we aren't the *only*, you know? That bank is writing deposit slips to more than the *Saints.* I know what we put in, and I hear what is taken out. Those numbers most definitely don't match."

"Never thought of that," I said. "Maybe we got hung up on the fact that the Chief keeps busting everyone *but* you. But it was your guys that rousted us at the bank, so that made me think motorcycle club, although the inside muscle was Asian."

"Yeah. Fuck all of that," Baker said. "We don't hire out for muscle, and the associate level guys don't play nicely with others. Our control is at the top—we audit the books." He drank more beer, but there was no way to tell how many he had had. At least not that I could see, but I was going drink for drink. His eyes were clear and his voice even; I hoped mine were the same.

"Let me help you with the math, Dirt. We own about 70% of the market, whatever market you can think of—so our deposits are substantial. We make the money and the bank picks it up; it gets loaned to whales and paid back with interest and a fee-- $50K on a million, plus the interest. We get the interest and the bank gets the fee. And our money gets paid back into something like two hundred different bank accounts we have at every bank you can think of—home and abroad."

"It's slick," I said. "Like Dial-A-Dope on steroids."

Baker smiled at the Dial-A-Dope reference, and toasted me. "Simpler times, Ryan, simpler times."

He put our empty wing and rib plates behind the bar. "Understand, we needed scale. Our operation is so successful that we had to have somewhere to offload cash and not draw additional attention to ourselves." He grabbed a clean cloth and wiped down the bar, the entire rectangle. He stopped and chatted with a few guests, and even poured a few drinks. When he was back where I was sitting, he said simply *"Brandi's* and *No. 5*, on their own, do nearly $500,000 a month in what the law hypocritically defines as illegal transactions. Ours are the best and the most lucrative, but there are six *Wolves* hang outs within two football throws of this bar." He threw the damp cloth into a bar sink. "Maybe a bit further, depending on who's throwing."

He switched my beer glass for a full one, this one a lighter colour. "Coffee Lager," he said. It was also excellent. "Have you figured out the volume of the third of the market we don't control?" he asked, but didn't wait for a response. "Fuck it, Dirt, *everybody* has deposit slips for Chesapeake Financial.

"And part of our cost of doing business is cash payments to authorities in blue, you know? And I don't think they want their books audited—I laugh every time she goes on TV to disclose the amount confiscated during a bust. Whatever drugs are confiscated, I buy most of them from the cops at a discounted rate and the confiscated money is not making it to evidence. All that money is going to the bank, Dirt." He laughed. "Take it to the bank."

As soon as he mentioned TV, I knew who he was talking about.

"And they," he said, "approached me. One of Xhang's giant pet turtles, but it was obvious who sent him. 'We can make things very easy or very hard for you', he said. He laid it out and I chose easy—diversification is always a good thing. Two weeks later, I'm meeting with her brother at a VPD sponsored BBQ." He laughed. "Talk about subtle."

I let that sit for a second or two. "It was all speculation until you said that."

"Hey, Dirt," he said, "Galileo said that 'all truths are easy to understand once they are discovered; the point is to discover them'. You already knew there was a bank. Maybe you needed a push, but you know the truth."

We finished the beer in front of us, and another arrived.

"I'm fucking tired, Dirt. Do you get that?"

"I get tired, AB," I said. "I know tired."

 We were silent for half a beer.

"Okay," Baker said. "I admit to nothing, but I won't be heart-broken if the *Saints* are inconvenienced financially for a while. "Which we won't be," he added. "We'll lose the money we make in lending fees and interest for a while, but that is barely outpacing the service charges we pay. Casino gets a cut, bank gets a cut, and her hand keeps getting stickier." I knew who he meant. "And there's a cost to pay for the protection services we don't need, and apparently don't prevent people like you from walking into the bank during office hours." He moved his glass in circles, spreading the condensation across his freshly wiped bar. "Something else will show up," he said.

He turned half-way on his stool and looked at me until I returned the turn. There, knee to knee, Anthony 'Agony' Baker, leader of the notorious *Silent Saints Motorcycle Club*, said "Help me help you, Dirt. I don't want to do this forever." He turned back to the bar. "Whatever happens," he said, "you will never run out of beer. Wherever you go." He emptied his beer glass. "Just one fucking second of happiness," he said. "Doesn't seem too much to ask, does it?"

I won't swear to this, but I think he added "Dad".

*****

I might have had two or twelve or twenty more beer with Baker. No one was counting or paying or driving, and we talked about a lot of things I would have thought I was incapable of talking about. I told him about what I'd learned in therapy, that fear of never getting back to San Francisco made me drink so that failure became inevitable. How I drove people away who knew me before because I thought that's what they would expect me to be moving forward, when really it was me with the expectations. And Baker told me about the endless hell of trying to run his club within some sort of moral code he could live with.

"I'm not the least bit religious, Dirt. How could I be? But I've made decisions I would wish on no man. I dream about Pistol every night, but I wouldn't change what I did." Pistol was the elephant who showed Jim pictures of his sister on stage at *Brandi's*, the guy Kyle had to prevent Jim from killing. Some things have a way of working themselves out, and everybody carries different weight.

At last call, two VPD officers walked in. Baker didn't even try to hide the envelope he passed them. In return, they were happy to drive me to the hotel.

Baker and I shook hands. He pulled me close. "I want out, Dirt," Baker said. "I want out."

I left a $50 on the bar for the bartender and the cops drove me home.

*****

The *Pan Pacific* suite was very nice, but it was only two bed rooms. While I was drinking beer and eating ribs and chicken wings with Agony Baker, Karen and Rileigh had moved into my bedroom, which relegated me to a pull out in the central living room. Robyn joined me; maybe that was why that pull-out felt far more like home than my place in Calgary.

In the morning, Karen readied Rileigh for school, and when they left, Nesha did a lot of whining.

"Gonna have to get a kid," Kyle said, "just to shut that dog up."

Everybody ignored him, for which I was grateful. "Hey," Terri said from the kitchen, "they've got *Kopi Luwak* coffee. Who wants a cup?"

After the night with Baker, coffee was exactly what I needed. "Pour me two," I said.

"Yes for me too, please," Kyle said.

Seemed like the coffee took a long time to make, but it was quicker to go through the coffee maker than it was to go through the monkey's butt. "*Kopi Luwak is what?*" I yelled. "At some point, before we drink it, you have to tell us that a monkey shit out the beans."

Robyn just laughed. "I don't think she does," she said.

"I told you what I was making," Terri added. "You guys said

yes."

"Where's your cup?" Kyle asked her.

"I'm not drinking coffee that comes out of a monkey's ass," Terri said.

*****

While I had been taking turns with Baker playing therapist the previous evening, Terri had finished her story. She gave us each a copy and asked us for our thoughts. "Quickly," she said. "I need to turn it in before 10 so they can complete the layout and artwork."

Karen had already provided her thoughts. "It's perfect," she said. "Explosive and indignant. I love it."

> **Dedicated to Mya James. We miss you.**
>
> *Vancouver Police Chief Tara Callan has made it a mission to clean Vancouver streets of drugs and crime. She has celebrated many public wins and is a stickler for transparency. But how much is real, and how much is show?*
>
> *Despite many federal and local law enforcement studies that suggest Vancouver is Ground Zero for millions of illegal cash activities on a monthly basis, the Chief continues to promote the idea that highly publicized busts like the recent one of a* Grave Wolves *safe house in North Vancouver are keeping the streets clear of drugs, guns and criminals.*
>
> *Calgary investigator Ryan Simms, however, has found undeniable proof that Ground Zero is alive and well and exists with the Chief's tacit approval. In short, Simms has found evidence that the VPD and multiple inter-jurisdictional Task Forces either cannot find or choose to ignore. Simms*

has evidence that a private underground bank exists in the Lower Mainland and washes millions of dollars a year and he has evidence of who runs the bank and where it is located. This evidence will be shared with a Federal Money Laundering Task Force later today.

"Could have mentioned my name a few more times here," I said. "Maybe tossed in my address and social insurance number."

As detailed in prior Vancouver Sun *stories, the Vancouver Model washes millions of dollars per year through legitimate and controlled casinos—by some provincial estimates, up to $500 million per year.*

Deposits are made, and then the bank lends money to gamblers, or 'whales', who brazenly take suitcases and hockey bags and duffel bags of twenties and fifties to Lower Mainland casinos and change the cash for chips. For cash transactions, no proof of the money's origin is required.

When cashed, the chips are deposited into a Personal Gaming Account, or PGA, which is required by BC Casinos for any transactions over $10,000. When these PGA's are cashed out, however, they are done so by bank draft or cheque; as a result, previously suspicious cash—most definitely the result of illegal activity—is now clean. This money is then deposited into legitimate bank accounts, the house (or, in this case, the underground bank) is paid interest and transaction fees and the process, like the laundry it represents, starts its own repeat cycle.

According to Simms, one man controls all of this action.

Once this evidence has been provided to the appropriate authorities, we will make this information public. The information Simms possesses has been validated by at least one ranking member of the Provincial Prosecutor's office.

Sure of the physical location of this bank due to Simms' efforts, federal authorities are planning a raid of the underground bank hoping to finally put a dent in the un-ending and illegal money laundering business.

The cash cycled through this laundry is predominantly the result of drug trafficking, and is provided almost exclusively by motorcycle clubs such as, but not solely, the Silent Saints *controlled by Anthony Agony Baker. According to Simms, however, another source of funds is money confiscated by police departments across the Lower Mainland through arrests and raids.*

This has long been rumoured in the criminal community; in fact, the Grave Wolves *actually filed a notice of appeal last year to request full disclosure of assets and cash confiscated versus what was disclosed in court. The* Wolves *contend that while $2.4 M was turned in as evidence, more than $7M in cash and equipment was confiscated. Where, they and now others ask, is the missing money?*

As a result of this notice of appeal, Provincial Prosecutors have called for a complete audit of all money confiscated and disclosed by law enforcement throughout the province. Two huge questions will be asked after this audit is complete: if money is missing, where did it go? And if money is missing, who is responsible for repayment?

This second question was asked specifically in a highly-publicized trial in Hamilton last year, where a 17-year veteran officer was found guilty of taking bribes and even selling confiscated equipment to drug dealers. In addition to a 14-year prison sentence, Det. Const. Kevin Forsite was fined $250,000. If not paid within twelve months of sentencing, Forsite will have another three years added to his sentence.

The Lower Mainland remains awash in drugs and cash.

Multiple attempts have been made by civilian authorities to stem the flood of cash; most notably by Gareth Davis, former civilian lead of the Joint Investigation Gaming Investigation Team (JIGIT). Mr. Davis, soon after making his concerns and evidence public after being rebuked by his employer, was killed last week in a hail of gunfire outside his Marpole home. His four year old son was also killed in the daylight attack. No arrests have been made and Vancouver Police continue to state that Mr. Davis was not the intended target. Two known gang members, far off their turf, were killed that same morning and one injured.

On a rainy night In April of last year, VPD Constable Jim Edwards was murdered at Crab Park in an explosion that also killed a man named Denis Sault. Constable Edwards was a vocal critic of Chief Callan and a virulent and eager tormentor of the Saints Motorcycle Club, *whom he believed to be responsible for the death of his younger sister —an assertion that cannot be proven.*

Interestingly, Mr. Sault was a partner at Engs & Associates in Vancouver and was solely responsible for auditing the books of the BC Lottery Commission. Before he was murdered, Mr. Sault had confided to Mr. Davis that he had some startling news and Engs & Associates had even called a press conference for later that week. The press conference was never held.

And last week, there was a fourth violent death that seemingly connects with the Vancouver Model. Sarah James, a twenty-seven year old lab technician from City Centre, was killed when the car she borrowed for the day was destroyed by a bomb connected to the ignition switch. The owner of that car is this reporter.

Suspicion for these acts has been cast on the Silent Saints, *who are undoubtedly guilty of many things. Ryan Simms, however, by trying to convict the* Saints *of these acts has done the opposite. Simms has the necessary evidence to clear the* Saints *of these deaths and instead has cast doubt on a Richmond resident who is, as they say, known to the law—and has a direct relationship with the Vancouver Chief of Police. As charges have not been laid, the Vancouver Sun will not be naming this person at this time.*

Chief Callan was appointed in August of 1996, shortly after the prior chief was terminated for inappropriate conduct, abuse of power and misuse of public funds. But have things in Vancouver improved? Access to information requests have revealed that the Public Police Oversight Committee (PPOC) has *investigated the Chief's department on seven separate occasions.*

These numbers, however, are likely an understatement as the committee itself cites a lack of cooperation within the VPD and an attitude of 'entitlement, obfuscation and improper oversight and internal control'.

The findings of the PPOC *are not pretty. In fact, their published report indicates that the VPD is violently linked to the criminals the Chief says they are protecting us from. The committee states that the improper release of police information to criminals 'to prevent or minimize the results of planned police activity has been the most common type of corrupt behaviour, followed by fraud, misuse of police officer status, theft and interference with the judicial process.' Ironically, Chief Callan filed similar charges against her former employer, the Regional District of Durham Police Department.*

That was the end to what was going to be the front page story. Inside, there would be numerous articles, all written by Terri, detailing the information we had learned about the Chief's background and time in Hamilton and in-depth articles about the structure of the Saints and other motorcycle clubs. There would also be flow charts detailing the Vancouver Model and, potentially to seem balanced, a summary of the Chief's drug busts. There would be a full reporting of everything that had happened to that police force, explaining how the Chief made her bones, so to speak. Another reporter had been dispatched to speak to executives of Engs & Associates to learn any possible details of what Sault was going to share.

When we were all finished reading, I said "Go ahead and press send. That's masterful work."

"Who picks you up first?" Terri replied. "Callan, Zags or one of Baker's crew trying to impress the boss?"

"Won't be the *Saints*," I said.

*****

The next day, the Canadian Security Intelligence Service and a national team of RCMP officers—without knowledge or consent from the VPD—raided Chesapeake Financial. Expecting to find millions in cash in an underground bank, they found nothing but an empty office and two bundles of cash. One was wrapped in a publicity shot of Terri and the other was wrapped in an old game photo of Robyn, a clear and obvious fuck you to the cops. And probably me, come to think of it.

The feds were displeased, to say the least. Terri and her editors received quite a few calls from Federal lawyers threatening all kinds of things that simply weren't true—in Canada, as in the States, laws that protect reporters and their sources are sacrosanct. There are no laws against hot air, though, and Terri and her paper heard a lot of that.

I was on less firm legal ground, we thought, but despite the hard time Terri's bosses were getting, nobody in law enforcement seemed that upset with me. Political bluster, we thought, of the fury surrounding Terri, or some serious cover-your-ass.

Collectively, we knew that there was one huge gap in our thinking to this point and we were just waiting for somebody of importance to bring it up. We knew that the Chief was Faas Xhang's sister and that Xhang was of questionable moral character and we knew that Xhang was involved with Chesapeake Financial—but we had no conclusive proof that Chesapeake Financial was Ground Zero, only conjecture. Although the bricks of cash wrapped in pictures of Robyn and Terri seemed a strong indication we were correct.

Because of this, Karen had asked a good friend of hers to represent me—and all of us, if necessary— legally and he had agreed without hesitation. Karen can be compelling. The Feds did ask me to come in—not for questioning, but 'to share my thoughts and information'. It was a ten-minute walk to the office space they were using, part of the Revenue Canada building on West Hastings.

My new counsel, an impeccable and distinguished Vancouver socialite named Scott Wirth, noted with irony how wrapping the left behind cash in pictures of me legitimized our 'conclusive speculation'. Scott spent the day with me at RCMP headquarters and while hanging out with anyone for seventeen straight hours is often difficult, hanging with Scott was far from the worst day I've ever had—and it was significantly better than I had expected it to be. Probably a four out of ten overall when I was expecting a negative twelve.

Scott had a perfectly trimmed Van Dyke beard and longish red hair swept straight back. In an immaculately tailored grey window-pane three piece suit and white shirt that never wrinkled, he was the living embodiment of a Southern gentleman. The feds seemed to enjoy our—or at least Scott's—company. They were obviously interested in the work my friends and I had done collectively, but there was nothing dismissive or condescending about them in any way. In fact, in some ways, they were grateful. And they fed us well—no cafeteria food, they actually brought us Hon's. It took a while, but I finally got my shrimp in garlic sauce. And a fork.

"You've certainly sped this action up," one of the Feds said. I met so many, I couldn't keep track of their names or titles or the acronyms they represented. Very few were in uniform. "The advantage of being a private citizen."

"We've had our eyes out west for quite some time," another said. "But anytime we felt we were close to something, a witness or evidence would disappear or we were convinced to wait for an even bigger opportunity that somehow never came."

We ate lunch in a board room, cops and people in suits coming and going. I met Stephanie Page, Deputy Director of Criminal Investigations, who said "We really did think it was your buddy Jim. We were set to take action." She was surprisingly petite yet formidable. *Like the Chief.* I was glad I was on Page's side. "We were saddened by his death because we thought it took away our case." She looked at me and raised her eyebrows. "That sounded harsh—we are very sorry he is gone, but it helps that we know now it was for the right reasons. Does that make sense?"

I told her that it did. After that, Scott and I were alone. "Is this for real?" I asked. "Or are they playing me for something?"

"I think it's real," he said. "If it's misdirection, it's being managed beautifully. My sense is that it's genuine admiration." He dipped his head slightly and frowned. "Maybe appreciation rather than admiration." He put his hand in the air and made a circling gesture with his index finger. "All these people," he said, "look at how many have come and gone today. I need a program to keep them straight, and not one person has criticized you. No bad cop, worse cop."

"I noticed that," I said. "Only good cop, friendly cop."

"I believe that they're impressed. You and your crew have done something in a matter of days that apparently these alphabet organizations have been working on for a number of years." He nodded at me. "And you're a good client. I haven't had to tell you to shut up once."

When the day was done and there was nobody left to talk to, Stephanie, the petite Deputy Director of Criminal Investigations, sent me home with a box of homemade dog treats.

She did have one piece of advice: "Leave it to us now. We'll bring this home."

I wish I'd been able to comply.

CHAPTER 16

As soon as we left the RCMP building, I heard my dog howl. Kyle was driving his Dad's classic 1978 Dodge Power Wagon and they were across the street parked in an obvious no parking or loading zone. Scott and I shook hands. "Nobody I'd rather spend a day at a police station with," I said. He laughed and gave my hand an extra shake.

"Back at you," he said. "Next time we hang, let's do it somewhere in the sun."

Kyle and I did the man hug thing and Nesha was relieving herself on some weeds. We watched Scott turn south in his vintage 1966 British Racing Green Jaguar E-Type. "If that's his winter car, I can't wait to see what he drives in the summer," Kyle said.

"Probably a Bronco," I said. "Any word on mine?"

"Lonnie finished it yesterday," he said. "Detailed it too." He shook his head in mock sadness. "You Ford guys, I don't get it." He handed me the keys. "I picked these up earlier, he said he'd leave it outside the gate." He looked at Nesha and shook his head. "You can take this fur monster home in it. She rode in the bed and still managed to get hair in the cab."

I smiled, and tossed the keys in the air. "Everything is coming up Dirt," I said. "Like Joaquin Andujar said, 'it's great to be alive, because when you're dead, you can't drink beer'."

"Pitcher for the Cardinals, right?" he asked. I nodded. "Was he the same guy who said the only real sports are softball, golf and bowling because you can drink when you play them."

"Our kind of guy," I said. "Our kind of guy."

There was a light mist falling, one that just becomes part of an early Vancouver spring. My sister calls it a dry rain, you can walk in it for hours and not be soaked, but you can't escape it. My truck was exactly where promised. Nesha seemed happy to see it, but she also seemed sad to know that she would be riding inside again. From being in the open bed of Kyle's truck for less than five minutes, her coat was glistening under the streetlights.

The Bronco was facing east and Kyle was facing west. We bumped fists. "See you at the hotel, Dirt Bag."

I was a little later than anticipated. But, then again, so was he.

*****

The Bronco was parked on River Road in Richmond, almost directly under the Knight Street Bridge. Right there, at another intersection of Vancouver and Richmond, River Road itself can go hours on the brightest of days without seeing the sun because of how it's dominated by the shadows of the on and off ramps of the bridge and high-rise condos and airport hotels. Despite this perpetual darkness, the area itself is a thriving community of river-based businesses—salvage yards, marine mechanics, tow yards, equipment manufacturers and suppliers, and tug boat docks.

On the river side, though, away from the shadows, it's a different world. Businesses, yes—boat yards and docks and fuel stations, but also grass and willow trees and picnic tables for the employees. I know the area well because Kyle and I spent five winters working on the river tugs for Mr. Richards—I even spent two additional winters there after I didn't need the money. His old business, *Alley Cat Towing*, was directly in front

283

of me, maybe half a kilometre down the road.

After Mr. Richards' death, *Alley Cat* was absorbed by his brother, also a tug boat operator. The business is now called *Richards' Salvage & Tug* and it's this business that now calls the dilapidated river side cottage and dock home. They do pay a respectful amount of homage to *Alley Cat;* in fact, I know from being there in the past that the first thing you see when you enter the office is a picture of Jean Claude Van Damme jumping on to one of the *Alley Cat* tugs—Jean Claude shot a movie there once. By all accounts, he was a pretty cool guy.

Nesha had never met Mr. Richards, but she agreed to go and visit his old dock and buildings.

So, really, everything that happened from there is her fault.

Visiting *Alley Cat* took me in the opposite direction of where Kyle was headed. To get home directly, I would have needed to turn around and follow him, but I wanted a trip down memory lane and figured I'd earned it. Pulling into the parking lot, I'd forgotten how big it was. The lot itself is half gravel and half cement. Nose to nose parking on the cement half is delineated by six inch high concrete barriers. At the far east of the lot is the original cottage, converted into haphazard office space, and to the left of that are three full size storage containers placed in a jumbled U shape. This is where all the day to day equipment is stored for the tugs—marine rope and bollards, pike poles and chains, camper locks and axes. And cans and cans of coffee—Folger's Crystals when I worked there.

Behind the storage units is a ten-foot high chain link fence, a fifteen foot drop, and then the Fraser River. I never knew if the fence was to keep people away from the river, or sea creatures away from the people. The ramp down to the well-maintained dock is generally in rough shape, with asphalt roofing tiles and 1x2s nailed down for traction. At the dock, there are always three or four good-sized tugs either coming on or going off shift or waiting to be repaired.

I rolled down my window, and from the sound of the river to my left, it was clearly flooding. The boats need to work the high tide, so we were about an hour away from the parking lot and neighbourhood springing to life. I was actually surprised there were no cars in the lot.

Surprise instantly became fear as every piece of glass in my truck—and in a Bronco, there is a significant amount of glass —shattered, including the just replaced side window, as two smallish SUVs won a three-way game of chicken that I didn't know I was playing.

The cars might have been Honda CRVs, I'm not really sure as everything happened so fast. But they obviously approached with no lights and hit me from both sides. Front and side airbags deployed and most assuredly saved my life, if not my surgically repaired shoulder. The tail gate sprung, and Nesha —panicked—jumped for it, taking off into the night. *Good luck finding her. Black dog, black night. I hope she stays out of the river; it's running too fast.* And then, reality set in: *what the fuck just happened?*

The windshield had somehow stayed mostly intact and in place, but with SUVs parked rudely inside my truck on the driver and passenger sides, my only exit option was to follow Nesha. Which I did. I think I managed it gracefully, but the two James Bond sized villains I had met at Chesapeake Financial might say differently. *What do they know? I am always graceful. Let's see them get out of that truck. Fat fucks.*

I took a physical inventory, and received a barely passing grade. I was bleeding fairly heavily from the forehead and my left shoulder, the one that took on Wrigley Field, was definitely separated. And there was something wrong with my right knee. *Have to stay off the basketball court for a while—sorry Robyn. But head wounds bleed and you're right handed. All good.*

There are worse outcomes of simultaneous T-bone collisions. "Hey guys," I said, "glad you're here. Is Mr. Chesapeake ready to meet me now?"

On my way out of the Bronco, my hand had found an old bat and I had grabbed it. I'd forgotten I even had it, but was glad to have it now—although I wasn't sure how much protection it would offer against these two guys. I was about to find out. They weren't hiding their guns, so I made no effort to hide my bat—a game used Adirondack Big Stick, signed by an old Giants teammate, Matt Williams.

"Did you see which way my dog ran?" I asked. "She loves to swim, but the river is moving too fast for her. Maybe I'll just go after her. I'll come by your office tomorrow—looks like there's something you want to discuss."

They raised their guns so they were pointing at my chest, which I took as an invitation to stay. "Guys, my dog," I said. "Come on now, have a heart. She's not from around here."

Suddenly we were all bathed in the bright lights of a sports car's high beams. I had also not heard this one coming. *Must be the mist muffling sounds.*

"You'll stay," one of the guys said. "See what the boss wants with you."

"This Chesapeake guy," I said, "what the fuck is his problem?"

At that point, the dialogue became predictable:

"You're the guy with a problem."

"Don't think so, I'm not morbidly obese."

Like that, but with fewer laughs than expected.

And then I did something I didn't know I could do—I swung a baseball bat at another person with clear and obvious intent. I looked at the guy on my left, and then swung the bat as hard as I could at the guy on the right. He started to fall, and even the mist didn't muffle the sound of his arm breaking; in the headlights, I could also see the bright white bone splinters from the compound fracture. I've always had a short, compact swing and, one handed, it was even more so. I had plenty of time to reload and take another swing, this time at a knee—and I heard that break too.

His gun was in a pool of darkness at our feet. I couldn't see it, but I could see his head and I took a half-swing at that. I hoped a half-swing wouldn't kill him but would help him sleep for a while to think about life choices. *Where's the gun? Gun. Why the fuck haven't I been shot?*

The answer to that one was simple. I hadn't been shot because my 100 pound dog was hanging off my other new friend's shooting arm. I'm not going to lie—it looked like it hurt. A lot. Nesha wasn't letting go; in fact, I thought she might rip his arm out of the socket, and I had surprisingly mixed feelings on that. And unlike with the *Saints* in Golden, Nesha's attack was absolutely silent.

Until it wasn't. To this day, I have no idea which happened first—Nesha's guttural scream as her opponent stabbed her in the back with what turned out to be a 4-1/4" gut hook blade, or his head disappearing in a burst of red and white and grey.

Standing over Nesha was Anthony Baker. I could see smoke coming from the muzzle of his gun. I ran to my dog, and as I fell to the ground to comfort her—*she's alive*—there was a very loud noise behind me and then Baker made a very strange noise in front of me. I could taste copper, and realized that it was the sense of blood—Baker's, Nesha's, mine. Baker lay bleeding in a pool of Nesha's blood. "Shoulder and chest," he said. "Bad." And then Anthony 'Agony' Baker, leader of the notorious *Silent Saints Motorcycle Club*, did the strangest thing. "I'll stay with her, Dirt. She won't be alone. But the bad guy is getting away."

He was right. Whoever shot Baker did so from the car with the headlights, which were now gone. In their place, I could see tail lights—and then they stopped. The engine revved manically. *It's going to red-line for sure.* I followed the sound and saw that the car was low, a brand new BMW M Roadster, and it was stuck on one of the concrete parking barriers. *Nice driving.* The motor was revving uselessly and all four tires were spinning, six inches off the ground.

I kissed my dog and grabbed the bat. "Dirt," Baker said. "Maybe take one of those." He used his good hand to point at a nice selection of guns lying on the ground.

"Right," I said. "If I drop the bat, I can hit him with one of those."

"Or you could shoot him," he replied. "What I would do."

I went to hand him my phone. I wanted to say "Call it in" like they always say on cop shows, but he beat me to it. "Already done," he said. "No cops. But Kyle is on his way, and he's bringing a vet. I have one who makes house calls; ironically, he's used to working on people." He was talking fine, although strained, and there was no blood in his mouth. From my life around sprains and strains and contusions, I diagnosed him as stable.

The BMW's engine was still revving. *More gas isn't getting you off that barricade. I hope you fight as dumb as you drive.* "Hey, AB," I said, "how do I use one of these things? Isn't there like a safety or something?"

He winced, I assume from the pain and not my ignorance; he was bleeding quite heavily, as was my dog. But, god love her, her tail was wagging, albeit slowly. "Take mine," he said and tried to slide it to me with his foot. "The safety is already off."

*****

I don't know anything about anything—I know nothing about trucks or cars, I'm easy prey for salespeople, I know nothing about women, and in a matter of a very few seasons, I forgot how to hit a curveball. But even I knew that, whoever was in that beached car, had the potential to take the night on an even greater turn for the worst. *Why aren't they shooting?*

The car was sixty yards away. Far enough away that I could hit it easily by throwing rocks, but probably not so easily by shooting bullets. But that certainly didn't mean whoever was in the car couldn't and wouldn't shoot me like they had Baker. *Maybe they'll throw rocks back and it will be a fair fight.*

"If we wait," Baker said, "my guys will be here and take care of this. He thinks he's pinned down, so he won't get out. I assume he's making calls for some help." Waiting for Baker's guy suddenly seemed like the prudent course of action and I was about to agree, but then Nesha convulsed. She whimpered, there was blood coming from her nose, and I was sure I was going to lose her.

I always had thought that the expression 'seeing red' was hyperbole; I can tell you for sure that it is not. With the world tinted red, light in the centre and darker around the edges, I picked up the other two guns and had Baker check the safeties. They were all off—or on, I'm not sure. Either way, they were in a position to be fired. I put them both in the pocket of my hoodie—*who needs a holster?*—and then thought better of that idea. I gave a gun to Baker. "She's alive when I get back, understand? Protect her." What could he say to that?

The pain in my left shoulder was excruciating and the shoulder itself felt like it was hanging by tendons. It was most certainly being kept in place by my sweatshirt, but at least my left hand could hold the bat. I considered my options and chose stealth. So I counted to three and ran at the car as fast as

I could while shooting all the bullets out of the first gun. Some of them might have hit the car, I don't know. No windows or taillights broke, but maybe I shot the hell out of the trunk. There was a lot of noise.

When I was even with the car, since it was in my right hand, I turned the gun around to smash the driver-side window. Instead, I burned the hell out of my hand on the muzzle and dropped the gun in a puddle. I figured that probably wasn't good for it, but figured Baker would understand. Using the bat, I hit my third home run of the night and the window shattered into a million pieces that looked like diamonds falling onto a velvet board.

The guy inside did have a gun, but my stealth attack under a hail of bullets had worked, and he didn't use it. While glass was still falling, he scrambled across the seats and exited through the passenger side door. He did not run and I was grateful. If he had, I certainly wouldn't have caught him.

"Fass," I said as the Chief's brother walked around the car, "nice shoes." And they were really nice—white and red leather Puma driving shoes with a minimum sole so that the person wearing them could really feel the pedals. "Didn't help you, though, did they? Don't need driving shoes when your car isn't on the ground." *If I don't get into a car chase with him, maybe we'll be okay.*

He saw that I wasn't armed and assumed he had me. He stepped close, and then took another half-step. With the size difference, I assumed he needed to close the gap before doing any of that crazy martial arts stuff. I decided not to wait and used the bat to knock the gun out of his hand. *Thank you Matt.* "Used to having people do the heavy lifting for you, I guess." I'm pretty sure he was wearing the same red Adidas track suit Kyle and I had seen him in the other day, but it could have been my vision.

Even after looking at his gun on the ground and kicking it as far away as I could, I embarrassingly had forgotten about the back up in the pocket of my sweatshirt. Xhang did have a very nasty looking knife—maybe an eight inch serrated blade with a hook at the end. In fact, he had two. "You brought knives to a bat fight," I said.

He did some of those fast and fancy knife movements you see in movies, but neither of us moved. We were six feet apart, too far for me to reach with the bat now but certainly close enough for him to throw a knife and put an end to a less than stellar evening.

"You're not walking away," he said. "Everyone else we will deal with directly, over time." The Chief's brother's English was almost perfect. But not quite. There was a natural accent trying to come through that he was trying to avoid—the result was less than he hoped. His voice was memorable. But I'd never heard it before. "Why," he asked, "why the fuck do you give a fuck?" Slight accent or not, his swearing was perfect.

"I had the same conversation with your sister the other day," I said. At 'sister', he gave a definite tell, a quick twitch to his head as he looked away and then back. "You need to give me more to go on. Why exactly what?" I was proud of myself for not swearing; seems it would have been forgiven under the circumstances. *Taking the high road.*

"You could have stayed in Calgary," he said. "One dead cop in Vancouver, who cares? You didn't."

"Truth hurts," I said, truthfully. "You got me there. But that also kind of explains why I couldn't stay in Calgary. Plus," I added as a reminder, "you've killed six more since Jim—including a four-year old kid."

He shrugged. That seemed a particularly cold response. My fear rose to another level, yet I still didn't think about the gun in my pocket. *Ground Zero,* I thought. *This is Ground Zero. Fuck all those other Ground Zeros.* "Is it too late to talk about my investments?" I asked.

"If you'd left well enough alone, nobody gets hurt. This is on you," he said. I had trouble with that logic.

"Not on me," I said. "Not in any way. This is all you and your fucked up sister. Your mom must have been a real bitch." *So much for the high road.*

I ran a quick calculation of my odds in fighting this guy. Then I ran them again, with no improvement. *Even if I knew how to fight, I can't fight this guy. Baker's down, Nesha's down. I'm on my own with a guy I told the world is the single biggest money launder in Canada.* I looked at the knives. *I don't think he likes me.*

The rain had intensified, and the blades were dripping. My vision had cleared, so at least the rain didn't look red. *This guy is a multiple champion of a ridiculous number of combative sports, and I kicked a guy in the balls a couple of days ago. The knives will be red soon enough.*

And then the yard exploded in engine noise and light. Not police lights, just head lights. But lots of them. First into the lot was Kyle in his Dad's truck, followed by the red and blue trucks Karen and I had seen in Golden.

"Should have brought more bad guys," I said to Xhang. He neither agreed nor disagreed, he just ran. *Crazy shit happens when you're sober.* His options were limited as Baker's guys were behind me, so he couldn't head for the street. Instead, he made a decision that I am sure he would like to reconsider—he headed for the water and vaulted the eight-foot security gate at the top of the ramp like it was nothing. I didn't hesitate— at least I don't think I hesitated. *Baker said he's got a vet.* But unlike Xhang, I didn't climb the gate—I still knew the security code.

Despite the asphalt tiles and 1x2s, the ramp was slick. But Xhang's driving shoes held up, and he navigated it easily. Once on the dock, though, his options were limited. Two river tugs, the *Celtic* and *Jesse Richards* were tied up and accessible, but Xhang didn't strike me as knowing his way around 40-foot working tugs. I was right, he ran past them both.

The dock at the Richards' operation is essentially a huge T, with the horizontal bar being significantly longer than the vertical. On the land side of the dock are a number of boat houses—basically sheds floating on the water with no bottom. From the dock, there are man doors into these buildings, but they were locked. With no bottoms, getting in there wouldn't have helped him anyway.

Xhang, from what he thought was a position of strength even five minutes ago, had now limited himself to three options. One, he could try and swim. In a flooding tide on a working river, I really hoped he wouldn't choose this option. Two—and this is the option I would have chosen—since we were the only two people on the dock, he could have made a stand and fought me for dock supremacy. I can pretty much guarantee that, even if I finally remembered the gun in my pocket, he would have won. Or, three, he could jump onto the string of cedar log booms chained to the dock. This option presented Xhang with the least upside and, fortunately for me, it's the one he chose. Perhaps he thought that the booms would act as a bridge and take him to dry land once he made it across. That's not how it works.

Almost like he didn't think this through. True, I wasn't wearing cork boots—essentially, Wellingtons with spikes, an absolute necessity for walking on booms—but Xhang was wearing actual driving shoes. And I'd spent seven winters working on log booms. A log boom is simply a rectangle of logs, free floating and trapped inside four boom sticks—the outside perimeter of the boom. Each boom stick has an O-ring, maybe eight inches in diameter, drilled into it and River Rats—the guys who get paid to climb the booms in all kinds of horrible weather and river conditions—use forty-pound link chains to either attach or separate one boom to or from another. The chains themselves have a toggle at one end and an O ring at the other and the toggle is passed through the boom stick ring and then attached to itself. Somehow, it is never a bright, sunny day when you work the booms.

The Fraser River is the Highway 401 of rivers. In BC, stretches of the Fraser are vital for tug-boats to get log booms—cedar, fir, poplar, pine, and the giant cypress—to the Pacific Ocean to be transported around the world. BC logs have long been valued internationally because of their availability and governmentally deflated prices, although recently, increased tariffs have put a damper on the industry.

Companies around the world order these booms and each boom is called a section. So a company in Louisiana might order fourteen sections of fir, and a company in Japan might need seventeen sections of cedar.

Because of this, the tidal flats of the Fraser, from New Westminster, past the Musqueam Indian Band and ending at the water surrounding the University of BC campus, are an ever changing log-boom parking lot. Companies like *Alley Cat Towing* and *Richards' Tug* are well-paid valets, conduits from the current owner of the booms to the future owner of the booms. Storage of the booms is like a game of Battleship, except completely devoid of all obvious logic. Booms are owned by individual companies, but stored collectively. Each boom is stored according to Battleship principals, so when a company needs A2, river tugs need to identify that section, cut it free, and wait at the mouth of the Fraser for the boom to be picked up by a larger, Ocean going, boat.

This is the choice Xhang made, and I am eternally grateful. The logs inside a boom are generally consistent in length and diameter. There are exceptions, and cedar, given the size of some of the trees that are logged, is often that. The string Xhang had chosen to climb onto was nothing more than a remainder bin—some of the logs were showing six to eight feet above the water, others were maybe a foot. River Rats hate these booms, especially at night and especially on a flooding tide in the rain, because they are so hard to navigate. Often, when you jump down from a larger log, you will come across a seal and sometimes even a sea lion. They are not happy to see you. *Score one for me; he's going to drown.*

In the flooding tide, the tail end of the cedar boom was straining for the open water. The toe end of the boom was struggling against its chains. This would be helpful for either the *Celtic* or the *Jesse Richards,* whichever boat was going to cut it free and take it to the mouth of the Georgia Straight, where they would hand the string to an ocean tug who would tow it up or down the Pacific depending on final destination.

To this day, I don't know why I did what I did next: I released the chains securing the four-section boom to the dock. Knowing how expensive the chains are, I laid them carefully on the dock for the Richards' guys to pick up later. Perhaps letting the boom go actually made sense—once floating free on the Fraser, where was Xhang going to go? It would take a tug to catch him and that certainly could have meant cops or Coast Guard or other authorities to bring it all home. It could have ended right there. So why did I jump on and join him for the ride?

It didn't take long for Xhang to get into trouble. Truthfully, he might have been okay on a fir boom, something relatively flat. But this uneven cedar boom, with some huge logs, on a choppy and windy night on a running tide, was too much for him. He slipped early and often and fell hard each time. Fortunately for him, each time he fell, he was inside the boom rather than river side where he would have been swept away. As it was, he fell in open water between floating logs and the danger of logs shifting and crushing him was real. It happens two or three times a year to guys who work the booms for a living, and they are comfortable with the circumstances. Xhang did not look comfortable on the logs or in the water, let alone with the chop and the cold. *I don't think he can swim.* He fell again and managed to pull himself onto a smaller log and stand.

If he'd just stayed put, admitted temporary defeat and said 'No Mas', my conscience would be a lot clearer than it is today. This is the darkness separate from the night. Xhang did none of those things. Instead, with nowhere to go in an environment he simply did not understand, he tried to run. *Fight or flight, I guess.*

River Rats learn early to spot sinkers: logs floating at the surface, but water logged and unable to carry any weight. Step on a sinker, down you go. And if the boom closes over you, you might not make it out. Faas Xhang was a lot of things, maybe even a rat, but he wasn't a River Rat. Cold and wet and probably scared and certainly disoriented on the boom and in the mist, he stepped on a sinker. For the third time that night, I heard a bone break.

Xhang was trapped. When he felt the log beneath him start to sink, he made a desperate lunge for another stick. With nothing solid to push off, however, he really just sunk the log he was on and fell in an awkward and painful position. His left leg was out of the water, mostly wrapped around a mid-sized log, but the rest of him was in the water. I could only see his torso, his right leg was stuck between two logs and as the logs moved in the water, I could hear the bones grinding.

I surprised myself with the coldness of my words. "Drop the

knives in the water and I will think about helping you." I was too close to him, and he was incredibly strong. Instead of dropping the knives in the Fraser River like I'd asked, he used one of them to stab me in the right leg. *Fight or flight.* The blade went in my calf and the hook on the end came out my shin. Somehow, he missed bone, but the pain was a solid eight. *Definitely no basketball.* I may have screamed—maybe the pain was a nine—but if I did, only Xhang could hear it and I'd stopped caring about him a few boom sections ago.

My leg gave way, but I was safe where I was, assuming I stayed out of his reach. I sat on a decent sized log and put my calf in the freezing cold water to hopefully stop the bleeding. As I sat, imagining the designs the blood made in the water, I noticed the weight of the gun in my sweatshirt pocket. *I am so stupid. I could have ended this before it started, probably wouldn't have even needed to fire it.*

"Listen," I said to Xhang, "I have a gun and you don't." I showed it to him. He didn't seem impressed but, to be fair, he had more immediate concerns. "You are badly injured and in the water, trapped between logs and I am not." I rocked the log I was sitting on to emphasize the point and, again, I could hear his leg bones grind. In the resulting wave, with his mouth wide open from screaming, Xhang drank more river water. "I am walking away right now, the only question is will you be in the water or on a boom when I go?"

At that, I remembered our rather untenable predicament— alone, on a log boom untethered in a river flowing north of four knots an hour, with nothing to stop us but sand bars, bridge abatements, shipping containers or land. I wasn't looking forward to the landing. Or remaining free and hitting the open ocean. But whatever happened, I would probably be okay; Xhang, on the other hand, was in a lot of trouble for a lot of reasons.

And I wasn't sure how much I wanted to help. Purely out of spite and frustration, I rocked the log again. Over his screams, I heard the distinctive diesel growl of the *Jesse Richards*. This run away cedar boom was worth about forty grand. I wasn't surprised that the lads had made retrieving it the first order of business once they got to work and noticed it was gone. I was surprised, however, when I heard Kyle behind me.

"This is so fucking tiresome," he said, but his voice was light. "Bad guy's associates are defeated by the good guy; good guy gets into trouble with the head bad guy; good guy's friend's show up; right wins over wrong; we all go home and wished we hadn't eaten so much popcorn."

"Which are we?" an obviously sea-sick Orangutan asked. He was trying to balance himself with an eight-foot pike pole on the rolling logs, but each time he planted the pole, he lost balance trying to pull it free.

"Go," Kyle said to me. "These guys will help you to the *Jesse*, she's idling off starboard," he said. I noticed then that Black Beard was on the boom as well, looking far more comfortable than Orangutan.

"Used to work for *SeaSpan*," he said. "The *Celtic* is already hooked on at the tail end. It's where we came from."

"Nobody gets an ocean cruise today," Kyle said. Black Beard also had a pike pole, and he had hooked it through Xhang's jacket to keep his head above water.

"He'll have hypothermia soon," I said.

Kyle reached for the gun in my hand, but I pulled it away. "I've been through three years of not caring about being alive, Kyle. Now, I'm past that and these guys tried to take it away." I was waving the gun around, and included Black Beard and Orangutan in the 'these guys' comment. "For what?"

"Money," Kyle said. "It's always money."

"Fuck that. He stays in the water." I tried to grab Black Beard's pike pole, but he was too quick. More likely, I was too slow. "Push him in all the way. Nobody has to know. I know you guys have done it before." I'm pretty sure I was on the verge of having a break down. "Orangutan goes in too."

"No he doesn't," Kyle said. "No he doesn't. Whatever happens here, you'll know." He reached for the gun again. "You had trouble with losing baseball, Dirt. You think you can live with murder?"

"So what? Maybe I won't like myself very much, but I've gotten used to that. I've had practice. And it's worth it for the hell that these fuckers have put my friends through. And I wasn't here, Kyle, I wasn't here when you guys needed me."

"Ryan," he said. "Listen to me. If you want a pity party, we'll do it later. We can sell tickets. But you are here now, when it mattered. But you need to go. Now. They will take care of this."

"They stabbed my fucking dog," I said.

"Go get her," Kyle said. "Take care of her." Xhang was struggling, his leg grip on the wet log was slipping and Black Beard wasn't trying his hardest to keep him afloat.

"You don't want this," Black Beard said. "Go. We're here 'cause the boss says to be here. This is what we do, not you."

I looked at Black Beard. I understood the words he used, but they were problematic. I had to figure them out, quickly. "Nesha's alive?" I asked Kyle.

"She is. Baker is with her. Go, Ryan. It's over."

And I went. I needed Kyle's help to walk, but I went, Blackbeard's words ringing in my ears.

Four hours later, Baker called. It was all over but the telling.

CHAPTER 17

O r almost over. Eight hours after Baker called, our original crew was together at the hotel. The same vet that had saved Nesha's life had set my shoulder, cleaned and sutured my calf, and put seventeen stitches in my scalp. To get the knife out of my leg, they actually had to break the hook off while the knife was still in place. "If we take it out," the vet said, "you probably lose the leg, the damage will be that great." I passed out from the pain. "For the best," the vet said. He had given me some OxyContin, but I wasn't going to mess with that stuff. Instead, I was self-medicating with left over T3s that were probably expired and copious amounts of beer.

Baker's bartender had supplied the beer. He had delivered so much that it was clear Baker intended to keep his promise of my never having to buy beer again. Baker himself was going to be okay. His shoulder was basically ruined and he was in for months, maybe years, of surgery and rehabilitation, but he was smiling when I saw him. "Some rehabilitation will do me good," he said. "My guy did your window," he told me. "I asked him to put a tracker on you. Figured you would need the help." I shook his hand and haven't seen him since.

Nesha was lucky. Baker had kept her warm and done his best to stop her bleeding, even while he himself came close to bleeding out. She'd been stabbed with the same kind of knife that Xhang had used on me, but smaller. Her wound track was so large, however, from her twisting and fighting even after being stabbed, that the vet was able to remove the knife without causing additional damage. She had internal and external stiches, more than one hundred in all and a disgusting looking drainage tube that I had to keep clear.

At the hotel, Terri had phoned her editor and given him a summary of what had happened. Perhaps coincidently, we had been upgraded to an even larger Fairmont suite, this one with four bedrooms and six gas fireplaces. Kyle carried Nesha into the front hall and it was obvious where she was to go. With her own room, Rileigh had made a bed of feather pillows and down duvets, big enough for two. I had no concerns about the dog having an addictive personality, so she was drugged out of her mind when Kyle laid her beside Rileigh. Instantly, Rileigh and Nesha were both smiling.

"Thank God," Kyle said after we closed the bedroom door. "You, I could do without, but having to tell that kid that Nesha was gone... no fucking way I was going to do that. I would have given the dog my own blood if necessary."

In the main living room, Karen turned on the fire place as there was something comforting about the flames, even though it wasn't cold. We kept the lights low, and since we were all standing, there was a significant amount of hugging and crying. I am almost sure they were all tears of relief and maybe joy. Robyn was being very quiet, but she was sitting close, tucked very carefully into my right side. I drank myself to sleep.

The next day, Stephanie Page had questions, of course, but seemed in no hurry to ask them. "When's a good time to come by?" she asked. "I'm busy tomorrow, maybe the day after. So much to see and do in Vancouver," she said. "I'm going to be sad to leave. Can you guys get into any more trouble so I can stay?"

We made no promises.

Neither Kyle nor I knew what happened to Xhang. He wasn't on the boom when the *Jesse* secured it, and neither were Orangutan or Black Beard. I know this was on Robyn's mind. "You walked away," she said after she was convinced I was going to be alright. "You basically left him to die."

I thought, but didn't say, that was probably true. There was no him or me defence available with Xhang. This was an entirely different set of circumstances than with the henchman Nesha attacked and Baker had killed or the one I crippled for life. What we did was troubling, but I sensed I would come to terms with it before Robyn did. For now, we just held each other, as Kyle held Terri. Karen, alone out of all of us, looked the happiest with everything. Once Terri's story ran, and Page and the feds had their press conference, Jim's reputation would be restored. No more black cloud and suspicion. Karen was going to donate all of Jim's pension and benefits to The Fallen, a program she was setting up to help the surviving families of Canadian police officers killed in the line of duty.

*****

The next day, Stephanie Page came to us at the hotel. Scott Wirth joined us as well, just in case. It was a Sunday, and the sun was shining. That particular day, Vancouver was in its absolute glory, showing off for the world to see. It was fifteen degrees, everything was green and lush, and there was snow on the mountains. There were bicycles and roller blades and skateboards everywhere. "How did you ever leave this place?" Stephanie asked.

I looked at Robyn and Kyle, friends for almost our entire lives, and at Karen and Terri, and then Rileigh getting ready for one last swim in the hotel pool. "Might have been a mistake," I said.

"There's a lot to still sort through," the Deputy Director of Criminal Investigations said to us. "There is probably some reward money—excuse me, we call it 'recovery' now."

I cut her off and spoke for all of us. "None of us really care about that, Stephanie. If it turns out there is some, it goes to that little girl right there."

Right at that moment, Rileigh was trying to explain to Nesha why she couldn't go swimming. "I could get you into the pool," Rileigh told her, "but you are injured and have to rest. I promise not to have *very* much fun without you."

"Understood," Stephanie said. "Duly noted." She had a few basic questions for Terri and Karen about their research and the reliability of their sources. Terri was under no obligation to disclose anything, of course, but confirmed that her information was solid. Karen had no issue in handing Stephanie a copy of everything she had accumulated. Scott did some grumbling over that, but his heart wasn't in it.

"It was the Chief herself who sent the message to change your shift that day, Kyle," Stephanie told us. "The henchman you wounded at the dock ratted the other one out—apparently, that one was responsible for getting Sault to the scene. We won't ever know how that was done, especially since the call to dispatch says that Sault was still alive when Jim got to him."

"On the subject of henchmen," Scott said, "and not to be flippant, but as noted, the Xhang enterprise is short one now. Do we anticipate any legal difficulty because of this?"

Page smiled. "We do not." She looked directly at Scott. "Anything untoward that happened on land would clearly be characterized as self-defence, and the crews of both boats confirm that the boom broke loose and they were tasked with securing said boom and retrieving an injured man. How, or why, Ryan was out there alone remains a mystery of no real importance currently." She smiled with full force. Scott took notice. "That two of Baker's employees were moonlighting on those exact tugs is an incredible coincidence, but does support the assertion that the *Saints* are down-sizing."

I hadn't known how the adventure on the river had been explained. *Thanks Black Beard. Sorry about your shirt.*

When we started talking about what happened on the boom, Robyn and Terri both excused themselves. Stephanie knew what wasn't being said about what had happened there. "Give them time," she said. "They weren't there and it's a tough thing to process. They will come to terms with it." She dropped her shoulders and looked at each of us again, sadness evident on her face. "Or maybe they won't. I hope they do. You two are on the side of good; not everybody is." She nodded curtly. "That will probably be enough."

At that, Page pulled some papers from her briefcase. "Ultimately," she said, "here's what we can now prove. The Chief was sand-bagging *Saint* operations to keep them out of court, and she was stealing the treasury blind. We are still working out how and how much and who else was involved but the threat of incarceration has a tremendous influence on police officers. Jail is not a good place for former cops.

"Baker and his *Saints* were the primary funding for Chesapeake, but not the only customers. The bank worked exactly as Terri described it. Denis Sault was killed because he was going to go public with information regarding the Casino accounts. Gareth Davis was killed because he had all the information necessary to piece everything together—obviously, the whole scene surrounding his murder, and his son's, was a smoke-screen. Turns out the Vietnamese gangbangers on scene had been set up as well—by Xhang's goons.

"Mya was killed by mistake. Obviously the target was Terri, and the intention was to stop the story from being published. We know Xhang's group did that as well." She stood up and shook our hands: Kyle, then me, then Scott.

"Gentleman, your Federal government thanks you. The only questions left unanswered are where the hell is Baker, and where is all that money?" She winked. "You wouldn't happen to know, would you?"

We all said no. For Kyle and me, that was only a lie to the second question. We had no idea where Baker had gone.

*****

After Stephanie and Scott left, Kyle and I went to pack. As I was looking for my sweatshirts, Robyn closed the door to the bedroom I was in. "We need to talk," she said. "I'm at a loss as to what to do." She took both of my hands in hers, and my heart stopped. "I love you, Dirt. God help me, I do. And I'm proud of you for what you've done—what we've done, I guess."

She fell silent and let my hands drop. "And I wasn't on the boom with you, and I can only imagine what actually happened there has cost you personally." She was crying. "But you left that man to die. You knew what was going to happen as soon as Baker's guys showed up."

"Nesha," I said.

Robyn cut me off. "I love that dog as much as you do. I'm forever grateful that you were able to save her. But that is not why you left Xhang." She hugged me quickly, letting go with some force. Her tears were hot on my skin. "How can I be so proud of you and my brother and so disappointed at the same time, Dirt? How is that fucking possible? Or fair?"

I said nothing. What do you speak to truth?

CHAPTER 18

Time moved forward, as it does, but there were two chapters left unwritten.

The first was completed two days after the chaos on the log boom when Page's team of hand-picked officers went to Vancouver Chief of Police Tara Callan's Jericho Beach residence and found her body, single gunshot to the head. She was sprawled over a glass topped desk in her study. Adam Robillard's sources, some of whom were there, told him that there was no note, but the Chief was slumped over a thirty-year old family photo: father, step-mother, five year old Tara and a new step-brother—hopefully in much happier times. There was no suicide note, but there was a full confession.

The second chapter is more complicated and may, in fact, never be over. When I saw Baker at the hospital, he slipped me an envelope. It was so thin, the only way I knew it wasn't empty is that there was a very firm and clear outline of a key inside.

Scott, my Vancouver lawyer, pretended that I hadn't mentioned the envelope or key to him. "When you met with Mr. Baker," he said, "immediately after you were both involved in a tragic and violent criminal assault against your persons, there is no legal reason to believe that what was shared between the two of you was anything more than commiseration for the events and relief to be alive, especially given that you were both intricately responsible for the others survival." I really didn't know what that meant, but I took it to mean that the key could remain a secret, at least until I didn't want it to be.

The legal ramifications of what has happened will take years to resolve. Scott remains on retainer, and now and then we do have a drink when the sun is shining and the weather is warm. None of us face any legal difficulties; in fact, we were all awarded meritorious medals of honour by the new Vancouver Chief of Police two months after he was appointed. Even the dog got one, and whenever Rileigh is over to play, one of them wears it. It took that long because Adam Robillard wasn't sure he wanted to unretire and move back to the city.

Anthony Baker simply disappeared. But maybe six weeks ago, I received a package of forwarded mail from Ivy Green. Included was a post card from Prince Edward Island. On the front was a picture of a salt marsh and red sand beach and blue Atlantic Ocean, a colour very different from the green of the Pacific. On the picture, somebody had drawn a simple building on the shore line. On the back, there was a recipe for Clam Chowder and the words 'wish you were here.'

I haven't shown this postcard to anyone. But I do really enjoy Clam Chowder and have always wanted to see Atlantic Canada again. Few people know this, but I was born in Prince Edward Island, although we only lived there until I was two before moving across the country and landing in Vancouver.

The Bronco was quite obviously ruined. I replaced it with a 2001 Ford Expedition and added all the same features. The Expedition is a bigger vehicle and it's everything I need and probably more, but I miss the Bronco—it was my last connection to the major leagues as I'd bought it with my signing bonus. I'd used the majority of that money to pay off my mother's mortgage and buy the land in Roberts Creek, about twenty minutes outside of Sechelt on BC's Sunshine Coast.

I did finally visit my Mom.

I'm living on the land in Roberts Creek now. Kyle moved his fifth-wheel to the edge of my property, and I am incorporating my shoulder re-hab into cutting down trees and clearing the land like he and I had talked about a life time ago. I'm letting Jamie run the bar in Calgary; he's better at than I ever was. I'm focusing on the cabin and Nesha's recovery. Because of how deep the wound was and how many muscles were impacted, has been slower. Her hair has grown in white around the wound track. From a distance, she looks like a giant, off-centre skunk.

Kyle is back at work, promoted, and comes up to help every chance he can. It's funny to see Kyle dote on the dog, but he does. I speak to Robyn almost every day, but I haven't seen her since the medal ceremony. It hurts us both, but I understand. We are all struggling with my decision to walk away —with Kyle—and leave Faas Xhang with Baker's men. I think I have come to peace with it; at least as much peace as I will ever have over something so horrible. I am surprised that my struggle has been easier than Robyn's, but I've had hard work and ocean air to distract me.

Terri wrote her article, and word on the street is that the Pulitzer is a foregone conclusion. It's a legitimately crazy and compelling story. She and Kyle are no longer together; I know it hurts him and Karen tells me it hurts Terri, but—again— what can you do? Terri and Robyn weren't there, in the rain, on the logs... it was us versus them in the most primal of ways. Until the log boom. That, I could have seen through to the end. *We move on.*

Karen and Rileigh are doing well; they come over maybe every other weekend and Rileigh and Nesha explore Roberts Creek, very slowly, and swim in the ocean. Apparently, the salt water and swimming are good for Nesha's recovery. Rileigh takes that very seriously.

There is one glaring omission from Terri's article, and Terri is complicit in its absence. The key Baker gave me? It opens the door to an abandoned water pumping station on the Vancouver side of the Fraser River, near the Fraserview Golf Course. The station itself is a rectangle, maybe a six foot by six foot piece of concrete above ground with a front door that is down three cement stairs. Underground, the space is about twenty feet long and eight feet high by the same six feet wide. All machinery has been removed. The fact that the abandoned pumping station is empty of all pipes and machinery is important, because in their absence, Kyle and I found bags and bags of cash. Hockey bags, duffel bags, IKEA bags, shopping bags. We stopped counting at $4.5 million and we may not have been a third of the way done. All the bags are now in my possession.

The only thing Scott said is "at least I know I'm getting paid." Andrew Robillard said "That's going to be complicated" and asked for some time to think about it. He hasn't said anything since. Stephanie Page made a trip back to Vancouver and asked Kyle and I to meet her downtown one night. She drank maybe four too many Bellinis. "One of you pay the tab," she said and kissed us both good-bye. "I know you can afford it." Neither of us has talked to her since.

Karen sees value in the money, for the good that it can do. Terri agrees, but is conflicted. She knows that we have told the police about it—at the Provincial and Federal levels—and the reality is this: if the money is surrendered, it will cease to exist. Nothing good will come from it. Robyn simply said "you're the one who bled for it, Dirt. You should do what you think is right, and I will support that."

That was not as helpful as she thought it would be.

None of us need the money, and there are so many people who do. So that is the answer we arrived at; the how still needs to be worked out. There's time, I think, to do this right—look at how much has happened in four years. *A life lost, a life found, a life being lived.*

*****

August 2000

For deckhand Mario Haute, this particular Thursday was shaping up to be a day like any other summer day— warmer than most but just as long. Until he stepped on the body. Six hours into what was shaping up to be a fourteen-hour shift, he slipped silently off the rear deck of the forty-foot tug *Expected,* crossed a smooth fir boom and took two steps onto a Cypress boom where he came face to face with mortality. Not his, fortunately, but someone's and frightening just the same. Faas Xhang, what was left of him, had been found.

I didn't know about this until days after it happened. I was in Roberts Creek with the dog and Kyle. I was under a bit of a time crunch, and we were making good progress getting the fallen trees to the mill, drinking less than I would have expected, and not talking much. Excavators were coming in a week to dig the foundation pit, so we had a schedule to keep. I had hired out the foundation work, as well as the rough plumbing and electrical. Everything else, I was going to do myself, from framing to finishing. I had the time, in between jobs as I was, but that first machine was getting ready to roll.

I had splurged for a satellite, and Kyle and I were inside his fifth-wheel watching the Seattle Mariners at home against the Texas Rangers. Raul Ibanez and Jay Buhner had just gone back to back for Seattle. Dave Niehaus' call was still reverberating around the trailer: "My, oh my!"

All the windows were open, and when the trailer was silent again, I thought I heard a car door slam, maybe two. Kyle and I had long ago cleared a path to where the cabin was going to be, but the trailer was quite a distance from the road and situated in a natural clearing. There was no vehicle access to where we were as we had dropped a bunch of trees in the way, so hearing cars was unusual. But the dog didn't bark and her tail was wagging, so I assumed I was mistaken.

I had taken some marinated pork chops out of the fridge and was looking for ingredients for a quick potato salad when there was a knock at the door. It was a good thing I had made extra.

On the other side of the door, Robyn and Terri were standing with brand new tool belts and the bottle of champagne we had bought months ago. "Got any tools we can borrow?" Robyn asked.

As luck would have it, we did.

Manufactured by Amazon.ca
Bolton, ON